Some part of Murdock's mind had been keeping track of targets going down, just like in the Fun House back at Little Creek. He'd counted fifteen floppers . . . was that right? Four . . . eight . . . ten . . . right. Fifteen down. That left three.

There! A shadow breaking from beneath one of the trucks, running toward the left. Murdock fired, missed, fired again. The burst smacked chips from the monastery wall close by the corner of the building. The militiaman lurched to a halt, spun about, and thrust his arms in the air. *"Molim!"* the Serb shrieked, his hands waving above his head. A teenager, Murdock thought. He was babbling incoherently, tears streaming down his face, plainly terrified of these black apparitions that had materialized out of the night. *"Ne! Ne! Molim!"*

"Sorry," Murdock said, and he squeezed the H&K's trigger once more. "Nothing personal . . ."

SEAL TEAM SEVEN

SPECTER

The SEAL TEAM SEVEN Series

SEAL TEAM SEVEN

SPECTER

1

Friday, March 3

0012 hours
Beach, 10 kilometers east of Dubrovnik
Croatia

The figure slid ashore with the roll of the surf, garbed all in black, glistening in the wan light of a new-risen last-quarter moon partly masked by scattered clouds, and with the oily sheen of phosphorescence off the sea. It might have been an oil-coated chunk of flotsam washed in by the tide—or a corpse—but the eyes, the whites like ice behind the nonreflective plate of the face mask, were very much alive, shifting back and forth to scan the length of beach.

The next wave brought a second armed and black-clad figure ashore, five meters to the left. The first signaled the second with silent, slashing movements of one hand: *Check that way.*

Both figures clutched knapsacks before them as though black nylon could provide cover from hostile fire; both held the sleek, black deadliness of H&K MP5SD3 submachine guns in gloved hands. The men lay belly-down in the sand as surf boiled and frothed around their bodies, using the knapsacks as firing rests for their weapons' muzzle-heavy barrels.

The beach, barely visible in the uncertain moonlight, looked deserted save for those two figures. A line of poplars,

1

dimly visible against moon-brightened clouds, marked the side of a highway paralleling the coast to the north, thirty meters ahead.

Thunder boomed and rumbled in the distance. To the left, westward, the sky was aglow with light reflected from low-lying clouds, light that wavered and flickered like the pulse of distant lightning.

Lieutenant Blake Murdock slithered a few more meters up the beach, then, still alert for movement or any sign of life, stripped off his face mask. From a waterproof pouch in the knapsack, he extracted an AN/PVS-7 night-vision device and slipped it down over his head.

They weighed a pound and a half and they sharply reduced his field of vision, but when the NVD goggles were switched on they pierced near-total darkness, transforming it into green-tinted day. Details hidden at first by darkness sprang into sharp relief: a low stone wall at the top of the beach; a small fishing boat pulled up on the sand a hundred meters to the east; the seashore clutter of civilization—lumps of sea-hardened oil, plastic six-pack rings, crumpled aluminum cans, tangles of fish line or plastic net, plastic jugs—marking the tide line between wet and dry sand. The beach, as expected, was empty. Satellite surveillance suggested that this strip of the Dalmatian coast east of Dubrovnik was at best only intermittently patrolled.

Murdock checked his swim buddy, who stared back at him with the hard-edged, mechanical-insect face of a man wearing NVD goggles. Chief Machinist's Mate Tom "Razor" Roselli gave Murdock a gloved thumbs-up: *Looks clear.*

Murdock signaled back: *Affirmative—move out.*

Flat on their bellies, the two men crawled the rest of the way up the beach until they reached the shelter of the seawall, where they stashed fins, face masks, and rebreathers. Both wore black nomex flight suits over wet suits. It was late winter, and both air and sea were bitingly cold despite the warm, southerly surface current off the Dalmatian coast. Murdock could feel the first signs of exposure after his long swim, the tingling numbness in his fingers, the faint trembling of his lower lip. He'd endured far worse than this during BUD/S training, though, a calculated set of tortures and privations that had shown just how far he could push himself in the wet and cold. He could keep on pushing for a long time yet.

He had to. They still had a long way to go.

Roselli produced a Global Positioning System receiver and carefully studied its luminous digital readout. After a moment, he snapped Murdock a thumbs-up. Their trip north in a CRRC from the U.S.S. *Nassau*, followed by a two-kilometer swim in ink-black water, had put them ashore precisely on target.

Communicating solely by gesture, the two black figures separated, crawling in opposite directions until they were twenty meters apart. Chemical light sticks, pulled from their packs and ignited with a shake, were planted in the sand, their pale green luminescence marking a landing zone visible only from the sea.

Then the two men settled down to silently watch . . . and wait.

They were U.S. Navy SEALs, members of the elite, high-tech warrior teams that took their name from the acronym for SEa, Air, and Land. Blake Murdock, the commanding officer of the Third Platoon, SEAL Team Seven, had been the platoon leader for nearly eight months now.

He crouched in the sand, alive to the night, to the stink of garbage and rotting fish on the beach, to the chill of the offshore breeze cooling his soggy flight suit, to the rough, gritty hardness of the stone wall pressed against his back. Though unusual and officially discouraged, the practice of having a CO come ashore first on an op was not unheard of in the Teams. During the Vietnam War, many SEAL platoon leaders regularly took point, officially because they could react more swiftly to the unexpected from that position. Few SEALs cared for official reasons, though, and the truth of the matter was that taking point was just one more way of

demonstrating the special bond most SEAL officers shared
with their men. Murdock had trained constantly with his
people since assuming command of Third Platoon. More,
he'd been in combat with them. Being first man ashore on
a hostile beach was nothing compared to that.

Besides, he'd wanted to assess the situation himself,
through his own eyes, before committing the rest of the
squad.

The pulsing glow to the west brightened and quickened,
and seconds later, the far-thunder rumble grew louder, more
insistent. Some of the light took on a silver-white tinge—
artillery flares, Murdock thought—mingled with the flash
of antiaircraft tracers and the sullen, ember-red illumination
of burning buildings. The Serbs were shelling the port city of
Dubrovnik. Again. The rumble of the bombardment sounded
like that of a summer storm, save that it went on and on,
without letup.

Damn them, Murdock thought, but he wasn't even sure
who he was damning most at the moment: the dozens of
militia and warlord factions that were so bloodily intent on
carving up the mountainous territory of what had once been
Yugoslavia, or the Washington bureaucrats and politicians
who seemed so pathetically unable to do anything at all
about the ongoing slaughter.

This latest round in the age-old bloodshed involving the
Balkan's religious, ethnic, and political factions had been
going on virtually without letup for several years now. The
power vacuum left by the collapse of Communism in
Europe had led to increasingly violent clashes among the
patchwork states and populations that over eighty years
earlier had given the world a new word: *balkanization.*
Serbs and Croats, Bosnians and Albanians, Slovenians and
Montenegrans, Muslims and Christians, Monarchists and
Communists, and more seemed hell-bent on drowning these
ancient mountains in blood. So far, the United States,
NATO, and the United Nations all had failed repeatedly to
find a peaceful solution; and with each failure, the possibility that the fighting in the Balkans would touch off a

larger, bloodier European war—as it had in 1914—loomed larger, more certain, more deadly.

To make matters worse, U.S. foreign policy had been unusually inept lately. The current Administration vacillated almost comically between chest-puffing bluster and appeasement, threatening air strikes one week, calling for sanctions and no-fly zones the next, then promising political concessions and millions in foreign aid after that. The indecisiveness bitterly angered Murdock, as it did most of the men in the Teams. Hell, the tragedy now playing itself out, especially up the coast to the west, was enough to leave anyone with a love of America and of history furious. Modern Dubrovnik had once been an independent city-state republic called Ragusa, the first foreign government in the world to recognize the infant United States of America in 1776. If ever a place deserved meaningful help from the U.S., it was Dubrovnik.

Murdock had first learned that historical tidbit while watching a news special on ACN about the fighting in Bosnia and Croatia, and he'd researched it some on his own since. The son of a U.S. congressman from Virginia, he had been unable to grow up without acquiring a love of American history that delighted in squirreling away such nuggets. If nothing else, his knowledge of history often gave him a reassuring sense of who he was and what he was doing. Unfortunately, it could also lead to intense frustration when he saw people who should have known better proving Santayana's maxim: Those who cannot remember the past are condemned to repeat it.

Still, Murdock was realist enough to know that it was irresponsible to launch a war over what amounted to ancient history. The real crime was that Washington could not decide on a single course of action and then stick to it. As always, the real victims of that indecisiveness were the civilians, the innocents caught at ground zero . . . and the American combat forces committed piecemeal to the meat grinder, usually with no clear goals and no definite or coherent policy.

Forces like Third Platoon, SEAL Seven.

Headlights flared down the road to the east, and Murdock and Roselli hunkered down lower, invisible in the wall's shadow. A moment later, a truck rumbled past on the highway meters beyond the wall; a heavy vehicle from the sound of it, almost certainly military. With a clash of badly worn gears, the noise dwindled away toward the west. Probably a truck carrying supplies to the Serbian forces besieging Dubrovnik.

A triple metallic click caught his attention. Turning his head toward Roselli, he saw the SEAL point down the beach. Murdock looked in the indicated direction. . . .

Yes! There! Even with the NVDs they were almost invisible against the water, but Murdock could see the rest of the platoon now, a low, black, almost shapeless mass rising and falling with the rolling surf as it made its way steadily shoreward. As it neared the beach, the mass resolved itself into what the Navy called an inflatable boat, small—or IBS for short—and what SEALs usually called a CRRC, for Combat Rubber Raiding Craft. Five men—the rest of Third Platoon's Blue Squad—occupied the raft. An outboard engine was attached to the motor mount, but since even the most silent-running of outboards made some noise, the SEALs had opted to make the approach the old-fashioned way, leaning out over the rubber sides to wield their paddles. At the edge of the surf line, the SEALs rolled out of the craft, snatched it up by its carry handles as though half a ton of IBS and gear was virtually weightless, and dashed through the spray and up onto the beach. Reaching the seawall halfway between Murdock and Roselli, they dropped the raft and began unloading weapons and equipment. Keeping low to avoid showing his head above the wall, Murdock duckwalked across to join the newcomers.

"Lieutenant." The one-word greeting was a whisper, more felt than heard, easily lost beneath the hiss of the surf and the rumble of artillery fire to the west.

"Hey, Mac," Murdock replied as quietly. Master Chief Engineman George "Big Mac" MacKenzie was the oldest of

Blue Squad's old hands, an NCO who'd been in the Navy for sixteen years now and in the Teams for eleven. A big-boned, powerfully muscled Texan, he normally hefted Blue Squad's SAW. This op, however, required stealth and speed rather than raw firepower; he'd left his usual M-60 machine gun behind in favor of a sound-suppressed M-16.

"Quiet beach?"

"Nothing so far."

Mac's teeth flashed white in the darkness against the black and green of his paint-smeared face. "Shit, L-T. Half expected to find ACN waiting for us."

The reference was an old in-joke within the Navy's Special Warfare command. When SEALs and Marine Recon personnel had slipped ashore at Mogadishu in 1992, just before America's intervention in Somalia, they'd found a small army of reporters, news cameramen, and lights waiting for them on the beach. SEALs liked to keep a low profile, and the screwup continued to be a source of wry, sometimes bitter humor within the Teams.

"Looks like we're not going to be on the evening news this time," Murdock replied, grinning. "C'mon. Get the gear broken out and let's diddy."

"Aye, aye, L-T."

It took less than ten minutes for the IBS, twelve feet long, six wide, and weighing 289 pounds minus its load of men and equipment, to disappear completely beneath the loose sand. The five newly arrived SEALs worked furiously while Murdock and Roselli continued to mount watch. The Chemlite sticks were retrieved, stowed, and buried, and two men made their way back down the beach with a pair of brushes, with which they carefully wiped out every footprint, every trace of the team's arrival.

Gathered once more in the shadow of the seawall, the platoon divvied up the gear and weapons they needed to carry with them. Tactical radios were donned and checked, and the squad's HST-4 C2 element sat-comm gear was carefully unpacked. Murdock took advantage of the time to go to each of the men, whispering a few well-chosen words as he checked their rigs and assault vest loadouts.

The TO&E roster for SEAL Seven's Third Platoon currently called for two squads—Blue and Gold—of seven men each. For this op, Blue Squad had been assigned to the landing party, while Gold waited in reserve aboard the amphibious assault ship *Nassau*, now on patrol in the Adriatic a few miles off the coast. Besides Roselli and MacKenzie, Blue Squad included Hull Technician First Class Juan Garcia, the dark-haired demolitions expert known as "Boomer" to the rest; Quartermaster First Class Martin "Magic" Brown, the team's sniper; Electrician's Mate Second Class William Higgins, the squad's radioman, whose quiet and somewhat erudite manner had landed him the nickname "Professor"; and Hospital Corpsman Second Class James Ellsworth, whose calling had inevitably given him the handle "Doc."

Good men, all of them. A little wild on liberty, sometimes, especially Doc and Razor, but they were the very best. In their black nomex and heavily laden combat vests, with their camo-painted faces and mismatched assortment of booney hats and watch caps and scarves, they were a frightening-looking lot. The camo paint liberally smeared on their faces—in Magic's case the stuff was pasted on so thick it was impossible to tell that the man was black—gave them all an eerily nightmarish quality. Murdock was proud to be in their number.

He just wished this mission counted for something. The thunder in the west was growing louder, more insistent.

As the final checks were made, Higgins radioed the team's initial entry report over the sat-comm gear, a single code word condensed to a burst transmission fired into the sky by the press of a button. Too tight and too quick for any eavesdroppers to get a fix, the code word would alert both Gold Squad, back aboard the *Nassau*, and the senior officers of NAVSPECWARGRU-Two and USSOCOM, who were listening in back at the Pentagon, that Blue Squad was on the beach and proceeding with the mission.

Ready now, their swim gear buried in the sand with the IBS, their weapons and combat loads checked out and ready, the SEALs one by one rolled over the top of the wall, then hurried across the highway. On the far side was open forest. The squad moved in patrol order, five meters between each man. Boomer took point, followed by Mac, the compass man with the GPS. Next came Murdock, then Higgins with the radio. Doc, Razor, and Magic brought up the rear. Only the point man and the tail gunner wore NVDs; the goggles could be hard on the eyes if they were worn for an extended period of time, and for a long trek through the night Murdock wanted the majority of the squad to have full use of their peripheral vision.

Their destination lay some six kilometers inland, just across the border.

Nearly all of this part of the Dalmatian coast had originally belonged to Croatia. The bulk of that state lay well to the north, enfolding Bosnia-Hercegovina between the slender horns of a crescent. Here, the southern horn dwindled away to almost nothing, a thin sliver of beach and coastal highway that isolated Bosnia from the sea save for one narrow passage at Neum, between Dubrovnik and Split.

West and south of Bosnia lay the new Federated Republic of Yugoslavia—which was to say Serbia and a scattering of smaller states from Vojvodina in the north to Montenegro and Macedonia in the south. Of all the Yugoslav republics, Serbia had kept the closest semblance to the old Communist regime and had proven itself more than willing to keep fighting to maintain Serbian hegemony over the Balkans.

And squarely between the Federated Republic and Croatia lay tragic Bosnia-Hercegovina, a triangular block of mountainous land both shared and claimed by Croats, Serbians, and Muslim Bosnians. It was there that the Yugoslav civil war had been most savagely fought since early 1991, there that the world had first heard the sickening phrase "ethnic cleansing." Now Bosnia was being divvied up between the Serbs and the Croats, with eager help from Bosnian Serbs openly armed and supported by the remnant of the Yugoslav federation. Lately, Serbians and Croatians, after a period of halfhearted cooperation against the Muslims, had begun fighting each other again, squabbling over the dismembered corpse of Bosnia as the UN, NATO, and the United States all helplessly watched, proposed partition plans, and attempted to impose laughably short-lived truces. The resulting tangle of territories defined by ethnic groups, religions, and nationalistic loyalties made even the most convoluted gerrymanderings of political districts back in the States look tame by comparison.

Like many Americans, Murdock had for a long time been uncertain about just what role the United States should play in the Balkans, when he thought about it at all. On the one hand were the stories of the atrocities, especially those reportedly committed by the Serbs against the Muslims— stories of whole village populations rounded up, packed aboard cattle cars, and shipped to concentration camps where starvation, beatings, torture, and mass executions were being used to exterminate an entire people. Stories of children being thrown beneath tank tracks, stories of the wholesale slaughter of men and the systematic rape of women, in a campaign designed to empty entire districts for Serb occupation.

Stories, in other words, that sounded chillingly like another type of "ethnic cleansing" carried on by another supposedly civilized nation half a century earlier.

On the other hand, there was the feeling that the United States had no business getting involved in this quagmire. The animosities in this tortured hodgepodge of states and peoples went back a long, long way. Those mountains looming into the eastern sky had been bathed in blood time after time over the centuries. The anarchist who'd started World War I by assassinating Archduke Ferdinand had done so on the anniversary of a Serbian defeat at the hands of the Ottoman Turks in 1389. The Serbs still called the Bosniaks "Turks," bringing to mind the centuries of misrule by the Ottoman Empire. These people had *long* memories.

Could anything the United States did make any difference here at all?

Murdock didn't know . . . and, in fact, the politics of this war, the decisions in Washington that had brought him onto this beach, were not his concern. He and his men had a mission to carry out.

According to the briefing Third Platoon had received yesterday aboard the *Nassau*, this particular stretch of Croatia, together with most of the former Bosnian territory inland, was now under the control of the Serbian Volunteer Guard—a local militia unit composed of pro-Serb Bosnians—and a Serbian motorized infantry brigade. The Serbs were trying yet again to seize Dubrovnik. When Yugoslavia had started breaking up in 1991, Croatia had grabbed all of the former Yugoslav naval bases save one, the Montenegran port at Kotor, sixty kilometers east of Dubrovnik. Now, the Serb-dominated Yugoslav Republic was trying to get some of those ports back, as well as to seize the initiative in the squabble with Croatia over the Bosnian corpse.

A rusted wire fence marked the official boundary between Croatia and Bosnia, but since the entire area was under Serbian control at the moment, the border was not patrolled. After a careful reconnaissance, searching for mines, patrols, or automated sensors, the SEALs crossed the wire into Bosnia halfway between the village of Mjini and Cilipi International, the shut-down airport twenty kilometers east of Dubrovnik.

There'd been a number of SEAL ops into the Balkans in recent months, all of them highly classified, with missions ranging from scouting out antiaircraft batteries to pulling full recons on stretches of the Adriatic coast that might become landing beaches if the decision was made to send in the Marines. Blue Squad's orders this night were to slip ashore unseen, rendezvous at the St. Anastasias Dominican monastery with a local contact in the pay of the CIA, and collect from him a list of Serbian units in the area and their deployments. The information might—*might*—be useful soon, in the event that the President decided to punish Serbian aggression by ordering air strikes.

A spook job, then. The SEALs and the Company had a long working partnership, one begun during World War II between the SEALs' forerunners in the old Underwater Demolition Teams and the CIA's predecessors with the OSS. Though he'd been on plenty of intelligence ops before—maybe *because* he'd been on plenty of them before—Murdock didn't like this sort of mission. For one thing, the civilian agency rarely had its priorities straight. Agency suits were as likely to request some routine bit of intel-gathering that could as easily have been handled by satellite as they were to load the team down with a dozen conflicting mission requirements, an often deadly misuse of assets. For another, Langley too often showed a nasty tendency to regard combat teams as expendable.

Murdock did not regard his men as expendable. He'd argued hard against this mission when Captain Coburn, SEAL Seven's skipper, had asked him to take it on. In the end, he'd accepted it, though. While SEAL commanders were notorious throughout the Navy for their willingness to argue orders that they considered impossible or suicidal, mission refusals nonetheless didn't look good on a Team's quarterly reports. It could mean cuts in the NAVSPECWAR budget, and with the fierce competition for money in a fast-shrinking military, that could mean the end of careers, even the end of the Teams.

Beyond the wire border was a pine forest and the start of a steep climb up the southern flank of Gora Orjen, the forest-covered line of mountains that walled the coastal strip off from the interior highlands between Dubrovnik and Kotor. As Murdock started to climb, he wondered if survival of the SEALs had really come down to nothing more than this, the willingness of low-man-on-the-totem-pole officers like himself to accept dubious missions.

Well, at least his was not one of those Agency Rambo ops piggybacking everything onto the field team from beach reconnaissance to a hostage rescue. Blue Squad had a single objective this time, a single mission to carry out. According to Frank Fletcher, the Agency's combat team handler aboard the *Nassau*, it was a quick-in, quick-out piece of cake. Murdock would have felt more confident of that assessment had he not known that a hell of a lot of similar ops had gone badly wrong in the past.

"A piece of cake," in Company parlance, all too often was rock-hard, fire-hot, and frosted with blood.

2

"Something's wrong, L-T. We got uninvited guests."

Murdock closed his eyes and gave an almost inaudible groan. "Okay, Razor. Let's hear it."

The squad had stopped for a rest and a position check just down the hill from the monastery, and Murdock had sent Razor and Magic on ahead to check out the objective. Now Roselli was back, and the expression on his painted face, just visible in the cloud-muffled moonlight, told Murdock that things were turning sour.

"The objective's there, all right. But it looks like some bad guys've set up shop to do some serious drinking."

"What, soldiers?"

"If you can call 'em that. For all I know they could be bandits. They don't look much like regular forces."

Murdock reached for his rucksack and extracted his NVD goggles. "Okay. I'll come have a look."

Silently, the two crawled upslope across a carpet of pine needles and patches of old snow. At the forest's edge, pine trees gave way to uncut brush and brambles, a perfect screen for the stealthily watching SEALs. Brown was still there, behind a fallen tree trunk, studying the scene through his NVDs.

There was the monastery, just as Roselli had said, a once-proud, gray stone structure now crumbled into ruin. Living quarters to the left, with a chapel under an impressive white dome to the right, and beyond that a small, rock-walled cemetery. Mortar fire and artillery shells had brought much of the building down in a tumble of broken stone, though the facade was still standing, as was most of the chapel. The monks had fled years ago, as had most of the other inhabitants of the area. The mountain road that wound past the monastery grounds to the left was one of the main supply routes used by Serbian forces coming west out of Montenegro.

Slowly, careful not to make even a rustle in the under-brush, Murdock pushed aside some of the weeds. The light from a bonfire burning inside a fifty-five-gallon drum was dazzling to his night optics, and he thumbed down the gain.

Yeah, Razor had been dead on. These weren't regular troops, though the truck parked to the right of the monas-tery's front steps was military, an ancient and mud-spattered UAZ-66, a one-ton transport that had probably been a hand-me-down from the Soviets. Murdock counted nine soldiers in all, two standing guard in the back of the truck with AK-47s, the rest sitting on the crumbling stone steps or standing around the fire, which they were feeding with scraps of wood and broken furniture.

Regular troops would have been more uniform in their appearance. This bunch sported a ragged mismatch of uniforms and civilian clothing; their weapons included military AK-47s and bolt-action sporting rifles; the crude flag painted on the door of their truck was Serbian. Chances were these were Bosnian Serbs, possibly members of the Serb Volunteers, possibly Chetniks or Beli Orlori or mem-bers of one of the other pro-Serb, anti-Muslim militias. No one appeared to be in charge, and if any of them wore rank devices, Murdock couldn't make them out. All were un-shaven and dirty-looking. Several brandished unlabeled glass bottles half-filled with clear liquid, and the mingled tangs of cheap alcohol and cigarette smoke were sharp in the air.

Murdock peeled back the Velcro cover on his luminous watch dial, checking the time. Zero-two-twenty-six, over two hours since they'd come ashore, less than four and a half hours until sunrise. Damn it, why had the Serbs decided to do their goldbricking *here,* of all the goddamned spots on the Adriatic coast?

The minutes crawled past, and the militiamen showed no sign of moving on. Three of them broke into a ragged and off-key Slavic-sounding song, while the others passed a bottle around.

What to do? The SEALs were supposed to meet their CIA contact here, at this monastery, between 0230 and 0300 hours. They'd deliberately arrived a little early so that they could check the ruins out first, to make certain there was no waiting ambush. Well, this looked like no ambush Murdock had ever seen, but that didn't help any. When the contact, code-name "Gypsy," showed up, things were going to get damned interesting.

Normally, in a rendezvous like this one, there would have been an alternate meeting site, but Fletcher hadn't been able to designate one. Apparently, communications with CIA assets inside Bosnia were less than ideal at the moment, and Murdock had been told that just setting up this meet had been difficult. Murdock considered splitting his squad and posting them on the mountain road, one up the hill, the other below, with orders to intercept any vehicle with a lone occupant approaching the monastery, but rejected that as too chancy. The SEALs had no idea which direction Gypsy was coming from, or even whether he would be on the road at all. He could be coming up through the woods as the SEALs had, on foot, and might even be watching somewhere nearby, waiting for the noisy party on the monastery steps to break up.

Besides, there was no way to know how Gypsy might react to three or four black-clad, face-painted commandos leaping out of the woods to stop his vehicle. Somehow, Murdock thought that Fletcher and his bosses back at Langley, Virginia, would take a dim view of the SEALs getting caught in a firefight with their man in Bosnia. All things considered, it would be safer to wait here and hope the militiamen got bored and left. Damn it, they must have to answer to *someone*. Sooner or later they would have to go back to base or show up for roll call or whatever it was that paramilitary play-soldiers did when they weren't hunting Croats or Bosnian Muslims. The question was whether or not Gypsy would put in an appearance after they'd gone.

Cautiously, Roselli and Murdock inched back from the edge of the woods. "Looks like a damned convention," Roselli complained. "Who invited *them?*"

Murdock consulted his watch again: zero-two-twenty-eight. While Murdock hoped that Gypsy was in fact hidden in the woods somewhere waiting it out like the SEALs, there was every possibility that the Company asset would blunder into the Serb militia. Should he call in a report? No . . . no time now, and there'd be time enough later, whatever happened. "Go back and get the others," he told Roselli. "Fill them in. Have them come up quiet, radios open, channel A. But no chatter. Got it?"

"Right, L-T."

"On the double. But *quiet*."

"Aye, aye, sir."

Returning to the edge of the woods once more, Murdock took up position to Brown's right. "Looks like they're waiting for someone, Lieutenant," Brown observed. "Don't know what they're sayin', but a couple of 'em keep lookin' at their watches an' then out toward the road. You think they're waiting for Gypsy?"

"If they are, they're being remarkably casual about it, Magic. It's certainly not an ambush."

"Yeah. Maybe—"

"Shh!"

Headlights glared on the main road, then swung sharply across the facade of the monastery. A second truck—

another UAZ, engine roaring as the driver downshifted—
bumped off the main road and turned sharply onto the dirt
drive running in front of the monastery. With a squeak of
ancient springs and a clatter of gnashing gears, it pulled up
directly in front of the monastery door, where it was greeted
by the other soldiers with cheers and friendly, bantering
calls. Like the first, this second truck bore a painted Serbian
flag on the door. The cover had been removed from the rear
bed, and Murdock could make out a number of heads behind
the glare of the vehicle's headlights. As lights and engine
switched off, Murdock could see another ten soldiers in the
back of the truck, plus two more up front. No . . . scratch
that. Three of the people in back were civilians.

Women.

Murdock felt a cold, icy slickness in his belly as the
soldiers began piling out of the truck. It was a rape party.
The women were prisoners, their hands tied behind their
backs, their clothing torn and disheveled; the men were
laughing and joking with one another as they shoved their
captives toward the back of the truck, then handed them
down over the tailgate one after another, kicking and
wailing, into the waiting hands of the soldiers already on the
ground. One woman was probably in her thirties. The other
two were younger—teenagers, Murdock thought, though
they were so scrawny and bedraggled that it was hard to
tell. The two other men stayed in the back of the first truck,
standing guard with their AKs, while the rest began crowd-
ing around the women.

"Lieutenant!" Brown breathed, his mouth inches from
Murdock's ear, the whisper so soft it was almost drowned by
the raucous laughter twenty meters away. *"Lieutenant!
What're we gonna do?"*

Silently, Murdock laid one finger across his lips and
shook his head, a dark warning. There was nothing they
could do at the moment, not without jeopardizing the
mission. A firefight here might draw down the full force of
whatever Serb warlord ruled this stretch of forested Balkan
mountainsides. Gypsy could be captured. One or more of

the team might be captured . . . and wouldn't the trial of a
U.S. Navy SEAL look good on Serbian television? Belgrade
had been itching for a confrontation with the Americans,
something that would help Yugoslavia's neo-Communist
dictatorship pull together the popular support they needed to
stay in power . . . and to keep the war in Bosnia going.
The situation, Murdock thought, was a damned international
incident begging to happen.

He felt Roselli moving up on his right, felt the SEAL
tense as he saw what was happening in front of the
monastery. He laid a steadying hand on the SEAL's shoulder. *Not yet.*

It looked like the militiamen were planning on going
about this methodically. They'd taken one of the younger
girls and dragged her off away from the others. Two men
disappeared through the monastery's door and reappeared a
moment later, lugging a torn, water-stained mattress between them.

This, Murdock thought with a trembling, barely contained fury, was the reality of war in the Balkans, something
the politicians and the Beltway bureaucrats never seemed
able to squarely face. For years now, as the Yugoslav civil
war ground on, sometimes hot, sometimes merely simmer-
ing, rape had been commonly practiced by both sides, but it
was the Serbs who'd transformed rape into state policy, a
means of demoralizing civilians and forging closer bonds
among troops of uncertain loyalties, a way of emptying
cities of enemy ethnic populations, and even one aspect of
the detestable notion of "ethnic cleansing." Muslim women
had been the most frequent targets. These people were
probably Muslims, though since Bosniak women did not
wear the chador there was no way to single them out. The
younger girl who had been separated from the others was
wearing Western-style blue jeans, and the other two wore
casual dresses. None had coats against the cold, night air.
Likely they'd either been snatched from their homes in
some village or taken from one of the huge, Serb-controlled

camps that more and more were beginning to resemble places with names like Buchenwald and Auschwitz.

While some of the men held the other two women apart, next to the fire, others dragged the third to the mattress. It took three of them to pin her down on her back while a fourth peeled off her jeans. When her legs were bare, a ponderously fat militiaman with a Josef Stalin mustache began using a bayonet to slice away her blouse; the others laughed and hooted wildly as the girl screamed, thrashing about in their grip. The older woman shouted something, her voice shrill and cracking. A big soldier in crossed ammo bandoliers and an ill-fitting fur schapska backhanded her savagely, and her shout was broken off in a muffled sob. A young militiaman with a thin, straggly mustache grabbed the other teenage girl from behind, tearing at her sweater as he dragged her to the ground. His comrades howled with laughter and urged him on.

Murdock touched his tongue to lips suddenly gone dry. There was no question about intervening; similar dramas were being played out daily throughout the former Republic of Bosnia, and the SEALs could not possibly stop the rape that had become a special Cain's mark of this war. Hell, at this point intervention was as likely to get the women killed as anything else. But to be forced to lie there in the bushes and watch, helpless to do anything at all . . .

Another set of headlights bathed the stone facade of the monastery as a second vehicle swung off the main road. This one was an open-topped jeep, also of Russian manufacture, and it had only a single passenger. Swiftly, Murdock raised his hand to cut off the glare from the headlights, enabling him to study the driver. Oh, Christ, yes . . . a short, wiry-looking man with glasses and a dapper mustache, identical to the man in the photograph he'd been shown yesterday. It was Gypsy, damn him, blundering headlong into the Serb party without bothering to scout the place first, and obviously as surprised by the presence of the soldiers as the SEALs had been. Two of the soldiers standing by the fire hurried out from between the parked trucks, signaling for him to stop and get out of his vehicle. Both kept their AK-47s trained on his chest.

"Shit, Lieutenant!" Roselli whispered fiercely. "That's fuckin' torn it!"

Murdock checked to see that his tactical radio was on. It was. "Blue Squad," he snapped, whispering into the microphone by his cheek. "Ready front!" He was thinking furiously. If they waited, Gypsy might be shot or arrested. So far as the mission requirements went, the balance had just shifted in favor of intervention. "Hasty ambush, single shot, stealthy, mark your targets. Magic, you take the two with our man. I'll drop the guys in the truck. After that, targets of opportunity. Professor, Doc, security, and backup. Rest of you, stand ready, on my signal. Acknowledge."

"Blue two, roger."

"Blue three, okay."

"Four, acknowledged."

"Blue five, rog."

"Six, ready to rock."

"Seven, rog."

Everyone was ready. Murdock paused, squinting across the barrel of his H&K, checking with his thumb that the fire-selector switch was set to the single red pimple marking single-shot fire. Of all SEAL combat ops, the two most nerve-wrackingly uncertain were those where hostages were scattered among the targets, and those where the attack had to be sprung without prior planning, the so-called hasty ambush, and this attack combined elements of both.

Gypsy was out of his jeep now, his hands raised. One of the soldiers was holding out his hand, demanding something—papers or identification, probably. Not that papers would help the man. Serb rape gangs and the officers above them didn't like the glare of publicity. A stranger who blundered in on a scene like this would probably be arrested at the very least, and quite probably killed. Gypsy was supposed to be a member of the SDA, the Muslim-dominated Bosnian Party for Democratic Action. If he was

Muslim and these militiamen found him out, he was a dead man.

Normally, even in a hasty ambush, each man in the squad would have been assigned a different sector, one overlapping the fire sectors of his buddies to left and right, and would open up on full-auto rock-and-roll. With civilian hostages in the line of fire, though, they couldn't risk indiscriminate fire; they would have to target and drop each enemy soldier separately. With eighteen enemy troops and only five shooters, it was a damn-near dead certainty that some, at least, would manage to escape. That was what the backup element, Professor and Doc, was for, to catch runners leaking through the kill zone.

The cardinal rule of this type of ambush was to put down the most dangerous targets first. Ignoring the thrashing of the girl, the rhythmic movements and grunts of the soldier on top of her, the coarse jeers of the men holding her down, Murdock selected one of the two men standing watch in the back of the truck.

Not that they were mounting an especially observant watch. Both were leaning against the side of the truck bed on folded arms, grinning and laughing like the rest as they watched the show taking place between the trucks. At a range of, Murdock estimated, fifteen meters, he picked an aim point inches below the spot he wanted to hit, just in front of the right ear of one of the men and below the line of his fatigue cap. It was a difficult shot for a submachine gun, but the way the targets were leaning against the side of the truck, it was safer going for a headshot than to aim for a center of mass he couldn't see behind a metal barrier that would almost certainly deflect a subsonic 9mm round.

Draw in a breath . . . let part of it out . . . a long, careful squeeze . . .

The suppressed H&K gave a sharp-edged cough, and the shot punched through the man's forehead just as he turned to say something to his partner on the truck. The impact slapped him back across the roof of the UAZ's cab with a neat, round hole just beneath his hat brim; his friend was just starting to turn to face the dead man, not even aware yet that something was wrong, when a second round drilled through the base of his neck, shattering vertebrae with a crack that sounded larger and louder than the shot itself. Murdock followed that shot with a second make-sure round to the back of the falling man's head, then shifted targets.

With Murdock's first shot the signal, all five SEALs were shooting now, sending round after round snapping into the bewildered, close-packed gaggle of militia troops in a sudden, devastating fusillade. The sound-suppressed shots were far louder than television thrillers portrayed them, reminding Murdock of the noise made by someone beating a rug, but without the ear-splitting crack of the bullet breaking the sound barrier.

The man demanding Gypsy's papers dropped to his knees, as Gypsy, his glasses and face and overcoat splattered with blood, screamed. The other armed militiaman spun toward the gunfire, his AK coming up to his shoulder just as Brown punched two rounds squarely into his chest.

The SEAL volley scythed through the Serb militiamen, dropping them one after another. A soldier in greatcoat and steel helmet fumbled for his AK, then slumped against the truck's flag-painted door; the camo-garbed man next to him gave a gasp that ended in a strangled gurgle as blood sprayed from his opened throat. A bearded soldier backlit by the fire fumbled with the AK slung muzzle-down over his back; by the time he had the weapon twisted around to where he could use it, four rounds from two different directions had slammed into his chest, pitching him back against the fifty-five-gallon drum, and then drum and body together hit the pavement with a thud and a clatter, spilling burning wood across the ground. Nearby, the big soldier on top of the naked girl lurched to his knees, his trousers bunched ridiculously around his ankles as he yelled something that could only be an obscenity and groped for a rifle, and then three bloody holes popped open across his face in one-two-three succession. The back of his head exploded; the girl shrieked hysterically as he collapsed in a bloody-headed sprawl across her legs. The soldiers holding her let go and rose in a confused tangle, colliding with one another and then going down, as splatters of their blood flicked across the stones at their backs. Two broke and made a dash for the cemetery wall off to the right. Murdock pivoted, taking careful aim, leading his target. His first round missed; his second caught the lead runner and flopped him facedown in the grass. His companion leaped over the still-rolling body, raced for the wall, then spun kicking as Doc opened up from the trees to the right with a well-aimed, three-round burst.

In front of the monastery door, a bearded soldier had grabbed the older woman from behind. Now, using her as a shield, he was edging sideways up the steps and toward the monastery door, but before he could reach it a bloody third eye winked open just above the bridge of his nose, and he flopped back against the massive wood door of the building in a gory splatter of blood and brains. SEALs trained long and hard to make difficult shots past the shoulders of human shields.

Murdock shifted his H&K left and right. No clear targets . . . no clear targets. . . .

"Razor! Boomer!" Murdock called over the tactical channel. He thumbed his magazine release, dropping a partly full mag, snapped a full one into its place. "With me! Bounding overwatch!" Rising, he stepped from the brush, H&K held tightly against his shoulder as he rushed forward, thumbing his H&K's selector to three-shot-burst mode. He reached the closest truck, then waited as Boomer and Razor dashed up from the treeline, weapons at their shoulders. Bodies lay everywhere. Most were motionless, but a screaming militiaman writhed head-down on the monastery steps, both hands clutching at a baseball-sized hole in his stomach. His shirt and the stone steps beneath him were covered with blood that looked black through the NVDs. Murdock fired once, putting three closely spaced rounds through the wounded man's skull, and the screaming stopped.

That particular scream, at any rate. The naked girl was

still alternately shrieking and gasping as she struggled to free herself from beneath the dead weight of the man lying across her legs. Gypsy was kneeling beside his jeep, eyes wide and staring, moaning and rocking back and forth. The other two women were leaning against one another on the blood-smeared monastery steps, sobbing hysterically. "Mac!" he yelled over the tactical channel. "Get Gypsy down and safe!"

"Right, L-T!"

Some part of Murdock's mind had been keeping track of targets going down, just like in the Fun House back at Little Creek. He'd counted fifteen floppers . . . was that right? Four . . . eight . . . ten . . . right. Fifteen down. That left three. Sound-suppressed shots snapped out nearby. . . .

"Blue five," Boomer's voice sounded over the radio. "One flopper. He's down."

Shit! Where were they?

There! A shadow breaking from beneath one of the trucks, running toward the left. Murdock fired, missed, and fired again. The burst smacked chips from the monastery wall close by the corner of the building. The militiaman lurched to a halt, spun about, and thrust his arms into the air. *"Molim!"* the Serb shrieked, his hands waving above his head. It was the young one with the attempt at a mustache. He didn't look any older than the girl he'd been pawing . . . a teenager, seventeen or eighteen, Murdock thought. He was babbling incoherently, tears streaming down his face, plainly terrified of these black apparitions that had materialized out of the night. *"Ne! Ne! Molim!"*

"Sorry," Murdock said, and he squeezed the H&K's trigger once more. "Nothing personal. . . ."

He checked his watch. The firefight, from first shot to last, had taken just fifteen seconds.

3

**0235 hours
St. Anastasias Monastery
Southern Bosnia**

"Jesus!" Roselli said. "L-T, you killed him!"

"Damn straight." Murdock checked the kid's right hand. On the back of his wrist were the letters CCCC—Cyrillic initials that stood for "Only Solidarity Can Save the Serbs."

So much hatred in this land. "Doc! Professor! I think we're still missing one. Any sign of him?"

"Negative, L-T," Doc's voice came back.

"Same here, sir."

"Okay. Doc, you come in and help Mac. Professor, you swing around to the rear of the building. Magic, you go with him . . . and check inside the building too. Look sharp and stay together. Mac? How's Gypsy?"

Mac had the CIA contact flat on the ground now. The man was trembling, his face and coat covered with blood.

"Shaken up, but I think he'll be okay. All that blood's not his, thank God. He got splashed by the bad guy next to him."

"Roger that. Anybody in the squad hurt?"

"Hell," Roselli said. "I don't think the sons of bitches even got off one shot."

Hadn't they? In the adrenaline-pulsing heat of the fire-

27

fight, Murdock hadn't even noticed. Now that he thought about it, though, he realized he hadn't heard any unsuppressed gunfire . . . just the harsh thumps of the SEAL H&Ks and M-16s.

Doc came trotting up as Murdock peeled off the NVDs, now grown intolerably heavy. "Doc, check our boy out."

"Right, L-T."

Murdock and Roselli went to the women next, freeing the one still trapped on the mattress, then using their SEAL diving knives to cut the twine that had been used to bind the wrists of all three. Roselli produced a relatively clean overcoat from somewhere and draped it over the girl's shivering, bony shoulders. *"Silovana sam,"* she said in a low and trembling voice, repeating the words over and over. *"Silovana sam. . . ."*

"Take charge here, Razor," Murdock said. "See if any of them speak English, see if you can get sense out of them. Check with Doc if you think they need meds or anything."

"Sure thing, L-T."

Murdock wished he had someone in the squad who spoke Serbo-Croatian. Normally they'd have had a linguist along, but this op had been too rushed to cover the fine points. Besides, as Fletcher had happily pointed out, Gypsy spoke English and the SEAL squad would not be interacting with anyone else ashore, civilian or military.

Yeah, right.

0248 hours
St. Anastasias Chapel
Southern Bosnia

It was sheer chance that they'd missed him. *Narednik* Andonov Jankovic had been leaning against the wall of the monastery, close beside the southeast corner, when his friends and comrades had begun collapsing left and right, mouths gaping, heads exploding, blood and gore spraying everywhere, all to the almost melodious chuffing ring of sound-suppressed gunfire.

Jankovic's rank of *narednik* was equivalent to that of a

senior sergeant, and though he wasn't in uniform he was still an active-duty member of the JNA, the Yugoslav National Army. Six months ago, he'd been seconded to the Serbian Volunteer Guard as an "advisor," one of thousands of JNA regulars assigned to keep the pro-Serb militias in line. With decent training and fifteen years' military experience, he'd acted instinctively when the militia troops started to fall, rolling around the corner of the building, then scrambling for cover as quickly as he could go. Judging by where the fire was coming from, he thought that one of the parked trucks had shielded him from view, but he couldn't be sure he hadn't been seen; he'd plunged into a shell hole in the side of the monastery's chapel, emerging inside the sacristy. By the time he reached the apse, the sounds of the firefight outside had died away.

The chapel had been torn by shell fire and was open to the sky. The icons, the altar, and most of the furniture had been all carried off, either by the original Dominican brothers when they'd fled, or by looters looking for gold or firewood later on. No place to hide . . . no place good enough, anyway. He scrambled through a gap in the north wall, vaulted an ironwork fence outside, and scrambled into the chill shadows beneath the trees beyond. The snow lay in patches . . . careful not to leave tracks. Where to go? Where to—

In the woods! A snowbank! Plunging into the snow behind a tangle of fallen branches, he lay there, panting hard, trying to control the heart-pounding terror that had propelled him into the forest. God, God, God, who *were* these people? Not Turks, surely . . . as he thought of the Bosnian Muslims. The UN arms blockade still prevented the Muslims from receiving more than a trickle of weapons from outside, and certainly they wouldn't have silenced guns.

What was that? Jankovic was sure he'd seen movement, close by the east side of the monastery's chapel. Holding very still in the snow, scarcely breathing, he watched a patch of darkness moving against darkness. The shape revealed itself against a bare patch of wall dimly illuminated by the glowing sky . . . but only for an instant.

Jankovic tried to digest what he'd just seen. The shape had been . . . nightmarishly alien, terrifying, with some kind of harness or vest heavy with equipment, with something like goggles or a camera over its face. A second shadow joined the first. They moved so stealthily, so silently, that Jankovic kept losing sight of them. He wanted to run, but he suppressed the urge, knowing that if he so much as moved, they would see him.

Russian Spetsnaz? The only Russians in Yugoslavia, apart from a UN brigade present solely for cosmetic purposes, were advisors secretly helping the JNA. Americans, then?

Everything he'd been told about the Americans said that they were cowards, afraid to fight save from behind the screen of their near-magical technology. Jankovic's superiors warned almost daily of the danger of American air strikes, impressing on the men the need to capture any downed pilots alive. But ground troops? It seemed impossible.

But as Jankovic lay in the snow, watching the two shadows quartering the grounds behind the monastery, he became convinced that they must be Americans, possibly even their legendary Delta Force. They had so much expensive equipment—personal radios, night-vision goggles, silenced submachine guns—they *must* be Americans, because only Americans could afford that kind of lavish, high-tech gadgetry.

Did their gadgetry include infrared goggles? Could they see him beneath his blanket of snow? Jankovic had worked with Russian IR equipment and knew that his body heat must be glowing as brightly as a bonfire against the cold ground. Even starlight optics allowed some vision at infrared wavelengths. If they saw him . . .

But no, the shadows moved within ten meters of his hiding place, giving no evidence of having seen him.

Silently, the shadows passed him by, circled the west end of the monastery, and vanished.

Even so, it was several minutes before Jankovic could force trembling legs to support him. He didn't dare head for the road, not when more of the invaders could have an ambush posted there. Instead, he started climbing the mountain behind the monastery. The road angled back across the face of the mountain, perhaps five hundred meters up the slope, and from there it was another three kilometers to a local militia outpost.

There was a radio there, and he'd be able to call for help. This was definitely a job for the JNA, and they would have to work fast to trap these high-tech shadows, before they could make their escape.

0252 hours
St. Anastasias Monastery
Southern Bosnia

Magic and Professor showed up a few minutes later, silently materializing out of the darkness like wraiths. "No trace of that runner, L-T," Magic said. "He must've decided it was time to get the hell out of Dodge."

"Shit, that son of a bitch's feet won't touch the ground twice before he hits the Bulgarian border," Doc said, coming up on Murdock from behind. "Skipper? Our spook friend checks out okay. I gave him a one-grain tab of phenobarb to kind of quiet him down, like."

"Okay, Doc. See to the women, will you?"

Doc's painted face split in a toothy grin. "Hey, my pleasure, Skipper."

"Cut the crap, Doc. They've just been through hell and they don't need any shit from you."

The smile vanished. "Aye, aye, sir."

Damn, he hadn't meant to snap at Doc. The guy had a wild rep with the ladies on liberty, but on duty he was always strictly professional, except for his sometimes quirky sense of humor.

The aftereffects of the firefight, and the fact that one of

the bad guys had escaped, had Murdock on edge. He hurried
over to where Mac was sitting on the ground with the CIA
man. Squatting next to him, Murdock tried to give a
reassuring smile, an expression that he knew well could not
be all that reassuring delivered through all of this camo face
paint.

"You're Gypsy?"

The man seemed to be trying to focus on Murdock. His
glasses were still blood-smeared. "Uh . . . *ya sam* Gypsy,"
the man said. "You . . . you Nomad?"

That was the proper recognition code, Gypsy and Nomad,
sign and countersign. "I'm Nomad."

The man gestured vaguely at the jeep. "Papers, in there."

They found what they'd come for on the floor of the
jeep, a briefcase bulging with typewritten papers. Not
originals; from the look of them, they'd have been stamped
secret if they were. They appeared to be carefully compiled
lists of troops, regular forces and militias, personnel rosters,
TO&E breakdowns, headquarters sites, SAM positions,
artillery placements. . . .

"You use, *ne?*" Gypsy said as Murdock carefully clicked
the briefcase shut. "You send jets, kill many Christians, kill
many Chetnik bastards, *da?*"

Murdock looked back at the monastery and at the bodies
littering the ground. "Kill many Christians," he said, his
voice hard. *"Da."*

"Hvala. Vrlo ste lyubazni."

0342 hours
Checkpoint Orandzasta
Southern Bosnia
The Mi-8 transport helicopter descended toward the clearing, a broad stretch of open and relatively level ground on
the otherwise thickly forested mountainside that had been
the site of a logging operation several years earlier. Several
vehicles had been lined up to either side of the roadway,
their headlights illuminating the touchdown point.

Brigadni Djeneral Vuk Mihajlovic remained in his seat as

the helicopter touched down, a crew member slid open the cabin door on the right side, and his aides and bodyguards clambered out into the night. He didn't like flying, especially at night, and especially as parts shortages and wear and tear claimed more and more of the aging aircraft purchased years ago from the then-Soviet Union. Still, it was the only way a brigade general could maintain personal control of his command, and this time it sounded as though he'd happened upon a special piece of luck.

JNA helicopters in Bosnia tended to fly only short hops nowadays, sticking to hair-raising, low-level flights through mountain passes and valleys just in case NATO or the Americans decided to enforce their ludicrous and arbitrary no-fly-zone decrees. Mihajlovic had been en route from Kotor to the headquarters of his Third Regiment in the hills outside Dubrovnik when the Mi-8's pilot had picked up an urgent radio call from Checkpoint Orandzasta. Normally, he would have ordered the pilot to ignore the signal, but the caller had used a code phrase that indicated he was a JNA advisor with the militias. He'd then reported an ambush on Bosnian-Serb forces that he claimed had been launched by American commandos.

That seemed unlikely. Almost certainly, what the caller had blundered into was a raid by one or another of the anti-Serb militias, probably Croats with the paramilitary HOS, the so-called Croatian Defense Army. There was almost nothing left of the Bosnian Muslin forces, not enough to have caused the slaughter the JNA advisor was screaming about over the radio.

In any case, since Mihajlovic happened to be in the area, it wouldn't hurt to stop and find out what was going on. Mihajlovic was a hands-on type of commander, Russian-trained, popular with his troops. It wouldn't hurt to check on the man's story, especially if the Croats were up to something unpleasant. A commando raid against the naval base at Kotor was a definite possibility, as were guerrilla-style raids against the Serbian supply lines through the mountains above Dubrovnik.

Careful not to give the appearance of unseemly haste, he
unbuckled from his jump seat and stepped out of the
helicopter. With head bent to avoid the still-turning rotors,
he walked toward the building nearby, a decrepit-looking
shack that had been the office for the lumbering company
here and that now served as Checkpoint Orange.

He was met outside the building's front door by two men,
both in dirty mismatches of Soviet-style and Yugoslav army
uniforms. *"Dobro yutro,"* he greeted them. "What seems to
be the trouble?"

"Good morning, Brigade General," the older of the two
men said. "I am Captain Balaban, in command of this post.
I—"

"Sir! Senior Sergeant Jankovic," the other man said,
abruptly interrupting the militia officer. "I am a JNA advisor
with these people."

"You are the one who reported an attack," Mihajlovic
said, ignoring Balaban. The militiamen tended to be disor-
ganized and more often than not exaggerated the situation,
whatever it was. But the JNA sergeant looked reliable
enough.

"Yes, sir. American commandos wiped out a section of
Serbian Volunteer Guards not five kilometers from here."

"And how is it you escaped, Sergeant?"

"The chances of war, General. That . . . and I was able
to react swiftly when the attack started." He glanced briefly
at Balaban. "The militia handled themselves as well as
could be expected under the circumstances. The attackers
were almost certainly American commandos. They opened
fire suddenly, without warning, when most of our men did
not even have their weapons."

"Um. What makes you think the attackers were Americans?"

"Their equipment, my General." He went on to describe
the attack, and what he had seen of the two commandos, in
precise detail. He did not say—and Mihajlovic did not
ask—just what the Bosnian militiamen had been doing at
the ruined monastery in the first place, other than to mention

that the unit had been standing down, with minimal security measures in place. In all probability they'd been engaged in what the JNA high command euphemistically called "pacification," breaking the stubborn Bosnian-Muslim will to resist, and the Serb general did not care to know too many of the details.

Sometimes, terrible things had to be done to further a cause, to achieve a necessary goal.

When Jankovic had completed his report, Mihajlovic was more than half certain that the sergeant had, indeed, seen Americans . . . or at least a contingent of NATO commandos. The description of their uniforms—black coveralls, combat harnesses, low-light goggles, silenced automatic weapons—sounded very much like the British SAS, though there were no reports that any Special Air Service detachments were stationed anywhere near the Adriatic just now. German GSG-9 was another possibility; the Germans had been taking a keen interest in military developments in the Balkans, though they were still unwilling to operate outside of the guidelines set by NATO. Americans? Very possible. Delta Force, Army Rangers . . .

But what could Americans be after at a ruined Bosnian monastery? Jankovic had mentioned a civilian who'd driven up moments before the ambush. That could be significant. A curfew was in effect throughout Bosnia and coastal Croatia; a civilian out in the middle of the night, alone at a place that should have been deserted, was extremely suspicious . . . and supported Jankovic's contention that the attackers were foreign commandos. "You did not see what became of the civilian," he said bluntly.

"No, my General. I know only that he was there in the custody of two of my men when the attack began."

"And the attack took place . . ." He consulted his watch. "Just over an hour ago?"

"Yes, sir. I remember looking at my watch when the civilian drove up. It was two-thirty-five."

"Then these invaders, whoever they are, are still in the area. Come with me, Sergeant."

"Yes, sir. Where are we going?"

"To find these commandos, of course. I would like to know what they find so interesting about a deserted, tumbledown church."

0345 hours
St. Anastasias Monastery
Southern Bosnia

"L-T?"

"Yeah, Razor."

"We got the brass policed, L-T," Roselli said. He'd found the lieutenant standing next to the highway, staring up the mountain, a distracted look on his face. "We're clean."

"Okay. Get your gear together and let's move. It's time to get the hell out of Dodge!"

Roselli, frankly, wasn't sure what to make of the L-T. He'd thought he'd known the man pretty well; eight months of close, hard training and two combat deployments—one in the Indian Ocean, the other just a few days later at the Iranian naval port at Bandar Abbas—were enough to make brothers out of any two men, whatever the differences in their backgrounds or families. Now, though, he wasn't so sure.

It was, he knew, the way Murdock had gunned down that Serb militiaman, right at the end of the firefight. Oh, the fact of the killing alone wasn't the problem. SEALs, like covert forces tasked with counterinsurgency/counterterrorism worldwide, frequently had to get into tight places and out again without being seen and without jeopardizing the op's success by dragging along prisoners. The written orders for this mission had directed Blue Squad to handle prisoners "according to SOP," a bit of verbal misdirection that meant they would not be taking prisoners.

But Lieutenant Blake Murdock was not just another SEAL platoon leader, whatever he might tell the guys. He was the son of Congressman Charles Fitzhugh Murdock of Virginia, and Roselli knew damned well that there was a lot riding on that relationship. According to the scuttlebutt, the

elder Murdock hadn't wanted his son to go into Navy
Special Warfare in the first place, and had done damn near
all he could to get him out. The L-T was a stubborn son of
a bitch, though, and the story was that he'd joined the teams
in defiance of his dad's wishes.

But man, if the story got out that Murdock personally had
blown away a bad guy after he'd tried to surrender, the
political fallout would be inconceivable. At the very least it
would end the younger Murdock's career . . . and maybe
the elder Murdock's career as well. There were plenty in
Congress who felt that SEALs and elite units like them were
anachronisms, necessary, possibly, during the Cold War, but
embarrassing and even dangerous in this enlightened day of
world peace and military cutbacks.

Besides, the L-T just wasn't that cold. Oh, Murdock
could be hard when he had to be; he ran a tight platoon and
didn't let the guys slack off for a minute. But he was also
less intense than a lot of SEALs, and he didn't come across
as a stone killer. He'd been to Annapolis—an honest-to-
God ring-knocker—and he looked more like a fighter jock
or an XO aboard some supply ship or, hell, like a *lawyer*
than he did a SEAL. Athletic—lean and wiry rather than
muscular—and clean-cut, clear-eyed, nonsmoker, nondrinker,
kind of on the quiet side. And sometimes, like now, he got
real quiet . . . and then you never knew what was going to
go down.

He'd talked to that spook local for quite a while, then
tried to use him as a translator with the women, none of
whom spoke any English. That hadn't worked out very well,
because the women were still in shock and Gypsy had been
real anxious to be on his way. Before he'd let the guy go,
though, he'd made him promise to take the girls along, get
them out of the area. Gypsy hadn't wanted to do that, but
Murdock had told him that the CIA would find out if he
didn't take them someplace safe . . . and then the SEALs
would come for *him*.

Then he'd made the guy wait even longer while he had
some of the guys take shirts and coats from some of the Serb

bodies, ones that weren't too badly bloodied, and give them to the women who'd had their clothing cut up.

That was scarcely the manner of a cold-blooded killer, or even of a SEAL officer who thought of nothing but the mission.

For the next half hour, Murdock had had the SEALs picking up all the spent brass from the firefight and bagging it. The 9mm rounds fired by H&Ks were common throughout Europe, but the .223 rounds fired by the M-16s carried by Mac and Magic were unmistakably NATO. Perhaps he should have insisted that everyone carry local weapons, like AKs, but damn it, there wasn't supposed to have been a firefight in the first place. The weapons were insurance against the unthinkable . . . to be used only as a last resort.

Now their concern was exfiltration, getting out with the minimum fuss possible. He'd ordered Doc and Higgins to gather up the bodies and dump them in the two trucks, after which Mac had siphoned off a couple of liters of gasoline and doused both vehicles and their contents. There was no way to hide what had happened here tonight, but Murdock clearly hoped to leave as few traces behind as possible.

"Everything's set," MacKenzie said, as Roselli shrugged into his assault vest. "The squad's ready to move out."

"Okay. Touch off the trucks and let's go."

MacKenzie stayed behind long enough to toss a couple of thermite grenades into the backs of the trucks. The SEALs were already well into the woods when the incendiaries went off, and the night-black forest behind them lit up brighter than day.

They were moving single file down the slope moments later when Murdock stopped, letting the rest of the men file past him. Roselli had the next-to-the-last position, just ahead of Mac. "L-T?" he asked as he came up to where Murdock was standing. "You okay?"

"I keep thinking I hear something," Murdock said. He looked worried.

Roselli stopped and listened too. He could hear the roar of the fire, but far off now. There was nothing else. . . .

No, there was something. Roselli heard it too, a kind of dull, clattering noise.

"Chopper," Murdock said. *"Damn* that was fast!"

"Maybe they're just passing by."

"Maybe. And maybe they're stopping to have a look at our handiwork." Murdock reached up and touched his tactical radio's transmit switch. "Blue Squad! The dogs are out. Let's take it double-time!"

Roselli could hear the helicopter clearly now, a pulsing *whop-whop-whop* sounding through the forest from higher up on the hill.

Murdock hadn't been kidding. The hunt was on, and the SEAL squad was the prey.

4

St. Anastasias Monastery
Southern Bosnia

"My General," the aide said. "This does not look like the work of Turk rabble."

Mihajlovic nodded, watching the flames in front of the monastery dwindle. "I am beginning to agree. Sergeant."

"Da, moy Djeneral!"

"You say you were just there, by the southeast corner, when the attack occurred?"

"Yes, sir."

"And the commandos must have been there . . . hidden in the brush at the tree line."

"Yes, sir."

There was little left of two military trucks save for the charred and twisted frames. There were no bodies lying around as Jankovic had claimed, but there was plenty of evidence of a massacre—splatters of blood on the ground and on the front wall of the monastery, bullet scars on the stone.

"You are right, Major," Mihajlovic said thoughtfully to his aide. "Someone has gone to considerable trouble to clean up after himself." He'd already had the men with him using flashlights to scour the area for empty brass casings that would have identified the weapons the intruders had used, but so far they'd found nothing, no shells, no discarded equipment or wrappers or food tins, *nothing* that would have told Mihajlovic who had been here. "Muslim militia would not have been so thorough. Even Croats would simply have ambushed our people, then melted away into the forest. Besides, I suspect they would have left some bodies about as a kind of calling card, *ne?*"

The bodies of the militia troopers and their weapons, he thought, had probably been dumped in the trucks before the fires had been set. The attackers could be anywhere now, hidden by the night and the forest.

But they would not have gotten far. The fire was still burning; it couldn't have been set more than thirty minutes or so ago . . . and maybe less. That meant that the invaders were still close, within two or three kilometers at the most.

"Major, if the intruders were, indeed, Americans or other members of NATO," Mihajlovic continued after a thoughtful moment, "then they are on their way to an extraction point. It is up to us to guess where that extraction point might be."

"Extraction, my General . . . by helicopter?"

"Possible . . . possible. We shall alert the Air Force, have them watch for incursions in the area by low-flying, unidentified aircraft."

Helicopter extraction did seem the most likely way out for the intruders . . . but Mihajlovic had been giving the situation some hard thought during the past few minutes, and he was not convinced of that scenario. Despite their bluster, NATO had not been enforcing their no-fly zones lately, yet their AWACs aircraft must be tracking the Yugoslav aircraft that were being employed against Dubrovnik. It didn't make sense to risk a helicopter extraction in heavily wooded, mountainous terrain, in a region where Yugoslav interceptors were active.

So . . . would extraction be more likely by air . . . or by sea? American Special Warfare groups commonly used both means of exfiltration. The Americans were good at undersea incursions, made from submarines . . . their Special Forces, their SEALs . . .

SEALs. Their Navy commandos. With the fighting at Dubrovnik, even with fighter cover the Americans would have been foolish to risk their special forces aircraft to SAM and antiaircraft fire. And St. Anastasias was only six kilometers from the sea.

"Both of you, come with me." Paced by Jankovic and the aide, Mihajlovic returned to the helicopter, which had landed on the main road just outside the monastery turnoff. In the back of the main cabin, he selected a map case from a storage rack and pulled out a military topo map covering the region between Kotor and Dubrovnik. Using a pocket flashlight, he studied the terrain carefully for a moment. "Sergeant Jankovic?"

"Da, moy Djeneral!"

"How would you like another chance against these mysterious commandos?"

Jankovic hesitated, and Mihajlovic could almost hear the wheels turning as the man considered his reply. He couldn't be eager to face those black attackers again.

"I would welcome the opportunity, my General. Of course."

Mihajlovic pointed to a spot on the map. "They almost certainly came ashore somewhere about here . . . east of Dubrovnik. I suspect that they have hidden diving gear somewhere along the coast. All we need to do is put down a force along M2." He dragged his fingertip along the coastal highway on the map. "Patrol from here to here and we will have our frogmen trapped, high and dry like a beached fish."

"Do we have troops enough available for such an operation?" the aide wondered. "That's a good five or six kilometers of highway."

"We can bring JNA regulars from the front lines at Dubrovnik, Major. I will give the necessary commands at

once. Sergeant, you may draw a weapon and join my escort.
I will be heading this operation personally."

"Yes, sir!"

The timing, Mihajlovic thought, would be tight . . . but
he was pretty sure they could pull it off. More than revenge
was riding here. If these frogman commandos were Americans, he wanted to take one or more of them prisoner. With
solid evidence of covert American military action on
Yugoslav soil, Belgrade might well be able to break the
coalition of European and UN forces arrayed against Serbia
in this damned, festering civil war. It would mean disgrace
for the Americans, a propaganda victory for Greater Serbia, a
promotion and an opening of political goals for himself.

In fact, it would tie in perfectly with Operation Dvorak,
which had many of the same goals. A victory here would
nicely complement his operation in Macedonia—a complex
plot that had been in preparation for months now and was
due to reach a climax in only a few more days.

Would this affect the timing of Dvorak at all? He didn't
think so. It probably couldn't have been better if he'd
planned it this way from the beginning.

And all he needed to do was to capture a handful of
lightly armed men before they could reach the safety of the
sea.

0437 hours
East of Dubrovnik
Southern Bosnia
They'd alternated running and walking down the flank of
the Gora Orjen, using a ground-eating pace across the open,
pine-needle-covered forest floor to put as much distance as
possible between them and their pursuers. The hunt was
definitely on. Possibly the missing militia trooper had
managed to call for help; more likely, a passing JNA
helicopter had sighted the burning trucks and come to
investigate. Either way, the Serbian military command in
the Dubrovnik area would be alerted. At the very least, there
would be patrols out, both on foot in the forest and in

vehicles along the road. If the JNA commander decided to risk the threat of NATO air involvement, he would have helicopters up as well, both transports carrying squads of soldiers, and gunships.

At least that's what Murdock knew he would do if he were in the enemy commander's place.

They reached the edge of the forest just above the border fence, and Murdock called a halt. The coastal highway lay another four kilometers down the hill, across an open, gently descending field. Beyond that was the seawall and the beach.

They'd emerged from the woods within a few hundred meters of where they'd gone in. As the other SEALs took up position crouched in a defensive perimeter about the area, Murdock and MacKenzie both checked the GPS, pinpointing their position and giving them a fix on where they'd left their equipment.

"So," MacKenzie said. "What do you think? Looks clear."

"Yeah, it does. I think to be on the safe side, though, we should call in. Higgins!"

The squad's radioman crawled over to them. "Yeah, L-T?"

"Break out the sat-comm gear, Prof. We're going to phone home."

"Will do."

It took only a few minutes to set up the sat-comm system's antenna, which was stowed in a pocket of one of the rucksacks like a folded-up umbrella. With legs and arms extended, it sat on the ground, facing south, its dish just seventeen inches across. A coaxial cable extending from the back of the antenna was plugged into Higgins's HST-4 unit.

Using a small manual, the *Equatorial Satellite Pointing Guide*, Higgins began lining up the antenna while the commo gear ran through its automated self-checks and calibrations. When he heard a tiny peep, the antenna was properly aligned with one of the military communications satellites in geosynchronous orbit above the equator.

"Ready to transmit, Skipper," he said.

"Okay. Give him a sit-rep. Tell 'em we have the package and we're four klicks from the beach, but that we got into a firefight and could have bad guys on our tail."

"Yes, sir."

As Higgins began speaking in low, measured tones into his microphone, Murdock unpacked a pair of 7x40 binoculars and began to carefully study the highway below. Low-light gear didn't help much at ranges over 150 meters; there were still situations where relatively old-fashioned equipment was more useful than modern, high-tech toys.

MacKenzie was also using binoculars to sweep the landscape. "Don't see a damned thing, Skipper."

"Affirmative. Looks quiet." Murdock lowered the binoculars. "Well, only one way to find out. Professor?"

"We got an acknowledge, L-T. They say Night Rider's on the way. ETA thirty minutes. They've also alerted Gold Squad. They're getting wet right now."

"We can't wait that long, not with the road still clear. Pack up your gear, Prof. We're moving."

"Aye, aye, Skipper."

Minutes later, the SEAL squad was back across the border and moving down the open slope, walking now, because the ground was more uneven than it had been in the forest, with numerous boot-sized holes masked by the long, dead grass. Magic had the point position now, followed by Mac and Murdock. The clouds overhead had thickened during the past hour, until the sky was almost completely overcast. The light of the moon had been lost completely; the only illumination in the sky now at all was the sullen glow over Dubrovnik.

A rumbling sounded out of the east, swiftly growing louder. Magic gave a sharp whistle, and the SEALs went to ground, making themselves as nearly as possible a part of the cold, hard landscape. The rumble neared . . . then exploded overhead, as thunderous as an exploding shell. The ground seemed to shake, and then the sound was dwindling away once more.

Two aircraft. Murdock could see their afterburners glowing like paired stars beneath the cloud canopy as they roared toward Dubrovnik. "Anybody see what they were?" he asked.

"Negative, L-T," Roselli said from somewhere behind. "But they sure as shit were goin' somewhere in a hurry."

"Maybe," Doc said, "they were afraid of bein' recognized."

The aircraft *might* have been friendlies. NATO and the U.S. had been attempting to enforce no-fly zones over Bosnia and the Adriatic coast, but with a notable lack of success. It was just as likely that those had been Serbian MiGs out of Kotor or Titograd, on their way to attack Croat positions at Dubrovnik or further up the coast.

Or . . .

"On your feet, people," Murdock called. "Fast!"

Or they could be air assets brought in to cover Serbian ground forces, especially airmobile troops.

"You think those guys were looking for us?" Mac asked.

"Maybe. They could be flying ground support. Even if they weren't, I think it's time we found a less hostile environment."

Though SEALs, unlike their UDT forebears, were trained to operate well inland from the beach, their training constantly emphasized that the sea was the SEAL's natural habitat. When things started to get hot ashore, the water offered cover, security, and escape. The sea lay just ahead, black, featureless, and welcoming, picking up just a hint of the sky glow from the direction of Dubrovnik.

Another forty minutes and they'd be there.

0501 hours
East of Dubrovnik
Croatia

Narednik Jankovic's grip on his newly acquired AKM assault rifle tightened as he leaned over to stare out the Mi-8's circular window. It was still too dark to see anything but a faint blur that might have been surf washing up the shelf of the beach. The transport was racing along through the night at an altitude of less than one hundred meters; somewhere just ahead, the second helicopter, the one with General Mihajlovic aboard, was also paralleling the coastline east from Dubrovnik.

The general, Jankovic reflected, certainly knew how to get things moving. They'd flown to the Serbian lines just outside Dubrovnik, and within minutes Mihajlovic had rounded up sixty troops, forming up what he'd referred to as an "ad hoc counterterrorist team." More troops were on the way by road, packed into trucks commandeered at the Serbian camp. Mihajlovic seemed fanatical on the subject of finding the intruders and running them to earth.

Jankovic wondered if the fact that the man's name was Mihajlovic had anything to do with it. Dragoljub Mihajlovic had been a colonel on the Yugoslav Army general staff during World War II, the man who had organized the original Chetniks. He'd been shot by the Communists in 1946—naturally enough since the Chetniks had in some cases openly collaborated with the Nazis, especially late in the war.

Well, it probably meant nothing. Mihajlovic was a common Serb name. But the general was old enough to be a son or a nephew of old Dragoljub, and such a connection would go a long way toward explaining his ambition . . . and his enthusiasm for this mission.

Jankovic almost hoped the commandos, whoever they were, had already made good their escape. Their ruthless and deadly efficiency at the monastery had burned the warning into Jankovic's brain. These were not men to trifle with, not men to put into a corner where their only option was to fight their way out.

"Hey! Sergeant!"

Jankovic turned from the window. The *kaplar*—the corporal—sitting in the next seat grinned at him hopefully.

"Yeah?"

"I hear you actually saw some of these terrorists we're supposed to be hunting. What were they like, huh?"

"Dangerous," Jankovic said. "Extremely dangerous."

0504 hours
Above the beach east of Dubrovnik
Croatia

"Chopper incoming!" Roselli called. "Take cover!"

The SEAL squad went to ground, still a full hundred meters short of the highway. The helicopter . . . no, *two* helicopters were coming in low from the west, with running lights blinking, with searchlights on and painting the road beneath them with dazzling white shafts. The lead aircraft flew past the SEALs' hiding place, racing toward the east. Its rotor wash set clouds of sand swirling in its wake, illuminated by the glare of its spotlight.

Roselli lay stretched out on the ground next to Murdock, his H&K's stock pressed to his shoulder. "Whatcha say, L-T?" he asked. "Shall we take 'em?"

"Negative, Razor," Murdock replied. "Some of those Mi-8s sport a fair amount of armor. All we'd do is pinpoint our position."

"Shit. What I wouldn't give right now for a couple of LAWs."

"Just sit tight. We'll wait 'em out."

"I dunno, L-T. Looks like that second bird's gonna touch down right over there."

As the lead Mi-8 vanished toward the east, the second aircraft was flaring out, nose high, settling down toward the road in a whirl of windblown sand. The line of poplar trees beyond whipped frantically in the breeze. As the helo's wheels hit the pavement, the cabin door on the port side slid open, and soldiers armed with AK assault rifles began piling out.

"How many you figure?" Boomer asked from nearby.

"A Hip's normal troop complement is thirty-two," Murdock replied. "Hip" was the NATO desgination for the Mi-8 in its troop-transport role. "But I guarantee you there'll be more coming down the road by truck any time now. This'll just be the advance guard."

"Looks like first-string JNA stuff," Roselli said. "They must want us pretty damned bad."

Murdock reached behind him and pulled out his night-vision set, pulled off his hat, and settle the goggles over his head. Roselli already had his goggles on his head, pushed up above his eyes, so he simply slid them down into place and switched them on.

The NVDs didn't make the helicopters that much clearer, not with all the flying sand and dust and the sweep of searchlights, but the soldiers sprang into sharp relief. "No night-vision gear, L-T."

"I see, Razor. That gives us a chance."

It was a little like being the invisible man, Roselli thought. You could see them, but they couldn't see you, wouldn't even know you were there unless you did something stupid like step on a branch or fall over your own two feet. All of the SEALs were wearing the NVDs now, and the scene below them glowed in eerily shining greens, blacks and silvers.

"Here! L-T!" Higgins said. "They're forming up and coming this way!"

While perhaps half of the Yugoslavian troops stayed near the helicopter, the rest were drawing out in a long line along the highway, with eight or ten meters separating each man from his neighbors. NCOs wielded flashlights and barked commands. Sixteen men started forward, walking up the hill toward the waiting SEALs.

"We could go around them, Lieutenant," Mac pointed out. "Cross there, to the left, then move back up the beach behind the wall."

"I don't think so," Murdock replied. "Look there."

A convoy was coming up the road from the direction of Dubrovnik, seven Army trucks, each crowded with troops. From the look of things, they were dropping men off along the road. One stopped several hundred meters further on. Five more grumbled past the tableau on the highway below, edging past the point where the helicopter blocked the road, then racing further toward the east as though they were in pursuit of the other helicopter. The seventh truck pulled to a halt just before it reached the Hip, and men began piling out, calling noisily to one another and tossing helmets and weapons down from the back of the vehicle.

"Definitely regular army," Murdock said, studying the men through his binoculars.

"They sure are loud," Roselli said. "You'd think they wanted us to know they were there."

"They may want to spook us back up the mountain," Mac pointed out.

"Yeah, or they may not care," Magic said. "Shit, they've got an army down there."

"So what?" Roselli replied. "Since when is an army a match for seven SEALs?"

The line of men grew longer as men ran up the hill to join it . . . and longer . . . and longer still. Flashlights probed and stabbed the darkness, flashing now toward the waiting SEALs, then away. The troops were closer now, perhaps fifty meters, and a searchlight mounted inside the helicopter's cockpit was being directed at the hillside.

"A cordon," Murdock said, his voice grim. "They know we're up here somewhere. They mean to stretch out a cordon and catch us like fish in a net."

5

Roselli waited, watching the soldier he'd picked out moving closer. The Serb troops were still noisy as they tramped up the hill through the field, but the shouts and catcalls had died away as each of the soldiers concentrated on his steps across the slightly uneven ground with its holes and unexpected mounds of matted grass.

There was no time to try to sidestep the search cordon. In the open field, there was just light enough that one of the advancing soldiers would spot a running, black-clad shape even without night-vision gear. The only option, then, was to sit tight and let the cordon pass. It was Roselli's job to make sure the opening between one soldier and the next was big enough for the SEALs to slip through unobserved.

One of the soldiers was moving directly toward Roselli's position. Had he been just a few meters to either side, Roselli would have let him pass, but there was too great a risk that he might see one of the SEALs lying flat on the ground . . . or step on one.

Roselli tensed, the dull ebon length of his diving knife held tight in his hand. The soldier walked slowly closer, paused two meters away, listening, then took another step—

The SEAL swept up from the ground, left hand sweeping around the soldier's head, hand clamping down over nose and mouth, right hand gripping the knife, snapping up and sharply down. Roselli went for a straight stabbing take-down, rather than a chancier and noisier throat slash, angling the knife down at the hollow of the Serb's throat as he snapped the chin back. The blade slid smoothly through the half-circle described by the man's first rib, making a tiny *chink* as it scraped down the inside of his right clavicle and snicked through the subclavian artery. The man shuddered in Roselli's grip. Shoving the knife's hilt hard back toward his jaw sent the blade slicing into the heart; angling it sharply forward again cut through windpipe and esophagus and the thoracic vertebra with a faint, dry, cracking sound. The soldier went dead-limp, and Roselli lowered him gently, gently to the ground.

Five meters to the left, Magic Brown silently merged with a second Yugoslavian soldier. The diving knife flicked, a razor-edged blur; there was a quiet, almost regretful sigh, and then Magic eased that body too onto the grass. To left and right, the other Yugoslavs kept walking, unaware of the two deaths in the middle of their line.

Roselli and Brown maintained their positions over the bodies, knives drawn, as the SEALs one by one slipped through the gap opened in the enemy's search line. They moved as silently as the wind, with only a faint rustle in the grass to betray their movement, and with the Hip's rotors still slowly turning the noise was easily lost. Moments later, the SEALs reached the road, gathering in a ditch on the north side of the road about eighty meters east of the helicopter.

They used hand and squeeze signals only to coordinate their movements. There was a terrible danger here, of the helicopter turning its searchlight on the road, or of vehicles approaching with headlights on. They could clearly hear the Serb soldiers who'd remained with the helicopter talking by the seawall just a few tens of meters away. Mac went first, his big bulk slipping across the pavement as lightly as a ballerina, edging past the line of poplars, then rolling across the seawall and onto the seaward side. Next went Magic . . . then Higgins . . . Doc . . . Boomer . . . the L-T. Roselli went last, backing across the road with his H&K raised, ready to return fire if someone spotted them.

On the seaward side of the wall, the SEALs lay flat on the sand. Their buried IBS and diving gear, as nearly as Roselli could tell, were on the far side of the helicopter, perhaps 100 or 120 meters up the beach to the west. Touching Murdock lightly on the sleeve, Roselli looked into the expressionless lenses of the lieutenant's night-vision gear and silently signaled: *To the raft?*

Murdock's mouth, just visible beneath his goggles, twisted in a frown. He shook his head, then pointed down the shelf of the beach toward the surf: *No. We'll go out that way.*

Roselli accepted Murdock's decision, but he felt a stab of disappointment nonetheless. SEALs prided themselves in coming and going along hostile shores and leaving no trace of their visit. If they abandoned the raft, together with two sets of rebreather apparatus and seven pairs of masks and fins, someone would be certain to find it sooner or later. The next good gale or storm surge would uncover it . . . as would a careful search by the local military using mine sweepers or metal detectors. Besides, there was the SEAL warrior's image to uphold. Swimming back to the *Nassau* without even their duck fins would be a little too much like being chased out with their figurative tails between their legs.

It would be a long swim too without their fins and masks. *Nassau* was on station just beyond the old Yugoslavian twelve-mile limit. While a twelve-mile swim wasn't out of the question for SEALs, even after a rugged mission ashore, their best bet would be to link up with Gold Squad and the second CRRC. Twelve miles in the open sea with neither fins nor floatation devices was going to be murder, pure and simple.

Before they could even think about swimming back to the ship, though, they would have to get across the beach. The tide had gone out since the SEALs had arrived on this beach over five hours earlier. Mediterranean tides rarely rose or fell as far as their oceanic cousins, but the gradual slope of the beach along this particular stretch of the Dalmatian coast meant that even a small difference between the high- and low-water levels could expose quite a lot of beach. Roselli estimated that the beach was eighty meters wide now, more than twice what it had been when they'd come ashore.

Another helicopter rattled overhead, traveling west to east and sweeping the beach with its searchlight as it went.

This could get damned tricky.

0514 hours
On Highway M2 east of Dubrovnik

Narednik Jankovic walked along the north side of the seawall, trying hard to see everywhere in the darkness at once. His comrades, members of the Third JNA Mechanized Infantry Brigade, had laughed at his belief that the infiltrators they were searching for were Americans.

They'd laughed harder still when he described the slaughter at the monastery . . . had it only been three hours ago? After all the Srpska Dobrovoljacki Straza—the Serb Volunteer Guard—while made up of fellow Serbs, was nonetheless a militia, good for hunting down Bosniaks but not all that good in a stand-up fight. Caught in an ambush by professionals, of course they'd been wiped out. But that sort of thing could never happen to regular army troops.

Jankovic wasn't so sure. A great many members of the various Serbian militias had been JNA men like him, allowed to leave the army expressly so they could join the militias or to serve as "advisors." Bosnia-Hercegovina had a sizable Serb population which did not want to live under either Muslim or Croat domination should Bosnia become either free or a Croat protectorate. Letting Bosnian-Serb troops leave the JNA to join the militias had been an easy means of keeping Bosnia—most of it, at any rate—under Yugoslav, that is to say, under *Serbian* control. While JNA troops might joke about their Bosnian brothers, the difference between the members of any Serb militia unit and the Yugoslav National Army had nothing to do with bravery, skill . . . or with determination. Indeed, many in the militia, especially the NCOs, were like Jankovic, still officially with the national army but serving on special attached duty with the Bosnians.

He wondered if General Mihajlovic was right in his guess that the SEALs must be headed for this particular stretch of beach. If so, the commandos could be anywhere . . . though they hadn't really had time yet to travel all the way down the Gora Orjen. Likely they were still up there, somewhere in that pine forest above the highway. He wondered if they were watching him right now, and shivered.

"Jankovic!" a young JNA *poruchnik*, a senior lieutenant, called from further down the sea wall. "Get over here!"

"Da, moy Poruchnik," Jankovic called back. He broke into a trot and hurried to join the group.

The lieutenant and several troops were gathered together on the seaward side of the wall. One of the men had a mine detector, while the others were on their knees, scooping out a shallow hole in the sand with their hands. There was something in the hole. . . .

"Jankovic!" the lieutenant said, grinning. "Do you think this might have been left here by your friends?"

He turned his flashlight on the object in the hole, his beam mingling with those of several of the men standing nearby. It looked like an inflatable boat, jet black in color, with a small engine carefully wrapped in plastic mounted on the rear.

"It could be, Lieutenant," Jankovic replied. "Are there any markings?"

"None. It could even have been left here by Big Brother Slav."

"Somehow, sir, I doubt very much that this is Russian."

"Agreed. I thought you would like to see that your wild story has some vindication." He laughed. "When we catch them, we'll have to teach them a lesson for littering our beautiful Adriatic beaches!"

"What now, Lieutenant?" the man with the mine detector asked.

The officer pointed up the beach. "We keep looking. There may be more than one of these. You two . . ." He pointed out two of the men. "Stay here, and stand guard. Jankovic's monsters could be just a few meters away, waiting for their chance to sneak back and claim their property!"

Everyone save the two "volunteers" laughed, and Jankovic smiled. "Stay alert," he told them. Then he turned away and started following the man with the mine detector.

0515 hours
On the beach east of Dubrovnik
Croatia

Murdock had been seriously worried about options for some time now. Back at the monastery, he could have called for a helicopter pickup, but he'd thought it wise to get clear of the area. Subsequent developments had proved him right on that one; there were too many Serb helicopters about, too many airmobile troops, to risk an incursion by U.S. Marine or Navy helos off the *Nassau*.

Okay. Next he could have headed straight for the beach, or he could have taken his men in some other direction, moving deeper into the forest-clad slopes of the Gora Orjen. They could have found a place to hole up, maybe call for a pickup the next night, or the night after that. He'd chosen to return to the beach. At first there'd been no indication that the Yugoslavs were onto them; once the JNA helo touched down at the monastery, it had seemed safer to try to make a run for the sea, before the locals could figure out that was where the SEALs might be headed.

A bad call . . . but the best he could have made under the circumstances. Once confronted by Yugoslavian troops and helos between the SEAL squad and the sea, he'd again been forced to make a choice—either to head back into the hills or to try to get around or through the enemy line.

There are no certainties in combat. None. In a difficult tactical situation there is no way to know in advance which of several possible options is the right one. As one of the SEAL instructors with Murdock's BUD/S class had put it once, "If you end up dead, chances are you made the wrong choice."

The entire trek back down the mountain from the monastery, though, had been one combat decision after another. So far, all seven SEALs were still alive, which was something, but Murdock had the feeling that he was being backed into a tighter and tighter corner, with fewer and fewer doors leading out. SEAL tactical training emphasized taking the initiative; it was supposed to be the SEAL team that set the ambush, the SEALs that forced the enemy to react to them, not the other way around.

Never mind. The sea was almost within reach. Mac and Magic had already started down the shingle of the beach, crawling flat on their bellies, spacing themselves well apart. Murdock had already lost sight of Mac, and thought he must have reached the surf line by now. Chief MacKenzie was carrying the waterproof rucksack holding Gypsy's briefcase—another cold tactical decision on Murdock's part. Of all the men in the squad, Murdock thought that the big, muscular Texan had the best chance of making it back to *Nassau* with the CIA's prize intact.

Another pair of jets thundered low overhead, and Murdock peered up into the overcast sky, trying to see them. Nothing. Were they Yugoslav? Or fighter cover for the SEAL exfiltration?

Less than five meters away, just on the other side of the seawall, a Serbian soldier stepped out from the shadow of a poplar and peered up toward the sky as well. Satisfied, apparently, that the aircraft were either friendly or, at least, not interested in him, he slung his AKM and produced a pack of cigarettes. A moment later, a match flared briefly between his cupped hands.

Murdock reached out, squeezed Higgins's arm, and pointed: *You're next. Go!* Higgins began slithering down the beach, following in Magic's wake. They had to get off this beach. There were far too many Serbs wandering around in the dark. Sooner or later . . .

Roselli tapped Murdock's arm three times, and pointed: *Look! They've found something!*

Murdock looked along the seawall toward the west. Sure enough, close by the wall and seventy meters away, a group of Serb soldiers were laughing, as some shouted at each other.

They'd found the IBS. The SEALs had to move, *now*. He tapped Doc on the arm, and pointed: *Go! Go!*

The excitement was spreading among the Yugoslavs, like ripples in a pool. Someone aboard the Hip was angling the helicopter's searchlight toward the beach now. The circle of illumination danced momentarily across the white breakers offshore, then skittered up the beach, briefly touching the line of weed and flotsam marking the high-tide line. The long, black shadows cast by the poplars between the helo and the beach moved across the sand like vast, silent finger shadows on a wall.

Briefly, Murdock considered putting a suppressed round through that damned light and making a running break for it in the ensuing confusion, but decided against it. Once bullets started flying across that beach, the SEALs' lives would be hanging purely on chance and on the Serbs' reaction. He wanted to maintain control of the situation for as long as he possibly could.

Only Boomer, Razor, and Murdock were left at the top of the beach. A group of Yugoslav soldiers was coming toward them now, moving along both sides of the seawall with weapons unslung and at the ready. One of them had what looked like an old-fashioned mine detector, a WWII-vintage treasure-finder mounted on the end of a long pole. The helicopter's searchlight danced along the sand in front of them as though leading the way, moving across the sand toward the SEALs.

The light caught Doc, starkly illuminating him where he lay on the sand, twenty meters from the wall. . . .

"*Sta ye to!*" someone shouted. An instant later, gunfire cracked and crashed and stuttered in the night, at least eight Yugoslav soldiers opening up with automatic weapons on full rock-and-roll.

On the beach, Doc leaped to his feet and dove headfirst out of the light, as sand erupted about him in a flurry of geysering impacts. Other soldiers, further up the hill and on the highway near the helicopter, opened fire as well. The Serb who'd been smoking a cigarette near the remaining SEALs by the seawall suddenly lurched to the side, the cigarette spinning from his mouth like a tiny orange meteor. He collapsed on the ground screaming, cut down by friendly fire.

The Serbs with the mine detector were moving down the beach now, still firing wildly as the helo's searchlight swept back and forth, trying to nail Doc. Murdock snicked his fire-control lever to full auto, then rose to a half crouch, H&K raised to his shoulder. "Go!" he shouted. "Go! Go!" He aimed at the close-packed mass of Serb troops and squeezed the trigger, sending a long volley slashing into them from the flank. Someone screamed . . . and then someone else spun wildly, his AKM still firing on rock-and-roll. The result was a deadly, bloody chaos as men were hit both by Murdock's volley and by the uncontrolled, full-auto fire of their own people. The thick-muzzled weapon bucked in Murdock's hands with a muffled, hissing clatter as the receiver bolt cycled rapidly back and forth. The Serb with the mine detector slumped over and collided with a companion, then collapsed backward onto the sand, his metal sensor lying across his chest. The man beside him got off one more wild burst with his AK before Murdock caught him squarely in the chest. Other men dove for cover or staggered and fell.

Murdock burned off half a thirty-round magazine in a little over a second, then spun to the right, shifting targets to the searchlight that was swinging now to capture him in its glare. The dazzle from the spotlight was blinding through the low-light goggles, but Murdock had squeezed his eyes shut behind the rubber-padded objective lenses and was firing at where he estimated the light must be. An instant later, he sensed the light beating against his eyelids flare and go out. Hit!

When he opened his eyes again, his low-light optics revealed an all-out battle, with at least thirty men firing in almost every direction. Bullets clipped the stone wall nearby and whispered overhead with a sound like ripping paper. The familiar flat crack of AKMs fired on full auto filled the night, as did the hard, jutting stab of their muzzle flashes.

Doc and Razor were halfway down the beach, running flat out. Garcia was hanging back, firing his H&K in precise, carefully aimed three-round bursts.

"Boomer!" Murdock called over the tactical radio. "Get your ass off this beach!" Garcia didn't appear to hear. Shit, was his radio off? "Boomer! Acknowledge!"

Murdock started to run toward the SEAL, crouched far over and moving with an easy, long-legged stride. Bullets struck the sand near Garcia, but he stayed in position, leaning into his submachine gun as he continued to mark down Yugoslav soldiers. When he saw Murdock, he lowered his weapon and grinned beneath his NVD goggles. His tactical radio, a small box strapped to his assault vest high up on his left shoulder, had been smashed open by a stray round.

"C'mon, L-T!" Garcia called. "You've got to—"

. . . and then Boomer was flung back, arms outstretched, subgun flying, as a round struck his chest with a vicious-sounding *thwack*.

"Oh, *shit*!" Murdock fired another burst, then dropped to one knee at Garcia's side. "Boomer! Boomer, can you hear me?"

The bullet had gone through the SEAL's upper chest, in the front, out the back, clean through his flak vest. There was a lot of blood, and Boomer appeared to be unconscious.

With one arm, Murdock hoisted the wounded SEAL to his feet, then began staggering down the beach. Bullets hissed and thudded in the sand to either side, and something snapped at his left sleeve. The water! They had to reach the water! . . .

But as the gunfire at their backs increased in manic intensity, Murdock didn't think they were going to make it. . . .

6

**0518 hours
In Croatian airspace
Southeast of Dubrovnik**

The AC-130U Specter was the direct descendant of the
Spooky gunships so beloved of ground troops during the
Vietnam War. The Spookys had been C-47s, WWII-era
cargo planes mounting a deadly trio of 7.62 miniguns
pointed out their left door and windows.

So effective had they been in close air support of ground
troops that the U.S. Air Force had expanded on the idea. The
AC-130U Specter gunship was a very specially modified
C-130 Hercules, an ungainly transport remade into the
image of a special warfare warrior. The 130U model
mounted a single 25mm five-barreled General Electric
Gau-12U Gatling Gun. Fed by a two-canister automated
loader system, the high-speed gun could deliver a rate of fire
of either 3600 or 4200 rounds per minute. The Specter also
mounted a 40mm cannon and a 105mm howitzer, and all
weapons were linked to laser range finders, an infrared
sensor, radar, low-light television, and a sophisticated fire-
control computer. All three weapons were mounted in the
aircraft's port side, like the broadside of some ancient war
galleon. Forward, a soundproofed battle control center

65

sported an impressive array of television monitors, computers, radar screens, and IR sensor displays.

It was there that Major Peter K. Selby, the aircraft's fire control officer, sat with two sensor operators, scanning banks of television monitors. Three particular display monitors showed what the gunship's weapons were pointed at. The images on the screens were indistinguishable from those of a black-and-white television set, save that each was centered on a set of crosshairs. Viewed in infrared, the scene below was day bright, unusual only in the fact that the engines of the Mi-8 Hip and an army truck parked nearby were glowing as brightly as a neon sign.

"Looks like they're having a damned party down there," Selby said. "You got 'em sorted yet?"

"No, sir," one of the sensor operators said. "Somebody's mad at someone, though. There's a hell lot of shooting going on down there."

Selby nodded. He could see several groups of men moving across the beach, and the muzzle flashes from their automatic weapons were distinctly visible. A helicopter was parked on the highway near a line of trees, and there was a hell of a lot of activity along the coast highway.

"Any sign of antiair assets?"

"Negative, sir. Not so far. The Harriers have been circling for ten minutes, though, inviting them to come out and play."

The Specter gunship, flying low and slow, would be an easy target for enemy aircraft. Escort for this mission was being flown by a pair of Marine Harrier IIs flying off the *Nassau*. Any sign of Yugoslav MiGs, SAMs, or mobile flak, and the Harriers would pounce like a couple of hawks.

"Okay, then we can probably assume we're clear." Selby said. "Let's see if we can raise our guys." Reaching to an overhead console, he switched on a radio, adjusted the frequency, then picked up a hand microphone. "Nomad, Nomad," he called. "This is Night Rider. Do you copy? Over."

There was no immediate answer. The angle of the scene

revealed on the TV monitors slowly changed as the Specter gunship circled the battle on the beach at a range of over two miles, and at an altitude of eight thousand feet, just above the lowest layer of clouds. The Specter's infrared optics penetrated the overcast almost as easily as it penetrated the night.

"Nomad, Nomad, this is Night Rider. Do you copy? Over."

"Night Rider! Night Rider!" sounded from an overhead speaker. The voice coming over the air-ground channel was scratchy with static, and Selby thought he could hear the thud and rattle of gunfire in the distance. "This is Nomad. Go ahead!"

It was a strange feeling to be talking to a man who was, at that moment, under fire. Selby had experienced the strangeness of this high-tech participation in battle before, during Desert Storm, and he'd never gotten over it. Here, aboard the AC-130, the only sound was the drone of the aircraft's engines, the hum of electronics, the low voices of the sensor operators. Except for the tilt to the deck, he might as well have been in an air-conditioned room in the Pentagon basement. The man he was talking to, just a few miles away, was fighting for his life.

"Nomad, we are circling your approximate position at eight thousand. Understand you might need assistance, over."

"Night Rider, Nomad, that is affirmative," the voice came back. "Wait one while we sort ourselves out for you."

"Roger that. Night Rider, standing by." He turned to one of the sensor operators. "Let's back off a bit and see if we can get a shot of more of the beach, okay?"

"Yes, sir."

The scene receded as the operator adjusted the lens magnification. Damn, there sure as hell was some kind of a ruckus going on down there. Selby could see dozens of men, and a lot of gunfire. But on infrared TV, all uniforms looked alike and there was no way to pick out the ones worn by Navy SEALs.

"There, sir," Sergeant Zanowski, the senior operator, said. "Clear signal. There's another."

Three . . . no, five bright stars had appeared on the screen, three up on the beach, two more by the edge of the black water. There were two more now, also in the water. Each SEAL was wearing a standard survival vest strobe attached to his assault vest, but capped with an IR filter. Switched on, the light was invisible to the hostiles, but it showed up clearly to the AC-130's IR cameras.

"Nomad, this is Night Rider. I see seven lights on the beach or in the water. Confirm your ID with a flash, over."

"Roger, Night Rider."

The IR lights flicked off one by one, then flicked on again.

"Okay, Nomad, we confirm your position. Everybody else is a bad guy. Heads down! Here come the goodies!"

"Roger that, Night Rider."

Selby reached for an intercom switch. "Colonel Carlotti," he said. "We have Nomad on the screen and we have positive identification."

"Very well, Major. You have my permission to fire."

"Gunners, this is Major Selby. Hang onto your jockstraps, boys. We've got firing command! Sergeant Zanowski?"

"Locked in, sir. The computer has it." The sensor operator grinned as he flicked off a row of switches, releasing the last of the armament safeties. "Firing phasers . . ."

The actual firing was done by the aircraft's computer.

0519 hours
On the beach southeast of Dubrovnik

"Blue Squad!" Murdock yelled. "Hit the deck and stay down! We've got incoming!"

"Yeah, big time!" Roselli added, and then the night lit up with fire.

At 3,600 rounds per minute, the high-velocity shells were shrieking out of the sky at a rate of sixty per second, each 25mm projectile traveling practically nose-to-tail with its neighbors in a solid stream of lead and high explosives.

Fired at night, the rotary Gatling cannon seemed to be loosing a bolt of white-hot lightning . . . or the phaser beam of a popular TV and movie science-fiction series.

The beam slashed in from over the sea, illuminating the clouds as it burned through them, then passed above the heads of the SEALs with a shrill, air-shaking howl that was palpable. The AC-130's warload for this pass was HEI— high explosive incendiary—and where those rounds hit there was destruction, instant, accurate, and devastatingly total. Poplar trees shuddered, cracked, and exploded left and right; part of the seawall dissolved in hurtling chunks of broken concrete; portions of the highway buckled and vanished in a searing cascade of explosions that swept across dirt and wall and pavement in a deadly, sparkling dance. The Mi-8 helicopter, its rotors still slowly turning as it rested on the highway, seemed to crumple like a deflating toy, sagging to the side before on-board fuel reserves were touched off and the aircraft fireballed. Thunderous explosions lit up the night as brightly as that shaft of glowing fire raining down from the sky. The Hip's five-bladed rotor lifted up off the helicopter's rotor shaft and cartwheeled through the air; an instant later, the sky-fire brushed across the military truck parked nearby, and that vehicle added its touch of flame to the firestorm raging over the Hip's spectacularly dissolving framework.

And men died. They died as the stream from the sky touched them and shredded their bodies in whirling fragments; died as their uniforms burst into flames; died as bits and pieces of metal or chunks of stone or shards stripped from ricocheting bullets scythed through them like volleys of machine-gun fire. The noise was deafening, overwhelming, a thunderous cacophony piled atop the buzzsaw shriek of incandescent shells. . . .

Murdock lay facedown on the beach, covering Garcia's body with his own as Roselli lay nearby, refusing to look up into that hellfire from the sky. With the Specter gunship's fire computer-directed, it was accurate to within five feet of the chosen target across a range of almost one mile. With an eerie and terrible mathematical precision, the Specter drew a curtain of flame and death between the SEALs and their foes.

When the fire ceased, scant seconds after it had begun, the silence was more unnerving in a way than the noise and flame had been. The beach was brilliantly lit now by the Hip's funeral pyre, but all gunfire had ceased.

"C'mon, Razor," Murdock said. "Help me get Boomer to the water."

"What about his weapon?"

"Forget it. Give me a hand!"

"Right, L-T."

Together, they half carried, half dragged Garcia toward the water's edge. They were met there by Doc and Magic, who'd swum back ashore when they realized that Murdock and the others were under fire. "I got him, L-T," Doc said. As Murdock, Roselli, and Magic formed a half perimeter at the surf's edge, Doc broke out his medical kit and began working on Garcia's wounds. A terrible sound could be heard now wavering above the crackle of flames, a low, monotonous moaning sound, a chorus of many voices from many terribly wounded men. Murdock could see several Serb soldiers moving against the firelight near the seawall, but he held his fire. If the Yugoslavs could see the SEALs where they were gathered at the edge of the water, they were ignoring them. More likely, the fire had so ruined their night vision that they couldn't see a thing right now beyond the immediate circle illuminated by the fire. Besides, they must have all they could handle right now, tending to their wounded.

"That's all I can do for him now," Doc said moments later. "We gotta get a medevac for him, stat."

"Well, we can't medevac him from here," Murdock replied. "Let's get him off the beach and into the water."

They discarded NVDs and boots, automatic weapons and ammo, Kevlar jackets and most of their assault vest loadouts as soon as they were past the wave line and well into deep water, keeping only their knives, radios, and survival gear.

They took turns, one man pulling Garcia along with one arm
thrown across his shoulder and chest, while another swam
alongside to make sure the unconscious man's head stayed
above water. Where the air had felt chilly, the sea seemed
almost warm, though Murdock knew that was an illusion.
They struck out from the shore, angling slightly south to
counter the south-to-north offshore current. A twelve-mile
swim with a badly wounded man. They'd never make it,
unless . . .

Roselli grabbed Murdock's arm and pointed. "Hey! L-T!
Look! It's Gold Squad!"

Murdock was almost too tired to look, so drained was he
by the brutal intensity of that short firefight on the beach. He
let Roselli turn him in the water, however, until he could just
make out the indistinct forms of more night-cloaked SEALs
riding low in a pair of CRRCs.

"Lieutenant Murdock!" Lieutenant j.g. DeWitt, Third
Platoon's XO and the leader of Gold Squad, called. "Here!"

Hands grabbed at Murdock's arms. "No," he said. "Get
Boomer on board. . . ."

"We got him, L-T. Come on."

"Christ, Two-Eyes!" Murdock said as he was rolled out
of the water and onto the raft. DeWitt's team nickname was
drawn from his position as platoon "2IC," the second-in-
command. "I don't think those people like us."

"From out here it sounded like you boys got quite a
reception."

"That's nothing to the reception we're gonna get at the
debrief," Murdock said. "You pick up Mac?"

"He's in the other raft, L-T. With the package. A chopper's on the way from *Nassau*. God, it's good to see you
guys. You had me worried!"

"That," Murdock said with feeling, "makes two of us."

0556 hours
On the beach southeast of Dubrovnik
Narednik Jankovic was the first one to find the blood, a
coagulated patch on the beach close to the high-tide line.

Most of it had already been absorbed by the sand, but there was no mistaking the slick, dark stain that remained as he turned his flashlight on it. Footprints were visible as well, along with a submachine gun dropped by one of the invaders.

He studied that weapon carefully. *Heckler und Koch* . . . though the fact that it was a German gun meant nothing. H&K made some of the finest firearms in the world, and plenty of people, from the British SAS to a dozen European and Mideast terrorist groups, used them. The SD3 model, with integral sound suppressor too. The very best. He had the feeling that if he were to disassemble the weapon, he would find that every serial number on every part had been removed or was otherwise untraceable.

He turned his flash back on the blood and the ragged, double line of footprints moving down the shelf of the beach toward the water's edge. Those footprints closely flanked twin furrows that were most likely where a dead or wounded man's toes had plowed through the wet sand as he was dragged along. There was some more blood further along . . . and there . . . and there. There was something oddly comforting about that stain on the beach and the furrows in the sand, evidence that these commandos were human. They *could* be fought, could be shot and killed.

Jankovic needed that reassurance just now. The slaughter on the beach had been indescribable. In almost four years of fighting Bosniaks, Jankovic had seen plenty of death and suffering, but never, *never* had he seen anything to match the horror that he'd seen tonight. The faceless enemy had killed or wounded a dozen men in seconds, then somehow called down death incarnate from out of the overcast sky.

They can *die. They* can *be killed.*

Jankovic clung to that simple and comforting thought.

0945 hours
Intelligence Department
U.S.S. *Nassau*

"Then what happened, Chief Roselli?"

Roselli's glance traveled from Dulaney, the Navy officer

who'd been running the debriefing, to the three civilians in the steel-walled compartment, then across the table to Commander George Presley, *Nassau*'s Combat Information Officer.

"Well, sir," Roselli said slowly, looking back at Commander Dulaney. "The Skipper started around the front of the truck on the left. I think he popped a couple of shots at the runner. I'm not sure."

"Did the man stop?"

"I think he did, sir. I'm pretty sure he was turning around."

"And Lieutenant Murdock shot him?" one of the civilians asked.

Damned suit, Roselli thought. "Uh, yes, sir."

"I see. Was he armed?"

"I don't know, sir. I was still quite a ways back and couldn't see real well. The truck was in the way."

"Do you know if any of the militia soldiers at the monastery tried to surrender?"

"Not that I know of, sir. It was all over pretty fast. If any of 'em wanted to, I doubt that they could have."

"What do you mean by that, Roselli?" Fletcher, the boss suit, asked. "That you weren't taking prisoners?"

"No, sir. I just mean we were in there just taking initials, 'cause we were moving too fast to take names."

"Did you understand, Chief," Fletcher said, "that your rules of engagement required you not to fire unless you were fired upon? That Lieutenant Murdock violated the ROEs by ordering you to open fire?"

"Well, we didn't have much fuckin' choice—"

"Chief!" Dulaney said sharply. "Please."

"Well, it's true! Excuse me, sir, but your agent would've been dead if we hadn't opened up when we did, and the whole op would've been for nothing."

Fletcher leaned over and whispered something to Dulaney.

"Very well, Chief," Dulaney said a moment later. "You may go."

"Thank you, sir."

Fletcher glanced down at a notebook in his hand. "And would you have, ah, Quartermaster First Class Martin Brown step in here, please?"

"Right, sure thing. Uh . . . listen, about the L-T—"

"That is all, Chief. Thank you."

"I just wanted to say that he—"

"That will be *all*, Roselli."

"Aye, aye, sir." Roselli rose, took a last look at the men gathered there, and walked out of the compartment. In the passageway outside, Prof, Doc, and Magic were waiting for him.

Just four hours ago, they'd been plucked from the sea off the Adriatic coast by a Navy SH-60 Seahawk off the *Nassau*. Flown back to the amphibious assault ship's flight deck, they'd been greeted before they even climbed out of the helo by a team of hospital corpsmen and a ship's doctor who'd bundled Garcia, strapped into a Stokes wire-frame stretcher, off to sick bay. While they were still climbing off the helo, they'd been met by Commander Dulaney himself, who'd told them they had two hours to get cleaned up and squared away for their debriefing.

Dulaney had not looked pleased.

When the SEALs had reported aboard the *Nassau* two weeks earlier, they'd brought full seabags as well as their combat gear; even SEALs couldn't run around aboard ship in their combat blacks all the time, and Murdock had always been a stickler for doing things the Navy way. "The fewer waves, the better," he'd told the platoon more than once, and so the SEALs had showered and shaved and changed into their blues.

Roselli had felt like he was under a damned magnifying glass throughout the briefing. *Something* had gone sour besides the mission itself, and he couldn't tell what it was.

"So how'd it go, Razor?" Magic asked.

"I'm not sure. Feels like they're railroading the Skipper, though." He jerked his thumb over his shoulder. "You're up next, Magic."

"Wish me luck, guys." The big SEAL sniper tugged at the bottom of his blue jumper, took a deep breath, and stepped through the compartment door.

"Shit," Doc said after the door had clanged shut. He folded his arms and leaned back against the bulkhead. "Here we go with the munchkin madness again."

"Aw," Prof added in a mincing, little boy's voice. "Are they upset that we bwoke their itty-bitty rules of engagement?"

"Something like that. Where's Mac and the L-T?"

"They went up on the flight deck. Something about needing some air."

"Don't blame 'em," Roselli said. "Maybe I'll join them. Uh, any word on Boomer?"

"Nope. He's still in sick bay. I imagine they'll fly him out today. Pneumothroax and he lost a lot of blood. They'll want him in a hospital Stateside pronto."

"Damn bad luck," Roselli said.

"Yeah, well, it happens," Higgins said. "He knew the odds when he got his Budweiser."

Roselli reached up and fingered the heavy, ugly gold emblem pinned to his dress blue jacket, just above its neatly ordered rows of colored ribbons. Eagle with outstretched wings. Anchor. Trident. Old-fashioned flintlock pistol. The "Budweiser" emblem that marked a man as a SEAL. "I guess so. Any word on what's going down? I feel like we're up for court-martial or worse. Mac got the package back okay, didn't he?"

"Turned it over to Dulaney soon as we stepped aboard," Higgins said. "Of course, things have been real tense with the Serbs all along. Maybe they're afraid that firefight's going to touch off some worse fighting."

"Well, shit," Roselli said with feeling. "Bring 'em on! Let's stop with the pussyfooting and settle this thing, right?"

"Rules of engagement," Doc snorted. "Who do they think they're shittin' anyway?"

0951 hours
Crew's lounge
U.S.S. Nassau

Murdock and MacKenzie had not stayed on the flight deck
for long. *Nassau* was in the middle of full flight deck ops,
using her catapult to hurl Marine Harriers into the sky one
after another. The noise on the flight deck was so loud that
anyone without protective headgear would have been deaf-
ened in moments, and ordinary conversation, certainly, was
impossible. Too, the stink of jet fuel made that "fresh air"
Murdock had spoken of rather hard to find. After being
confronted by a chief aviation boatswain's mate who told
them both point blank that unless they had some specific
business on *his* flight deck they'd both be pleased to go play
tourist someplace the hell else, they decided to take the
man's advice and find a spot for themselves somewhere out
of the way.

The crew's lounge, aft and three levels down from the
LPH's flight deck, normally didn't cater to either officers or
master chief petty officers, and from the looks they were
getting, Murdock decided that there probably wasn't any
place aboard this ship where he and MacKenzie could
unwind, at least not without collecting stares. A ship, even
one as large as the *Nassau* with a complement of 58 officers,
882 enlisted men, and 1,924 Marines, is a tight, tiny
community where nearly everyone knows nearly everyone
else, and where the only thing faster than radio communications is shipboard scuttlebutt. The SEALs had attracted a
lot of attention since they'd come aboard two weeks ago,
and Murdock still wasn't used to always being watched.

Screw it. He wanted a cola and he wanted someplace to
sit and talk with Mac. They ignored the looks, got their
drinks from a coin-operated machine near the compartment's
forward door, and found themselves a table. The compartment was not too crowded at this hour of the morning. Two
sailors were bent over a couple of arcade games aft, and
several more were sitting on a sofa, watching television.

"They seemed pretty bent out of shape, Skipper," Mac said as they sat back in their seats. "They were hitting me with questions about the firefight at the monastery, and about you capping that guy who tried to surrender. How the hell did they find out about that?"

"Easy," Murdock said. "I told 'em. Hell, I'm not going to lie about something like that."

Mac shook his head. "Sometimes, Boss, you're just too much the frigging straight arrow."

"Hell, I didn't like doing it, but there was no way I was going to risk the mission screwing around with prisoners," Murdock said. "But I don't think that was what was bugging them. It was more like they were worried about, I don't know. What evidence we might have left behind."

"What, like our IBS? Boomer's piece? That stuff's all sterile."

"I know. It's just—"

Murdock stopped in mid-sentence, staring at the television monitor across the compartment.

"Lieutenant? What is it?"

Murdock gestured toward the TV. *Nassau* sported her own TV studio on board, but most programming was picked up from Armed Forces Network broadcasts and piped through the ship's closed-circuit network.

At the moment, an attractive, dark-haired, professional-looking woman was on the screen. Visible behind her was the familiar-looking facade of the St. Anastasias Monastery.

"Oh, *shit*," Murdock said.

"Hey, son," Mac called to the sailors watching the program. "Could one of you turn that up, please?"

A second class obliged, and Murdock listened to the newscaster's words, comprehension dawning.

". . . ian officials claim that American commandos carried out the predawn raid as a deliberate provocation against the Federal Republic of Yugoslavia. One observer had this to say. . . ."

The woman was replaced on the screen by a military

officer, an older man with the single star of a Serbian
brigadier general on his gold-heavy epaulets.

"We are convinced this, this unprovoked attack is part of
American campaign to win UN approval for further air
strikes against Serb forces in Bosnia," the man said in
heavily accented English. A subtitle appeared at the bottom
of the screen, identifying him as General V. Mihajlovic.
"We invite United Nations to come here, come see evidence
of American aggression in Serbian internal affairs."

The general's face was replaced by a shot of the burned-
out trucks in front of the monastery. Greasy black smoke
was still curling from the wreckage. "So far," the woman
reporter continued in a voice-over, "American officials here
have refused to answer any questions about the incident, or
to confirm that American aircraft took part a few hours later
in an airstrike against Yugoslavian ground troops near the
coast.

"For ACN, this is Marsha Shakarian, Mjini, Yugoslavia."

"That explains it," Murdock said. "The news networks
got the story before the CIA."

"It's happened before, Boss."

"But that means they're going into ass-covering mode. I
think the shit's about to hit the fan."

7

Monday, March 6

1015 hours
Salonika International Airport
Greece

A chilly wind had been blowing all morning, whipping down off the Khortiatis Mountains with a bitter reminder that winter wasn't quite finished yet. The sky, contrary to the usual blue-sky standards of Greece, was low and overcast, and prone to periodic flurries of snow.

Despite the unpromising weather, however, Congresswoman Ellen Louise Kingston had found an audience for herself. The reporters had been waiting for her just outside the passenger terminal, and as she emerged through the big double doors onto the painted walkway leading to her plane, they started shouting questions to her.

"Congresswoman! What do you think the chances are for peace in the Balkans?"

"Congresswoman Kingston! Does your government plan to launch new air strikes against the Bosnian Serbs?"

"Will the United States bomb Belgrade?"

"Have you consulted with America's NATO allies?"

Kingston stopped, smiling and waving for the cameras that clicked and whirred with each gesture, each motion she made. She was tall, with a regal and aristocratic bearing. Though she was only in her early fifties, her once-dark hair had turned to lustrous silver years before, and she'd left it that way to emphasize her maturity. She faced the cluster of eager reporters, the ranked microphones, and the glaring lights of cameras with practiced ease, a general marshaling her troops. Her tail—her escort of Greek security officials, two American Secret Service men, aides, secretaries, and staffers—piled up behind her in a confused huddle.

"Ms. Kingston," her chief aide said. "We really ought to board the plane."

"There's time, Bunny," Kingston told her, still waving. The reporters were crowded up against a metal railing that held them back, but camera lenses and microphones snaked across, probing toward her face.

"Congresswoman! Please!" a woman reporter shouted. Kingston recognized her—Marsha Shakarian, one of ACN's top foreign correspondents. "What about those bombing raids against Serbia?"

"Ladies and gentlemen," Kingston said, holding up both hands. "As I told you all in my press conference last week, I am just here in Greece on a fact-finding mission. I knew nothing about these terrible atrocities taking place in Bosnia during my visit. No, I've not consulted with NATO, though certainly I've discussed the situation with members of the Athens government and Greece, of course, is a NATO member."

A man with a BBC press card pinned to his lapel shoved a microphone toward her. "Madam Congresswoman, what do you say to General Mihajlovic's charges that the United States is deliberately provoking an international incident?"

"The United States does not want war in the Balkans," Kingston replied. "Indeed, any national interests we have in the region would be best served by peace. The attack on that Yugoslavian monastery was carried out without the knowledge of Congress and without the sanction of the American people. The moment I get back to Washington, I intend to look into this whole situation and demand a full accounting. The Cold War is over. So is the era of cowboy politics and shooting from the hip. I believe America has a very constructive role to play in the Balkans, and that role does not include bombers, aircraft carriers, and commandos!"

"Does that mean that Americans *were* involved in the attack?"

"No comment. Yes—in the back."

"Madam Congresswoman. There are unconfirmed reports that the raid the other night was carried out by American Special Forces. Officials in Belgrade have suggested that one of our heavily armed gunships fired on one of their patrols, killing thirty men and wounding many more. That's not the sort of thing that can be covered up, is it?"

"No, it isn't. And as I said, I am going to launch a full investigation when I get back."

"A follow-up, if I may. There are also reports that the operation may have been carried out by either Marine Recon forces or the Navy SEALs, operating off one of our Marine amphibious ships in the Adriatic. In view of your public position on these elite units in the past, would you care to make a statement?"

"Certainly. I have no information about what units may or may not have carried out this aggression in Yugoslavia. However, as soon as I return to Washington, I shall demand answers. If Americans were involved, this represents a shocking misuse of force. It is high time that these, these elite murder squads like the SEALs and the Rangers were disbanded. We do not need them any longer. They are the direct cause of a disproportionate drain on the tax monies allocated to the military. I might add that most senior officers in the Pentagon are united in their feeling that elite units such as the Navy SEALs funnel the best men, the most expensive equipment, and the lion's share of the money away from our regular forces. At best, this is an unproductive use of precious national assets. At worst, it's a potentially dangerous and terribly misguided attempt to circumvent clearly established national policy. I would like to see this insanity ended and I intend to do all in my power to make that happen."

"Congresswoman Kingston, is it your contention that all

covert operations should be under direct Congressional control? That sort of thing has always been the prerogative of the President."

"Yes, it has, and look what trouble it's got us into. President Kennedy and the Bay of Pigs. President Carter and the hostage rescue in Iran. And they were both Democrats." There was a ripple of polite laughter in the crowd, and she waited for it to die down. "Seriously, it's high time the people, and by that I mean Congress, be given total and complete oversight of the use of *all* of our military forces, and a say in how they're used. It's not as though we have a world-class enemy like the Soviet Union to worry about anymore, is it? We spend billions on the Army Special Forces, the Army Rangers, and Navy SEALs, and God knows how many other special warfare units, and what does it get us? Not one thing! That's taxpayer money being shoveled into a bottomless hole, and I intend to put a stop to it!"

"Madam Kingston!"

"Congresswoman Kingston!"

"That's all. I'm getting cold and I have a plane to catch!" Deliberately avoiding the questions and demands shouted after her, still smiling and waving, Kingston turned and walked on, her following straggling along after. The waiting airplane was an Olympic Airlines NAMC YS-11, one of the old-fashioned two-engine turboprops used on Greek domestic flights. Her schedule called for her to fly back to Athens that morning for a meeting with Constantine Mitsotakis, the Greek Prime Minister, that afternoon. After that, there would be a special chartered flight back to Dulles International and a meeting with the Select Committee on Monday.

Climbing the boarding ladder to the rear passenger door, Kingston entered the plane, where she was greeted by Colonel Ted Winters, her U.S. Army watchdog, and by *Lochagos* Dyonisios Mantzaros, her principal shadow from the DEA.

Not the U.S. Drug Enforcement Administration, of course. She smiled at the thought. The Dimona Eidikon Apostolon, or Special Mission Platoon, was a fifty-man unit established in the mid-1970s as a Greek SWAT and hostage-rescue unit within the Athens City Police. Its responsibilities had been extended recently to include airport security and protection for visiting dignitaries. Mantzaros and five of his agents had been dogging her every step since she'd arrived in Greece last week, all of them dressed in identical dark business suits, dark, narrow ties, and dark glasses, costumes that virtually screamed security force. The two men contrasted sharply with one another, Mantzaros being short, pudgy, and olive-skinned, while Winters was tall, bone-skinny, and so pale that Kingston had kidded him once about all the time he must spend in the White House basement.

"Well, well," she said, grinning at them. "If it isn't Tweedledee and Tweedledum. Been waiting for me long, fellas?"

"Congresswoman," Winters said, his mouth set hard and expressionless. Winters, she knew, didn't approve of her . . . or at least he didn't approve of her politics, which were liberal Democrat and anti-military. That was okay by her. She disliked Winters. She disliked all military personnel . . . or, to be completely fair, she disliked the military mind-set, the testosterone-drugged fascination for expensive toys and loud noises and macho confrontations with unpleasant strangers.

"The pilot said to tell you, Congresswoman," Mantzaros said, and he nearly bowed as he spoke, "that we will be able to take off as soon as you are ready."

"Thank you, Captain," she told Mantzaros. "I'll ride up there in the lounge."

"Of course, Congresswoman." And this time he did bow, ushering her forward up the aisle.

Normally seating sixty passengers, this particular aircraft had been modified for VIP use, with half of the five-abreast seats removed to make room for a comfortable lounge area forward. She allowed Mantzaros to escort her to one of the comfortable lounge seats behind a polished, wood-surfaced table. Barbara Jean Allison, her chief aide, handed Kingston her briefcase, then slid in next to her.

"Thanks, Bunny. What we got . . . about a half-hour flight?"

"Thirty-five to forty minutes, Ms. Kingston."

Winters slid into a seat across the table from them. "You never let up, do you, Madam Congresswoman?"

"What do you mean?"

"I was listening to your little off-the-cuff speech to those reporters. I wonder if it was wise blasting the U.S. military for what happened in Bosnia the other day when you don't even know if we were responsible."

"Oh, we're responsible, Colonel. You can take it from me."

His eyebrows crept up on his forehead. "You're sure of your information, ma'am?"

"Always," she said. "I heard some things before we left Washington. Ever hear of something called Operation Blue Arrow?"

"No. And I don't think you should be discussing code names with someone who hasn't been cleared to hear them."

"Colonel, do you think I give two pins for that macho-military bullshit?"

"No, ma'am, but you should. There're reasons for it. Damned good ones."

"God. Sometimes I just don't believe you people." She turned away, staring out the window. The plane's turboprops were firing up. There was a cough, then a roar as the right engine revved up to speed. "Anyway, Colonel, I didn't tell them we did it. When someone asked me if we did, I said, 'No comment.' "

"Uh-huh. And let them read between the lines. I thought you wanted to stop a war out here, not start one."

"You're out of line, Colonel."

"*I'm* out of line?" He laughed, but his eyes struck angry sparks.

"Yes, you are." She sighed and leaned back in her seat. "You know, Colonel, for way too long the American military has had its own way. It's about time the Pentagon realized that the Cold War is over, that the old way of doing things is gone for good, and a good thing too!"

Mantzaros and one of the American Secret Service men walked up to her seat. "Everything okay, ma'am?" the Secret Service man asked. The American agent was almost indistinguishable from the Greek DEA people, right down to the conservative suit and the dark glasses.

"Just fine, Franklin. Thanks."

"Pilot says to tell you we'll be taking off in about five minutes."

"Very well."

"Tell me, Colonel," she asked a moment later. "What's your opinion of the Special Forces?"

Winters almost smiled . . . almost. "To be honest, I'd have to say they're more trouble than they're worth."

"Expensive."

"That . . . and it's hard to maintain discipline in an organization that *must* have discipline to operate effectively, when there are units within that organization that claim to be better than everybody else."

"If I remember from your record, Colonel, you were in the Army Special Forces."

"That was quite a while ago. Yes, ma'am. I was."

"A green beanie. And you don't believe in special-warfare units?"

"Oh, there are places where special warfare is important, sure. Especially in counterinsurgency operations, training local forces, stuff like that. But I never have liked the elitist attitude behind some of the special-ops people. Like I say, it interferes with discipline."

"It is also an intolerable drain on our tax dollars," Kingston said, warming to the subject. "And a drain of our best men. I've heard even the Army Special Forces complain a lot about their best men volunteering for Delta Force."

"Yes, ma'am, that's true."

"Well, I'll tell you something, Colonel. Someone up in the Adriatic really put his foot in it the other day. I've wanted to see the special-warfare people put out to pasture for a long time now. And I think someone has just given me the weapons I need to see that done!"

For several minutes now, the NAMC had been taxiing slowly along the runway. Now, the roar of the aircraft's engines thundered louder and louder, until Kingston could feel the fuselage shuddering around her. There was a gentle shove of acceleration, and then the aircraft lifted clear of the runway, rising higher and higher. The airport dropped away astern, replaced by the steel-gray waters of the Thermaic Gulf. North, across the bay, she could see the city of Salonika, could even pick out the stubby thrust of the city's famous White Tower on the waterfront. Then the panorama was blotted out by a dark gray fog that grew swiftly lighter. Moments later, sunshine exploded in through the windows; the plane was above the cloud deck now, banking gently toward the right.

For the first time in several days, Kingston allowed herself a less than optimistic thought. Things were not going well here, with her mission, with the people she'd been seeing. She wondered if her presence here was making any difference at all.

It was this damnable situation in the Balkans, a situation already critical, and rapidly going out of control. She was beginning to think that nothing that she, Washington, NATO, or anybody could do was going to be of any help. And how the hell was she supposed to do her job when those military buffoons insisted on playing their games?

Several times during the past year, NATO—under pressure from the U.S.—had launched punitive air strikes against the Bosnian Serbs in an attempt to stop their wholesale slaughter of Bosnian Muslims. Somehow, that war had continued . . . and lately two new wars had been added to the flames already devouring the Balkans. One was the renewed warfare between Croatia and Serbia; for some time now, the Croatians had been rounding up Bosnian Croatians who'd fled their war-torn homeland and forcing them to "volunteer" for service in the various Croat militias, first to fight the Bosnian Muslims, and lately to take on the Serbian militias as well.

The second new outbreak of fighting was even more worrisome, for it threatened to spill over across the borders of the various states that once had made up Yugoslavia and engulf other nations in the region. If that happened, well, all of those impassioned speeches she'd delivered in the House about how large military forces were no longer necessary now that the Soviet Union was gone could very well blow up in her face. The United States was a hairbreadth from war, and sometimes it seemed like every step her country took was exactly the wrong one. . . .

The root of this latest problem was an ancient and unhappy land called Macedonia, divided since 1913 when the Treaty of Bucharest had partitioned the nation among its four neighbors. The biggest chunk had gone to Serbia, and after World War II it had been incorporated as a republic within the Yugoslav Federation. Smaller slices had been gobbled up by Albania to the west and Bulgaria in the east. The southern portion had gone to Greece, which itself had won independence from the Ottoman Turks only eighty-three years before.

Greek Macedonia today was the largest single region in Greece, as well as its most productive. Salonika, its capital, was the second largest city in Greece. There were still those who wanted to see a united and independent Macedonia, however; the International Macedonian Revolutionary Organization, the IMRO, had waged a bitter terrorist war throughout the first half of the twentieth century to achieve that end. Early in World War II, Bulgaria's claims to Macedonia had led to that nation's alliance with Nazi Germany and her occupation of Macedonia in 1941.

With the breakup of Yugoslavia, Macedonia had again become a potential problem in the area. Yugoslav Macedonia had declared its independence and applied for membership with the UN; Greece had blocked the application, insisting that it had all rights to the ancient name "Macedonia," which it was not going to share with this northern

upstart. The matter had been only partly resolved when the
two parties had finally agreed that the new republic would
be called "The Former Yugoslav Republic of Macedonia," a
temporary compromise that pleased no one. With independence from Serbia in April of 1993 had come UN peace-
keeping troops, including three hundred Americans, and the
UN-mandated requirement to maintain an embargo against
what was left of Yugoslavia . . . an economic disaster for
an area that depended on trade with Serbia for survival.

But Macedonia was at the very center of a potential
international firestorm. Serbia wanted Macedonia back, a
part of the historical "Greater Serbia." Greece too wanted
northern Macedonia to again come under Serbian rule,
because a free Slavic Macedonia gave too many ideas to
Greek Macedonians. The IMRO still existed and still had
the goal of liberating all of Macedonia, north and south, and
uniting it as an independent nation.

For that reason, Greece and Serbia were cooperating with
one another on the problem, for both nations had reasons to
keep a lid on Macedonian nationalism. Other countries in
the region, though, saw it differently. Bulgaria was flexing
its muscles with a rather cynical demand for Macedonian
independence. Bulgaria's claim to Macedonia went back
before World War I. It was no secret that Sofia had its eye
on the possibility of a Greater Bulgaria, one that included at
the very least northern Macedonia. Albania felt the same,
and for the same reason, with the added twist that Tiranë
had a long-unsettled grudge with Serbia over Kosovo
Province, which once had belonged to Albania and still had
a large, ethnic Albanian population. Turkey, the bitter
historical enemy of Greece, supported Macedonian independence, if only to see Greek power in the region weak-
ened.

And as for the Macedonians, well, they saw themselves
as the heirs of Alexander the Great, even if they were
historically Slavs for the most part rather than Greeks. Most
saw no reason why their national pride and character should
be stifled, especially now that the world was changing and

nationalistic ideals were blowing freely in the wind. All too many Macedonians, on both sides of the Greek-former-Yugoslav border, Kingston thought, would love to see an independent Macedonia that stretched clear from Serbia to the Aegean, from Bulgaria to the Adriatic.

And in all of that political turmoil and suffering, all of that bluster, threat, and counterthreat, there were painfully few options that did not lead to a war that would ravage every nation from Croatia and Hungary to Greece, Albania, and Turkey. Once that happened, an even larger war, one involving NATO and the United States, and probably Russia as well, was a near certainty.

And the damned U.S. military had just gone and stuck a pin in Serbia. It was enough to make a grown Congress-woman cuss.

"Oh, shit," Winters said suddenly.

"I beg your pardon?"

"Uh, sorry, Congresswoman." Winters leaned across the empty seat beside him and peered out the plane's window. Kingston glanced out her own window curiously. Every-thing looked perfectly normal to her. Sunlight dazzled off a solid mass of snow-white clouds, seemingly just below the plane's wings.

"Colonel, what *is* the matter?"

"That's damned peculiar. . . ."

"Is there a problem, Colonel Winters?" Mantzaros asked, walking up the cabin's central passage.

"Damn right there is," Winters muttered, more to himself than to those within earshot.

"Colonel, please," Kingston said tiredly. "I'm in no mood for your military theatrics."

"Beg your pardon, Congresswoman, but we're flying the wrong way."

She laughed. "Really? Your Boy Scout manual told you to check for moss on the north side of the plane?"

"No, but common sense tells me that if the sun is behind us and to the right at ten o'clock in the morning, we must be flying northwest. And we've been flying northwest for a good five minutes now."

"But Athens—"

"Is south of Salonika," Winters said. "Actually a little east of south. We're flying almost exactly in the wrong direction."

Mantzaros gave a start at that, performing an almost comical double take. Reaching inside his suit coat, he dragged out an automatic pistol, then jerked the slide back with a sharp *snick-snick.*

"Gentlemen, please," Kingston said.

"Maybe the pilot's just detouring around a storm or something," Bunny said. But she looked scared.

"I checked with the met office at the airport," Winters said. "No storms between there and Athens. Agent Mantzaros?"

"I think perhaps I should check up front," the Greek DEA man said.

"I think that's an excellent idea," Winters said, rising. "Let's go have a word with the pilot."

"That won't be necessary," one of Mantzaros's men said, brushing through the curtain at the front of the passenger compartment. He was holding an ugly-looking automatic weapon which he kept centered on his boss's chest. Kingston searched for the gun's name. What was the thing called? *Uzi,* that was it.

"Stavrianos!" Mantzaros cried, eyes widening behind his comic-opera dark glasses. *"Ti kaneteh? Then kantalamvano!"*

"Skasmos!" The DEA man kept the Uzi pointed at Mantzaros in one hand as he held out the other, palm up. *"Thos moo toh! Grigora!"*

His dark features growing darker still, Mantzaros slowly handed his pistol to the DEA man butt first.

"Kalos." He gestured toward a seat behind the VIP lounge with the pistol, then dropped the weapon into his pocket. *"Kathesate!"*

"What the fuck is the meaning of this, you bastard?" Winters demanded.

The man with the Uzi whipped the ugly weapon around, catching the colonel on the side of his head, just behind his left eye. Kingston winced at the crack of metal striking skin over bone. Winters gasped and dropped to his knees clutching his head.

"Colonel!" she exclaimed. There was blood . . . a *lot* of blood, welling up from a cut just behind the officer's left eye.

"I advise you to watch your language, Colonel Winters," the man said smoothly. "There is a lady present." With his free hand, he reached out and grabbed Winters by the hair, shoving him back against the table and pinning him there with his bloody head all the way back. He brought the muzzle of the Uzi down and pressed it against Winters's throat.

"No!" Bunny cried. "What are you doing? You can't do that!"

"We already have, Miss Allison. My, ah, associates and I are now in command of this aircraft."

"Son . . . of a . . . bitch . . ." Winters gasped against the pressure of the gun's barrel resting on his Adam's apple.

The man pulled Winters's head up, then slammed it viciously down on the table again. Winters reached for the gun, but the man stepped easily back out of reach.

"As I say, we are in charge now. All of you would be well advised to stay in your seats and remain silent. You will not be hurt if you do precisely what I say."

"Who are you?" Kingston demanded. "What is it you want?"

The man smiled. "I am Mikos Stavrianos," he said, turning his gun on her. "I am a member of the EMA . . . and what we want, Congresswoman, is you."

8

Tuesday, March 7

0840 hours
Briefing room, Ops
U.S.S. *Nassau*

"Get in here."

Murdock opened the door and stepped through into the briefing room. Part of *Nassau*'s Operations suite, it was a typically stark shipboard compartment, gray-walled and with a tile deck. PLAT monitors—television monitors showing activity on the flight deck looking both forward and aft—hung from several strategic points on the cable- and conduit-cluttered overhead, and the center of the room was dominated by a large table.

There were maps on the table, but they were covered by a sheet. Murdock, who'd been anticipating worse and worse personal outcomes for himself in regard to this meeting, wondered what that meant.

Were they going to kick him out of the Teams?

A number of naval officers were in the compartment, gathered around the table or sitting in chairs or sofas near the bulkheads. Most were members of *Nassau*'s Operations staff, including Commander George Presley, from CIC, and Commander Randolph R. Garrett, the red-bearded head of *Nassau*'s Intelligence Center.

There were some surprises waiting for Murdock there as

well. Captain Phillip Coburn was the commanding officer of
SEAL Seven, an old-time SEAL who'd begun with Team
Two in Vietnam, back in 1969. Commander George Monroe
was Coburn's executive officer, while Senior Chief Ed
Hawkins was on Coburn's administrative staff.

Two of the men Murdock did not know . . . the only
two enlisted men in the compartment. One was a tall,
athletic-looking electronics technician first class, square-
jawed, blond, and blue-eyed. The other was a machinist's
mate second, a head shorter than the other petty officer, with
black hair and an intense, dark gaze. Both wore the SEAL
Budweiser on their dress blue uniform jumpers.

Murdock zeroed in on Coburn, however. "Captain Coburn,"
Murdock said, trying to control his surprise. "I, ah, I thought
you were at Little Creek. Sir."

"I was, until Blue Arrow got hot. I've read the report, and
Commander Presley filled me in when I came aboard this
morning. Tell me something, son. Was there any way on
God's green earth you could have avoided that firefight at
the monastery?"

"Certainly there was, sir. I gave the order to fire. I could
have ordered my men to hold their fire. The decision was
mine."

"And?"

"Sir?"

"Why did you do it? Open fire, I mean."

"Two soldiers had detained Gypsy, our contact, our
whole reason for going in. Judging from the nature of what
was going on at the time, I thought it likely that they would
shoot him. At the very least they would have arrested him
on some pretext."

"Yes, and searched his vehicle."

"They would have found the briefcase, sir, yes."

"I don't know if anyone bothered to tell you, Lieutenant,"
Monroe said, "but the Agency has its package. Fletcher flew
back to Langley with it soon as you brought it aboard. By all
accounts, *they're* happy about this mess at least."

"I take it you've seen some of the late-breaking news stories, Lieutenant," Coburn said.

"Yes, sir. It sounds like the Serbs are playing up our presence there in a pretty big way."

"You got that straight," Coburn said. He leaned back against the table, his arms folded. "That general . . . what's his name?"

"Mihajlovic."

"Mihajlovic, right. He's telling the whole world, live on ACN TV, that—pick one—the Marines, the Green Berets, the SEALs, the CIA, or all four are out to overthrow the legitimate government of the Yugoslav Republic. He's been showing off that CRRC you left on the beach, by the way."

"We had no choice on that, sir. They were parked practically on top of it."

"Was there any way for you to have avoided contact with the enemy at the beach?"

"Well, I could have holed up in the woods for a day or two. Or chosen a different extraction point. But there seemed to be no reason for either until we were already committed. I . . . I'm really not sure what else I could have done, sir."

Coburn held up a hand, shaking his head. "Don't sweat it, son. I just wanted to hear it from you. Missions of this type never go as smoothly as they do in the movies, do they?"

Murdock quirked an eyebrow. Where was this leading? "No, sir. Never."

"Mihajlovic can't *prove* anything," Senior Chief Hawkins put in. "All the gear was sterile. You didn't leave anyone behind."

"By the way," Coburn said. "Speaking of that, I saw Garcia at Bethesda before flying out here. Doctors say he's going to make it."

They'd medevaced Garcia off the *Nassau* that same day, first to Naples, then back to the National Naval Medical Center at Bethesda, just inside the Washington Beltway. "That's good news, sir," Murdock said.

"Yes. Yes, it is. Good work bringing him off the beach like that."

"SEALs take care of their own, sir."

"Yes, they do." Coburn unfolded his arms and exchanged looks with several of the other officers. "Gentlemen? Any further questions for this young man?"

"Not on the last mission," Garrett said, scratching his beard. "But I can't wait to hear how he's going to manage this next one."

Coburn looked at the expression on Murdock's face and laughed. "What did you think, son? That we were going to court-martial you? Maybe keelhaul your ass out of the Navy?"

"Something like that, sir. We were supposed to go in quiet. In and out, no hear-um, no see-um. We screwed up. *I* screwed up."

"Bullshit. The gods of war screwed up this time, if anybody did. You did everything right, Lieutenant. Sometimes even right just ain't good enough."

"That's not to say there won't be some administrative fallout over this," Monroe put in. "Like they say, shit runs downhill, and there are some very unhappy people at some very high levels in this affair. Right now, there is some very high-level ass-covering underway in Washington. I'm afraid you haven't heard the last of it."

"But to get to you they have to go through me," Coburn said quietly. "So don't worry about it too much. How have you and your men been getting on since your picnic on the beach?"

The abrupt change of tack in the discussion caught Murdock by surprise. "Eh? Fine, sir. We've been keeping them busy, cleaning weapons and gear, calisthenics, and so on."

"Ready for a new assignment?"

"Absolutely."

"Good." He glanced across the compartment at the two enlisted men. "Pardon my manners. I should introduce these two. Lieutenant Murdock, this is Petty Officer Stepano,

Petty Officer Papagos. They've volunteered for this operation, and if you agree to help us out here, they'll be assigned to your unit. Stepano speaks Serbo-Croatian, Bulgarian, and Macedonian. Papagos speaks Greek. You'll likely need both of them where you're going."

"Welcome aboard," Murdock told them.

"A pleasure, Lieutenant," Stepano said.

"Yeah, Lieutenant," Papagos added. "We heard a lot about your outfit."

Coburn turned to the table and lifted the sheet off the maps. Murdock had expected them to be charts of the Adriatic coast and inland, where Blue Squad had been operating a few nights ago, but these maps covered an area farther south. He immediately recognized the convoluted coastline of northern Greece, the indentation of Thermaic Bay at Salonika, the rugged mountains inland that formed the natural border between the Greek and Slavic Macedonias. A red line had been drawn on one of the charts, from the airport south of Salonika northwest. It ended with a roughly circled region in the mountains just south of the border, not far from the Greek towns of Orme and Edessa.

"Yesterday morning," Coburn said softly, "a Greek passenger aircraft was hijacked. Olympic Lines domestic flight, a twin-engine turboprop. There were no radioed demands, no negotiations. Shortly after takeoff, the aircraft simply left its flight path and started flying toward the border with Yugoslav Macedonia. It was intercepted by a flight of Greek Mirage F-1s about here." He pointed to the map halfway along the line, near the town of Arabyssos.

"My God. They didn't shoot it down, did they?"

"No. But the hijacked aircraft ignored all radio calls and all threats to shoot it down. It began flying very low, following the mountain valleys toward the border. They lost it somewhere north of Edessa."

"Radar?"

"We were tracking the aircraft from a Hawkeye on radar picket duty off the *Jefferson*, but they weren't able to hang onto it. That terrain . . ." He brushed his forefinger along the border. "The mountains aren't necessarily all that high. This one on the border is twenty-five hundred meters. But it's rugged. There was also some pretty heavy-duty jamming in the area by Macedonian forces."

"Macedonians, sir? Or Serbians?"

Coburn gave a hard smile. "Good question, and one we don't really know the answer to yet. Former Yugoslav Macedonia is technically independent. We still have a small peacekeeper force there. But the Serbs still think of the place as theirs. The Macedonians themselves aren't Greeks, like most people think. They're Slavs, like the Serbs. It's entirely possible that Serbia is mixed up in this."

Murdock studied the map for a moment. "If you never had radio contact with the aircraft, how do you know it was a hijacking?"

"We know." Coburn paused, staring at the largest topo map, one that showed the entire stretch of Macedonia, from the Kosovo-Serbian border to Salonika. "Lieutenant, what I am about to divulge is classified top secret. My orders were to keep you in the dark about certain aspects of this mission until you had already accepted the assignment. That's why the nonsense with the sheets when you came in.

"I'm going to stick my neck out a bit on this one, though, and tell you something that must remain within these four bulkheads. God knows, it'll come out soon enough anyway. ACN is probably drawing up its special news bulletin logo right now."

"Yes, sir?"

"One of the passengers on that aircraft was Congress-woman Ellen Kingston from California, a member of the House Military Affairs Committee."

"My God . . ."

"Her plane was a chartered VIP special, nobody aboard but her, her entourage, and both Greek and American security. This wasn't just a random one-of-the-passengers-has-a-gun hijacking. They were clearly after her in particular."

"This is starting to sound a little crazy," Murdock said, shaking his head.

"We've received a list of the people who should have been on board," Chief Hawkins said. He handed a computer printout across the table to Murdock. "Besides the distinguished lady from California, we have nine congressional staffers, five males, four females. Two U.S. Secret Service men assigned to Ms. Kingston more or less permanently. A U.S. Army colonel, a military liaison officer out of the American embassy staff in Athens. Three other American military personnel, two males, one female, all officers of the colonel's personal staff. Six Greek DEA men. And the crew of the aircraft, of course, all Greek. Pilot, copilot, engineer, three female attendants, one security man."

"With all of that security aboard," Murdock wondered, "how the hell did the bad guys get aboard in the first place?"

"That, Lieutenant, is a question we would very much like answered. Since there is no evidence that anyone forced their way aboard at the airport at Salonika, there really are only two possibilities. A number of armed terrorists could have been hidden aboard the plane before the passengers boarded."

"Or it was an inside job," Murdock said, reaching out and picking up a deck plan schematic of an NAMC YS-11 lying on the table among the maps. "Either the aircraft's crew or the Greek security element."

"That's what we think. Right now, the CIA and Army Intelligence are probably going over the personnel folders of those security men with microscopes. Meanwhile, we've been given a mission alert and told to start planning an immediate op."

Murdock laid the aircraft schematic down and turned his attention once again to the map of the Greek border. "Question, Captain."

"Yes?"

"Why us? I mean, I'm delighted, I'm sure . . . but that aircraft's last known heading is taking it into a country that's completely landlocked. According to this map, there are exactly two airfields that handle commercial traffic, one up here in the capital at . . . what is that? Skopje?"

"Pronounced 'Skop-yay,'" Coburn corrected him gently.

"*Skopje*, right. And the other one's down here, tucked in between the mountains, these lakes, and the inland border of Albania."

"Ohrid," Commander Garrett said. "Used to be a heavy tourist area, until the war sent the tourist trade to hell. Then it was the site of a round of Balkan peace talks that failed."

"And you're wondering why the SEALs are in on this," Coburn said.

"The question had crossed my mind. This looks like the sort of dreamsheet op the Delta boys would kill for."

"And the Army Rangers, and Airborne, and the Army Special Forces, and the Marines, and the Air Force 7th Special Operations Squadron up at Rhein-Main, and probably half a dozen special-warfare commando groups you and I have never even heard of. Right now, I imagine there's something very like a feeding frenzy going on back at the Pentagon, as all of the services line up for a piece of this one.

"The one advantage we have right now over all the rest is, we're here. And they aren't."

"Delta Force will probably get their tickets punched on this one," Monroe said. "They have a team ready for immediate deployment, and local caches of arms and equipment. They were alerted as soon as we got word that the aircraft was off course and are probably working out scenarios right this moment. And you're right, of course. While the SEALs' combat responsibilities do extend inland, Skopje is one hundred sixty kilometers from the Adriatic. That's pretty dry, even for a SEAL."

"What Navy Intelligence is interested in," Coburn said, "is what went down at Salonika International two days ago. Even if this was an inside job, there had to be people at the airport who were in on it. Greek Military Intelligence is following that angle. And we're going to help them. But diplomatically."

"Sir?"

"To start with, we want your team to go into Salonika. Have a look around. Work with the Greek DEA. That's why we dug up Papagos here. Speaks Greek like a native."

"That's me, Lieutenant," Papagos said with a bright grin. "Nick the Greek Papagos."

"Where you from, Papagos?"

"Chicago. South Side. But my parents was from the old country, see? Patrai, down on the Peloponnisos."

"You ever been to Greece?"

"Me, sir? Never. I joined the Navy t'see the world, y'know? But I speak the lingo okay. *Milao ellenika.*"

"How about you, uh, Stepano?" Murdock asked.

"I am Serb," the blond ET replied. Murdock could hear a fairly thick East European accent. "From Pittsburgh now, sir. Originally Belgrade."

"Josip Stepano was Yugoslavian," Coburn said. "Got into some trouble with the local police and had to skip the country. Naturalized citizen."

"I have been American fifteen years now," Stepano said, and Murdock could heard the pride in his voice.

"Well, I'm real happy to meet both of you," Murdock said. "Looks like we're going to need you guys. Salonika, huh?"

"That's right," Coburn replied. "How much do you know about our relations with Greece just now?"

"Prickly. That's about all I know."

"Prickly describes it quite nicely. Greece is a member of NATO, of course. So is Turkey, though, and Turkey and Greece are bitter blood enemies. Ottoman Turkey ruled Greece until the early 1800s. There were lots of massacres on both sides, and believe me, both sides have long memories.

"Then there's the Macedonian problem. You see, when Yugoslavian Macedonia voted independence for itself and applied for UN recognition a couple of years ago, we supported it, while Greece opposed it. The whole Macedonian question is very, very touchy so far as Athens is concerned. They'd like nothing better than to see the Serbs control Yugoslav Macedonia. An independent Macedonia might give their *own* Macedonians some unpleasant ideas."

"Like independence?"

"Exactly. Our relations with the Greeks have not exactly been pleasant lately. When the Pan-Hellenic Socialists came to power under Papandreou in 1981, the government went pretty far to the left, anti-European Community, anti-U.S., anti-NATO. The center-rightists took a slim parliamentary majority in 1990, but they've been just barely hanging on. The Greek economy is in a shambles. There have been threats of another military coup, like the one that ended the monarchy back in '67."

"I'm afraid the current Greek government has no particular reason to love us," Garrett explained. "There have been some unhappy incidents. One of our ships accidentally fired a missile into a Greek destroyer in 1992, during some joint maneuvers. Bad business, that. Besides, Washington has been leaning pretty hard on them for a long time to keep the lid on the Turkey-Greece conflict. Lately we've been leaning on them some more, trying to get them to bend our way over Yugoslav-Macedonian independence and to keep imposing sanctions against Serbia. And last year, Greece slapped an embargo on Yugoslav Macedonia, which, of course, is landlocked. Most of their oil comes in through Salonika. We've been at odds with Athens over that too."

"At the moment," Coburn said, "Greece tolerates us and is willing to cooperate on most matters, at least at a distance. But that toleration probably won't extend to allowing a major military presence in their territory. If Washington pulls its typical big-brother act, sends in the Marines or a division or two of Army troops, most Greeks are going to see that as the ugly Americans throwing their weight around, impugning their military's abilities—"

"Impugning their manhood," Presley put in. The others laughed.

"The Athens government won't like the implication that they're weak. Their armed forces won't like the implication that they can't keep order or handle their own military problems. We're going to have to tread very carefully over there."

"I take it we're going to have to cooperate with the Greeks on this one," Murdock said.

"So far as investigating the hijacking, which involved Greek security personnel and a Greek airliner over Greek territory, yes. Definitely. If it turns out the hijackers are in Yugoslav Macedonia, the picture may be different, but we're going to have to start south of the border. Our embassy in Athens has started the ball rolling so far as putting small U.S. military teams into Greece to work with local military and law enforcement agencies."

"Well, who the hell are the bad guys anyway?" Murdock wanted to know. "We must have some ideas, some place to start."

"We do," Garrett said. "There are several active Macedonian pro-independence movements going on both sides of the Greek border. The ones north of the border have a longer history, and more practice. The ones south of the border didn't really get restive until their cousins up north kicked over their traces, but they're making up for their late start with plenty of enthusiasm. Our best guess right now is that one of the Macedonian independence groups is behind the hijacking."

"What groups?" Murdock wanted to know. He disliked the idea of trying to come to grips with a faceless enemy. "Who are they?"

"The International Macedonian Revolutionary Organization is a good bet," Garrett said. The IMRO's been around since, oh, 1893 or so. First they fought the Turks. Then they fought the Serbs. And there are reportedly some splinter groups."

"The EMA's one of the biggest," Presley said. "They've been making a nuisance of themselves lately. Car bombings, assassinations, that sort of thing."

Murdock blinked. "EMA?"

"A Greek acronym for a phrase that translates as 'United

Macedonian Struggle,'" Garrett said. "We think they're a
Greek offshoot of the Slavic IMRO."

Murdock shook his head unhappily. "I thought the
Macedonians were Slavic, not Greek. Or am I missing
something?"

Coburn laughed. "Son, you've just grasped the essentials
of Balkan politics. No label can ever do justice to a
hodgepodge mix of Serbian, Romanian, Bulgarian, and
Greek Slavs." He stopped, took a deep breath, and began
counting off names on his fingers. "Not to mention Albanians, Greeks, Turks, Croats, Hungarian Magyars, Greek
Orthodox, Macedonian Orthodox, Serb Orthodox, Muslim,
Catholic, atheist, and the Lord alone knows what else, most
of them hating everyone else in the neighborhood. In this
case, most Macedonians *are* Slavs . . . but there are plenty
of Greeks who would like to see Greek Macedonia independent for one reason or another."

"The worst part of all of this," Garrett went on, "is the
number of outside parties who have an interest in Balkan
politics. Italy is poised to become the money man for the
emerging Balkan republics, something like Japan in Asia
today, and they have a vested interest in Trieste, up the
Adriatic coast here. Austria and Hungary both want to
see Slovenia stay independent, and that independence would
be threatened if the war spread. Russia has a keen interest, of
course. Yugoslavia was an ally, an arms and energy market,
and a fellow Communist state, even if old Tito never saw eye
to eye with the Kremlin. Besides, Russian Slavs don't want to
see their South Slav cousins—that's what Yugoslavia means,
by the way, 'South Slav'—they don't want to see them pushed
around."

"The Russian ultra-nationalists," Presley said, "have been
talking about re-imposing the socialist workers' paradise on
the whole region. They're afraid all-out war in the Balkans
could spill over into Moldova, Ukraine, and even Russia
itself. Besides, there are all of those lovely warm-water
ports on the Adriatic. Dubrovnik, Kotor, Split, and all the
rest."

"Then there's Turkey," Coburn said, "which would love an excuse to get into a general war with Greece, even if they are both members of NATO. We've got literally dozens of players in this show, all with hard reasons to either back or block Macedonian unity."

"Sounds like that old cliche, the Balkan powder keg," Murdock said.

"If you want cliches," Coburn said, "try this one. The Ellen Kingston hijacking is the fuse, and it's burning damned short now. Fumble this one and we touch the whole damned mess off."

"What do you think the terrorists, whoever is behind it, what do you think they're trying to accomplish?"

"Lieutenant, that's anybody's guess right now," Garrett said, smiling through his beard. "We probably won't know until they do try to contact us. Chances are they'll have a list of political demands. You know, U.S. recognition of a Greater Macedonia, or something like that. Maybe leverage from Washington against Athens."

"And then there's the Armageddon scenario," Presley said.

"Armageddon scenario? What's that?"

"The idea that someone, the EMA or the Serbs or some other damned bunch of malcontents, actually *wants* a general war, that they kidnapped Kingston because they knew we would intervene militarily. You see, if Bulgaria, Greece, Turkey, Italy, Russia, and the United States, along with most of the other nations of Europe, all wound up involved in a devastating war, maybe they—whoever 'they' might be—could have a chance to move in and set up as the local tough kids on the block."

"There are some in Belgrade," Garrett said, "who have actually been boasting that the first World War started in the Balkans . . . and that the third one will too."

"Good God, why?"

"Is matter of pride," Stepano said. "Serbs, some Serbs anyway, see themselves as martyrs, as victims of centuries of persecution. By Turks. By Nazis. Now by Americans."

"What," Murdock said, "because we're trying to stop the slaughter of the Bosnian Muslims?"

Stepano shrugged. "They see it as their chance to get even. Like I say, they think they're victims. It is . . . it is insanity."

" 'They?' " Garrett said. "Aren't you a Serb?"

"I," Stepano said, straightening a bit, "am *American.* Sir."

"Good man," Murdock said. "It's going to be good to have you with us." He meant it. The complexities and the passions of Balkan politics left him feeling cold and a little lost.

And this mission was one where getting lost—just one little screwup—could mean not only the loss of his team, but the beginning of World War III.

9

Wednesday, March 8

0820 hours
Carrier Onboard Delivery aircraft
En route to U.S.S. *Thomas Jefferson*

The C-2A Greyhound was a twin-engine turboprop, a cargo aircraft designed around an enlarged E-2 Hawkeye fuselage. Popularly known as COD, for Carrier Onboard Delivery, the Greyhound was a vital link in American aircraft carrier operations, ferrying supplies, personnel, and mail to and from the big CVNs while they were at sea. Murdock and the rest of Third Platoon had boarded the aircraft aboard the *Nassau* early that morning. Now they were lounging in the hard folding seats that lined the Greyhound's cargo compartment, flying south along the west coast of Greece.

The men of SEAL Seven, Third Platoon, were relaxed and happy, enjoying both the flight and the prospect of what Jaybird Sterling laughingly called a "yesterday's mission." "The only easy day was yesterday" ran the refrain from the BUD/S training, and that same spirit permeated most SEAL operations in the field as well. Some few SEAL operations, though, involved civilian clothes and tourist strolls through cities rather than twelve-mile swims or crawling through mud. The men gloried in what they referred to as a government-paid vacation, working leave, or liberty with strings attached.

All of both Blue and Gold Squads were aboard the COD aircraft, as well as the two new men Coburn had brought with him from Norfolk. Gold Squad's leader was Third Platoon's XO, Lieutenant j.g. Ed DeWitt, while the senior petty officer was Boatswain's Mate Chief Ben Kosciuszko. TM2 Eric Nicholson, GM1 Miguel "Rattler" Fernandez, RM1 Ron "Bearcat" Holt, MN2 "Scotty" Frazier, and MM2 David "Jaybird" Sterling made up the rest of the Gold Squad's muster list.

"So what do you know about this Solomos guy?" Jaybird asked Murdock after they'd been airborne for a time. "Is he Greek military?"

"I gather he used to be in the Greek paratroopers," Murdock replied, "so he's been there and knows the score."

"He probably already knows how to break into locked Volkswagens, Jaybird," Magic said, and the rest of the men in the Greyhound laughed.

Machinist's Mate Second Class David Sterling joined in the laughter, and Murdock nodded approval. Sterling was relatively new as a SEAL, but he'd been accepted by the platoon and by now was an old hand. He'd completed BUD/S training eight months ago, just in time for the op aboard that Japanese plutonium ship in the Indian Ocean. He'd won his Budweiser after the usual six months' probationary period in a wildly memorable party in Norfolk two months ago. The nickname "Jaybird" was the result of an incident involving a pretty girl, a locked Volkswagen, and skinny-dipping in the ocean off the beach at La Jolla, California, just after his SEAL training had been completed.

"How do you read it, Skipper?" MacKenzie asked. "We going to have problems with the locals? Or is all the unpleasantness higher up than down here at grunt level?"

"Don't know, Mac. We'll just have to play that as it comes. But I want all you guys to remember the captain's last word on the matter. It's low profile, right? Greek jails aren't as pleasant and comfy as the city jail back in Norfolk."

"Don't worry, Skipper," Chief Kosciuszko said, a deliberate growl in his voice. "These puppies'll behave or they're gonna think it's Hell Week all over again. Right, people?"

"Yes, Mother," Doc cracked, and the cargo compartment rang with hoots and laughter.

Murdock had given all of his men the option of backing out of this one. While working with local police in Salonika didn't sound like hardship duty, Murdock felt that he ought to give them a choice . . . and to let them know that this op felt wrong. It wasn't something he could put into words. After considerable thought, he'd decided that his bad feelings about the mission probably centered on the fact that, first off, their mission goals were uncomfortably vague. And even more problematical, they would be operating in a host country that didn't really want them, against enemies that weren't even identified yet, and on the fringes of a war—several wars, really—that promised to be as messy as Vietnam . . . in spades.

Every man in the Third Platoon had volunteered, despite Murdock's warnings. The banter among the men now as they flew south was a confirmation of what Murdock already knew. Morale was good, despite Garcia's having been wounded, something that was always tough on a unit as close-knit as this one. They were tight, hard, and ready.

At the moment, conversation had drifted from what Kosciuszko would do to them if they screwed up to times they'd been in trouble generally. Jaybird told them again about the administrative mess he'd been in after the affair with the skinny-dipping in La Jolla, ending with his being arrested by a female cop while driving through town in his VW completely naked. Roselli and Holt repeated the story about the time in Norfolk when they'd been arrested by the local police after threatening to chuck a hotel manager out of a fifth-story window, when Mac had had to come down and bail them out.

"So, Stepano," Roselli called, shouting to be heard above both the roar of the Greyhound's engines and the laughter and applause that followed his tale. "We heard tell you were in some sort of trouble back in Yugoslavia. What was it, some problem with the government?"

When Stepano didn't answer immediately, Murdock leaned closer to the big Serb-American. "You don't have to tell 'em anything if you don't want to."

"Oh, is no problem, Lieutenant," Stepano replied. "I was just thinking. Was not government trouble, exactly. You see, there was this girl. . . ."

"Ah."

"Okay!" Doc shouted. "This boy's gonna fit right in!"

"It was still serious thing, Lieutenant. They were threatening me with Goli Otok. You see, she was daughter of a member of Central Committee. . . ."

Murdock shook his head. "Sorry. Goli . . . what?"

"Goli Otok," Stepano repeated. "One of two islands in the Adriatic, not so far from Trieste, you see? Goli Otok was torture prison for men, run by Tito's secret police. Sveti Grgur was same thing, only for women prisoners. There were awful stories. . . ."

Stepano bit his lower lip, then settled back in his seat. "Is not really so funny a story," he said, finally. "That was why I left Yugoslavia, though. I was eighteen."

His mood momentarily darkened the atmosphere within the COD's compartment, but not for very long. Doc began telling a story about a girl he'd known in Norfolk who was the daughter of an admiral, and soon the cargo compartment was again ringing with the SEALs' shouts and laughter.

But the exchange had left Murdock thoughtful. He'd heard the fear behind Stepano's words. How did the Serb feel about going back to his old neighborhood, Murdock wondered. Those "torture prisons" he'd mentioned probably belonged to Croatia now, and Tito's secret police would have evolved into something else. But there would be other Goli Otoks in place in what was left of Yugoslavia, and knowing the socialist bureaucratic mind, Murdock was sure that there were still plenty of records stuffed in a file folder someplace in Belgrade with Stepano's name on it.

It might be a good idea to make sure that Stepano stayed

in Greece, should the team need to cross over into Serbian-controlled areas. Of course, the whole reason Stepano was along was to provide translation if they did end up across the border. Murdock shook his head. He sure as hell wouldn't want to be in Stepano's place right now.

God, why had the big Serb volunteered for this anyway?

The nuclear aircraft carrier *Thomas Jefferson*, CVN 74, had been on patrol in the eastern Med, but as soon as word had been received that Congresswoman Kingston's flight had been hijacked, the *Jeff* had put about and headed north, entering the sparkling blue waters of the Saronic Gulf early on the morning of March 7 and anchoring in the roads off Pireas, the port facility for the city of Athens.

The supercarrier, nucleus of Carrier Battle Group 14, was the visible, physical manifestation of America's military might, a symbol of both reassurance and warning to the Greek government that the United States was *extremely* concerned about the incident. *Jefferson* also provided a way station for the SEALs en route from the Adriatic. The COD touched down in a barely controlled crash on the *Jeff*'s flight deck, tail hook snagging the number-three arrestor wire and dragging the big aircraft to a halt. SEAL Seven's Third Platoon did not linger aboard the carrier for long, however. After a short briefing with a military attaché officer from the American Embassy, during which they received the necessary papers and travel permits and made arrangements for the secret shipment of weapons and other gear to Salonika, the SEALs had gone ashore in one of *Jefferson*'s liberty boats, a Mike boat lowered alongside the temporary dock floated off the carrier's stern.

All fifteen men wore civilian clothes. Looking at them, for the first time Murdock wished he'd allowed more latitude for his men in their grooming standards. MGS, or "Modified Grooming Standards," had been a sore point in the SEAL community for some time. Some units, like the notorious SEAL Six, encouraged their men to wear beards, mustaches, and long hair—long enough to warrant pony-tails—precisely so that the Team members didn't look like military personnel. Some Team commanders stressed MGS as a means of letting their men operate undercover; others, and Murdock was among them, had always stressed traditional Navy grooming standards, both to avoid making waves with other naval personnel, and because long hair or face fuzz could be a hazard for SEALs. Murdock had ordered more than one man in his platoon to shave his facial hair because of the danger that a mustache might prevent a watertight seal between skin and face mask.

Aboard the Mike boat, however, Murdock was painfully aware that his people all *looked* like sailors, clean-cut, clean-shaven, their hair closely trimmed. With their short hair and their powerful, athletic frames—Bearcat Holt, especially, had the physique of a bodybuilder—they could only be military personnel or members of some traveling international sports team. That could well turn out to be a handicap on this op.

To reduce the chances of being spotted for what they were, Murdock had the platoon split up as soon as they were ashore. Fifteen muscular young men traveling together looked like a military unit on a secret mission; two or three such men together were not at all unusual in a country where, despite tensions with Washington, American marines and sailors often went ashore on liberty in their civvies. Murdock did veto Doc's grinning suggestion that they round up some girls to make their disguises more complete.

Travel arrangements had already been made through the embassy, but only six of them—Murdock, DeWitt, Papagos, Sterling, Brown, and Roselli—would take the chartered flight north. The rest would make their own ways north to Salonika, never traveling more than three at a time, some aboard various commercial aircraft flights from Hellenica International, the others taking buses, rented cars, or the Greek OSE railway. The embassy officer had told them that rooms had been booked for them at a hotel called the Vergina, on Monastiriou Street northwest of central Salonika, not far from the railway station.

They were met at the Salonika airport by two men, who

stepped forward as soon as Murdock and the SEALs with him stepped through the door into the airport arrivals area. One, clearly, was a local, with dark eyes, hair, and skin and a brushy black mustache. He wore a conservative suit beneath an open trench coat, garb that somehow communicated the idea of "police" or "secret service" without actually displaying a badge. The other man, Murdock was willing to bet, was American . . . and almost certainly military, despite his sports shirt, slacks, and the tourist's 35mm camera around his neck. He was as tall and as muscular as Stepano, and he had the same clean-shaven, square-jawed, brush-cut look that described most of Murdock's SEALs.

"Lieutenant Murdock?" the small, dark man asked. His English was clipped and precise.

"That's me."

"I am Captain Solomos," the man said. "DEA, the Special Mission Platoon. Welcome to Salonika."

"It's good to be here, Captain," Murdock replied, extending his hand. "I wish it could be under happier circumstances."

"Indeed. May I present a compatriot of yours. Captain John Beasley, U.S. Army."

"Captain." Murdock shook hands with Beasley. His grip was strong, his eyes cold, pale, and hard.

"Lieutenant."

Solomos eyed the five men standing with Murdock. "This is your entire team?"

"Not quite. The others will be along directly."

"How many?"

"A few more." Solomos's face darkened, and Murdock added, "Nine more, to be precise."

"On a different flight?"

"Some of them. They'll all be here by noon tomorrow. Why?"

Solomos frowned. "I don't like so many of your men wandering around . . . aimlessly."

"I assure you, sir, that their wanderings won't be aimless."

"Yes, well, I assure *you* that my government's investigation into this incident is proceeding with perfect efficiency. There was really no need of your government to send, ah, additional troops."

"We're not really here as troops, Captain Solomos," Murdock said smoothly. "My government agrees that this incident should be closed with the least possible fuss and publicity. To that end, they've sent us as observers. We're under orders to keep a low profile and not to get in your way, sir."

"Hmpf. I have worked with your government before, Lieutenant. Most recently with *your* DEA, your Drug Enforcement Administration, on an operation against a heroin-smuggling pipeline supposedly passing through here from Turkey. Their idea of 'keeping a low profile' was a pitched gun battle with narcoterrorists that left three people dead, one of them one of my best men."

"Well, we're not hunting narcoterrorists, are we, Captain Solomos? Uh, shouldn't we find a more private place if we're going to talk?" He gestured at the crowded concourse. "This is kind of busy."

"There is really nothing more to be said, Lieutenant. I give you a friendly warning, nothing more. This regrettable affair is a Greek internal matter. We need neither your observations nor your help. Come. I have a driver standing by to take you to your hotel."

"That stuck-up little bastard," Sterling said, ninety minutes later at their hotel.

"Take it easy, Jaybird," Murdock said. "He's just doing his job, and he hasn't had that many good experiences with Americans."

They'd checked in with the desk clerk at the Vergina, then gathered in the room Murdock and DeWitt would be sharing. Jaybird and Roselli were facing each other on one of the beds, sitting cross-legged on the mattress as they assembled two pistols. The weapons, 9mm Smith & Wessons, had been broken down into dozens of individual pieces, and the pieces carefully hidden in their carry-on luggage. The larger and easily recognizable sections, like the frames and the loaded magazines, had been carefully positioned inside the luggage so that if they were X-rayed at a security checkpoint, their narrow facings were turned toward the camera, and they were bundled with other odd, mechanical-looking gadgets like alarm clocks and radios.

The scary part was that the elaborate preparations might not have been necessary. Murdock had carried loaded weapons through airport checkpoints plenty of times. Some airports—and those in Greece were among them—were notorious for their lax security measures. More often than not, all that was necessary was a U.S. fifty-dollar bill slipped into the right open palm. More than one terrorist had smuggled weapons aboard a target passenger liner at Athens's Hellenica International, and the security personnel tended to be even more careless on domestic flights, which were not so likely to be the targets of a terrorist operation.

"I'm still trying to figure that big U.S. Army guy," Roselli said, moving a slide into the guide grooves on the frame of the pistol he was working on. "Who the hell was he?"

"One guess," Murdock said, "beginning with the Greek letter delta."

"Aw, shit," DeWitt said. "Delta Force? Here?"

"I'm pretty sure of it. He could be Special Forces, like Solomos said, but there was something about his eyes, the way he was studying us. My guess is that Captain John Beasley is on a scouting trip, just like we are. Looking over the lay of the land for a Delta element."

"SEALs and Delta Force," Jaybird said, grinning. "Now this could get interesting."

"Just so we all remember we're on the same team," Murdock cautioned. "This isn't a goddamned competition."

"Yeah, well, just so the Delta guys remember that too," Brown said. "If they get stuffy about jurisdiction . . ."

"We'll worry about that when it happens," Murdock said. "Weapons okay?"

Roselli snicked back the slide on his Smith & Wesson, chambering a round, then dropped the magazine and snicked the slide again, catching the round as it spun from the ejection port, clearing the weapon. "All set here."

"And here," Jaybird said, holding up the other pistol and snapping a loaded magazine into the grip. "I'd be a hell of a lot happier with an M-60 about now, but . . ."

"We should have our other weapons tomorrow, through the Consulate."

Weapons had been a major concern. The Greek government had point-blank denied the Navy permission to arm its people ashore, a reasonable enough request, perhaps, in light of their contention that they didn't need American help. There were ways around such restrictions, however, and Murdock was not about to embark on a mission involving unknown terrorists with his men not armed. He imagined that this wouldn't be the first time that small arms had been smuggled into the country hidden within diplomatic pouches. There would be trouble only if any of the SEALs were actually caught and arrested by the local authorities while carrying a weapon.

"Well, gentlemen?" Murdock said, standing and going to the window. It was beginning to get dark outside, and the city lights were coming on. "Who feels like a little evening constitutional into town?"

Roselli and Murdock carried the two pistols, tucked into their waistbands at the smalls of their backs, hidden by the fall of their untucked shirttails and windbreakers. They strolled toward the center of Salonika along the Leoforos Nikis, the Avenue of Victory, a promenade that ran along the seafront from the long customs house above the harbor southeast to the White Tower. The tower, a massive, whitewashed structure thirty-five meters tall, was the city's best-known landmark. According to a tourist's guidebook Murdock had picked up in *Jefferson*'s ship's store before going ashore, it had been built by the Turks in 1430. In 1826, a number of rebel janissaries had been imprisoned and killed there, and the place had become known as the Bloody

Tower. In what was for them an unusual display of public relations sense, the Turks had then whitewashed the entire building, renaming it the Beyaz Kule, the White Tower.

To their right, the harbor was aglitter with the reflected lights from hundreds of ships and pleasure craft anchored out in the gulf, or behind the long breakwater pier that enclosed Salonika's inner harbor in front of the customs house.

"So what's your handle, Nick?" Roselli asked Papagos as they walked along the smooth, gray promenade.

"He told me 'Nick the Greek,'" Murdock said, grinning. He continued to study the layout of the city, however, as they talked. Traffic was heavy in Salonika's city center, and even though the tourist season didn't get into full swing until later in the year, there were a number of tourists evident on the streets and seated at the numerous sidewalk restaurants and cafes along the way.

"Hey, Nick the Greek?" Roselli said, laughing. "That right?"

"Either that or 'Nick the Geek,'" he said cheerfully. "But them that calls me that lives to regret it. *Usually* they live anyways. Once in a while they don't pull through, know what I'm sayin'?"

"Okay, okay," Brown said, grinning. "We'll be careful. Wouldn't want to start no international incidents."

"What's Stepano's handle?" DeWitt wanted to know.

"I heard some SEALs calling him 'Steponit' back at Little Creek," Papagos said. "He told me they called him that 'cause he was big, dumb, and slow."

"Dumb?"

"Don't you believe it. Steponit ain't dumb. In fact, the guy's a Grade-A genius when it comes to electronics. He just talks a little slow, is all. Not like me, y'know?"

"Speak of the devil," DeWitt said. "Isn't that him up there?"

"Sure enough," Roselli said. "And Mac and Scotty. They were flying in behind us, weren't they?"

"Yeah," Brown said. "Who're the two bad dudes with them, though?"

"Son of a bitch," Murdock said. "One of 'em's our friend Captain Beasley."

"Maybe his buddy's big-D too," DeWitt said,

Murdock glanced up and down the street. No one appeared to be paying any attention to them. "Let's go join the party and find out, huh?"

As they walked up to the four men on the promenade, Murdock took the time to study the two strangers. Beasley had exchanged his Japanese camera for a pair of big 7x40 binoculars hanging by their strap around his neck. The other man clearly had something bulky concealed beneath his half-zipped nylon jacket, tucked away beneath his left arm.

"Mac!" Murdock called as they came near. "Scotty! Stepano! Fancy meeting you guys here. What's going on?"

Beasley turned, studying Murdock through narrowed eyes. "Good evening, Lieutenant. I was just telling your men here that they're a little out of their element."

"Actually, he called us froggies," Mac said in a hurt voice. "Not very friendly at all."

"We don't want any trouble," Beasley's companion said. He smacked one meaty fist into his palm. "We got some bad guys staked out here, and you SEALies are just gonna get in the way."

"Cut the shit," Murdock snapped, his voice going cold. "We're both after the same thing, and that's information that'll let Kingston get rescued. I don't give a shit who does the rescuing, but if you Army assholes get that woman killed while you're playing your damned games . . ."

"Nobody said anything about games."

"Good. Now it seems to me that your people and mine can cooperate, Captain, or we can do this strictly by the book, which would cramp everyone's style. What's it going to be?"

"Captain," the second Army man said. "We can't let these sons of bitches—"

"You want to go by the regs, Captain? What's your date

of commission?" It was a bluff, because he wasn't about to involve Washington in something that would be better settled privately here and now. An Army captain and a Navy lieutenant were the same O-3 rank, and the threat of going regulation on this guy might give Murdock the wedge he needed.

"Easy, Lieutenant, easy," Beasley said. He looked Murdock up and down and seemed to arrive at some sort of a decision. "No point in getting hostile. But this is an Army op, and we would appreciate it if you would respect our jurisdiction."

"I will if you tell me what you've got."

Beasley considered that for a moment, then jerked his head forward. "Fair enough. Your word on that, Lieutenant?"

"My word, Beasley. We'll respect your jurisdiction."

"Okay. Come on. Having you people lined up in the open like you're passing in review makes me nervous."

"Where we going?" Magic asked.

The Army officer grinned. "Best place in town for a good view of the harbor," he said. "The White Tower, of course."

10

Rising above a small, public park on the waterfront, the White Tower might once have been a prison, but now it was a tourist attraction, complete with souvenir shop and a small museum. There were no tourists in the place, however, only more of Beasley's men. Murdock couldn't tell whether it was past the museum's hours, though, or if Beasley and his people had commandeered the place under authority granted them by Solomos and the local police. "Y'think maybe Notre Dame's team is visitin' today?" Papagos wondered, nodding toward one of the big, hard-muscled troopers in civilian clothes.

"Shh," DeWitt hissed. "Don't mention Notre Dame around Army. It's *not* a pretty picture."

"Keep it down, people," Murdock warned. "Papagos, Roselli, you two with me. The rest of you stay down here."

He stayed on Beasley's heels as they strode through the darkened museum, where mosaics and Byzantine gravestones and ranks of vases lurked in the shadowy surroundings. Past a black, iron grillwork held open by a civvies-clad trooper holding an Uzi submachine gun, stone steps wound

up the inside of the tower, toward the parapets over one
hundred feet above.

The White Tower had two observation levels, with a
smaller, central tower that rose another twenty feet above
the main parapets like the top layer of a wedding cake. They
emerged on this higher platform to a breathtaking view of
city and harbor. The wind had a cold bite to it, whipping
across the top of the tower out of the north.

Murdock paused, looking around to get his bearings.
North lay the city proper, an improbable mix of the old
Middle East and the modern West, church towers and
minarets mingled with apartments and office buildings.
Northeast, beyond a broad, tree-lined plaza, was a brilliantly
lit fairground, tents and temporary buildings spread out
beneath a tall communications tower.

Opposite, across a broad sweep from the northwest to
the south, were the sparkling waters of the Thermaic Gulf.
The waters close to the city were crowded with boats,
pleasure craft for the most part, though several freighters
and Greek naval vessels were moored by the inner harbor
pier.

Two more of Beasley's men—Murdock was certain now
that they were Delta—were crouched behind the crenelated
parapet of the tower, overlooking the bay. One was aiming
a rifle through one of the window-sized gaps in the wall, a
long-barreled Haskins M500 balanced on a bipod mounted
just ahead of the trigger. The weapon was slow—its
precision-milled bolt had to be removed to load each
round—but those rounds were .50-caliber monsters that
could take down a target at a range of better than two
kilometers. The Haskins mounted a bulky, low-light tele-
scopic scope, a Varo AN/PVS-4, giving it the look of
something out of science fiction. The spotter, kneeling at the
next opening to the right, was peering through a heavy,
tripod-mounted infrared surveillance scope.

"Hey, Captain," the spotter said as they emerged onto the
tower roof. "Who're these guys?"

"Navy," Beasley said. "But I think they're on our side this time."

"No shit?" The trooper shifted his face back to his scope.

"What's your target?" Murdock asked as they moved up to the wall. From the angle of the sniper's rifle and the spotter's scope, they were both watching one of the boats tied up in the outer harbor.

"Okay," Beasley said. "Here's the way it is. Our pal Solomos and his people got a pretty good lead. Seems two guys in their Special Missions Platoon have more money in their bank accounts than their government salaries could explain."

"Uh-oh."

"Yeah, uh-oh. First suspect's name is Eleni Trahanatzis. Young guy, twenty-three. No known political connections. He's still officially on the DEA roster, but apparently he took an extended leave of absence a couple of months ago. See that yacht tied up to the orange buoy, about seven hundred meters out?" He pointed, handing Murdock his binoculars. "That's his. He's been living there ever since."

Murdock took the binoculars and picked up the indicated boat. It wasn't quite what he thought of as a yacht, but it was bigger and fancier than a policeman's salary could afford, perhaps thirty feet long, with a flying bridge atop a large cabin, a well deck aft, a sun deck forward. Probably twin screws . . . and probably fast if it came to a chase. Murdock estimated that she'd be able to top forty or forty-five knots in calm seas.

"The guy's doing pretty well for himself," Murdock said, carefully studying the craft. Cabin lights were on, though he couldn't see through the closed curtains. A lone man sat in the well deck aft, smoking a cigarette. A cable passed over the bow and was secured to a mooring buoy. A Zodiac raft was tied to the craft's stern.

"Second guy is Stathis Vlachos," Beasley went on. "He's harder to pin down. Solomos says he retired from the DEA about two months ago, but he won't tell us where he worked or who he worked for. He's older, maybe thirty-five, and there's a hint that he got his job through some sort of pretty powerful political connections. Nephew of the Prime Minister, that sort of thing."

"Is he?"

"Not so far as we know. Washington is looking into it. No lurid details yet."

Through the binoculars, Murdock could make out the boat's name, written in Cyrillic letters. He could sound them out but didn't know what the word meant. "Papagos," he said quietly. "What's '*Glaros*'?"

"*Sea gull*, Lieutenant."

Beasley chuckled. "If you really want an eyeful," he said, "have a look through here. Move over, Hodge. Give our guests a peek."

The spotter grunted and moved aside. Murdock handed the binoculars to Roselli, then got down on his knees and put his eye to the glowing objective.

The *Glaros* was transformed, the boat's hull still visible, but overlaid now by ragged, glowing patterns of colored light that gave the vessel's interior an eerie, three-dimensional aspect, as though the hull were made of some substance not quite so transparent as glass. Most of the thermograph colors were shades of green and blue, but some oranges and yellows showed up as well. The water, being coolest, was black. Most of the boat's hull was ultramarine or deep purple, especially at the edges and along the waterline. The man on the after deck glowed bright yellow-orange, with a bright white spot marking the hot tip of his cigarette. The thermal image was so detailed that Murdock could see a pistol-shaped patch of blue obscuring part of the yellow of the man's chest.

The truly interesting part was forward, however, in the yacht's cabin. The thermographic imaging of this IR unit was sensitive enough to pick up minute variations of temperature, less than a tenth of a degree or so Celsius; with barriers as thin as curtains or the fiberglass hull of a boat, radiated heat from inside could be picked up from the outside. The image was fuzzy and not nearly so detailed as that of the man on deck, but Murdock could easily make out several shapes, seen through the hull in muted patterns of heat. That bright red glow was probably an alcohol or kerosene heater . . . and that smaller one a motor of some sort, possibly the exhaust fan from a small refrigerator. Other shapes nearby were in writhing, shifting motion.

"What in the world?" There appeared to be two brighter, horizontal patterns of warmth a few feet apart, and they . . .

"Hey, Navy," Hodge said in a flat, fake-Mexican accent. "You like feelthy peectures?"

"Definitely X-rated," the sniper said, his cheek still resting against the stock of his high-tech rifle. "Now that's what I call a *pleasure* boat."

With that as a clue, the thermal images resolved themselves in Murdock's mind, too fuzzy to be more than mildly titillating but obviously created by the body heat radiating from two couples lying side by side. One couple was engaged in some rather frenetic, rhythmic movement; the other seemed more relaxed . . . watching the show, perhaps.

"Okay," Murdock said. "We have five people on board, total?"

"That's right," Beasley said. "The guy on deck is paid help, a local thug named Katris. We think the other two hired him as muscle, or maybe he's just there to pilot the boat. Vlachos and Trahanatzis are in the cabin with a couple of girls from town."

"Girlfriends?" Murdock asked, turning away from the eyepiece. "Or professionals?"

"Nah, they're strictly amateurs," Hodge said. "Pickups at a bar."

"You've been following these guys around town, I gather."

"Ever since Solomos and his boys filled us in."

"What are you going to do about them?"

"Nothing, at the moment."

"Nothing?"

"The DEA has them under surveillance. We're under orders to stay clear until they complete their investigation."

Murdock turned his eye back to the thermograph eyepiece.
The hard-driving, rhythmic motion had ceased, though there
was still movement going on. "Shit," he said. "If Solomos and
his people think these two are tied in with the Kingston
hijacking, why don't they go in and grab them? I'd be kind of
interested in what they might have to say."

"So would we. But the Greeks are moving extra slow on
this one. All they have is a couple of their Special Missions
guys who might have outside sources of income. And I
gather there are some sticky political problems."

"Vlachos and his patron?"

"Worse. Friend Trahanatzis is the son of a rather wealthy
Greek shipping magnate. Not an Onassis, but pretty well-
to-do. And he's a steady contributor to the Greek Christian
Democrats."

"Wait a minute. I thought you said they couldn't explain
his bank balance. If Daddy's a millionaire . . ."

"Apparently Poppa T. wasn't pleased when Junior didn't
follow in the family business. Trahanatzis is on a tight
allowance. Why else would he take a job with the Athens
City Police, eh? But he has made some pretty sizable
deposits in the bank over the past couple of weeks."

"Okay. I follow."

"Yeah. Anyway, Solomos still doesn't want to have the
guy arrested, not with Poppa holding purse strings that just
might find their way into the police budget, see?"

"I'm beginning to. Whose name is the boat in? Trahanatzis?"

"Negative. Vlachos."

"Interesting."

"Guess who made the deposits in Trahanatzis's account?"

"Vlachos?"

"Bingo. We're pretty sure Vlachos is a link in the chain to
somebody higher up. We don't know who, though, and the
Greeks don't even want to guess. They're too afraid of what
they might find." Beasley's words were dry and tight, only
just hinting at the frustration he must be feeling.

Murdock rose, stepping back from the eyepiece and

motioning for Roselli and Papagos to take their turns. "Tell me something, Captain."

"Yeah?"

"Have you considered helping things along at all?"

"Of course. But we're operating under strict orders . . . *very* strict orders. This show belongs to the Greeks."

"Meanwhile, a member of the United States House of Representatives has been the prisoner of somebody, we don't even know who, for almost three days now."

"I hear you. Let me tell you something. I've leaned on our friend Solomos just about as hard as I can. I've been on the satellite horn every day to Washington, trying to get things moving from that end, so far with zero effect. I got from Athens, finally, permission to set up this OP to keep the suspects under surveillance. The sniper is my idea, and Solomos doesn't know about it. He'd shit if he did, I think, but Hodge and Kraus over there are my insurance in case Vlachos and his pal decide to do a fast fade. Right now, that's our number-one worry, that those two get spooked and decide to tear out of here in that high-performance motor yacht of theirs."

"Where would they go?"

"Shit, if they have friends in the police force, anywhere they want. That's the problem. If they wanted to just run for the border, well, Turkey is maybe fifteen hours by sea."

"So you figure a .50-caliber bullet through the engine might slow them up, eh? Good thinking. I take it the DEA is keeping tabs on the suspects too?"

Beasley nodded toward the white facade of a hotel overlooking the Leoforos Nikis. "For what it's worth, they've got a team up there. For all I know, they're keeping a closer watch on my team than they are on Vlachos and company."

"I dunno about that, Boss," Hodge said. He had just resumed his place at the IR scope. "Looks like they're going at it again over there. If it was me, I'd rather watch thermoporn than watch us watching thermoporn any day."

"You know, Captain Beasley," Murdock said, "if someone else went out there and made sure that our friends weren't going anywhere, you couldn't be accused of breaking the rules, could you?"

Beasley stared into Murdock's eyes for a long moment. "If this is some damned Navy scam . . ."

"No scam. Look, I'm talking about it with you . . . not just going out and doing it, right? You've been square with us, we'll reciprocate. I'm not even suggesting anything right now, just kind of wondering out loud. If somebody snatched those two before they could get away, before the Greeks let them get away . . ."

"Too risky." He shook his head emphatically. "Solomos would have a fit. My people could lose everything they've built up in this damned country."

"Not if it wasn't your fault."

"Eh?"

"Blame it all on us. You had no idea what those Navy sons of bitches were up to."

"What'll your superiors say?"

"Let us worry about that. What do you say?"

"Let's say I'd like to hear a bit more."

"Why don't we get off this roof, first? If Solomos is keeping an eye on you, we don't want him to get the idea we're plotting anything together, right?"

"Murdock, God help me, but I think I'm starting to like you."

"That shows your excellent taste. I'm really quite a likable fellow. Now, what we'll need is about twenty, thirty meters of lightweight nylon line."

"We have that."

"And a truck. Or any kind of covered vehicle. Actually, it might be better if we could rent a car someplace. . . ."

With Roselli and Papagos following, Murdock and Beasley descended the stairs into the White Tower, deep in conversation. On the roof behind them, Kraus and Hodge gave one another wondering looks, then returned to their surveillance.

2205 hours
Harbor pier
Salonika, Greece

Razor Roselli, Jaybird Sterling, and Murdock walked slowly along the pier, pretending an interest in the ships and small craft docked to either side, but keeping most of their attention focused on the *Glaros*, just visible from here on the far side of a buoy-moored sailboat.

"Anywhere along here'll be fine, Skipper," Roselli said. The black water lapped against the pier and the rust-streaked hulls of the ships. The stink of harbor water and diesel oil was thicker here than it had been back on the Leoforos Nikis promenade. Even this late in the evening, the streets of Salonika were busy. Roselli could hear the rumble and honk of traffic; somewhere in the direction of the city, the plucking lilt of bouzouki music was accompanying singing.

"You both still want to go through with this?" Murdock asked them. "You can still back out if you want."

"Nah," Razor said. "Things were getting kind of dull tonight, y'know?"

"Yeah," Jaybird added. "I could use a little midnight swim just to wake me up."

"With a water temperature of fifty-nine degrees, Jaybird, it ought to do just that. Okay. We're covered here." They stopped in the shadow of a Greek-registry freighter, its hull conveniently placed to block the three SEALs' activities from anyone who might be watching ashore. Murdock set down the gym bag he was carrying on a bollard, and Roselli and Jaybird began stripping off their street clothes.

They were wearing swim trunks beneath their trousers, and black T-shirts that would cut down on their visibility a bit in the dark. Mac had jury-rigged belts for them out of doubled-up lengths of nylon line. From the bag, Murdock handed them each a tightly knotted hank of line and a small, cloth bag, both of which they fastened to their belts. Both of them already wore their SEAL diving knives in black plastic scabbards strapped to their lower legs. They wore neither masks nor flippers; they'd not brought any of their diving gear along, and trying to find any in the city at this time of night—and at this time of year—would be both futile and suspicious. Instead, they wore canvas deck shoes with thick rubber soles, chosen because they would offer a decent grip on a smooth, wet surface.

"Okay, you too," Murdock said when they were ready. "Remember what I said. We don't want these guys dead, and we don't want an international incident. But I don't want them going anywhere before we have a chance to question them."

"Right, L-T," Roselli said. "Just leave it to us."

Jaybird entered the water first, lowering himself from the side of the dock feet-first and slipping beneath the inky surface with scarcely a ripple to mark his entry. Roselli went next. The water *was* cold . . . not as frigid as it had been on some memorable BUD/S exercises, perhaps, but with bite enough to sap a man's strength and endurance in less than an hour. Under normal conditions, Jaybird and Roselli would have worn wet suits for this, but their total immersion time shouldn't be more than an hour or a little more.

The water was so black and thick with suspended sediment that Roselli literally could not see his hands in front of his face. He swam just beneath the surface, arms extended, thrusting ahead with a powerful frog kick. When his lungs began to burn, he brought his head slowly up into the air and light. The *Glaros* was *there*. He would have to angle to the right a bit to keep the sailboat between him and his target.

Slipping beneath the surface once more, he kicked and drifted, kicked and drifted, concentrating on swimming a straight line . . . or as straight as he could manage completely blind. Sound was of no use underwater. The depths were alive with sounds, clanks and creaks and hollow-sounding bumps, mingled with the far-off *thud-thud-thud* of a ship's screws turning, but the sounds seemed to come from everywhere, giving no hint of their direction. When Roselli surfaced again, he was much closer to the sailboat he was using for cover. There was some sort of party going on aboard; he could hear the chink of glasses, the guffaw of men's laughter, the softer voice of a woman speaking.

But there was no one on deck to see Razor as he glided close beneath the sailboat's bow, then reached up to take hold of the mooring cable. Jaybird was by the buoy, hanging onto the cable, his head bobbing slowly up and down with the timing of his kicks. Roselli moved over to join him. They exchanged a glance, nodded, then began swimming again.

Glaros was now less than fifty meters away, its bow turned to face the two combat swimmers. Beyond, rising above the city, the White Tower stood guard over the harbor. Roselli suppressed the urge to grin and wave at the IR scope he knew was trained on him.

This final part of the swim would be made on the surface, lest one of them surface suddenly directly under the gaze of Katris, the guard. They moved carefully, raising scarcely a ripple as they breaststroked toward the moored power yacht.

2217 hours
Harbor pier
Salonika, Greece
Murdock checked his watch as he stepped off the pier and turned right onto the street that would lead him back to the promenade. DeWitt and Mac ought to have another hotel lined up by now, assuming they weren't all booked up. He hated leaving details like that to the last moment, but there hadn't been any choice this time. Still, though there were lots of tourists in town, this early in the season it couldn't be anything like peak attendance. In another couple of weeks, a huge annual tourist trade fair would be under way at those fairgrounds he'd glimpsed earlier, and then finding rooms at the last moment might be damn near impossible.

Just the same, he wished he could have taken care of those details first.

"Just a moment!" a sharp voice called out from the left. "You! Lieutenant Murdock! Stop, please!"

Captain Solomos hurried across the street, apparently having just left the hotel Beasley had identified as the location of the DEA's observation post. Three men were with him, in camouflage Greek Army uniforms, with M3 submachine guns—the World War II-era weapons sometimes known as "grease guns"—held at port arms.

"Captain Solomos," Murdock said as the officer trotted up to him. Damn, something was wrong. Solomos looked mad enough to spit nails. "How nice to see you again."

"Murdock! Where are the two men who were with you?"

"What men?"

"Don't give me that! You were seen." He jabbed a thumb over his shoulder. "From up there. You and two of your SEALs were walking toward the customs house forty minutes ago. Now you are alone."

"Oh, you must mean Sterling and Roselli. I don't know. Maybe they went on into the city for a drink. Or they could be back at the hotel. Did you check?"

"Don't give me any of your American arrogance." He pointed at the gym bag in Murdock's left hand. "What's in there?"

"Nothing."

Solomos reached for the handle. "Let me—"

Murdock's right hand flashed across and down, thumb and forefinger grasping Solomos's wrist and breaking it back in a lightning move that made the Greek officer gasp, then nearly go to his knees in a vain attempt to relieve the pressure.

"You know, I really thought a warrant was required for that sort of thing."

Solomos gasped again. The three soldiers with him raised their weapons, and Murdock heard the nasty sound of bolts being drawn back.

"I . . . advise . . . you . . . to let me . . . go . . ."

"Well, so much for the land of democracy." He released Solomos, who barked something in Greek at one of the soldiers. The man stepped forward and took the gym bag, unzipped it, and emptied the contents on the ground.

"What is this?"

"Two shirts, two pairs of trousers."

"I can see that. Whose are they?"

"Mine. I was looking for an all-night laundry."

"They are the street clothes your two men were wearing." Solomos, still rubbing his injured wrist, stepped past Murdock and stared for a long moment toward the boats at their harbor moorings. He snapped something unpleasant-sounding half under his breath, then reached under the tail of his jacket and hauled out a walkie-talkie. The soldiers continued to hold Murdock at gunpoint as Solomos spoke rapidly for a few moments, listened to a reply, then spoke again. Had he seen something in the water? Murdock couldn't tell, and he didn't dare turn and look to see if he could see anything himself. If he hadn't seen, though, he'd certainly guessed. The man was delivering a flurry of orders in rapid-fire Greek, and Murdock knew that none of it meant anything good.

That done, Solomos put the radio away and said something else to the soldiers. One of them prodded Murdock in the kidney with the grease gun. "Come," Solomos said. "We had better round up your accomplices at the White Tower."

"Accomplices?"

"Do not play games with me, Murdock. I can be a dangerous man."

"I'm sure."

"Your little game has accomplished nothing but to get you and your people expelled from this country. We wanted no part of your military 'advice' or 'observers' in the first place. Now, perhaps, we can do things without your meddling."

"Uh, Captain, if you don't mind my asking, what's this all about?"

"The DEA is moving tonight, Lieutenant. I've just radioed to my people to move in and arrest the suspects. But where I might have been inclined to permit you to question these people before, now you will just have to wait until my government communicates through channels with your government. I'm sorry that it must end this way, but I will not tolerate further interference in our internal affairs!"

Murdock heard a growl and turned to look toward the harbor, toward the right. There was the source . . . a big patrol boat, probably a military job, its engines booming in the otherwise quiet night, its searchlight glaring across the black water of the harbor like a great, white lighthouse beacon.

"Really, Captain," he said as one of the soldiers prodded him again. "I'd have thought you could have carried this off with less noise and fuss."

Before Solomos could answer, a burst of automatic gunfire chattered across the water.

11

Roselli was twenty meters from the *Glaros* when he heard the thunder of a big boat's engines, heard the sharp, barking rattle of automatic weapons fire. Bobbing in the water, he wiped his eyes with his hand, trying to clear them. The guard aboard the target boat had picked up what looked from here like an AKM assault rifle, run up to the craft's sun deck, and begun firing into the night. Roselli dove, expecting to hear the snapping impacts of bullets in the water around him . . . but when all he heard was the rapidly swelling throb of a boat's engines, he surfaced again.

Katris was aiming the AKM at something farther out in the harbor. Turning in the water, Roselli saw the target . . . a Dilos-class patrol boat bearing down on the anchorage, its bow rising above the white mustache of its bow wave. A searchlight glared from high up on its superstructure, and Roselli looked away to keep from being blinded.

A Dilos. He'd studied the different ship classes on the Greek Navy lists during the flight from the *Nassau* to the *Jefferson*. The Dilos class was a motor patrol craft twenty-nine meters long and displacing seventy-five tons. Armament would be a couple of 20mm machine guns, her top speed about twenty-seven knots. If the *Glaros* was able to get under way, the pleasure craft would outrun the larger boat easily, especially within this crowded anchorage where maneuverability was as definite a plus as speed.

Jaybird bobbed in the water a few meters to Roselli's left. Which direction . . . forward or back? The occupants of the *Glaros* were thoroughly alerted now, and getting onto her deck was not going to be easy. Roselli could see movement on her flying bridge now. Somebody must have emerged from the cabin and be working to get the boat moving.

The Greek patrol boat's engine throttled back, and the piercing ululation of a siren blanketed the harbor. Katris stooped swiftly, tugged at the mooring line which was looped over a cleat on the deck, and tossed it over the side. *Glaros* was drifting free now.

The guard stood upright again, raising the assault rifle to his shoulder for another burst. The patrol boat was not firing . . . a good decision, Roselli thought, since the city of Salonika lay directly behind the target. God, what shit-for-brains space cadet had engineered the tactics of *this* search and seizure?

Then, Katris's head literally exploded in a bloody spray of tissue, blood, and bone. The body went up on its toes, then toppled backward onto *Glaros*'s sun deck, blood fountaining across the forward cabin windows. One of the Delta guys on the White Tower had just reached out and touched someone with that big Haskins rifle. In the same moment, the *Glaros*'s engines coughed, then gunned to life.

Raising his hand from the water, Roselli caught Jaybird's attention with a wave, then vigorously pumped his fist up and down. Jaybird nodded, and the two SEALs plunged beneath the surface, swimming hard toward the thirty-foot boat. In the underwater blackness, the *Glaros*'s engines sounded deafeningly close. Kicking with powerful, scissoring strokes, Roselli swam until he sensed more than saw the hull of the boat just above his head. Moving by touch, he freed the tightly wrapped hank of nylon line that he wore on his belt, tugging the knot loose that held it together, then letting the line unfold.

The thunder of the *Glaros*'s engines pounded through the hull. With a heavy thump-*chunk*, the boat's pilot put the craft into gear, and the twin screws, motionless until that moment, churned to life. The boat began to move, and the pressure of its passing pummeled Roselli's body.

Turbulence from the spinning screws clawed at him, but he twisted to face them, moving his arm in an arc to spread the tangle of nylon line in front of him like a net. The deadly slice of the screws bore down on him fast; jackknifing, he brought his feet up and kicked, hard, shoving off from the keel of the moving boat. Its bow wave gave him added thrust, pushing him deeper into the water. The prop wash caught him and twisted him violently, but he kept kicking, swimming as hard as he could to get under and behind the churning of *Glaros*'s propellers. With the violent exertion, his body was demanding air, his chest aching, his heart hammering.

Then the thunder of the engines, the pounding of the screws, suddenly took on a new sound, a sharply rising whine of protest ending in a loud clunk. One of the screws was still turning, but the other had stopped, its shaft fouled by Roselli's line. Rising through the blackness, Roselli broke the surface five meters astern of the boat, mouth open, gulping down a full draught of cold, wonderful air.

Glaros was still moving but circling hard to the left, the Zodiac raft tied to her stern wallowing along in her wake. Beyond, the Greek patrol boat was looming closer, perhaps a hundred meters off, the dazzle of its searchlight bathing the motor yacht in a brilliant, blue-white glare. By the light, Roselli could see a man wearing white boxer shorts leaning over *Glaros*'s transom, a boat hook in his hands as he tried to poke and probe at the fouled starboard screw. Behind him was a dark-haired woman, bare-breasted, screaming in shrill terror. Smoke from the boat's exhaust boiled off the surface of the water. Suddenly, *Glaros*'s second engine whined, shrieked, then ground to a thump and silence, and the yacht went dead in the water. Jaybird surfaced a few meters away, close alongside the Zodiac, gasping for air.

The man with the boat hook shouted something in Greek, and Roselli hoped he wasn't calling for a gun. No . . . apparently the guy hadn't seen the swimmers yet. He was still trying to reach the screws with the hook, assuming, perhaps, that they'd been fouled by weed or by garbage floating in the harbor, and yelling at his partner up on the boat's flying bridge. He shouted again and *Glaros*'s engines whined, but failed to kick over.

Jackknifing once again, Roselli dove, swimming quickly toward the stern of the boat, passing beneath the Zodiac, then surfacing explosively within touching distance of the transom, looking straight up into the startled face of the man with the boat hook. Rising like a rocket out of the water, Roselli stretched out both arms, grabbed the shaft of the boat hook, and yanked hard. The man, caught off balance and completely by surprise, gave a loud wail as he soared headfirst off the stern of the *Glaros* and splashed into the sea.

Roselli's movement carried him up, then back under water. Kicking back to the surface, he launched himself toward *Glaros*'s fantail, grabbing the top of the transom and boosting himself up . . . then muscling himself up and over the top in an untidy somersault. He landed with a loud, wet thump in the boat's after well deck at the feet of the screaming woman.

"Easy! Easy!" Roselli yelled, holding up a hand, wondering if she understood English, but the woman kept screaming, her hands holding her head, her breasts dancing and bobbing wildly as she jumped up and down. Roselli was less interested at the moment in her movements, though, than he was in her safety. Snapping out with one foot and rolling to the side, he swept the girl's long, bare legs out from under her, spilling her to the deck with a startled bump. His boarding technique had been less than stealthy, and he didn't want innocent bystanders hit if the guy up on *Glaros*'s bridge decided to start shooting.

He unknotted the heavy cloth bag still dangling from his makeshift belt. Inside was one of the Smith & Wesson automatics, which he dragged out as he came to his feet. Flicking off the safety, he braced the pistol in both hands, aiming it up the well deck ladder toward the flying bridge, where the boat's pilot was still trying to get the engines started again. "*Stamatiste!*" he shouted, using his sole word of Greek. Papagos had coached him on it an hour ago. "*Stamatiste!* Stop!"

Taking the first three rungs of the ladder, Roselli moved halfway up to the flying bridge level, until he could see the entire deck. A man in trousers and an unbuttoned sports shirt stood at the control console, his hair in wild disarray, a .45-caliber Colt automatic clutched in one hand.

"*Stama-fucking-tiste,* you son of a bitch!"

The man turned and stared into the muzzle of Roselli's Smith & Wesson, and some of the wildness seemed to go out of him. He slumped into the pilot's seat, the Colt spilling from his hand and clattering onto the desk. He raised his hands as Roselli climbed up the rest of the way onto the bridge. Kicking the .45 away, he grabbed the man's collar and forced him facedown onto the deck. Standard takedown— Roselli kicked his legs apart, jammed one foot against his crotch, then kneeled on the guy's buttocks, using his left hand to check for other weapons beneath his shirt.

Where was Jaybird? Roselli didn't see him, but he did hear a frantic splashing and stole a glance aft. The woman, evidently, had recovered enough to make one rational decision, at least, and was swimming toward the promenade in a thrashing flurry of legs and arms. "Wonder what the indecent exposure laws are like in this town," he wondered half aloud. His prisoner rasped something in Greek, and Roselli roughly shoved the muzzle of his pistol against the base of his head to quiet him.

Seconds later, the patrol boat, engines throttling back,

rumbled slowly up to the *Glaros*, starboard side to, the searchlight sweeping the yacht from bow to stern. Squinting past the glare, Roselli could see a dozen armed men standing along her rail. A loud-hailer voice boomed something at him in Greek, and with a sharp chill Roselli realized that, so far as those guys were concerned, he was an armed man aboard a hostile craft.

"American!" he yelled as loud as he could. "U.S. Navy!"

"Put down the gun, Mr. Roselli," the loud-hailer voice barked in accented English.

Sailors on the Greek vessel were reaching down with boat hooks to grab *Glaros*'s rail and pull her up alongside. Roselli felt the deck shudder, heard the creak and scrape of the yacht as it bumped across the long, dirty white fenders hanging down the patrol boat's side.

"Roselli!" the voice called again. "Put down your gun or we fire!"

Shit! These guys were supposed to be on his side!

Carefully, ostentatiously, he placed his pistol on the bridge control console, then raised his hands and clasped them behind his head. He stayed on top of his prisoner, however, digging in with his knee to convince the man that it would be wiser not to move. "Don't even think about it, pal," he said, wondering if the man understood English at all.

Greek soldiers in camouflage uniforms began leaping aboard the *Glaros*, as sailors used boat hooks to draw the two vessels together. In a moment, both Roselli and his prisoner were being herded back down to the well deck at gunpoint.

The woman who'd dived overboard was gone. Some of the soldiers started searching the *Glaros*, and in moments he heard a piercing shriek from inside the cabin. Seconds later, the laughing soldiers emerged, pulling along a girl—she couldn't have been more than eighteen—wearing nothing but long blond hair and a terrified expression. There was no sign of Sterling, however, or of the man Roselli had tossed

over the side. As soldiers roughly handcuffed his wrists
behind his back, Roselli grinned.

The Zodiac that had been tied up astern of the *Glaros* was
gone, its mooring line snicked clean through by a SEAL
diving knife.

2315 hours
Harbor front
Salonika, Greece

Murdock stood on the promenade below the White Tower,
watching as the Greek patrol boat edged closer to the
promenade waterfront. Solomos stood beside him, scowl-
ing, while Brown and Papagos leaned against the tower
wall, under guard.

"Lieutenant," Solomos said quietly, "I am going to take
great personal pride in seeing you broken. You have
exceeded your authority, abused my hospitality, and threatened the success of my operation here."

Murdock said nothing. There would be no reasoning with
Solomos, not now. The man's pride had been injured, and
this was a nation that took pride very seriously indeed.

Politics. *Shit!*

Every so often, the SEALs were forced to operate in a
political environment, something quite different from the
sea, air, and land elements which they'd been trained to deal
with. Getting SEALs to behave diplomatically, or to follow
the rules, or to avoid stepping on toes, was difficult to say
the least.

Sometimes it was even dangerous.

In October of 1985, members of SEAL Team Six and the
Army's Delta Force had been deployed to Sicily in order to
carry out an assault on the cruise ship *Achille Lauro*, which
had been commandeered in the eastern Med by four
terrorists of the Palestine Liberation Front. A joint plan had
been conceived between the assault force and a team of
Italian commandos who were also participating. The SEALs
would board the cruise ship and take down the terrorists,
then allow the Italian team to come in and take the credit, a

ploy that had been used several times already by both the
SEALs and Delta to keep those units out of the spotlight of
media attention.

Before the operation went down, however, the terrorists
had surrendered after being promised safe passage by
Egypt. Only after the terrorists had gone ashore at Port Said
was it learned that they'd murdered one of the passengers,
an elderly American confined to a wheelchair, and thrown
his body overboard. Despite American protests, the Egyp-
tians allowed the terrorists—together with several PLO
negotiators and Abu Abbas, the terrorists' leader who was
posing as a negotiator, and four members of Egypt's Force
777 counterterror unit—to board an airliner for a flight to
the PLO's international headquarters in Tunisia.

In a swift and determined series of maneuvers, planned
and coordinated by Lieutenant Colonel Oliver North at the
White House, four F-14 Tomcats off the American carrier
U.S.S. *Saratoga* intercepted the Egyptian airliner and forced
it to land at a NATO military airfield at Sigonella, Sicily,
where the SEALs were waiting for them. Moving fast, the
SEALs had surrounded the aircraft on the runway, prepared
to fight with the terrorists if necessary.

Then a political complication had arisen. Italian *carabinieri* had appeared, surrounding the SEALs and ordering
them to stand down. The Italians were outraged that the
Americans had taken military action on their territory; for
their part, the SEALs thought that the Italians—who'd
caved in to terrorist threats in the past and not always
carried through with what they'd promised to do—would
let the hijackers escape.

A tense standoff ensued for nearly an hour, with the
Italians demanding the release of the airliner's occupants,
the SEALs refusing. A radio conversation on a tactical
channel overheard by several officials at the scene added a
new note of tension. Two SEALs were quietly discussing
whether or not to take out the Italians, and how best to go
about it. Only when the American Secretary of State

received assurances from Rome that the terrorists would be tried for murder did the SEALs—somewhat reluctantly—stand aside and let the *carabinieri* take charge of the prisoners. Even at that, the SEALs didn't give up the chase entirely. When the terrorists were flown to Rome, two of the SEALs followed close behind in a small plane, claiming engine trouble to enable them to land behind the other plane and maintain surveillance of the *carabinieri* and their prisoners.

Eventually, the terrorists were tried, though Abu Abbas—the mastermind of the original hijacking operation—had been allowed to walk away by Italian authorities almost as soon as he landed. The murderers received sentences of from fifteen to thirty years; Abu Abbas and two fellow-plotters were sentenced to life in prison *in absentia* . . . not that anyone expected that they would ever be brought to justice.

SEALs and international politics, Murdock reflected, simply did not mix.

The patrol boat *Lindos* was secured by lines passed down and slung over bollards rising from the pavement, and a gangplank was dropped over the side. A moment later, a line of six Greek soldiers came filing ashore, along with Roselli, one male prisoner, and a young woman wearing a sailor's dungaree shirt several sizes too large for her. All three were handcuffed with their hands behind their backs, and each was guided down the ramp by a Greek trooper.

"Come on, Captain," Murdock said to Solomos. "What's with the handcuffs?"

"Standard operating procedure, Lieutenant," Solomos said blandly. "All prisoners must be secured for their own protection and the protection of the arresting officers while they are being processed."

"You're not arresting my man, are you?"

"I am. I am arresting all of you. You will be held here in Salonika until my office can make arrangements to turn you over to American naval authorities."

"Aw, damn it all, Captain! How come?"

"Your interference has jeopardized a Greek counterterrorist operation and resulted in the escape of at least one suspect. Further, your activities triggered a gun battle in Salonika harbor, one in which innocent bystanders could have been killed. I will be very happy to see the last of you, Lieutenant."

"That's bullshit, Solomos, and you know it! You people weren't going to do a damned thing about those suspects, and the gun battle started when your damned soldiers charged in with searchlights and sirens!" He didn't mention that sniper shot from the tower that had taken out the gunman. Solomos didn't appear to be including the Delta Force team in his little tirade. Papagos and Brown were standing nearby, under guard but not yet handcuffed. Solomos's people appeared to be ignoring the Delta men still in their tower-top OP.

"We appear to be missing five of your men, Lieutenant," Solomos said. "There were nine of you. Where are the others?"

"Seeing the sights."

"At this hour of the night? I don't think so."

"Then they're bar-hopping. Maybe you should go check some of your local taverns. Or the whorehouses."

"I have a better idea. You may be more willing to discuss things with us in a reasonable manner at the police station." He reached into a back pocket and produced a pair of handcuffs. "Turn around, and place your hands behind you."

Murdock hesitated, as if he didn't quite know what to do, looking from Papagos to Brown to Roselli. Roselli gave him a broad wink, a sign that he, at least, thought things were going well.

Good . . .

They'd gone over as many of the possibilities as they could think of earlier, while planning this op with Beasley and the Delta people. He'd emphasized to both Roselli and Sterling that they needed at least one of those men off the yacht, no matter what. With all the lights and confusion, Murdock hadn't been able to see clearly what was happening when the patrol boat had drawn alongside the *Glaros*, but the fact that both Jaybird and one of the suspects were missing was a hopeful sign.

He just hoped Jaybird had indeed managed to carry off his part of things, or this whole show would all be for nothing.

12

"I said turn around! Hands behind you!"

"Oh, very well . . ." Murdock pivoted, turning his back to Solomos . . . but then continued the movement, hard and fast, ducking his head and snapping his leg up and around in a reversed roundhouse kick. His foot slammed into the DEA captain's gut, bending him double and lifting his toes clear of the pavement.

"Lochagos!" a soldier shouted, and then Magic's elbow slammed into his face not once but twice, so quickly the movement was a blur. Papagos sidestepped his guard, smashed down on the inside of the man's ankle, and stepped inside the muzzle of his M3 grease gun and snatched it away before the man's finger even reached the trigger. Roselli simply spun and threw a roundhouse kick into his startled guard's face, sending the man flying backward into the water. A second soldier was gaping at Solomos, who was still busily folding himself around Murdock's shoe, and never saw the two lightning kicks that caught him first in the stomach, then in the head.

Normally, trying an unarmed takedown of soldiers with automatic weapons was nothing less than an act of despera-

tion . . . and a great way to get somebody shot. Murdock
had taken the measure of these men, though, and decided
that if the SEALs were going to make a break, it had better
be now, while things were confused, rather than later . . .
quite probably inside a Greek prison cell. The soldiers, he
thought, were army troops brought in to assist the DEA, not
DEA men themselves. They were young and they were
inexperienced; it was clear from their milling about on the
dock that they didn't have the faintest idea what was going
on. No doubt they'd been rousted out of their barracks that
evening and told that they were helping the police, and they
still didn't know who or what their prisoners were.

They were finding out in a hurry. One-two-three, and
three more soldiers were down or disarmed. In the flurry of
confusion, the male prisoner off the *Glaros* saw an opportunity and started to run, but Razor calmly reached out with
one foot and tripped him, slamming him facedown into the
pavement.

"Drop 'em! Drop 'em!" Magic barked, gesturing with the
grease gun he'd lifted from one of his victims. The soldiers
gaped at each other, then at Magic, who shouted at Papagos
in frustration, "For Christ's sake, Nick, tell these guys to
drop 'em!" One by one, pistols and submachine guns
clattered onto the pavement, and men began raising their
hands in the air.

Murdock, meanwhile, had reached down and grabbed
Solomos by his hair, whipping him up and around with his
left arm about the man's throat, one extended right knuckle
pressed menacingly against the DEA captain's temple.
"Let's have the keys to Roselli's cuffs, Captain." The man
struggled, then tried to pull away, and Murdock increased
the pressure of his knuckle against his head. "Do it, or I'll
reach into your skull and pluck out your eyeballs from the
inside! *Do it!*"

Hastily, Solomos grabbed something, and a Greek sergeant unlocked Roselli's hands. The other soldiers stood in
a half circle around the SEALs, some looking confused or
scared, others furiously angry. Papagos made the rounds

then, gathering up the discarded weapons. Keeping three of the grease guns and several magazines, he dropped the rest over the side of the pier with a loud splash. After a moment's thought, Murdock also ordered them to unlock the girl's hands as well. She was almost certainly an innocent bystander, but Murdock had heard unpleasant things about what went on inside Greek jails. Besides, she might be persuaded to help with the other prisoner.

With a squealing of tires, a dark blue, four-door sedan bumped up onto the curb with Scotty Frazier at the wheel. Armed, then, the SEALs backed away, keeping their weapons trained both on the Greek soldiers and on the sailors watching helplessly from the deck of the patrol boat. Several tourists, those who hadn't already fled, stood nearby, watching as though the whole scenario had been arranged for their entertainment. Roselli helped the girl into the front seat, then slid in beside her. Magic and Papagos climbed into the back.

"Just to show you my heart's in the right place," Murdock told Solomos, reaching across the man's shoulder and plucking a Smith & Wesson .38 revolver from his shoulder holster, "you can have that one." He pointed at the prisoner who, face bloodied, was still lying on the concrete. Murdock had considered bringing the man along as well, but decided that he would be too likely to slow them up.

Besides, he owed Captain Beasley one; the Delta team must know what was going on down here but they hadn't intervened against the SEALs. Leaving the prisoner as an intelligence source for Delta would be a good way to say thank you.

"You will be court-martialed for this!" Solomos growled.

"Maybe, but it won't be your choice. Now why don't you work on finding out where the real bad guys took Ellen Kingston, okay? Otherwise we might have to come back here to discuss it with you, and I don't think you'd like that at all." He gave Solomos a hard shove, knocking him to the pavement, then dove into the open right rear door of the sedan. As the car lurched forward off the curb, he could hear

Solomos screaming up the wall of the tower. "Beasley! Shoot him! Beasley! *Shoot him!*"

Then the car was racing down the Leoforos Nikis, past the White Tower and then hard left onto the Ethnikis Aminas. "You know where you're going?" he asked Frazier from the back seat. Much of downtown Salonika was off-limits to cars in an attempt to control pollution, some parts just during the day, others at all times. The streets, most of them, were straight, but many crossed one another at confusing angles.

"No problem, Skipper," Frazier called back. "But we're going to want to ditch this heap before we get close to the new hotel."

"Right. What is it . . . a rental?"

"Uh, actually, Boss," Frazier said, sounding embarrassed, "Mac and me didn't have time to find a rental place, and anyway, Mac was worried about the paper trail, y'know?"

"So you stole it."

"Yeah. Well, borrowed it."

"Right. I should have guessed. You guys ever decided to leave the Navy, you've got a great career ahead of you in larceny and grand theft."

"Hey, be all that you can be," Roselli quipped.

"That's the damned Army, numb-nuts," Magic said.

"Aw, they won't mind if we borrow their slogan. We borrowed one of their suspects, didn't we?"

"Cap it," Murdock warned. He still didn't know if the girl spoke English, and he didn't want her to hear too much. "Let's find a place to stop, okay?"

Somewhere in the distance, a police siren was giving its odd, piercing, two-tone chant. The SEALs were going to have to work fast if they were to salvage anything out of this mess.

2340 hours
Harbor front customs house
Salonika, Greece

Jaybird throttled back on the Zodiac's engine, turning the steering handle slightly to guide the rubber boat gently past an anchored sailboat. The gasoline engine was louder than the SEAL could have wished, but there was still plenty of commotion going on across the harbor to the southeast, and he doubted that anybody was paying him any attention.

Ashore, two police cars hurried past, racing along the Leoforos Nikis toward the White Tower. He hoped Roselli was okay.

The operation this evening had been loosely planned and open-ended; ideally, Jaybird and Roselli were supposed to have grabbed Vlachos and Trahanatzis and gotten them ashore in the rubber Zodiac. Mac, DeWitt, Frazier, Stepano, and Papagos were supposed to find a new hotel, one hidden away in a secluded part of the city where Solomos and his people weren't likely to find them, then go out and boost a couple of cars. After that, Papagos was to join Magic and the L-T by the White Tower, where they would be watching the op go down with the Delta guys. Frazier would take one car and be their backup if they needed a fast getaway, Stepano would stay at the hotel, and Mac and DeWitt would take the other car and wait for Roselli and Jaybird to show up at the pier near the customs house.

Jaybird still wasn't sure what had gone wrong, though he suspected that that bastard Solomos was behind it. Maybe he'd seen the two SEALs making their final approach on the yacht from his OP overlooking the harbor. Maybe Jaybird and Roselli had simply been guilty of extremely bad timing, launching their snatch operation at the same time as a planned raid by the Greek police. Whatever the reason, the original plan had gone to hell as soon as that Greek patrol boat had come rumbling out of the night, searchlight glaring.

But SEALs were good at improvisation, and the possible need for improvisation had been worked into the plan. When one of the two men had come sailing over the *Glaros*'s transom and into the water, Sterling had drawn his diver's knife, grabbed him from behind, and delivered a short, sharp blow with the knife's pommel to the base of the guy's skull. He'd gone limp, and Sterling had rolled him into the Zodiac tied to *Glaros*'s stern.

While he was heaving the unconscious man's dead weight up into the raft, a half-naked woman had dived off the well deck, splashing into the harbor a few feet away, surfacing, then swimming rapidly toward the shore. Jaybird had ignored her. The plan had been for the SEALs to take the men and leave the women behind. Roselli was on the flying bridge at the moment, taking down the second man.

Freeing his pistol from the bag at his waist, Jaybird had prepared to board the yacht to give Roselli a hand, but the Greek patrol boat was bearing down on them fast. He'd heard the first loud-hailer challenge, and Roselli's reply. When the loud-hailer voice had shifted to English, demanding that Roselli drop his gun, Jaybird had decided that it was definitely time to start improvising.

Roselli wasn't going to be able to get away. The L-T had explained that they needed at least one prisoner—it didn't matter who—and they needed to get him away without Solomos and his people knowing about it, if possible. Roselli was busted, kneeling on top of his prisoner with his hands clasped behind his head. Jaybird knew that if he hung around for long, he'd be picked up too . . . and the SEALs would lose both prisoners.

Damn! What a choice! A SEAL never left his buddies . . . but this time around the mission demanded it. He'd reached up with his knife and cut the line, then watched for his chance to slip away.

With all the confusion, E&E had been surprisingly easy. That bright searchlight had actually helped, since it tended to ruin the night-vision of anyone watching the scene, either from shore or from the deck of the patrol boat. Treading water, watching for his chance, he'd waited until the Greek sailors were pulling the *Glaros* alongside, then swum beneath the loom of the patrol boat's bow, the Zodiac's mooring line clenched in his teeth. He'd towed the raft and its unconscious passenger until he was hidden in the shadow on the patrol boat's port side, while all of the troops and sailors aboard were gathered to starboard. Rolling into the raft, he'd checked the outboard motor's gas tank—nearly full—then cracked open the ignition and hot-wired the engine. As shouts and laughter had echoed across the water from the far side of the patrol boat, he'd eased open the throttle and motored slowly away, steering a course that would keep the Greek vessel between the Zodiac and watchers ashore for as long as possible. Using several other anchored boats for cover, sticking to shadows and darkness, he'd slowly zigzagged his way across the anchorage, first to the west, away from the waterfront, then north, steering by the lights from the city's customs building.

Now, very nearly forty minutes later, he was nearing the pier. There was quite a bit of light from the customs house, and some dockworkers were off-loading a cargo ship a hundred meters further down the pier, but the site selected for the rendezvous was deserted and dark. Slipping up to the pier in the shadow beneath a Liberian freighter, Jaybird cut the engine and drifted the last few feet. Mac materialized out of the shadows, tossing him a line and dragging him in.

"What the hell happened?" DeWitt looked worried as Jaybird scrambled out of the Zodiac.

"They got Razor," Jaybird said. Standing on the pier, he stared across the water, trying to see what was going on back at the anchorage. It looked like the patrol boat had taken the *Glaros* in tow, that both vessels were up against the waterfront close by the White Tower. There were lots of lights and the pulsing strobe of police car emergency lights. "Shit, I didn't want to leave—"

"You did right, Jaybird," Mac said. "Razor'll be okay. And you got our prisoner. Good work."

Not until that moment did Jaybird realize that he didn't know the identity of his prisoner. Vlachos or Trahanatzis? Not that it really mattered. Either man ought to be able to answer their questions . . . assuming they could make him talk. "Well, the police or whoever those guys are got the other one. And they got Roselli. Chief? Mr. DeWitt? What are we gonna do?"

"Let the Skipper worry about Roselli," Mac said. "We've got to get this guy to the hotel."

"You found a room?"

"Papagos did." DeWitt wrinkled his nose. "Not exactly the Hilton."

Together, they hauled the prisoner out of the Zodiac, tied his wrists and feet just in case he decided to wake up, and bundled him into an empty canvas laundry bag. The hotel was located beyond the White Tower from where they left the Zodiac, but they took a roundabout route to avoid passing the cluster of police cars and soldiers now spilling across the Leoforos Nikis.

It took twenty minutes to reach the place, called the Dimitriu, tucked away just off of Lampraki Street, southeast of the fairgrounds, only a few blocks from the city's Kaftanzoglion Stadium and on the opposite side of the city from the Vergina.

DeWitt had been right. The hotel was small and had a battered air to it, with its facade showing dark patches where the whitewash had crumbled away, but it was off the main thoroughfares and it had a fire escape in an alley in the back. The three of them snuck the bulky laundry bag up to the third-floor room through the back. Then Mac left again to dispose of the car in the stadium parking lot.

Jaybird, Stepano, and DeWitt settled down to wait, sitting in the dilapidated hotel room with the prisoner, saying nothing to each other.

Damn, Jaybird thought. *What else could I do? Why the hell couldn't Razor dive over the side and swim for it?*

Because the bastards would have searched for him, idiot, and probably caught you both.

He eyed the man, who was lying unconscious on the bed, still wearing nothing but a damn pair of boxer shorts.

"You'd better be worth it, you bastard," he said.

2324 hours
Kaftanzoglu Street
Salonika, Greece

"Parking garage," Magic said, pointing. "Turn in there."

At this time of night, there were few customers. They

turned up to the building's entrance, accepted a ticket from a sleepy-looking attendant, then drove to a far corner of the garage and parked. The huge, dimly lit concrete cavern offered a relatively secure spot to talk to the girl they'd rescued.

At the moment, she didn't seem all that sure that she *had* been rescued. Her name was Nikki Iatrides, and she spoke very little English. She answered Papagos's questions in Greek, speaking in a low, scared voice, and she seemed preoccupied with tugging the hem of her borrowed shirt as far down her bare thighs as she could manage.

Clearly, she was terrified; a night of fun and friendly sex aboard her boyfriend's yacht had ended in gunfire and the yacht crewman's blood splattered over the cabin windows. She'd tried hiding under a galley table, but soldiers had burst in and dragged her, naked, onto another boat filled with leering, gun-waving men. Someone had given her the shirt. Someone else had handcuffed her, then herded her ashore like an animal with Eleni and a stranger wearing swim trunks and a wet, black T-shirt. She didn't know what she'd done, she didn't know who the SEALs were, she simply wanted them not to hurt her.

Gently—as gently as he could, under the circumstances—Murdock questioned Nikki, with Papagos as interpreter. She told them that she was an office secretary for Trahanatzis Shipping and that that was how she'd gotten to know Eleni Trahanatzis, the boss's son. Though Eleni didn't work for his father, he was frequently in and out of the office, and she'd started dating him perhaps five months before. She didn't know anything about the IMRO or the EMA. She was a Macedonian Slav—with her pale blond hair and blue eyes she could hardly be anything else and still be Greek—but she knew nothing of politics and cared nothing about "that other Macedonia, across the border." She'd been born and raised in Lankadas, a village a few miles north of Salonika, and in her entire eighteen-year life she'd never even been as far away as Athens.

More than once during the interview, her low voice had

gotten louder and higher and louder and higher, and Papagos
had been forced to stop and spend long minutes trying to
calm her down. She had no idea what was going on. She'd
assumed that she and those with her were being arrested for
some reason . . . but why did *he*—and at that point she'd
turned and stared with wide, terrified eyes at Roselli, seated
beside her—why did he trip Eleni when he tried to run
away? Did it have anything to do with *narkoticos*, with
drugs? She'd started wondering about that when Eleni's
friend had started flashing so much money about. She didn't
use drugs, she didn't know about drugs, she didn't . . .

"Okay, okay," Murdock said. "Tell her she's not under
arrest. We just want to ask some questions, okay?" When
Papagos had spoken to her and she'd calmed down again, he
added, "Ask her about this Vlachos character. What does
she know about him?"

After speaking briefly with the girl and getting a considerably longer and more emotional reply, Papagos turned to
Murdock. "Interesting, Skipper. She met the guy through
her boyfriend Trahanatzis a couple of months ago. She
doesn't really like him, though."

"Why not?"

"Well, I'm reading between the lines here, but I get the
impression that Vlachos is a libidinous son of a bitch. It was
supposed to be a cozy, romantic weekend, with Nikki and
Trahanatzis and Vlachos and his girlfriend, Maria. Vlachos
wanted to turn it into an old-fashioned orgy, but Nikki here
just wanted to screw with her boyfriend. Trouble was,
Trahanatzis was awfully eager to impress Vlachos and was
pressing Nikki to, uh, be extra nice to him."

"Cute. Get her to tell you about Vlachos. Why doesn't she
like him?"

Papagos rattled off the question in Greek. Nikki's reply
was a long one, accompanied by quick, nervous hand
gestures. Once the words started coming, there was no
stopping them.

"She says he was boorish and loud and . . . and arro-
gant. Sounds like he thinks of himself as a real stud, a

God's-gift-to-women kind of guy. And he's prejudiced. It seems Nikki here has some friends, neighbors of her family's back in Lankadas, who are Muslims. Nice people, she says, just plain folks who helped out her father once when he was in some kind of trouble. Financial, I think. Anyway, Vlachos was always going on about Muslims . . . 'Turks,' he called them. Thought they were all terrorists and ought to be butchered like pigs. Uh . . . that's a pretty strong insult to a Muslim, Skipper."

"I know. Go on."

"That's about all. Something about the other three hiding all her clothes to make her fuck Vlachos. I'm not sure if she's telling the truth there, or making up a story to explain why she didn't have anything on when they dragged her out from under the table. I do know the poor kid's scared half to death. She's not faking that."

"Does she know where Vlachos is from?" Murdock asked.

A moment later, Papagos turned to Murdock, his eyes sparkling. "Bingo, Skipper. She says he never told her, but he speaks kind of clumsy Greek, like it's not his native tongue. Seems he speaks Macedonian, though. So does Nikki, enough to know he speaks it with a northern accent."

"Macedonian, eh?" The language, like the people, was Slavic, more closely related to Bulgarian than to Greek.

"Well, well," Roselli said. "A Macedonian who arranges sexy weekends aboard his yacht with members of the DEA."

"He was DEA too, remember," Murdock said. "Ask her, was he the only one she knew from up there?"

"He's the only one she knew well. She says there were these four other guys, all Greek Macedonians and all members of the DEA, that Vlachos and Trahanatzis entertained a lot. She only met them a couple of times, and Trahanatzis didn't seem to want her around those times."

"Nice guy."

"Yeah. Sounds like a real sweetheart. Anyway, sometimes

they got together on Vlachos's boat. Usually it was ashore, at some restaurant or other."

"Sounds like those four might be people we'd like to meet," Frazier said from behind the wheel. "If we could get names, I'll bet a month's paycheck that they're the same as four of the names on that list of DEA agents assigned to Kingston's flight."

"At least we have a direction to go in with our questions." Murdock reached into his trousers and extracted his wallet. They'd all been issued 100,000 drachmas—about $400 American—in spending money by their embassy contact aboard the *Jefferson* that morning. Murdock counted off 20,000 drachmas and handed them to the girl. "Tell her she's been an enormous help," he told Papagos. "Tell her we're sorry about what happened on the boat, but that Vlachos is a bad man and we're trying to find him. She can have the money to buy herself clothes, or to get her home, or for whatever else she needs."

"What about Solomos, Lieutenant?" Magic asked. "That bastard's going to be looking for her."

"I know. Can't be helped, though. Damned if we can adopt her. Tell you what, Nick. Tell her to try to stay away from the DEA and the soldiers, but that if she can find a local cop, someone from here in Salonika, she might be able to get him to help her." People were people, whatever their language. Just as Solomos didn't like the idea of Americans intruding on his turf, the chances were good that local cops didn't care for the elite Dimona coming along and carrying out paramilitary operations in their territory.

It was the best he could do for her . . . and he hated taking the added precaution of having Papagos tell her they were hunting for Vlachos, not that they already had him. If they did pick her up, that was what she would tell them . . . another fiction that might delay a police search by a precious few more hours.

If they were lucky, Jaybird, Mac, DeWitt, and Vlachos were already at the new hotel, waiting for them, while the police were searching the streets.

Nikki couldn't know about any of that, of course. She did seem grateful, though, now that these mysterious foreigners were letting her go when she'd been imagining the worst. When they all got out of the car, she came up to Murdock, stood on tiptoe, and kissed him on his cheek. *"Sas efharisto poli, kirie,"* she said, her eyes shining.

"Hey, L-T," Roselli called. "Who's your friend?"

"She says thank you very much," Papagos added.

"How do you say, 'You're welcome'?"

"Parakalo."

"Parakalo, Nikki."

"Hey, L-T," Roselli said, grinning as the girl hurried off, bare feet slapping on the concrete. "I think she kind of likes you."

"Shut up. Let's find that hotel."

13

Thursday, March 9

They left the parking garage in two groups to avoid attracting attention, sticking to side streets where possible and taking separate routes to the hotel. Frazier led Magic and Razor, while Papagos stayed with Murdock. Navigation through the city streets actually proved to be relatively simple, since both the communications antenna above the fairgrounds to the northwest and the huge sports stadium to the east were easily recognizable, easily spotted landmarks.

Murdock and Papagos were delayed only once, waiting for a few minutes in an alley as a police car cruised slowly past on Papaphi Street. They found the Dimitriu without trouble and slipped up the fire escape in back, to find that Frazier, Brown, and Roselli had gotten there just minutes before them, while Sterling, DeWitt, and MacKenzie had arrived with their prisoner nearly an hour earlier.

"So that's Stathis Vlachos," Murdock said.

"I think he may be starting to come around," DeWitt said. "From the size of that lump on the back of his head, I'd say Jaybird damned near took his head off."

"Stepano?" Murdock said, jerking his head toward the room's single small window. "Let's talk. Over here."

161

"Yes, sir."

Murdock began filling him in on what the SEALs had learned from Nikki in the car, speaking quietly so that if the prisoner was awake, he would not hear. "So he's Macedonian," he concluded. "Or, I should say rather, at least he speaks Macedonian. Don't know how much English he has, but the girl said his Greek wasn't all that good. I think he's from up north."

"I had already wondered about that, Lieutenant," Stepano said, his blue eyes flat and cold. "Judging by what Razor, Scotty, and Magic told me when they came in."

"I'd say this one is in your department."

"Yes." Stepano appeared to be studying the prisoner. They had him on the bed, still tied hand and foot, still wearing nothing but his boxer shorts. He did indeed appear to be coming around, moaning and twisting his head back and forth. "Sir . . . how rough can we be with him?"

Murdock sighed. "Son, that's a hard one, but I'd have to say you can be as rough as you need to be. We've *got* to know what he knows about the hijacking. The names of his mysterious friends in the DEA. Where he's from. Who he works for. And we've got to get the goods fast. Solomos is probably turning this city inside out right now looking for us, and we probably don't have more than, oh, let's say six hours. We might have more, but I don't want to stretch it too close."

"Maybe we can scare it out of him," Roselli said, joining them.

"Maybe," Murdock said. "Unfortunately, folks in this part of the world are used to the idea of torture. This guy couldn't be working for the Greek government and not be aware of what would happen if he got caught."

"Shit," Roselli said. "We're gonna torture the guy?"

"We can't," Murdock said. "Even if we wanted to, we can't." He pointed at the room's nearest inner wall. "These walls are only a little thicker than paper. If he starts screaming, we'll have Solomos and his men breaking down the door ten minutes later. Count on it."

"Is possible that we can use the fact that he is from Yugoslav Macedonia," Stepano said quietly, his accent noticeably thicker as he thought about the problem. "And . . . he does not know us, know who we are. What we are. I think I see way. . . ."

"He's all yours," Murdock said. He signaled to DeWitt, who was standing next to the bed. "Two-Eyes? Take everybody out except two volunteers."

"Me," Roselli said.

"I'll stay," Sterling said.

"Also, I need something," Stepano said. "Perhaps Papagos can get some from hotel desk. Or at all-night drugstore."

Papagos nodded. "Right, then," Murdock said. "Let's get this over with. We don't have much time."

After dispatching Papagos on his errand, they bound the still-groggy Stathis Vlachos to a wooden chair, using the handcuffs they'd taken off Roselli to secure his wrists behind his back, then binding his arms and torso to the chair's straight back with a length of nylon line left over from the evening's activities. Next they pulled off his shorts, then tied his ankles to the chair's rear legs, using more rope to spread his knees apart.

Stepano played the role of chief interrogator with the air of a man used to getting the answers he demanded. Roselli and Sterling carried out his instructions with the solemn air of men participating in some dark and mysterious ritual. Once, when Roselli moved a bit quickly while looping the rope around the legs of the chair, Stepano said, "Slowly, Razor, slowly. We want him to think about this, about what we are doing." Then he'd added something in Macedonian, possibly repeating his words for Vlachos's benefit.

When they were done, the man could move nothing but his head. His legs were spread open and tied, his genitals exposed and vulnerable. Murdock watched full awareness returning to the prisoner's eyes, saw a flash of panic there . . . replaced almost at once by a dark, urgent watchfulness.

They waited then for several moments, the silence in the

room growing heavier. There were two quick knocks at the door, and Papagos entered, carrying a brown paper bag.

"Place it on dresser, please," Stepano said. "Thank you."

Papagos did as he was told, then crossed the room to take his place next to Roselli and Jaybird. Murdock considered ordering him to leave, then decided against it. He had a right to see, to know.

God help us, he thought blackly. *We're becoming as bad as the sons of bitches we're fighting.*

Stepano stepped closer to the prisoner, leaning over until their faces were inches apart. He smiled, a hard, calculating expression. *"Kade e Gospogya Kingston?"*

The prisoner snarled something back, bared his teeth, and spat. He was brave, certainly, Murdock was willing to give him that. Murdock couldn't imagine himself spitting in the face of anyone if he'd been in the prisoner's place.

The smile fixed rigidly in place, Stepano pulled a handkerchief from his back pocket and wiped the spittle off his cheek. "Razor? Gag our friend, please."

Razor tore off a strip from the bedsheet, stepped behind the prisoner, then pulled the cloth taut between the man's teeth, knotting it tightly. Stepano stepped close again, still holding the handkerchief.

"Yas sum od Goli Otok," Stepano said, and his voice, though still low, was as hard and as cold as ice. *"Razbi-ram?"*

The prisoner's face went death white at the words "Goli Otok," the name, Murdock remembered, of one of the prison islands that Tito's secret police, evidently, had made notorious.

Stepano kept speaking, his voice low, almost gentle as he carefully and neatly twisted his handkerchief into a thick, white rope. Next he looped it beneath the prisoner's genitals, then tied it in a knot, drawing the ends very slowly tight. *"Dali ste zheneti, gospodin? Imate li devoyka? Ah! Zhal mi e!"*

Throughout all of this, the prisoner's eyes were starting from his head, as wide and as white as the gag in his mouth.

Stepano next crossed the room to the dresser and, careful to keep all of his movements in clear view of the prisoner, slowly produced a can of lighter fluid, the kind used in refillable cigarette lighters. He held it to his ear, shaking it, then nodding approval.

Returning to the prisoner, he showed him the can, uncapped it, then began to pour it, a small dribble at a time, onto the knotted handkerchief. All the while, Stepano kept talking, and four or five times Murdock caught again that dread name of Goli Otok.

Murdock didn't understand the spoken words, but he could certainly imagine what Stepano must be saying . . . something about *this* was the way it was done, back at that prison on Goli Otok, and *this* was what happened to someone Stepano had known. . . . Was the SEAL claiming to be a victim of Tito's torture prison, Murdock wondered, or one of the secret police's torturers? It hardly mattered; the gentle-sounding words coupled with the look on his face as he emptied the last of the lighter fluid onto the skin of the man's penis combined to create an atmosphere of utter and complete madness. The sharp stink of the liquid bit the air. The knotted handkerchief was sopping wet, as was the matted black hair on Vlachos's belly and groin. His genitals lay flaccid in a puddle of the stuff on the chair between his open thighs, and some of it was dripping onto the carpet. He was whimpering through the gag now, a quavering, horrible sound, scarcely human.

When the can was empty, Stepano set it aside, then fished about in his shirt pocket, producing at last a silver cigarette lighter. He held it delicately between thumb and forefinger, so close to the prisoner's face that his eyes crossed as he tried to focus on it.

"Kade e Gospogya Kingston, Vlachos?"

The pitch of Vlachos's whimpering went up an octave, his head thrashing back and forth, his eyes huge. There was blood on the gag now. He'd bitten his lip or tongue.

"If I didn't know better," Papagos said, "I'd swear he's trying to tell us something through that gag."

Deliberately, Stepano flicked the lighter open and struck a spark, keeping the lighter well above the prisoner's groin. Flame danced on the end of the wick, reflected brightly in the terrified mirrors of Vlachos's eyes.

"Jeez, Steponit," Roselli said. "Watch those fumes. . . ."

Stepano lowered the flame one inch . . . two . . .

"Kade e Gospogya Kingston!"

"You know, Steponit," Papagos said, "in Greece, when you jerk your head up and back, you mean 'no,' but when you turn your head to the side, like he's doing, you mean 'yes.' Is that what you're trying to say, Vlachos? You're trying to say yes, you'll talk?"

"Nah," Roselli said. "He's just shaking his head no, like he doesn't want a light."

Vlachos's reply was a shrill, muffled unintelligibility, but it was clear enough what he was trying to say. "Roselli," Murdock snapped. "The gag."

The gag came off and Vlachos launched into a torrent of words, sometimes in Greek, sometimes in Macedonian. Papagos stood beside Murdock, trying unsuccessfully to keep pace with a running translation.

"He says he and four of his friends with the Enomenai . . . ah, the United Macedonian Struggle . . . infiltrated the DEA . . . something, something . . . he's speaking Macedonian now. I don't . . . okay, the idea was to take the plane to Skopje. The plane . . . the crew, they're all at Skopje. The women . . . ah, the congresswoman and her people . . . they're taking them off some place. Ah . . . can't catch that. *'Ohridsko Ezero . . . Gorica . . . Gora . . . Gorazamak . . .'*"

"That's Lake Ohrid," Stepano said. "Gorica is a village on the shores of Lake Ohrid. Gorazamak is an Ottoman fortress nearby."

"Thank you, Mister Travel Guide," Sterling said.

"He's still speaking Macedonian now," Papagos said. "I'm not getting this at all."

"It is Serbo-Croatian," Stepano said. "Not Macedonian. He's saying . . . he's saying the Congresswoman and her

staff were supposed to be taken off the plane and transported
to this castle."

"Taking the most important hostages off someplace safe,"
Roselli said. "Someplace where we or Delta Force can't get
at them."

"There's no such place," Jaybird said.

Vlachos was continuing to talk, the words tumbling out
so quickly the prisoner began to stutter, his eyes still fixed
on that horrible yellow flame wavering atop Stepano's
cigarette lighter.

"He says that there was list of demands, due to be
delivered to the American embassy in Athens tomorrow . . .
ah, later today, rather. We were to recognize Macedonia as
including both Yugoslav and Greek Macedonia. Statement
of principle, he says. We were to recognize EMA as the
legitimate representatives of united Macedonia. This . . .
this is crazy, Lieutenant. What he is saying, we would never
do. . . ."

"Since when are terrorists considered sane? In any case,
he's not telling us the whole story."

"Eh?"

Murdock locked eyes with the prisoner. "Mr. Vlachos
here is not Macedonian. Or if he is, he's not working for
Macedonian independence."

"What then, Boss?" Papagos asked.

"What's his word for 'Serbian'?"

"Srpska."

The prisoner jumped at that word as though he'd been
jabbed. Eyes wide, he looked back and forth, from one
SEAL's face to another.

"Tell him we know he's Srpska."

Stepano's words prompted another torrent from Vlachos,
who was watching the cigarette lighter again as though his
life depended on his fixed concentration. When he stopped
talking, Stepano appeared to be considering what he'd said.
Then he flicked his hand, snapping the lighter shut. The
prisoner slumped back in the chair, eyes closed, sweat
beading his forehead.

"I think you have found something, Lieutenant," Stepano said. "Something important. Our friend here is not EMA, but he has been working closely with EMA cells in both Macedonias for a long time. As you guessed, he is Serbian . . . a Bosnian Serb, actually. His real name is Vlacovic, not Greek Vlachos."

"How the hell did you know *that,* L-T?" Roselli asked.

"Our L-T's a mind reader," Sterling said.

"Nope. It was just a guess, but an educated one. Earlier, when we were talking to Nikki? She said that Vlachos called Muslims 'Turks' and indicated that he didn't care much for them. That sounded like something a Bosnian Serb would say, not a Macedonia Slav who's spent most of his life hating Serbs."

"That's stretching things a bit, ain't it, Skipper?" Papagos asked. "Lots of folks in this part of the world don't like Muslims. Especially Greeks. They hate the Turks."

"Exactly. Which means they tend to identify Turks specifically with Turkey nowadays, not with all Muslims. At least, that was my read on it. And when Stepano said he'd started speaking Serbo-Croatian . . ." He shrugged.

Stepano nodded. "You guess right, sir. He is a Serb. Says he's a *potpukovnik*—that's lieutenant colonel—in Yugoslav Army."

"What the hell interest does Serbia have in Kingston?" Roselli asked.

"And why are the Serbs helping an outfit dedicated to Macedonia unity?" Sterling added. "I thought the Macedonians wanted rid of them."

"Politics and strange bedfellows, Jaybird," Murdock said, folding his arms. "Actually, now that I think about it . . ."

"Whatcha thinking, Skipper?"

"Another guess, Nick." But Murdock was excited now. He was right. He *had* to be. "Okay. Here's the way I see it. The EMA has been working against Greece for some time now. They have independence for northern Macedonia. What they want now is to shake Greek Macedonia free from Greece. Right?"

"Affirmative," Roselli said. "You're thinking the EMA is trying to make trouble between the U.S. and Greece."

"That's part of it. More than that, though, what do you think we would do once we found out that our congresswoman's flight was hijacked to Skopje?"

"Hell," Sterling said. "Delta Force would go in and kick ass."

"Exactly. Whose ass?"

"Christ!" Papagos said. "The EMA isn't that large. They must have most of their best people guarding the aircraft!"

"Delta Force goes into Skopje. Typical aircraft hostage rescue, just like Entebbe. The EMA never knows what hits them and probably loses every shooter guarding the hostages. Delta also gets enough intel from prisoners or from captured records or from debriefs of the hostages that they're able to nail all or most of the EMA's top people, probably within a few months. Hell, Serbian intelligence might even lend a hand, pass on a few files, a few names, whatever is necessary."

"And when the dust settles, there is no more United Macedonian Struggle," Stepano said.

"Sheesh," Roselli said. "That's twisted!"

"Ever heard of Byzantine politics, Razor?" Papagos asked. "Welcome to the land that spawned it."

"Oh, it gets even twistier, I imagine," Murdock continued. "Imagine Delta's surprise when they take down that aircraft and find that Ms. Kingston and her staff aren't there? There are recriminations. There's that trouble between Washington and Athens you mentioned, Razor. We find out the hijackers were infiltrators in the elite DEA. Sloppy, sloppy. And after that . . . I wonder what would have been next." He eyed Vlachos speculatively. "Maybe the Serbians holding Kingston at this castle threaten to kill the hostages one by one unless we abandon our support for Macedonia? That seems kind of blunt. I doubt they'd be quite that crude. Maybe instead they play it real cute and 'find' Kingston and her staff. They could claim they pulled off the hostage rescue of the century. That would make our

efforts look pretty dumb and encourage us not to meddle in
Balkan politics. Maybe they would claim we owed them a
big one, and win some concessions from us in Bosnia or in
their unresolved claims to Macedonia at the UN. Or maybe
they just figure it would make us look bad and them look
good to the world community at large, a colossal public-
relations ploy."

"I like the double-cross aspect," Papagos said. "The Serbs
get what they want from us, while we wipe out the EMA for
them and take the heat from the Greeks. Slick."

"Wait a minute," Jaybird said. "All of that assumes that
we found out enough to be able to launch an assault on the
Skopje airfield in the first place. They couldn't know we'd
pick up enough intel to make a hostage rescue even a
possibility."

"Sure they would," Murdock said cheerfully. "After
Solomos and the DEA finally got around to picking up Eleni
Trahanatzis and working him over in one of their basement
cells."

"Fuck . . . me," Roselli said, the words soft.

"Why else would Trahanatzis's bank account be so
obvious?" Murdock asked. "Kind of stupid, putting all that
money in an account where Greek intelligence would spot it
right off. I imagine Vlachos here, or Vlacovic, or whatever
the hell his name is, has been playing Trahanatzis like a
Stradivarius, setting him up for the fall. Solomos probably
got the word from someone higher up: 'Hands off until
Vlachos is out of the way.' He only moved tonight because
he thought we were going to screw things up."

"So once Vlachos is out of the way, Solomos and his
Keystone Cops move in," Sterling said. "They take Traha-
natzis apart a piece at a time until he tells them that the
EMA is holding the American congressperson at Skopje.
They pass that to Delta, and Delta moves in. Yeah, it fits.
God help me, it fits!"

"You know, this is a pretty big, pretty complicated plan,"
Roselli said. He grabbed Vlachos by his hair and pulled his

head back. "I don't think lover-boy here came up with it on his own, do you?"

"Ask him who he's working for," Murdock said.

Stepano barked a question. The prisoner sagged farther down against the ropes. Once he'd been broken, all of the fight appeared to have drained from him.

"*Da*," the man said. "*Brigadni Djeneral* Vuk Mihajlovic."

"Well, well," Roselli said. "Our friend from TV."

"Ask him how far the JNA is involved in this," Murdock said. "I want to know just what we're up against, and you can tell him that if he doesn't tell us the precise truth, he can kiss his balls good-bye."

The added threat didn't seem to make much of an impression. Vlachos's reply was a barely intelligible mumble.

"He says there are some Serb 'volunteers' helping the EMA. Sounds like ten or twelve shooters, max, guarding the plane at Skopje, some army regulars, some EMA freedom fighters. That castle on lake used to be some kind of a tourist attraction, but it's been closed for quite a while. Even the caretakers are gone. He's not sure how many men are up there, but he thinks it's supposed to be ten, maybe twenty, all regular JNA."

"You know," Roselli said, "Mihajlovic might be running things on the Serb side of the border, but he wouldn't have any pull with the Greeks. We must have two higher-ups, Mihajlovic to handle the Serbs, and somebody else with the Greeks . . . someone who helped plant those EMA infiltrators in the Dimona, someone to protect this bastard until they're ready to sacrifice Trahanatzis. Who would that be anyway?"

"I don't know," Murdock said. "I doubt that this guy knows. Frankly, that's one for the Greeks to worry about. We can pass all of this on to them, but our problem is finding Ms. Kingston."

They questioned Vlachos for another hour, checking answers, digging for inconsistencies, looking for signs that he might be lying about anything, even the smallest detail. Toward the end of the session, he became stubborn again, refusing to say more. Stepano flicked the lighter into flame, spat a Slavic curse, and dropped his hand toward Vlachos's groin.

Vlachos burst into another flood of begging, pleading, desperately ingratiating words as tears streamed down his face. By the time he was through answering the last of the SEALs' questions, Murdock was certain that they'd gotten everything out of him that there was to get.

"God, Stepano," Murdock said quietly after the big SEAL again closed the lighter. "I'm glad you're on our side."

"In this land," Stepano said quietly, "so very much depends on a man's . . . manliness. Like the *machismo* of Latin America. I . . . did not want to have to threaten him like that . . ."

"Would you have set him on fire?" Roselli asked. "No, don't answer that, Steponit. I don't think I want to know."

"There were moments," Stepano said, staring at the cigarette lighter still clutched in his hand, "when I thought I might. *Bog! Mi pomotchi! . . .* "

Tears were running down his face, as well as that of the prisoner. Stepano was trembling, shaking as his rigidly held inner control began to slip. His fists clenched, the muscles in his arms and back bulging as he struggled with what he'd just done.

God, what did Stepano just put himself through? Murdock wondered. He slipped an arm around the Serb's shoulders and squeezed. "It's okay, Stepano. You did good. We got what we needed, right?"

"Y-yes. But I *hate* this. . . ."

"Me too, my friend."

"This guy," Roselli said, slapping the back of Vlachos's head, "is a thorough-going bastard. Don't worry yourself over a scumbag like him."

"Believe me, Steponit," Papagos said. "What you did to him tonight is *nothing* compared to what the government security forces would have done. He got off light."

"Greek security'll still get a crack at him," Murdock said.

"We're turning him over to them?" Sterling asked,

nodding toward the sobbing, utterly broken man still tied to the chair.

"We can't take him with us," Murdock decided. "We'll leave him tied up and gagged just like he is, and put out a do-not-disturb sign on the door. We can telephone Solomos from the consulate and tell him where he can come pick him up."

"The consulate?" Roselli asked.

"I have a feeling they'll be able to put us in touch with Captain Beasley," Murdock said. "And we're going to need Delta's help for this one."

"Not to mention a good lawyer," Sterling said. "I'm not sure Solomos is going to let us out of the country after the way we put his tits through the ringer at the waterfront."

"Well," Murdock said, "some of what we picked up here tonight might serve as a peace offering. Look at it this way. We got the information without Solomos's interrogators having to mop up all that blood in their basement. Nice and neat. And if he's smart, he can use it to find the Greek Mr. Big in this plot."

"Shit," Roselli said. "What if Solomos is part of it?"

"I don't think he's *that* smart, Razor. Come on. Let's get our shit together and get the hell out of Dodge."

Minutes later, as they stepped out of the room, Papagos leaned back in and barked something at Vlachos in Greek. Murdock heard only the muffled groan of a reply.

"What'd you tell him?" Murdock asked.

"*Apagoretai to kapeisma,*" Papagos said, grinning wickedly. "That's 'No smoking.' Until somebody comes in and cleans him up, smoking just might be hazardous to his sex life."

14

The structure was small as Ottoman fortresses went, but it offered a commanding view of the lake from its cliff-side eyrie. Once it had protected a mountain road winding up through the Plachenska Mountains from the rug-making center at Korcë to the crossroads town of Uskup, later known as Skopje, 140 kilometers to the north.

That road had been closed for a long time now. The Albanian border lay just eighteen kilometers south at the tiny village of Ljubanista, and that tiny country had been shut off from the rest of the world since the end of World War II.

The lake itself was well known to geologists as the deepest in Europe, one of the oldest lakes in the world. At an altitude of 695 meters, nestled into the forested landscape between the Galicica Mountains to the east and the southern arm of the Jablanica Mountains to the west, Lake Ohrid itself formed part of the border between Albania and The Former Yugoslav Macedonia. Approximately a third of the lake, the southwest corner from just south of Ljubanista to the border crossing at Cafasan, belonged to Albania.

As his car wound south past the town of Gorica on a

175

narrow and poorly maintained road hugging the sheer, forested cliffs rising from the lake, *Brigadni Djeneral* Vuk Mihajlovic reflected that a more remote and private spot could scarcely be imagined. Struga Airport—which included a military air base, of course—offered access, but this narrow road and the forbidding terrain above and below it guaranteed the privacy of the force now holding Gorazamak Fortress. In recent years, the city of Ohrid had become something of a tourist center for this corner of Macedonia, and Gorazamak was one of some thirty so-called "cultural monuments" in the region. With civil war in Yugoslavia, however, and with the rise both of local terror groups like the EMA and of the threat of Serb-Yugoslav intervention in a state that clearly could not survive on its own, the tourists had vanished, taking their foreign currency elsewhere. So sharp had the economic collapse of the past couple of years been that many of the villages in the area were deserted now.

That was of no concern to Mihajlovic, who saw Macedonia as key both to the future of Greater Serbia and to his own personal future.

His driver turned left onto a dirt road that wound sharply up a steep, thickly forested hill. Several hundred meters into the woods, the road turned right into a clearing, offering a splendid view of the castle.

Gorazamak—the name was Serbo-Croat for "Mountain Castle"—was perched on a rocky cliff some fifty meters above the lakeshore road. It wasn't actually much of a castle as European castles went, with little to the place save an irregular, outer wall enclosing a five-story inner tower or keep. The place had been renovated perhaps fifteen years before and operated for a time as a hotel. It had gone out of business with Macedonian independence, and eventually had been purchased by Mihajlovic's agents. As a student of military history, Mihajlovic found a fine irony in the fact that a medieval castle, a type of fortification long obsolete in an age of airmobile troops and nuclear weapons, could once again play a part in a modern military operation.

The road ran across a narrow steel and concrete bridge spanning a natural moat, a crevice plunging straight to the boulders rising above the coast road below. Beyond was the massive gate tower that led to the courtyard or bailey. Soldiers in the gray Soviet-style uniforms of the home defense militia stopped them at the gate, looked over the driver's ID and papers, and checked Mihajlovic's face against a photograph before saluting and ushering the car through. Inside, military vehicles and a few civilian cars were parked alongside a low building to the left that had once been a stable. To the right, similar buildings served now as barracks for the outpost's fifty soldiers. Beyond, the tower loomed high in gray stone blocks against the evergreen forest of the higher slopes beyond.

Leaving the car with his driver, Mihajlovic strode across the flagstone pavement, up five steps, past two more sentries who saluted with crisp present arms, and through the high, vault-arched doorway opening into an impressive entry hall. The walls had been stripped bare of the banners and tapestries and museum relics that once had hung there, and the carpets once covering the floor and the broad, stone steps winding up either side of the room to a railed gallery overlooking the chamber had been removed. An unpleasantly anachronistic counter backed by racks and shelves to the left of the entrance as he walked in had once been manned by ticket-takers and stocked with souvenirs; now the area served as a guard post, where two men in the brown and gray camouflage of Yugoslavian Army uniforms stood watch, snapping to crisp attention as Mihajlovic walked in.

An aide hurried from the communications office, in a room leading off to the left. "My General!" the man called, and the sharp, military click of his boot heels echoed through the stone-walled chamber. "Welcome back!"

"Thank you, Ivo. Are our guests comfortable?"

"As comfortable as the circumstances permit, my General. They have been complaining of the lack of heat, the lack of privacy, and the poor food."

"You may tell them that their captivity will probably not

last much longer. It is important to keep their attention focused on release, rather than on attempts at escape." He looked at the aide sharply. "You have not permitted them to see those uniforms, have you?"

"No, my General. As you ordered, their guards and those who tend to their needs wear militia uniforms. I doubt that the women would know the difference. The American officer, however, probably would. He has several times questioned his jailor about military matters, trying to draw him out, I think."

"It may be best if that one does not survive his rescue. He is entirely too clever, too observant."

"His dossier says that he was a POW in Vietnam. No doubt he entertains fantasies of escape."

"Well, we shall discuss his fate later. And our troops? They are settled in?"

"All is in readiness, my General. As you ordered."

"Excellent, Ivo. Another week, I think, and the whole world shall know of the Macedonia terrorists and their hijacking of an American congresswoman. We shall give the Americans a couple of days to deal with the hijackers at Skopje, and then we shall show them how a hostage rescue *really* works."

"Yes, sir."

"In the meantime, I want—"

"General!" A man in a JNA sergeant's uniform appeared in the doorway to the communications center. "General Mihajlovic! You're here!"

"Yes, Sergeant. Just this moment. What is it?"

"Sir, a Priority One message has just come through. From Athens."

"Voice?"

"On the fax modem. They are running it through decryption now."

"I'll read it in there." Athens? What could he want? There was to be no communication with the Greek side of the operation until—

In the communications center, a female lieutenant looked

up from an IBM computer screen. "General! The message has just been cleared."

"Let me see."

Taking the woman's chair, Mihajlovic leaned forward and read the words written on the screen in glowing yellow phosphor.

> IMMEDIATE: VLACOVIC CAPTURED AND BROKEN, SALONIKA.
> EXPECT HRU ACTIVITY YOUR AREA.
>
> — ARISTOTLE

Damn the man! Why couldn't he have transmitted more information? When had Vlacovic been taken? And by who? Was it a screwup with the local authorities, or were the Americans already involved? Why couldn't that idiot Vlacovic have been silenced in prison before his interrogation? How much had the opposition learned from him? Was the HRU, the Hostage Rescue Unit, to be the American Delta Force, as had been assumed? Or were the Greeks behind it, or somebody else? It wasn't even beyond the realm of possibility that Vlacovic was playing at some game of his own. The first rule of operations in the twisted world of Balkan politics was *never trust anyone*.

And that, of course, applied even to Aristotle, even though Mihajlovic had groomed him for his current role himself. Had Aristotle betrayed the operation?

Doubtful. Not with those photographs and videotapes documenting Aristotle's rather bizarre sexual tastes in such lurid detail still safely locked away in the safe upstairs. If the man wanted to continue in Greek politics—if he even wanted to continue showing his face in public—he would continue to play the role in this drama Mihajlovic had assigned him.

For a moment, Mihajlovic toyed with the idea of contacting Aristotle in hopes of learning a few answers to go with the torrent of questions racing through his mind, then decided against it. He would assume the worst—that the

Americans had been the ones to take and interrogate Vlacovic—if only because only news of that urgency would have prompted Aristotle to break the agreed-upon protocol and send this message. And even assuming the worst, nothing had really changed. The timetable for Dvorak would have to be moved up a bit, that was all. And it would help to increase military security here at the castle.

"Ivo!"

Boot heels clicked at Mihajlovic's back. "Yes, my General!"

"Prepare the draft of an order. I wish to bring in more men, immediately. C and D companies, I believe, are still at the Struga airfield?"

"Yes, sir!"

"Have them brought to the castle immediately. And I will wish to review the deployment of our forces."

"At once, my General. The . . . hostage rescue? You are moving up the schedule?"

"Possibly. This . . ." He tapped the computer screen with the knuckle of his right forefinger. "This may force us to move a bit faster than we anticipated. I would still like the operation carried out after an American rescue attempt at Skopje, however, if possible."

The aide's eyes narrowed as he read the screen. "Ah. Is that wise, sir? I mean, if the Americans have learned that the Kingston woman is being held here, instead of at Skopje—"

"The Americans will still assault Skopje," Mihajlovic said. "They must. They cannot know whether or not all of the Americans have been removed from the aircraft and transported here, and they will want to make certain before launching an assault here. Furthermore, I expect they may wish to keep us uncertain about how much they know. The best way to do that would be to launch a rescue operation at the Skopje airport." He smiled. "It is even possible that they will think that the story that Kingston was brought here to be a fabrication. If I were they, *I* would not believe so fantastic a story, eh? It has all of the elements of a fairy tale, does it not? A castle on a mountain, the princess held prisoner in the dungeon."

"It lacks only the fire-breathing dragon, my General."

Mihajlovic laughed. "Forewarned is forearmed, as they say, my friend. With two more companies of soldiers in place, we will make anyone who comes calling believe that we have a regiment of dragons on this mountain. Come. Let us see about sending that order."

1440 hours
U.S.S. *Thomas Jefferson*
The Adriatic Sea

The Greyhound COD dropped out of leaden skies, descending at two hundred knots toward the roundoff of the supercarrier's flight deck. Wheels kissed steel, the tail hook snagged the number-two wire, and as twin turboprops howled protest, the aircraft lurched to a halt.

On board the COD, Murdock unhooked his safety harness.

"Haven't we been here before?" Mac said, peering out through one of the Greyhound's tiny windows. The edge of the flight deck just aft of the carrier's island was packed with aircraft, F-14 Tomcats and A-6 Intruders, their wings folded, their fuselages huddled together like huge, gray, nesting birds.

"That we have, Chief," Roselli said. "But I got a feelin'. . . ."

"What feeling, Razor?" Holt wanted to know.

"That we ain't gonna be aboard for very long. I'd keep my toothbrush handy if I was you guys."

"Shit," Jaybird said. "I'm just glad to be the hell out of Greece. I thought for a while they were going to give us a personal tour of their prison system."

"Me too, 'Bird," Papagos said. "Hey, I don't think Mr. Solomos likes us very much."

The others laughed, all except Stepano. Murdock decided

that it would be a good idea to keep a close eye on the big
Serb-American. Forcing him into the role of interrogator
back in Salonika might not have been such a good idea.

Screw it. If they hadn't done it, they wouldn't have found
out about Lake Ohrid. Murdock knew he would make the
same decision again if he had to.

All the same, Stepano would bear watching for a while.

Their escape from Greece had been somewhat anticli-
mactic. After leaving Vlachos tied up in the room at the
Dimitriu, they'd broken into small groups again and made
their way across town to the American Consulate, at number
59 on the Leoforos Nikis, back where the evening's excitement had begun. Two Greek soldiers were standing guard
out front, no doubt with orders to arrest any SEALs who
might show up. Roselli and Mac took them out, silently and
efficiently, leaving them unconscious, tied and gagged, and
lying behind a rubbish bin in an alley around the side of the
building.

At the consulate, Murdock made several phone calls,
using a password that both vouched for his security clearance and demonstrated the urgency of the situation. The last
call on his list put him through to Solomos, manning a
stakeout back at the Vergina Hotel. In the early morning
hours, Solomos had managed to pick up three more SEALs—
Rattler, Bearcat, and Doc—when they'd showed up at the
hotel in their rental car from Athens, but he'd lost them again
almost immediately. Murdock hadn't learned all of the details
yet, just something about a smoke grenade going off inside the
van the DEA men were using as a mobile headquarters.

But the rest of the SEALs would still be arriving
throughout the morning, and Murdock wanted to get them
all rounded up without further interference from Greek
security. Solomos refused to talk with Murdock when the
SEAL lieutenant got him on the phone, but an hour later
he'd been contacted by George Aristides, the Assistant
Director of the Greek Security Agency. Aristides, it turned
out, had just had a long conversation with *his* boss, the

Agency's Director, who in turn had just had a long conversation with the U.S. Secretary of State. The SEALs were to be released—all of them—and allowed to leave Greece at once without hindrance.

Solomos, Murdock imagined, was by that time probably delighted with the idea.

Once all of SEAL Seven's Third Platoon had been collected, they'd taken an Olympic charter flight to Hellenica, where they'd boarded the same Navy Greyhound that had brought them there the day before.

And now they were back aboard the *Jefferson*.

For ten hours that morning, ever since receiving an alert from the Chief of Naval Operations at the Pentagon, the *Jefferson* had been cruising north through heavy seas at thirty-five knots. Now she was on station, patrolling a racecourse-shaped oval midway between the heel of Italy's boot and the Greek island of Kerkyra, which curled protectively around the southern tip of Albania. Murdock and the other SEALs accepted the padded helmets known as "cranials" in Navy parlance, and life jackets, both of which they were required to don for their trip across the flight deck. *Jefferson* was at battle stations and in the middle of a hectic launch-and-recovery operation; under those conditions a carrier's flight deck was quite literally the most dangerous work environment on Earth.

Murdock stepped off the Greyhound and onto the deck. It had been raining not long ago, and the air was chilly and wet with the promise of another storm. Even through the cranial's built-in hearing protectors, his ears rang with the throbbing thunder of a catapult launch off one of the two waist cats. Preparations were under way at the second waist cat as well. The air shimmered from the jet wash, boiling above the raised rectangle of deck called a JBD, or jet-blast deflector, as the aviator aboard an F-14 Tomcat eased up the throttles on his chariot. A small mob of men in brightly and variously colored jerseys and helmets were in the midst of an intricate performance around the aircraft. At the launch officer's signal, they scattered, drawing back from their trembling gray charge.

Forward, the launch director waved, spun, pointed down the deck, then dropped to one knee with his thumb to the steel; at the signal, the Tomcat rushed forward, hurled down the slot of the catapult at an acceleration that took the aircraft from zero to 250 knots in less than two seconds. Steam spilled from the slot that guided the cat shuttle hooked to the Tomcat's nose wheel, almost as though the hurtling aircraft had set the deck afire behind it as it moved. Afterburners glaring like twin, orange-white eyes, the Tomcat flashed off the waist catapult, then ominously dipped below the level of the flight deck, vanishing from view. As Murdock watched, however, the aircraft reappeared a moment later, well ahead of the ship and climbing steadily, rising toward the gray ceiling on a trailing crescendo of thunder.

"Man," Murdock said, yelling to be heard both above the jet roar and the cranials everyone wore. "I don't know how they do that!"

"They might say the same thing about your job, Lieutenant!"

Murdock turned and found Captain Coburn standing there, along with Senior Chief Hawkins.

"Good afternoon, sir," Murdock said. He almost saluted . . . stopping himself when he remembered that he was still in civilian clothes. "We seem to keep bumping into one another out here."

"Hello, Blake. Ed. Welcome aboard. I hope your boys are rested after their shore leave in Greece."

"I'm not sure I like the sound of that," DeWitt said.

"Don't worry. You're gonna love this one. You two eaten yet?"

"No, sir," Murdock replied. "Things were kind of hectic in Athens."

"I can imagine. Come on. Hawk will take care of your boys and see that they're fed. I'll buy you lunch and fill you in on some of what's happening. At 1600 hours, we have a pre-mission briefing. Beaucoup braid. I'm beginning to think you guys like slamming your fists into hornets' nests."

"A mission?" Murdock asked. Adrenaline kicked his awareness to full on. "We're going back in?"

"Damn right you are. Any objections?"

"Not a one," Murdock replied. "Not a damned one."

They strode across the deck. Forward, thunder rolled again as a Tomcat roared off one of the bow cats. Closer at hand, the flight deck crew was bringing up another aircraft for launch off the first waist cat. This one was an E-2C Hawkeye, a twin turboprop plane that bore a distinct family resemblance to its Greyhound relation . . . except for the disk-shaped radome, over seven meters across, rising above its back like a flying saucer hitching a ride. The multi-hued deck personnel closed in; the dance on the deck continued, with yet another round.

Aft, another aircraft dropped out of the clouds toward *Jefferson*'s roundoff. Scant seconds, it seemed, after the COD had been nudged and prodded out of the way, an EA-6B Prowler electronic-warfare aircraft slammed into the deck in a barely controlled crash, yanked to a halt by the arrestor cable.

It was quieter inside, in the wardroom known as the Dirty Shirt Mess because officers didn't need to change out of flight suits or less-than-reputable uniforms to eat there. Murdock could still hear the roar-slam-*whoom* of aircraft taking off from *Jefferson*'s "roof," another aircraft launching or landing every minute or two. Coburn purchased meal tickets for the three of them, and they went through the line. Lunch today was hamburgers—"sliders" to carrier personnel—french fries, and coffee.

"Okay," Coburn told Murdock and DeWitt after they'd found a table and sat down. "CIA and Naval Intelligence bought your story about Kingston and some of her people being moved to Ohrid. There're some satellite photos that back you up, and it turns out the Company has a file on this

Mihajlovic bastard. He just might be looking for an opening at the top in Belgrade. Finding a way to humiliate the U.S. would grease his way to the top of the heap real well."

"I sense a 'but' in that, sir."

"Yup. Big time. But it works to our advantage, Lieutenant. It seems that Army Intelligence, the State Department, and the White House are all convinced that the honorable representative from California is still being held at Skopje."

"Shit."

"Not shit. We're going to take down both targets, a doubleheader. Or rather, Delta Force will be going into Skopje. *We'll* be hitting Lake Ohrid. If your people are ready, of course."

"We're ready, sir."

Damned straight they were ready. They'd discussed the possibility of another mission among themselves during the flight from Hellenica to the *Jefferson*. Something about the urgency in the air during their discussion that morning with the military liaison at the U.S. embassy had told Murdock that something big was on, probably an op. Normally, though, when one unit pulled recon, another would be brought in to carry off the op . . . and SEAL Seven's Third Platoon had already been in combat just a few short days before.

Coburn seemed to be reading Murdock's thoughts, or at least anticipating them.

"We have First Platoon on the way from Little Creek," he said. "And we've put Second Platoon on alert. But time is absolutely critical on this op. Bainbridge has been going ballistic. I think if we could insert you guys twenty minutes from now, it would still be about a week too late so far as he's concerned."

Murdock smiled. Bainbridge was Admiral Thomas Bainbridge, the commanding officer of NAVSPECWARGRU-Two, and the CO, therefore, of all East Coast SEALs.

"Problems with deployment?"

"The usual. Not enough airlift capability, and some gear

problems Stateside. First Platoon ought to be here late tomorrow afternoon, Second Platoon the day after that. SEAL Six has a team in Sicily right now, but they would need more men and they're not up to speed on the tacsit in Macedonia. *You* guys are here. Now. I've asked Admiral Bainbridge to send you in, and he gave the affirmative. So if your people agree, you're the ones."

"When?"

"Tonight."

Murdock whistled, and DeWitt spilled some of the coffee just as he was raising the mug to his lips.

"Good God!" DeWitt said. "You're not serious? Sir."

"Dead serious. If our intelligence is accurate, Kingston and at least four people, maybe more, are being held in an Ottoman castle on the east shore of Lake Ohrid. But the CIA concurs with your assessment, Lieutenant, that there is a mole, an infiltrator of some kind, at a high level of the Greek security system. The moment Greek DEA picked up your prisoner at that hotel, or very shortly afterwards, the mole knew that *we* knew, and he could make a pretty shrewd guess at how much we knew. We're betting he alerted the Lake Ohrid group."

"He wouldn't have been able to tell them much," Murdock pointed out.

"Maybe not, but he could tell them that we knew Kingston was there. That means two things. They'll probably beef up their security, for one. For another, if they had some sort of gimmick going with this hijacking—like staging a fake rescue, or killing the hostages and blaming it on the Greeks . . . that's another idea that's been in the wind, lately—then they'll likely move their timetable up. The Agency thinks they could try their move, whatever it is, by tomorrow."

"So we have to go in tonight," Murdock said quietly.

"I wish we could give you more time. But . . ." Coburn shrugged, picked up his hamburger, and took a bite out of it. "Anyway, you'll have two more platoons as backup. This'll be a strictly down-and-dirty, no-frills op. You go in, grab the hostages, and keep them safe against all comers until we figure out a way to get you out."

"Simple," DeWitt said. He was grinning.

"Oh, getting in is always simple," Coburn said. "It's getting out that's hard."

"Actually," Murdock added, "the trick is in getting out *alive*."

15

Friday, March 10

1220 hours
U.S.S. *Thomas Jefferson*
The Adriatic Sea

In the end, the mission had not gone down that night. A hold order had come through from Washington early that evening, delaying the op for twenty-four hours. At first, Murdock had been afraid that the delay would mean the op would be given to someone else, Delta possibly, or SEAL Seven's First Platoon, but it turned out his fears were groundless. Delta, he'd been told, was still working out its operations plan for the assault at Skopje, and both First and Second Platoons would be going into the backup slot for Third Platoon, as planned.

Murdock was relieved. Until the delay had thrown things into question, he'd not been aware of just how much he wanted this mission . . . not out of a sense of duty or an enjoyment of combat, but simply because, more and more, he was beginning to feel a personal involvement in the continuing nightmare that was the former Republic of Yugolsavia. He was thinking a lot about Garcia; one of the first things he'd done after coming aboard the *Jefferson* was to have Doc talk to some of the people in the carrier's medical department and get an update on Garcia's condition from Bethesda.

The word was that Garcia was out of intensive care, which was good news, but that there'd been extensive pulmonary damage, which was bad. SEALs needed good lungs, both for diving and for the kind of physical exertion routinely expected of them both on ops and in training. You *don't* run fourteen miles in 110 minutes with a crippled lung, and swimming two miles with fins in under seventy minutes is flatly impossible. Garcia would almost certainly be dropped from the SEAL program; there was even some doubt about whether he would be allowed to stay in the Navy.

But it wasn't just Garcia that had Murdock personally involved. There was Stepano, and the look on his face after he'd broken Vlachos that had made Murdock wonder if Stepano himself had been broken in some way. And there was the lingering feeling of being jerked around by the Greeks, and the knowledge that his people had been at risk because of traitors in their security force, and probably in their government as well.

And Murdock had also been thinking a lot about Nikki Iatrides during the past few hours, a nice girl from a small village who thought the Muslims living next door were "nice people" and "just plain folks." Most of the people in the Balkans, Murdock thought, must be pretty much the same, more than willing to get along with their neighbors so long as their neighbors were willing to get along with them. It was bastards like Vlachos and Mihajlovic and the Serbian rape gangs and the fanatic groups like the EMA and the proponents of "ethnic cleansing" that started wars and kept them going.

Maybe, when SEAL Seven paid a late-night visit to the occupants of Gorazamak, they could tip the balance just a wee bit in favor of the just plain folks.

At least that was the way Murdock was thinking about it, and that was why he was looking forward to this op, with all its dangers and all its uncertainties. Time after time in the past, he'd faced the certainty that the bad missions were the ones where people died or were crippled and no one could tell you why.

"This, gentlemen, is Gorazamak, seen from one hundred fifty miles up."

The room was dark, lit only by the glow off the slide-projection screen at the front, and crowded, an ad hoc theater for a highly classified slide show. The mission briefing was being held in *Jefferson*'s CVIC, naval shorthand for "Carrier Intelligence Center," and inevitably pronounced "civic." Present, representing SEAL Seven, were Murdock, DeWitt, and Coburn. This time around, the gold-braid-heavy assembly had been crashed by several petty officers as well, both MacKenzie and Ben Kosciuszko for Third Platoon, and Hawkins as Coburn's chief aide.

Representing Carrier Battle Group 14 were Rear Admiral Douglas Tarrant, the CBG commander, and Captain Jeremy Brandt, *Jefferson*'s CO. Another four-striper in the room was Captain Joseph Stramaglia, the carrier's CAG, an outdated acronym that meant he was commander of the carrier's air wing. Other officers included men from *Jefferson*'s Operations Department—from Intelligence, from Met, from Battle Ops. Squadron commanders were present as well.

At the moment, the floor had been turned over to Lieutenant Commander Arthur Lee, the air wing's intelligence officer, and he was going through a series of slides pulled from the latest batch of satellite photos transmitted to the carrier from NPIC, the CIA's National Photo Interpretation Center in Washington.

"In this shot," Lee was saying, a telescoping metal pointer in his right hand casting a pencil-thin shadow across the screen, "you can get a pretty good idea of how steep this cliff is. Our shadow triangulations and radar mapping jibe on this one for a change. You've got about twenty meters from the water to the road, here, then another fifty meters of sheer rock, almost straight up, from the road to the objective."

He pressed a control button in his left hand, and with a ratcheting click-*clunk*, the picture changed. It was the same

castle, obviously, but from a slightly higher angle, looking
down at a ribbon of white beach at the foot of the cliff. The
image was almost magically clear, a crisp black and white
that showed minute details of leaves and branches, all in
perfect focus. The perspective, looking down the cliff's
face, was dizzying.

"This one shows the beach below the castle. It's not very
wide, three meters maybe; and sandy. We think the sand was
trucked in and dumped, back when the place was a
rich-tourist mecca. Of course we can't show you, but the
lake is extremely deep—over nine hundred feet out toward
the center. Just imagine that cliff continuing, straight down,
for the length of another three football fields. The water is
remarkably clear. There are stories that you can see fish
seventy feet down. For that reason alone, our combat team
will have to approach at night."

Click-*clunk*.

"This is just east of the castle . . . the castle is out of the
picture, down here. Woods. Steep slopes. These objects
here . . . and here . . . and here are probably small bunkers. Since the sixteenth-century Ottomans didn't go in for
such things, we can assume they were late additions." A
polite ripple of laughter ran through the audience. "We can
also assume that the castle's present tenants are expecting
any assault to be made down off the mountain, through
these woods, and across this crest, rather than up from the
lake."

And that, Murdock thought, as he sat in a folding metal
chair with arms and legs crossed, was a damned good
assumption. Getting into that lake would take some damned
world-class parachutist skills. Getting up to the castle out
of the lake afterward would require world-class moun-
taineers . . . or mountain goats.

Well, SEALs could handle all of that, and more.

Click-*clunk*.

"Ah. This is one of my favorites. We're looking straight
down into the courtyard here. It's a stone-floored, walled-in
area approximately one hundred twenty meters north to

south, forty meters east to west. This is the gate, in the northwest wall, and this is the bridge across the canyon right outside the wall. These, as you can see, are trucks, Soviet-style jeeps, and private automobiles. If you look close, you can see that, yes, we *can* read license plate numbers from orbit."

That raised another laugh.

"There are some interesting features about this one. Look over here, in this little cul-de-sac around behind the stables. It's hard to make out without enhancement, but bear with me. This, right here, is the top of a man's hat, an officer's billed cap. These are his shoulders . . . arms . . . The way he's standing, we think he must be facing the wall while he takes a leak. Notice the shoulder boards here . . . and here. Now, these aren't in color and our resolving power falls short of what we'd need to make out details of a uniform, but very few of the militias or the shooters of groups like the EMA go in for shoulder boards, or anything like a real uniform. Most of them wear hand-me-downs, old Soviet-issue, and shoulder boards are a pain so they're usually the first to go when things get ragged. What we think we have here is an officer, possibly in the Macedonian Army, but much more likely he's JNA. If so, that would tend to confirm the idea that we may be up against Serbian regulars here, who've infiltrated into Macedonia as part of this, this rather fantastic plot. . . ."

The lecture droned on. Murdock paid attention with a part of his mind, but all of the hard decisions had already been made. The five of them, him, Ed, Mac, Kos, and Captain Coburn, had worked out a rough operations plan after lunch yesterday, then fleshed it out with some of the boys in Battle Ops afterward. The plan had been approved by Tarrant, who'd passed it on to Washington with his own recommendation.

Details, countless details, remained to be hashed out, but it had looked like this one was going to be a go. Then the hold order had been flashed from Washington, and everything was left hanging in the air.

Planning had proceeded, however, with the assumption that a go order would be forthcoming. That final seal of approval from Fort Fudge, as the Pentagon was sometimes known, was always the real chain-jerker. People on the front line, from Admiral Tarrant down to the newest swabbie recruit in the carrier's snipe gang, tended to work well as a team. They knew their jobs and they knew their responsibilities, and they'd been trained to carry them out with a minimum of supervision from on high. It was the REMFing munchkins and bean-counters and shit-for-brains pencil-pushers in Washington that scared Murdock.

And the *President* . . .

The current Administration was not known for its love of the military, nor for its clear-cut and unambiguous decisions regarding foreign policy and U.S. military intervention overseas. There'd been considerable speculation aboard the *Jefferson* about which way the White House was going to jump on this one. Murdock had kept his thoughts on the matter to himself and advised others who'd tried to draw him out to do the same. A good soldier follows orders, stays out of politics, and respects the office of his commander in chief even if he doesn't care for the man sitting in the Oval Office at the moment. . . .

None of which meant that Murdock couldn't entertain some pretty serious private reservations.

At least the delay allowed the SEALs to pack in one good night's sleep, and it gave them the chance to go over their equipment thoroughly. In the meantime, *Jefferson* had taken up her assigned position at the mouth of the Adriatic, a featureless point in the water nicknamed "Gyro Station." The name had originally been pronounced like the Greek word for the lamb and pita bread sandwich, *yee-ro*. Before long, though, popular usage and the realization that the word wouldn't carry well over radio had devolved it to gyro, as in a ship's gyroscopic navigation.

Though *Jefferson* would be the mission's combat control center, the SEALs would actually deploy from a land base. The San Vito Dei Normanni Air Station, located a few miles from Brundisium close to the tip of the heel of Italy's boot, had been selected as their staging area. Support aircraft and some necessary last-minute gear were being flown down from Rhein-Main, in Germany.

In the meantime, the SEALs carried out their pre-mission chores aboard the carrier, waiting, wondering what the word from Washington was going to be. Under Mac's critical eye, each man packed his own ram-air parachute, a tradition that had been started some years ago in SEAL Six. There was less likelihood of a mistake that way, with each man relying on his own eyes and hands and brain instead of those of some anonymous rigger who was just doing his job. The SEALs were "just doing their job" as well, but in their line of work, the smallest mistake could kill them. They'd spent the entire day so far going over all their weapons as well, breaking them down, cleaning them, loading out magazines, checking for wear, and drawing fresh suppressors for their Smith & Wesson 9mm automatics. Radios, sat-comm gear, signaling devices, maps, compasses, climbing rope and harnesses, gloves, boots, night-vision goggles, flashlights, first-aid kits, load-bearing vests, everything right down to their sticks of camo paint and the plastic binder handcuffs each man would carry—everything was checked and double-checked, then carefully packed in rucks and stowed aboard the waiting COD aircraft.

They also studied. Floor plans of Gorazamak were faxed via satellite from Washington to the *Jefferson*, and every man went over each sheet, memorizing stairs and blind corners, corridors, rooms, and closets. There was no guarantee that the interior of the place would look anything like these maps, of course. They were based on blueprint specs from a British firm that had renovated Gorazamak fifteen years ago, and it was possible that there'd been numerous changes made since. But load-bearing walls would be the same, as would stairways, especially those of the castle's original stonework that remained. Though Gorazamak had been built as a sixteenth-century fortified outpost, it had been refurbished as a pasha's summer cottage on the lake during the nineteenth century, then renovated again as a small combination of museum and hotel when tourism had become more important to the area than rug caravans from Korcë.

Now the tourists were gone . . . unless one wanted to count the SEALs that were already walking its corridors in their minds.

Murdock, meanwhile, along with DeWitt and the two senior chiefs, had continued with round after round of additional last-minute planning sessions in CVIC, as additional spy-sat photos were fed through from Washington. So far, there wasn't a lot on them that Murdock hadn't seen in the earlier shots.

Perhaps the oddest part about all of this was that Murdock had been sitting here for over an hour, leader of the SEAL team that would be the stars of this show, and no one had yet asked him anything about it. How he expected it to be, how he expected to be able to carry it out. He'd already accepted the mission and had contributed his part to the planning. It was up to others now to work out the support and logistical details, while he wondered how many more last-second changes might be implemented, changes that would affect him and his people as soon as they hit the ground.

"We're still working out the bugs in the pickup," Lee was saying, and that snapped Murdock's full attention back to the briefing. The satellite photo on the screen was another view of the courtyard, the irregularly shaped pavement inside the castle's walls. "An hour ago, another plan update came through from Washington. They're recommending that a Ranger team be inserted to seize control of the airport at Ohrid, some twenty kilometers from the primary objective. The advantage, of course, is that we can fly in a Combat Talon and land it at the airfield, pack the hostages and our ground team aboard, and fly them right out under fighter cover from the *Jefferson*. The downside, of course, is that we'll need another twenty-four-to-forty-eight-hour delay to implement it."

A chorus of groans ran through the compartment, followed by murmuring voices.

"They are also," Lee continued, "asking for clarification on the insert. Their feeling is that a helicopter insertion would be more viable than a HAHO."

The groans redoubled.

Admiral Tarrant stood up and strode toward the podium where Lee was standing. "As you were, people," he said as the CVIC's lights came up. "As you were! I agree with your, ah, unemotional assessment of the situation, and I believe that Washington will have to agree too, given a little more time to consider all of the implications. The time element in this operation is too critical to permit further delay." Tarrant scanned the audience, his eyes singling out Murdock. "Lieutenant Murdock? You and your people are going to be on point for this one. Do you have anything to add?"

"Good Lord. Ops is actually asking me what *I* think?"

The audience laughed. Murdock stood up and waited for the laughter to subside.

"So far as the infiltration goes, Admiral," he said when the room was quiet again, "we don't have any choice. A helo insert at the castle is definitely out. If they put us down outside the walls, the bad guys know we're coming. If they put us inside the walls, well . . . there's not a lot of room in there. If the chopper was knocked down on the approach, it would completely block that courtyard, not to mention screwing up the assault team's schedule.

"As for the extraction, I don't much care how you get us out, just so long as you do. I would definitely argue against any more delay. The longer we wait, the tougher things are going to be for us on the ground. We've already seen signs that they've been moving in more troops from Ohrid. I think we've got to go tonight, or not at all."

"Which extraction technique would you prefer . . . assuming, of course, that Washington gives us a vote?"

They'd been over this ground a good many times already. "I agree that the airport option offers the best safety if we can get the hostages to Ohrid. The trouble is, to get to the airfield we've got eighteen kilometers of narrow road, hemmed in between a lake and a mountain, followed by the city of Ohrid itself, then another two kilometers to the airport, and no alternate way of getting there. We know the opposition has a mechanized regiment in the area. Unless Washington's figuring on sending in half of the Army Special Forces to secure that road, I believe the risks of transporting the hostages over that route are unacceptable. There's the risk of ambush, either by troops already in place or by runners from the castle. There's also the danger of enemy air strikes, if any MiGs or Hips leak through our air cover. No offense, Captain Stramaglia, but your boys can't be everywhere at once."

The audience laughed again, including the CAG. *Jefferson*'s air wing would be tasked with assuring American control of the skies for this operation . . . but the best air superiority in the world couldn't guarantee protection from one or two hedge-hopping and determined enemy pilots. And Murdock had to consider *all* possibilities.

"So in my opinion, extraction both of the ground team and of the hostages has got to be from the castle. That has the advantage of giving my boys a defensible perimeter while we're waiting for the extraction aircraft, and better cover for the hostages.

"As for how we do it, well, we've discussed STABO, SPIE, and STAR extractions, but there are problems with all of those. If we use STAR, we can only take them out one or two at a time. If we use STABO or SPIE, we could get more people out faster, but the fact that the hostages aren't trained would almost certainly lead to people getting tangled up, and possibly hurt."

He was discussing the three primary means of recovering people from the ground without having to land an aircraft, all of them first implemented in Vietnam. STAR—Surface To Air Recovery—was the well-known technique requiring the evacuee to wear a harness attached to a helium weather balloon, which was snagged in midair by a low-flying MC-130 Combat Talon transport. The Army's STABO and the Navy's SPIE were means of inserting or extracting personnel using special harnesses attached to lines dangled beneath a helicopter.

"Besides," Murdock said with a grin, "none of those means of extraction is exactly in keeping with a congresswoman's sense of decorum and proper modesty." Laughter . . . and a smattering of applause. Murdock decided not to add that a STAR recovery would almost certainly have to be reserved for any of the hostages who were seriously wounded while they were being rescued. That was a very real possibility that the mission planners had to always keep at the backs of their minds.

"Absolutely the best extraction technique will be to use helos, coming in and landing right there in the castle's parking lot. It looks like that courtyard is just big enough for one helo to touch down at a time, especially if we move the cars out of the way. One chopper could take all the hostages, and then a second can move in and pick up the team when the first one's clear. We can wait to call the choppers in until the entire area is secure, so they don't have to face a hot LZ, and we'll have that beach below the castle as a backup, if a pickup in the courtyard proves impractical. There would be the usual hazards of flying out through hostile territory, especially after everyone in Europe figures out what's going down, but a couple of Pave Low IIIs ought to be stealthy enough to sneak in and sneak out again without getting tagged. Especially if the Navy does their part in the EW department, and if we have decent air cover off the carrier."

"I tend to agree," Admiral Tarrant said, "as does my ops staff. You can rest assured that I'll include your opinions in my next communication with Washington."

As they continued to discuss options, it struck Murdock what a monumental operation this actually was, a team effort involving some twelve thousand men aboard the seven ships of CBG 14, the pilots and ground crews of the Air Force Special Operations Squadron who would be responsible for inserting and recovering his men, the Delta team that would be hitting the hijacked aircraft at Skopje at the same time in order to avoid tipping off the opposition, and God alone knew how many thousands of other military and civilian personnel from Washington to Greece and back again who were working on this op, code-named Alexander.

Alexander, for the boy-king of Macedonia who'd conquered half the known world 2300 years before.

Murdock did not dwell on the thought that, while Alexander had been arguably the most spectacularly successful of all of history's conquerors and military figures, he had also died very young. . . .

At 1825 hours, the word came through at last.

Operation Alexander was *go*, and as originally planned.

2230 hours
San Vito Dei Normanni Air Station
Near Brundisium, Italy

The MC-130 Combat Talon aircraft, a Hercules especially augmented and equipped for this type of covert, deep-penetration mission, was waiting for them when they arrived at the Italian air base. Painted jet black, without identifying marks or insignia, it seemed to be a part of the night as the SEALs gathered up their parachutes and weapons loadouts and started filing up the huge aircraft's rear ramp.

They'd left the *Jefferson* to pursue her endless circles at Gyro Station, flying the COD on a short hop across the mouth of the Adriatic to San Vito. The MC-130, one of four deployed south from Rhein-Main, Germany, had arrived at San Vito just ahead of them and was already fueled and ready to go. Another, with a Delta team aboard, had already left on a roundabout route that would take it to Skopje.

Each man in the SEAL platoon had his own way of facing the possibility of death or injury or capture in the coming mission, from Doc's wisecracks to Mac's single-minded professionalism to the L-T's habit of going the rounds of his men, talking quietly with each. During the flight into San Vito, the Professor had been reading Polybius's account of the rise of the Roman Empire, of all things, while Roselli perused a dog-eared copy of last month's *Penthouse*. Holt, Nicholson, and Fernandez had exercised the warrior's historical ability to sleep anywhere, any time, while Frazier had quietly written a letter to his wife. Most of the rest had cracked jokes, told stories, or gone over their gear and weapons yet again.

ET1 Josip Stepano had not said much since the SEALs had left Salonika yesterday morning. He knew the L-T was worried about him, and he'd done his best to reassure Murdock that he was fine. But after completing all of his checks of personal gear, weapons, ammo, and chute, Stepano had done very little over the past few hours but think . . . and remember. He wondered often just how much he had in common with the other SEALs of the Team, especially when it came to motivation.

The Navy SEALs had the reputation of being hard-hitting, hard-drinking, fast-living superwarriors—and for the most part the rep was a well-deserved one. SEALs themselves often claimed that their unit's acronym stood not for SEa, Air, and Land, but for Sleep, EAt, and Live it up. You couldn't live as close to the edge as SEALs did every day and not have a bit of wildness to work off once in a while. Still, it seemed sometimes to Stepano that his fellow SEALs were more concerned with their warriors' fraternity than they were with the old-fashioned concept of patriotism.

Stepano was a patriot in every sense of the word. He loved his adopted country as only one who has escaped the nightmare of tyranny can. In lighter moments he joked about his love affair with a government official's daughter, but those moments were rare, the memories of the state police pounding on his father's door that night too fresh and sharp. His session as interrogator with Vlachos had brought back some of those memories with a fresh and blood-bright clarity.

He was American now and fiercely proud of that fact. A citizen when he was eighteen, he'd joined the Navy three years later. Because of his language skills, he'd been granted special clearance after an exhaustive background check, and that had led him first to Navy Intelligence, then to the SEALs.

But a man could never entirely escape his roots, that deep-down sense of who he was and where he'd come from originally.

Maybe . . . maybe what he and the others were going to do tonight would make some small difference in his homeland.

For Stepano, this operation had become intensely personal.

16

2315 hours
MC-130 Combat Talon
Over central Albania

In near-total darkness the fifteen SEALs sat facing one another across the cargo bay of the MC-130 Combat Talon aircraft. The drone of the four turboprops had been steady and unchanging since they'd lifted off from San Vito thirty minutes before. The aircraft's crew chief had ducked his head into the cargo deck moments before to announce that they'd just gone feet-dry.

Murdock turned and glanced at one of the small, round cabin windows, but there was nothing at all to be seen outside. The night was as black as the bottom of the sea. Perhaps later, when they got above this crap, he would be able to see some stars. . . .

For now, though, safety lay in flying low. Somewhere down there in that darkness, he knew, was Albania . . . yet another tiny Balkan nation with a bitterly unhappy past.

Under the tyrant Enver Hoxha, the tiny country—only about the size of Maryland—had closed itself off from the rest of the world, a small and bankrupt hermit kingdom in some ways more paranoid about contamination from without than North Korea. A hard-line Stalinist, Hoxha had ended relations with the Soviet Union in 1960 when

Khrushchev had demanded a naval base at Vlorë. His close relationship with Mao's China had ended in 1978, as China drifted toward liberalization. With Hoxha's death in 1985, however, rule had passed to Ramiz Alia, who slowly had begun to open the country to the West, privatizing industry and carrying out economic reforms. It was possible that Albania's long, self-imposed exile was nearly over.

In the meantime, Operation Alexander was taking direct and highly illegal advantage of the near-primitive state of Albania's military, especially their radar and tracking networks. Despite the rhetoric of Hoxha's ultra-Communists, the vast majority of the tiny country remained undeveloped. It had exactly one city of any real size—its capital, Tiranë—and one seaport, Durrës. Most of the land was mountainous and covered with pine forests, while twenty percent of the country's land area was coastal plain, swamp-ridden, and infested with malarial mosquitos. The Albanian military consisted of a 40,000-man force of regulars, with another 155,000 in the reserves, but that included just one tank brigade and eleven infantry brigades. Their air force was equipped with old J-6s and J-7s, purchased years ago from the Chinese, and they had only three squadrons of those, a total of about thirty fighters. Murdock had read once that Hoxha's idea of defending his country against invasion—or against contamination by foreign ideas, which for him amounted to much the same thing—was to build thousands of small, round pillboxes along his nation's borders with Greece and what was then Yugoslavia, and along the seacoast all the way from Konispol to the Buna River. Murdock had heard that the thirty-seven-kilometer highway from Durrës inland to Tiranë was lined with hundreds of bunkers that looked exactly like whitewashed igloos with gun slits.

Stone igloos, however, were no match for an invasion by the technological magic of late-twentieth-century America. The first invaders had been purely electronic, powerful jamming transmissions directed at coastal and inland radar installations by EA-6B Prowler electronic-warfare aircraft flying off the *Jefferson*. Soon, the invaders took on a more tangible substance, racing in from the sea, going feet-dry less than five hundred feet above the salt marshes behind the Karavastasë Lagoon.

They flew in tight groups of four aircraft, three F-14 Tomcats protecting each Prowler, and as they penetrated Albanian airspace, they spread a blizzard of fierce electronic snow that jammed every radar from the airport at Tiranë south to Berat. Albanian radar operators, both military and civilian, were used to near-constant breakdowns in an economy where new equipment was impossible to come by, and most simply logged the interference and ignored it. A few alerted superiors; a few of them actually wondered about the widespread breakdown. According to reports transmitted from circling Hawkeye early-warning radar planes, several flights of Chinese-made fighters were scrambled.

None of them found a thing.

Traveling at just below the speed of sound, the U.S. aircraft flew up the valley of the Devoll, across land that was empty for the most part of anything but mountains and pine forests. Behind them, traveling more slowly but still sheltered within their pattern of electronic jamming, came the night-black MC-130. North of the town of Gramsh, just before the mountains reared ahead into the twin peaks of Mali Shpat and Guri i Zi, the Combat Talon began climbing, lifting up off the deck and grabbing for altitude.

The optimum height for HAHO operations was 30,000 feet.

"Ten minutes, Lieutenant!" the jumpmaster yelled back at Murdock. "Met report's still clear. Report for the target is low overcast, wind from the northwest at five. We have a go from Olympus."

Murdock nodded, then signaled to his men. "Stand up! Equipment check!"

Each man went over his own equipment, and then, when he was through checked the gear of the man beside him, looking for loose straps or releases, checking pack bodies, watching for Irish pennants—hanging lengths of tie-off cords—or improperly positioned gear. Murdock and DeWitt then personally went from man to man, giving each a final, all-over inspection.

They said little. With the Combat Talon now climbing to drop altitude, the men had all switched to bottled oxygen from their bailout bottles; their faces were completely encased in breathing masks and helmet visors that gave them the look of fighter jocks.

Fighter pilots never flew as burdened as these SEALs, however. Each man wore both his main parachute and his reserve on his back, with a bundle consisting of his rucksack, an inflatable raft, and his secondary equipment load in front, secured between his waist and his knees by a quick-release harness. His bailout bottle, the size of a small fire extinguisher, was strapped to his left side; behind that, secured to the side of his chute pack and to his leg, was his main weapon. For most of them, this was either an M-16 or an H&K MP5SD3. Mac and Bearcat, however, were both carrying hogs—M-60E3 Maremont GPMGs—while Magic Brown sported a Remington Model 200 sniper's rifle and Doc and Rattler both were lugging H&K CAW automatic shotguns. Four of the men carried M203 40mm grenade launchers attached to their M-16s.

Besides all of this bulky gear, each man carried numerous smaller packages and parcels—a HAHO compass on his left wrist; a digital altimeter on his chest above his ruck; a tactical radio; a secondary weapon—for most a 9mm Beretta pistol with an extended magazine; an inflatable life vest; an Eagle Industries Tac III assault vest with pockets bulging with extra magazines, chemical light sticks, first-aid kit, and hand grenades; rappelling gear and line; night-observation gear; knife; all of this worn over black nomex coveralls and heavy gloves. The temperature outside was something like thirty below, and frostbite of unprotected skin was a serious danger.

Besides the gear every man carried for himself, there was special equipment divided up among the team, mostly extra ammunition for the 60-guns, but including Higgins's HST sat-comm and KY-57 encryption gear, and batteries. Sixty pounds was the recommended equipment load for a combat jump, but each SEAL on the Combat Talon was packing at least one hundred.

Murdock went to each man, gave his load a tug or a pat to make sure it was secure, and tried to think of something light or encouraging to say. He didn't care for pep talks, and he knew his men didn't either. Still, it helped if they knew he cared.

"Doc," he said, shaking his head in mock despair. "What the hell is a noncombatant doing with a damned shotgun?"

It was an old joke. Theoretically, hospital corpsmen didn't fight and didn't carry weapons, but no SEAL was a noncombatant, no matter what his rating had been before he'd volunteered for BUD/S.

Doc grinned behind his mask and shrugged—a difficult maneuver under all that gear. "What the hell, L-T," he said. "Doc Holliday packed a shotgun, so I reckon I will too."

Murdock moved to Stepano, standing next in line. "You okay, son?" was all he could think of to say.

"I am fine, Lieutenant," the Serb said. "Do not worry about me. Kick ass and take names!"

"That's the spirit, Steponit," Roselli called. "We're gonna hop and pop tonight!"

They were ready.

"Okay, people," Murdock said, shouting so that all of them could hear. "The weight's going. to be the critical factor. Remember, if. any of you pop your canopy and find yourself descending at more than eight meters per second, reach down and jettison your secondary gear. Just let it go. I'd rather do without the equipment than have to do without the man. You read me?"

"Loud and clear!" "Roger that!" "Affirmative, L-T!" the voices chorused back.

"DeWitt and I both have strobes. Watch for them when you're going in and guide on us. If you don't see us, for whatever reason, aim for the midpoint of the lake, right opposite the castle if you can manage it, then make for the beach below it. If you end up too far north or south, or if, God help you, you overshoot and touch down on the mountain somewhere, get down the best you can and rally at the castle. If you undershoot, well, I sure hope you've brushed up on your Albanian." When their laughing stopped, he added, "You might try *'Me falni,'* which I'm told means, 'I am very sorry I fell out of the sky and killed your cow.'"

"Ha!" Papagos shouted over the laughter. "And what if we land on the guy's daughter?"

"Well, you could also try, *'Une jam student,'* which means 'I am an innocent student traveling in your beautiful country.' Who knows? Maybe they'll believe you. If not, try to make it to the castle. If you can't, sit tight and put out your Mayday call. Somebody will be along to pick you up sooner or later."

"Right," Doc said. "Probably to make you pay for that cow."

"Or marry the daughter," Roselli added.

Humor, even the often obscene or grim gallows humor favored by SEALs, was a good measure of the men's spirits. Murdock noticed that neither Mac nor Kos joined in, but that was to be expected. They were older, and made steadier by their authority as the platoon's two senior NCOs. Stepano hadn't laughed either, though he'd smiled at the part about killing a cow.

"Two minutes!" the jumpmaster called to them. "Skipper says your approach vector will be zero-five-zero, range to target fifteen miles."

"Zero-five-zero, and fifteen miles. Affirmative. Everybody got that?" Helmeted heads nodded, gloved hands gave thumbs-up signs or clenched fists meaning *got it.*

"Okay!" the jumpmaster shouted. "We're opening up! Clear the aft compartment!"

With an ominous, grinding noise, the rear deck of the transport began dropping away, a hatch opening into the blackness of space. From where he was standing, Murdock could see that the waning moon had not yet risen, but there was sky-glow enough to illuminate the clouds far, far below.

It reminded Murdock piercingly of a snowfield, perhaps a scene on a Christmas card he'd received once. It was noisier now, both from the thunder of the Combat Talon's engines and from the roar of the wind rushing past the gape-mouthed opening.

Murdock checked his altimeter—32,800 feet—high to allow both for the altitude of the lake, and for the fact that since they were higher to compensate for the target's altitude, they would be falling through slightly thinner air.

The jumpmaster gave a signal. "Ten seconds! Get ready! Good luck, you guys! And good hunting!"

"HAHO! HAHO!" Doc sang. "It's off to work we go!"

The seconds passed . . . a light on the bulkhead winked green.

"Go! Go! Go!"

This was no one-at-a-time airborne leap like the static-line jumps of World War II. The entire platoon rushed down the broad ramp in two close-arrayed squads, each flinging itself as a single organism headlong into the night, then breaking up as its members spread arms and legs and snagged the currents of the sky. Murdock was last off the ramp, hurling himself headfirst into the darkness after his men. Wind battered and tugged at him, snapping at the sleeves and legs of his coveralls and at the equipment secured to his vest, threatening to yank him out of position and send him into a sprawling tumble, but he held himself poised against the storm, arms swept back, legs bent at the knees, back arched. The glorious, buoyant, flying sensation of free fall thrilled within, like a favorite piece of martial music . . . no . . . like Wagner's "Ride of the Valkyries."

For a HAHO jump, free fall lasted only eight or ten seconds, just enough time to clear the aircraft and to get clear of the other jumpers. Murdock watched the luminous flick of the seconds on his watch, then yanked the ripcord on his primary. A drogue popped free, fluttering behind him, steadying his fall . . . and then his chute unfolded after it, deploying slowly at first, then snagging the wind with a crack like thunder, the harness snapping at Murdock's thighs and chest and shoulders, yanking him upright, yanking him so hard it felt as though he'd just reversed course and was on his way back to the Combat Talon.

Silence. After the roar of the wind passed his helmet, the silence was shocking in its intensity, its completeness. Murdock dangled beneath the rectangular wing shape of his ram-air chute, suspended between a crystalline, star-powdered heaven and the faintly luminous clouds below.

HAHO—High Altitude, High Opening—as opposed to the more usual HALO—High Altitude, Low Opening. With HALO, a SEAL could leap from an aircraft at 30,000 feet, too high for anyone on the ground to hear the plane's engines, then ride thin air in free fall all the way to 2500 feet or less—about a two-minute trip, express only, no waiting. The chute jerked you up short within spitting distance of the ground and let you glide in the last few feet in death-dealing silence.

With HAHO it was different. His steerable chute let him extend the jump with a very favorable glide ratio, literally flying like a tiny, unpowered aircraft for as much as fifteen miles cross-country, a flight that would typically take seventy-five minutes . . . definitely life in the slow lane. His coveralls and much of his equipment were radar-absorbent, and the chute would reveal only a tiny cross section to watching enemy radar. They should be able to fly silently right across the border, and on this mission the decision to violate Albanian airspace provided a bonus. The planners back aboard *Jefferson* had thought it most unlikely that the enemy would be expecting an airborne assault from the direction of Albania. *Nobody* paid attention to Albania, especially these days with its increasingly nonexistent military. Likeliest would be an airmobile assault by helicopter coming out of the southeast, mountain-hopping across the rugged, forested border with Greece. Most of the enemy's attention, Murdock was willing to bet, would be focused in that direction, not to the west.

And he was betting on that . . . with the lives of

himself, his men, and the hostages they'd come to rescue as the stakes.

Course . . . course . . . Checking his compass, he determined that zero-five-zero was *that* way, about eighteen degrees to the left. Reaching up above his head, he grasped his steering toggles and lightly tugged downward on the left-hand control, watching the point on the horizon he'd picked swing around until it was directly ahead. To extend the range of a HAHO jump for as long and as far as possible, the rush of air across his chute had to flow unhindered between its two panels. That meant he had to leave the toggles in the extreme up position for as much of the trip as possible; each maneuver, left or right, cost him precious altitude. Stabilized, he seemed to be descending at about six meters per second, not bad at all considering how much gear he was carrying. Some of the others—the Professor and Mac and Bearcat—were packing much heavier loads. He hoped they didn't have to jettison.

It was astonishing, now that his free-fall flight was ended and he was drifting to earth, how alone he felt. The Combat Talon was gone, already lost in the night. Looking around, he thought he could make out several other chutes . . . though most of the fourteen other men were invisible, jet-black canopies against the blackness of the night. Looking up, he might, if he were lucky, catch one of his men when he occulted a star. Below, the cloud glow was so faint he would have to be pretty close to see a chute silhouetted against it. He wished he could talk to them, and they to him. Radio communication was possible, certainly, and the encryption gear would guard their words from eavesdroppers. But radio silence was the order of the day. Even encrypted, radio chatter might tell listeners that something was happening. They would save the radios until the fun began at the target.

An hour later, arms cramping from their grip on the control toggles, back aching with the dead weight of his rucksack dragging at his harness, he approached the clouds, which were rushing up toward him like a vast, fuzzy cotton floor. The cloud deck flashed past the bottoms of his boots, an indicator of just how quickly he was moving. The clouds were so thick, he almost expected to feel them drag at his legs as he sank into them, but there was nothing except a sudden close blackness that wiped away the stars and coated his visor with droplets of water that turned almost immediately to ice.

Damn! He couldn't see a thing . . . not even the altimeter on his chest. Releasing his riser, he scraped at his visor with his gloved hand, but there was ice on the glove too, and all he managed to do was smear the mess around. Finally, he reached up and unlocked the visor, sliding it up on his helmet. Blinking against the rush of cold, wet air, he checked his altimeter.

Sixteen hundred eighty-two meters . . . but that was set to register off sea level. Lake Ohrid was at an altitude of 695 meters, so he should be nine hundred eighty and some meters up—just over three thousand feet. Though his fall had slowed somewhat as he'd descended through increasingly denser air, he was still only about two minutes from touchdown.

Vision returned with startling suddenness as he punched out through the bottom of the clouds. Until that moment, he'd had no way at all of knowing whether he was steering a proper course, short of the rather abstract knowledge that he'd been steering the course given him before he'd left the aircraft, falling at a constant rate, across a known range.

"Damned if geometry doesn't work," he said aloud as the panorama swam into view below him. The scene was cloaked in darkness, of course, but that yawning, black emptiness below was water, and the lights of the castle were dancing off the surface eight kilometers—call it five miles—ahead. North, he could see the town of Ohrid, and beyond that, the lights of what must be the local airport. South were the lights of other towns, their glow outlining the vast, oval blackness of the lake. He'd fallen almost six miles across a distance of fifteen, with a lake seven miles wide and fifteen long as his target. With over one hundred square miles of water to land in, he was coming down almost perfectly on target, almost precisely in the middle of the lake.

Twisting in his harness, he searched for other SEALs but saw no one . . . not surprising given the night, their garb, and the fact that they were bound to have scattered a bit during the descent. Reaching up to his shoulder, he snapped on his strobe. The IR hood had been removed. While it was possible that someone ashore might see the pulsing flash of the light, the chances were slim across a distance of more than a mile or two, and in any case, an observer might well assume that he was watching a plane. Murdock looked left and right again. . . . *There!* A flashing red light, and not very far off either, though range was next to impossible to estimate at night. DeWitt was flying parallel to Murdock to the north and just a little below. Gently, Murdock dropped his left toggle slightly, easing his chute into a converging course with the other.

Now, please God, everybody else made it through, and everybody else can see our beacons. Murdock began to concentrate on his landing.

He checked his altimeter again. One hundred ten meters to go. He thought he could see the surface of the water now, sweeping past his feet at an alarming speed. Reaching down, he unsnapped his rucksack and secondary equipment bundles, then let them go. The shock of their release rocked him alarmingly, setting up a nasty oscillation, but he kept control and paid out the rest of the line, allowing his gear to dangle some twelve feet beneath his feet. Next he turned the quick release box to the unlocked position, pulled the safety pin, then opened the safety covers on his Capewell releases.

Closer now . . . and closer. The water was rushing toward him now, and he could see just how fast he was descending. Ten meters up he pulled down on both steering toggles, curling down the upper rear edge of his canopy like a gigantic set of flaps. The change in aerodynamics brought the front of the chute high, and for a moment, Murdock hung there in the sky, seeking the balance between a gentle landing . . . and spilling too much air too soon, which would plunge him hard into the lake.

Forward speed arrested, he dropped toward the lake. His equipment bundle struck with a splash, and then the strap holding it gave him a savage tug. The last of his forward velocity was killed by the drag of his rucksack in the water. The surface rushed up, his feet kicked up spray. . . .

17

At the last possible moment, Murdock squeezed the left-hand Capewell release and yanked down. The chute snapped free on that side, billowing up and spilling its remaining air. Murdock plunged into the water with a splash, bitterly cold, black water enveloping him as his rate of descent drove him down . . . down . . . still further down into the depths. The force of the landing tore the oxygen mask from his face. *God,* the water was cold. Despite his multiple layers, the water of that mountain lake was frigid.

Then his equipment strap yanked at his harness, this time from above and behind, threatening to turn him head-down. The pack included an inflatable rubber raft, a small one, just big enough to support one man and his equipment, and it had begun to inflate as soon as it hit the water. Still descending, Murdock twisted sideways in the water, and the strap was entangling him. Reaching behind his back, he found the gear release and squeezed it; with the jerk, the ruck broke loose, the strap trailing free in the water. His oxygen mask . . . where was his mask? Was it still attached? He fumbled with the right-side Capewell, trying to

215

release the chute entirely. What he didn't need at the moment was to become entangled underwater in its shrouds. There! He was clear!

A pull ring at his waist inflated the rubber flotation jacket he wore over his combat harness. He estimated, from the pressure on his sinuses and ears, that he must have descended a good forty or fifty feet down before he finally started to rise again. Holding his breath despite the pounding in his chest, the growing, squeezing sensation in his ribs, Murdock kicked toward the surface, kicking . . . kicking . . . and then he broke through into blessed, cold air.

Even without his rucksack, Murdock was still heavily weighted down. His MP5 weighed two and a half kilos with a loaded magazine; he had lots more magazines tucked into pockets in his assault vest, not to mention radio, grenades, and at least five kilos more of sundry equipment. Even with the life jacket, each moment, each second brought him closer to being dragged under and drowned.

One of the first ordeals undergone by recruits at BUD/S training at Coronado involves dropping them into a nine-foot-deep tank of water with their hands and feet tied, requiring them to sink to the bottom, then push themselves off and back to the surface. After that, they learn tricks . . . like donning a face mask, or swimming the entire fifty-meter length of the pool, hands tied. The process is called "drown-proofing," and it is designed to strip recruits of the panic reflex that is the usual cause of drowning.

Despite the weight, Murdock stayed at the surface, kicking hard and moving his arms, treading water until he spotted his flotation pack a few yards away. Moments later, he was lying across the raft, savoring air and the lack of any need to move.

As he lay there, bobbing low in the water, he heard someone splutter and gasp for breath, not far to his left. Gently, he began kicking, propelling his ungainly life preserver toward the sound. Softly, he called out the password: "Shadow."

"Bucephalus."

It was Nicholson—Torpedoman's Mate Second Class Eric "Red" Nicholson, of Gold Squad. "You okay?"

"Yeah. Swallowed a little water." He was shivering. "Damn, we were loaded a bit heavy that time, weren't we?"

"We've done worse."

The difference was that training was always different from the real thing. There were no instructors standing by, ready to share the mouthpiece from their scuba tanks, no divers ready to go in and pull you out if you found yourself facing something you could not handle. Even on a mission, SEALs generally tried to stage a "dip test," dropping into a water tank with their full equipment loadout as a buoyancy test. There'd been neither time nor facilities for that luxury this time around. They'd just been lucky that the waters of the lake were as calm as they were.

Working quickly, Nicholson and Murdock strapped their flotation packs together, then got rid of all excess weight. They gathered in their parachutes, bundled them with their reserve chutes and harnesses, and let them sink. Their bailout bottles and masks—Murdock found his mask had snagged somehow beneath his reserve chute pack—went too, sinking into nine hundred feet of water. They freed their weapons, balancing them atop the float packs. After that, they drifted motionless for a time, huddling together for warmth, with Murdock continuing to show his flashing beacon, but turned so that it could not be seen from shore. After five minutes, two other SEALs—Frazier and Sterling— paddled up, giving the recognition sign. After another five minutes, no one else had shown up. By this time the whole team ought to be down, and hypothermia in the cold water was becoming a serious concern.

Side by side, the four SEALs began kicking their raft of inflated nylon bundles toward the shore.

0035 hours
Gorazamak
Lake Ohrid

General Mihajlovic had not been able to sleep.

He liked Gorazamak, liked this mountain lake with its

clear air and rugged, beautiful terrain. Years ago, he'd come here as a tourist. He and Katrina, his young wife, had stayed at the Mladinski Center, up in Ohrid, and the two of them had done some marvelous hiking in the federal park that enclosed most of the mountains and forest to the east.

That had been in 1979 . . . or 1980? No, it had been the year before Tito had died, the year before the federation of republics that Tito had forged from the blood and agony of war had begun to unravel.

So much had changed in just fifteen years. A whole new world had come into being. And an old one had died.

He walked the stone parapets of the inner ward, a solitary watchtower overlooking the black waters of the lake. Blood and agony had returned to the Federation, despite the best efforts of Tito and everyone after him. *Katrina* . . .

In 1987, Slobodan Milosevic had become the leader of the Communist Party in Serbia, still a position of tremendous power despite the toppling of Communist regimes that had eventually reached even into the Kremlin. His public vision of a "Greater Serbia" had proven to be the trigger that had driven the two restive northern republics of the federation, Slovenia and Croatia, to elect non-Communist governments three years later, and to declare their independence. Within a year of that, Bosnia-Hercegovina and Macedonia had broken away as well. The Albanian population of Kosovo was restless, as always, and Bulgaria was again casting covetous eyes on Macedonia. The situation had been deteriorating faster than even the most gloomy of pessimists in Belgrade could have imagined.

Then, early in 1991, Serbian nationalists had staged demonstrations that verged on riots in several Croatian towns. They'd been deliberately incited by Milosevic's people, of course, with the aim of provoking either a pro-Serb military coup in Zagreb, or the implementation of martial law. When that failed, Serbia's state-controlled radio and TV stations had broadcast reports, all completely fabricated, that ethnic Serbians living in Croatia were being massacred, a prelude to reintroducing federal rule in the breakaway republic.

The plot had been badly mishandled. Those responsible had forgotten that many Serbs living in Serbia opposed the state as much as Croats living in Zagreb . . . and worse, that there were other forms of communication available besides the official news media, forms not under the state's control. The truth had gotten out, the clumsy lie had been revealed. A pro-democratic mob had besieged the TV studios in Belgrade, demanding that those at the station responsible for this blatant attempt to manipulate public opinion be fired. Milosevic had panicked and ordered the police to disperse the crowd. Hundreds had been arrested, and hundreds more badly beaten.

According to the official reports, only two had died in the riot that day, shot down outside the television studios when the police opened fire on the demonstrators. The actual number of fatalities, counting the casualties in Belgrade's back streets and those who had died in the SBD's interrogation chambers, had been higher than that. How much higher would probably never be known.

Damn it, Katrina hadn't even been involved! The shot that had struck her down hadn't even been aimed at her. She'd been sitting at a table in an outdoor cafe on Skadarska Street, and a stray bullet fired somewhere else in the city had found her, a senseless, random twist to the violence that flamed everywhere in Yugoslavia now, either openly, as in Bosnia, or quietly smoldering just beneath the surface.

Mihajlovic was determined to end that violence, one way or another. Milosevic was an idiot, pompous, strutting, narrow-minded, conscious only of his own power, alternately defying NATO and the West, then caving in to their demands. Yugoslavia needed a *strong* leader, one who had the full support of the Federation's 180,000-man, 2,000-tank army.

Someone like General Vuk Mihajlovic.

He walked to the parapets of Gorazamak, wondering how quickly he should advance things. The extra troops he'd

requested had arrived that morning. There was little more to
be done here. The annoying thing was that there still was no
word from Skopje. The Americans should have launched
their assault of the airport by now. Their Delta Force was
notorious for its speed of deployment, reaching anywhere in
the world within a couple of days at the most. What was
keeping them?

Perhaps what was needed was a higher level of visibility.
And of urgency. He could have one of the hostages at
Skopje shot. *That* would elicit a response. If necessary, the
congresswoman and some of her aides could be paraded in
front of the cameras. The thing could be staged so that it
looked like Skopje.

A white flash caught Mihajlovic's eye . . . a splash, he
thought, in the water almost directly below the castle. Lake
Ohrid was known all over Europe for the size of its trout.
That had been a big one.

When this was all over, it would be good to return here
for some fishing. If he could just put those memories to rest.

The interior of the ward was brightly lit, but up here on
the ramparts it was dark. A barely discernible shadow
stepped around the corner of an inner wall, blocking his
way.

"Halt!" a voice called out. "Who goes there?"

"Brigade General Mihajlovic."

"Advance and be recognized!"

Mihajlovic took the manual-prescribed two steps forward
and stopped. By the light from below, he could make out
the sentry's face now, a very young corporal from C
Company. He was wearing the somewhat shabby uniform of
a typical Macedonian militiaman, but his Automat M70A—a
Yugoslav-manufactured, folding-stock version of the ubiqui-
tous AK-47—was in gleaming, parade-perfect condition.

"Sir!" The man snapped to attention, the rifle flicking
from port arms to present arms with drill-book precision. "I
recognize you, sir!"

"Good evening, Corporal. At ease, at ease. I'm just out
for some fresh air."

"Yes, my General," the sentry said, relaxing only slightly.

"So. Quiet night?"

"Very quiet, sir." The sentry relaxed a bit more, enough to nod toward the lake. "I did see some lights out there . . . or I thought I did. They were too far away, though, for me to tell what they were, and they disappeared a few minutes later. I reported them and was told they were probably Albanian aircraft."

"No doubt. No doubt." Mihajlovic took the powerful 7x40 binoculars slung around his neck and raised them to his eyes, scanning the horizon slowly. There was little to see along the opposite shore of the lake now, with fewer lights than there were to the north and south. That patch of starlike lights almost directly opposite from the castle would be the Albanian village of Lin, just behind their border crossing at Cafasan. There was nothing else for the whole length of the lake until the village of Pogradec, twenty kilometers to the south, or the cluster of lights at Struga at the northern end of the lake.

After a moment, he lowered the binoculars, leaned against the cold, damp stone of the parapet, and helped himself to a Turkish cigarette. He did not offer the soldier one, of course. Too much familiarity between the officers and the men was not good for discipline.

"I see nothing now. Was it an aircraft, do you think? Or a boat?"

"I'm sorry, my General, but it was impossible even to tell that. I assumed that it was a low-flying aircraft. It was moving so slowly, it seemed very far away."

"Ah. Still, we've had some strange reports tonight from Ohrid Traffic Control," Mihajlovic said. He took a drag on the cigarette, and the tip flared a brilliant orange. "*Something's* going on over there. Radar jamming. Aircraft being scrambled. Lots of radio traffic between their military bases and Tiranë. It is possible that you saw one of their aircraft moving against the mountains. Or a small boat patrolling their end of the lake."

"Could it have anything to do with us, General?"

"I very much doubt it." He laughed. "Most likely their radar net is down again and Tiranë is getting panicky. But keep a sharp lookout nonetheless. Those people have no reason to love us and cannot be trusted. There is Kosovo, remember."

"Yes, my General." The man stiffened again to attention, boot heels clicking.

Kosovo, Mihajlovic reflected, was another of the Federation's restive republics, this one tucked in between Montenegro and Serbia in the north and Macedonia and northeastern Albania to the south. The cradle of Serbian civilization in the Middle Ages, and the center of their empire, Kosovo had later belonged to Albania, and today over eighty percent of its population was ethnic Albanian. In a region known for the long and bitter memories of its varied peoples, Kosovo was a festering wound that would cause more bloodshed one day.

All the more reason to reunite the Federation now under a strong and able hand.

"Carry on!"

"Yes, my General!"

It is for you, my Katrina, he thought, turning and walking away. *We* will *have an end to the killing. It is just too bad that there must be more killing before we—and you—can find peace.*

0035 hours
Over Gorazamak
Lake Ohrid

Doc pulled down his right steering toggle slightly, easing into a right-hand turn. Damn! The castle was reaching up for him right off the mountain, like it was trying to claw him from the sky.

Man, he must have overshot the DZ by a good five miles. It was these damned chutes, configured a bit larger than standard in order to support the heavier-than-usual weight carried by the SEAL jumpers. Once he'd lost his gear, there'd been no way to compensate for the greater lift.

He'd known he was in trouble right out of the aircraft, when he'd yanked his rip cord and, instead of a satisfying crack-and-snap hauling him upright, there'd been a sickening flutter and the heart-stopping rush of a too-fast descent, spiraling dizzily toward the right. Looking up, he'd not been able to see the canopy well enough in the darkness to know what had gone wrong; the chute had opened at least partly, or he'd still be in free fall.

The danger was that his canopy might have either twisted about its middle, a condition called the "Mae West" because of the chute's resemblance to a huge brassiere, or curled up on one side or the other in what was known as a "cigarette roll." In either case, the recommended procedure was for the jumper to immediately activate the reserve chute.

But the reserve was smaller than the main and not designed for extended HAHO flight. It would never take him as far as Lake Ohrid, and Doc had no desire to sample the inside of an Albanian jail. He decided to buy some time by jettisoning his ruck early. He had lots of time—hell, it would take him a couple of minutes to fall thirty thousand feet even without a half-open canopy. He was dropping at about twenty meters per second . . . that gave him better than eight minutes. *Plenty* of time.

As soon as he'd unstrapped the ruck from his legs, then hit the emergency release, his fall had slowed dramatically. Working at the toggles, he could feel the chute responding now to his guidance, and when he unsheathed the flashlight from his vest pocket and turned it on the canopy, everything looked all right, at least so far as he could see. Possibly one side of his chute had rolled under, but the shock of dropping the gear had freed it.

The problem was that his angle of approach had been calculated on his weight plus the better than one hundred pounds he'd been carrying. Without the ruck he was seventy-some pounds lighter, and dropping along a corresponding shallower descent path. Unfortunately, he had nothing to go on for navigation except for his compass, and that only showed direction, not how far he'd traveled. When

he finally dropped beneath the overcast, he saw that he'd
overshot the DZ by quite a bit; he was still over the lake, but
not by much . . . and that damned castle looked like it was
going to do its best to take him out.

He had too much forward speed to simply dump air and
drop. What he needed to do was pull a 180 before he
crashed into the castle walls or into the mountain beyond,
and get back where he belonged, out over the lake. And that
was going to take some doing . . . especially if his chute
had suffered any damage earlier.

He was across the beach now. *Shit!* There was a warm
updraft coming off the land. It felt as if he were actually
rising. Pulling harder on the toggle, he started to slip to the
left. Too late. He was going to hit. . . .

No . . . he was going to pass right over the damned
place! He felt awkward, as though he had no control at all.
It was damned frustrating, too. The castle was laid out
below him exactly the way it had looked in those satellite
photos, with a smaller, inner tower rising from the rear of a
roughly oval walled court. With a properly working chute,
he could have dropped in anywhere he pleased, touching
down right atop one of those stone parapets if he'd wanted.
Ram-air chutes gave a jumper unprecedented control and
accuracy whenever everything went right.

But of course, in combat things never went right, not one
hundred percent anyway, and that was why an op this
complex was using the middle of the lake as a DZ, instead
of down there inside the castle keep.

The scenery from up here was nothing less than magnifi-
cent, a literal bird's-eye view. Doc had read recently that the
Albanians' name for their own country was Shqiperia,
"the land of Eagles," and that the Albanians were Shqiptars,
"the Eagle Men." *Eagle Men, my ass,* he thought, a little
wildly under the surge of adrenaline coursing through his
system. *They ain't got nothing on me!*

As silently as a huge, gliding eagle, Doc swept over
Gorazamak's outer walls, still turning to the left, still high
enough that he was able to look down inside the enclosures.

He could see men down there easily . . . a sentry by the front gate, two more men standing together on one of the highest of the inner parapets. Those two were almost lost in the darkness above the light-bathed courtyard below, but Doc caught the flare of a lit cigarette. He was still above the highest of the walls, though considerably below an array of UHF antennas and communications masts on the roof. If he tangled up in those . . .

But then he was safely past, still slipping left, sliding clear of the loom of the fortress. Now his only worry was slamming into the side of the mountain . . . or landing in the damned trees.

The mountain bulked above the castle's rocky perch like a solid wall, some of it sheer stone cliffs like the heights below the fortress, most steep and rugged but not impassable, blanketed in thick forest growth. There was lots of snow on the ground, more than there'd been in Bosnia. It reflected light enough from the castle that Doc could easily see the branches reaching up for him, just below his boots.

During the fighting against Communist guerrillas in Malaysia in the early 1950s, the British SAS had developed a new type of parachute insertion, one tailored for the thick forest and jungle of the Malay Peninsula, called "tree jumping." The idea was to deliberately land in the woods, with your chute snagging you far up at the top of the tree canopy, where you could use a long length of line to lower yourself to the forest floor.

The idea hadn't worked out well, and the practice had soon been stopped. Too many troopers had impaled various parts of their anatomy. Doc had a superb imagination . . . not to mention a thorough medical understanding of just what could happen to a man landing in the treetops. He kept pulling down on the left-hand toggle. Could he tighten his turn . . . pull it back over the lake? . . .

No way. He was heading south now, half a mile or more clear of the castle but dropping so fast with his turning maneuver that he didn't have a prayer of reaching the water. Quickly, he assumed the emergency tree-landing position—

legs tight together to protect his crotch; left arm over his eyes, left hand in his right armpit, palm out; right arm over left arm, with right hand in the left armpit, palm out; head cocked to the left to protect his face and throat. . . .

He felt something brush along his left leg, snag at the shotgun strapped to his side . . . and then he was crashing down through branches in a series of jerks and jolts. Pain arced through his right leg like an electric shock. *Shit!* Then his canopy snagged hard and yanked him to a halt; a second later, his back slammed into the tree's trunk with a thump that left him stunned.

Doc held his tree-landing position until he'd stopped falling, then slowly relaxed. After the racket of his landing, it was almost blissfully quiet, except for the barking of a dog somewhere not too far off. The ground, he estimated, was thirty feet down. His right ankle was throbbing, whether broken or sprained, he couldn't tell yet. "The Eagle," he muttered softly to himself, "has landed. Almost."

And he didn't even have the climbing rope carried by those old SAS tree jumpers. There'd been line in his rucksack, but that was lying on a hillside somewhere in Albania right now, along with a flotation device, most of his shotgun ammo, and five hundred rounds of 7.62mm ammo for the 60-guns.

Shit, shit, shit, he thought, swaying slightly, then bumping again into the tree's trunk. *Now what?*

0038 hours
Lake Ohrid
Southwestern Macedonia
(Former Yugoslav Republic)
When they estimated they were a mile from the beach, they'd stopped, according to plan, waiting for another ten minutes. Though they were no longer showing beacons, which might have been visible from the castle at this range, the rallying point was well-enough defined by the lights from the castle that three more men were able to find them—Holt, Roselli, and Brown.

They swam the rest of the way in slowly, taking care not to break the surface with a carelessly kicking foot. They were almost certainly invisible from Gorazamak . . . but if they weren't, they would be no more suspicious than a mat of black, floating vegetation.

They didn't come ashore on the beach. There was too great a chance that they'd be observed from the walls above, even the possibility that it would be patrolled. Instead, the seven men aimed for the rocks south of the beach. The bottom came up swiftly to meet them there. Soon, their boots scraped against rocks, mud, and weed, and they crawled the last few yards on hands and knees through a thick wall of reeds, still shoving the raft before them.

"Shadow!" a voice called softly from the rocks, a welcome challenge.

"Bucephalus."

DeWitt and six more SEALs were already waiting for them at the rally point. Gold Squad's CO had splashed down closer to the shore than Murdock had, and some of the others—Mac, for instance—had come down just short of the shore. Only one SEAL was missing now, Doc Ellsworth, and he might be arriving at any moment.

The SEALs had just utilized two of their elements for their insertion, air and water. Quietly now, they began preparing to take on the land as well.

18

0104 hours
Below Gorazamak
Lake Ohrid, Macedonia
All of the SEALs had studied both maps and satellite
photographs of the stretch of lake shore directly beneath the
castle, knew it well enough to—literally in this case—find
the place in the dark. While the rest of the SEALs began
unpacking their assault gear, Roselli and Sterling pulled the
protective tape off their H&Ks, cleaned the weapons, and
snapped in thirty-round magazines. They broke two sets of
NVDs out of their waterproof cases, left all of their extra
ammo and gear with the rest of the team, and slipped off
into the darkness, moving uphill.

Now, twenty minutes later, they lay among the rocks on
the east side of the coast road, using their night-vision gear
to peer down on four soldiers standing guard at the entrance
to the approach road north of the castle. The soldiers,
completely unaware of the black-garbed commandos watching them from the blackness overhead, were not particularly
alert. One was pacing back and forth at the entrance to the
main road, nervously looking up and down the highway as
though he expected an assault to come from the north or the
south, rather than from across the lake. The other three
seemed to be ignoring the first, sitting and talking, smoking

pungent cigarettes and drinking something that was almost certainly not coffee from a couple of thermos bottles stashed in a rucksack.

Roselli wished that Stepano was with him to translate their conversation. Steponit, however, was on another reconnaissance, along with Red, Scotty, and the 21C. The two SEALs listened long enough to satisfy themselves that the sentries here were running on routine, that there was no alert out, no indication that the SEAL platoon's arrival had been detected. The nervous guy by the road was a kid, a teenager, and had the look of a new recruit taking his duties very seriously indeed. The other three, probably seasoned campaigners, were passing around a thermos and telling one another stories. From the gestures one was making with his hands and the laughs and declamations being made by the others, the subject was the favorite topic of all soldiers and sailors on duty late at night with no superiors listening in.

Soldiers' bull sessions, Roselli thought, were probably universal, the same no matter what the language or the nationality.

Quietly, he laid a hand on Sterling's arm and squeezed. Like shadows, the SEALs backed away from their observation nest above the storytellers.

It was time to get back to the others.

During their sweep of the area, Roselli and Sterling had managed to verify by Mark I eyeball much of the data already acquired through satellite photos. Spy satellites were incredible reconnaissance tools, allowing you to see fantastic detail from a hundred miles up. Many in the Pentagon and in the U.S. intelligence community swore by the high-tech voyeurs, claiming that the age of HUMINT, of intelligence acquired by human agents on the ground, was all but dead.

Few SEALs thought that way, however. There were still too many things that satellites couldn't do . . . like keep a particular sentry under observation for hours at a time, or catch the pungent whiff of a Russian-made cigarette in the darkness. Checking out an objective personally taught you things about the target, and about the enemy, that you never could have gleamed from the bright, flat, and sterile slickness of a photograph.

The highway, Roselli and Sterling had discovered, was not patrolled or covered by either ambushes or electronic surveillance for at least a hundred meters in either direction. Four men were standing guard at the cutoff road winding sharply up the mountain northwest of the castle. That was a new twist, one added since the last set of satellite photos had been faxed across to the *Jefferson*, and reason enough for the manned sweep.

What any raid or hostage-rescue assault such as this one required more than anything else was intelligence. How many soldiers occupied the castle? How many were on duty . . . and where were the off-duty troops quartered? Were there other approaches besides the road leading up to the front gate? Were there machine guns or other heavy weapons on those parapets, or were the troops carrying small arms only? Were there reinforcements closer than the air base at Ohrid?

Many of those questions could be answered by satellite, but not all, and even the best orbital reconnaissance gave, not fact, but probability and guesswork. And the most important questions for this kind of mission could not be addressed by satellite at all. Where were the hostages being kept? Were they being held in the same room, or were they dispersed throughout the objective? How heavily were they guarded? Were they all at Gorazamak, or might some of them have been taken elsewhere for added security?

Roselli and Sterling approached the SEAL base camp south of the beach, a rocky niche tucked away behind boulders and pine trees, close enough to the water that they could hear the steady *lap-lap-lap* of the waves against the shore.

DeWitt's team was scouting the approaches to the castle itself. The remaining SEALs had been stowing their gear and laying out the markers, tetrahedral reflectors that would show up on a properly set multi-mode radar like tiny suns and guide in Alexander's second element. A four-man cordon had been thrown out around the beachhead, to give early warning of the approach of hostiles.

And one man, Doc, was still missing.

Murdock was with Higgins and Kosciuszko, crouched over the sat-comm unit, speaking quietly into the microphone. "Copy that, Olympus," he was saying as Roselli and Sterling drew close. "We'll try to do our best to have things quiet by the time they get here. Alexander out."

"Skipper," Roselli said as Murdock handed the microphone back to Higgins. He slid the NVDs off his head and switched them off to save the batteries. "We're back."

"Let's have it, guys."

Quietly, turning a red-filtered flashlight on one of the NSA maps of the area faxed to them earlier from Washington, Roselli showed Murdock where he and Sterling had been. "Four sentries here," he said, pointing. "This part of the road is clear . . . and over here too. We made it as far up the hill above the main road as this part of the cliff. No other hostiles. No alarms. And no sign that we're expected."

"Okay," Murdock said, nodding. "Olympus says that Chariot is set to ride, but Achilles is late."

"Damn. How late, L-T?"

"We won't know until they get to San Vito, will we?" A grim smile showed in the darkness. "But we're to Charlie-Mike."

Continue mission. "I'd damn well say we'd better. Shit, L-T, we're close enough to smell the tangos. If they told us to abort and extract, I'd be damned tempted to develop fucking radio trouble."

"You and me both, Razor." A rustle in the vegetation upslope, and the softly whispered sign and countersign, warned of DeWitt's return.

"Hello, L-T," DeWitt said softly. "You guys here having a picnic on the beach?"

"Pull up a rock, Two-Eyes. Whatcha find?"

DeWitt took the NSA map, pulled a pencil from his vest, and began pointing out the route his patrol had taken.

"Two decent approaches, L-T, unless you're partial to going up the access road?"

"I don't think this time."

"Thought not. Okay, we got as far around the front of the castle as here. The structure really is built into the side of the mountain. The south slope isn't too bad . . . about thirty percent up through here, and we could climb that without too much difficulty. If we work our way up this cliff here, on the southeast corner, we could climb this rock face, fix lines to the edge about here, and rappel onto the outer ward wall."

"That's fine," Murdock said, studying the map. "Except that we'll be coming over the east wall, which seems to be where they expect us."

Gorazamak's weakness was the cliff rising behind its east wall, a tactical disadvantage that hadn't worried the Ottoman ruler who'd built it since the tower was little more than a police outpost on the road to Korcë, not a bastion expected to withstand a siege. The bad guys inside could be counted on to have the wall beneath the eastern cliffs thoroughly covered with fire.

"Right. Well, the other approach could be tricky with all the ice and snow, but it's up this way." He pointed to a narrow ravine northwest of the outer castle wall and south of the access road. A stone bridge crossed the ravine just outside Gorazamak's gate tower. "Red says he could scale that, no sweat, and drop lines to the rest of us. The ravine is pretty narrow in through here, more like a chimney than anything else. We climb up and come out by the bridge."

"Right outside the main gate?"

"Two possibilities. We take out the guards at the front gate quietly and walk right in. Or we climb the wall here . . . or here. The gate tower sticks out from the wall about a meter or so. We could pull a ninja-of-the-night stunt and go right over the top without being seen. Advantage too is that the power lines for the place go in right here, next to the gate."

"They'll have a generator."

"Which probably hasn't been used for a while. It'll take time to find the damned thing and crank it up."

Murdock nodded. Roselli could almost hear the wheels turning. When the L-T had first taken command of Third Platoon, Roselli had had his doubts about the man. Shit, the guy was a ring-knocker, an Academy grad, and though that kind of crap might sit well with the bean-counters at the Navy Department, it didn't mean a hell of a lot in the field. Men had died in combat because their officers were too tight-assed to blend well with their men.

The Teams were just that . . . *teams*, and a man's background or wealth or family or political connections didn't cut him a damned thing when it came to that special warrior's brotherhood shared by all who'd gone through BUD/S and won their Budweisers.

Murdock was different. He cared for his men, *loved* his men . . . and they loved him back. It wasn't a thing that most SEALs could put into words; hell, they wouldn't even try. But Roselli had seen the look in Murdock's eyes when they'd reached the beach earlier and confirmed that Ellsworth was missing.

At that moment, Roselli had known that he would follow Murdock *anywhere,* up the face of a sheer cliff, into a storm of automatic-weapons fire, straight into Hell if he had to. Because he cared for his people.

"You know," Murdock said softly, "it's just possible that we could manage both approaches. How about if we try this?"

0115 hours
North of Gorazamak
Lake Ohrid, Macedonia

It had taken Doc about ten minutes to get down out of that damned tree, but he'd finally made it. While he didn't have any climbing line on him, he had perhaps the next best thing. Carefully, he'd reached up to his shoulder and grabbed the rip cord for his reserve chute, yanking it out and down. With a rustle of nylon, his reserve had spilled from

the pack and dropped toward the ground. Next, Doc had
unlocked his harness quick release, and then, grasping hold
of his reserve chute's risers, he'd unsnapped his harness. His
chute had slipped a foot or two and the branches supporting
him had creaked and swayed alarmingly, but he'd managed
to slide all the way down the reserve, landing in the snow at
the base of the tree with an agonizing thump a moment later.

God, his ankle hurt. First things first, though. Swiftly, he
broke out his primary weapon, fished a magazine from his
load vest, and snapped it home. The H&K CAW had
originally been developed as a contender in the U.S.
military's search for a combat shotgun. It looked more like
a gadget out of science fiction than a serious weapon, all
clean lines and sharp angles and with a bullpup receiver in
the butt, set behind the hand grip. The ten-round box
magazine could be emptied one shot at a time, or with a
twice-per-second cyclic that was death incarnate at close
quarters.

Too bad most of his ammo was gone now. He had just
five loaded magazines for the thing tucked into various
pouches in his vest—four after he'd untaped the weapon
and snapped a mag into the receiver. Fifty rounds was
enough to do some serious hurt, but when they were gone
Doc would be left with his Beretta secondary, and four clips.
Alone, he wouldn't last long.

Weapon ready, he checked his ankle. He was pretty sure
from the feel of the thing that it was sprained rather than
broken. Gingerly manipulating it, he felt no crepitus—the
grinding sensation of two jagged ends of bone grating
across each other—and he could still flex it up and down,
though he couldn't move it back and forth. With care, he
could put weight on it; it hurt like hell when he tried, but he
could manage it. He could feel the ankle swelling inside his
boot.

Well, there was nothing for it then but to strap himself up
and make do. He didn't remove the boot; if the ankle
ballooned too much while he had it off he'd never get the
thing back on afterward. Instead, he unlaced the boot, then

relaced it as tightly as he could manage. After that, he found a branch—there were plenty lying nearby that had fallen when he'd hit the tree—and fashioned a splint out of two inch-thick sticks and a roll of gauze from his first-aid kit. Could he walk? He tried a mincing step, using his CAW as a crutch. Shit . . . he could walk, but not very well, and anything requiring climbing or jumping was definitely out. Facing south, he could make out a bit of a glow beyond the trees where the castle lay about a half a mile distant. The dogs were still barking.

His options were limited. He had his tactical radio, of course, but he was out of line-of-sight from the rest of the team and they might not hear him. Even if they did, he couldn't risk calling them until after the raid had started . . . and then they would be too busy to bother with him. So . . . he could sit tight and call in a rescue chopper once the second-wave elements arrived, but that could evolve into a pretty complicated rescue mission in its own right, especially if hostiles were running through these woods. He could hobble back down to the beach and signal for a pickup there.

Or he could make for the castle.

James Ellsworth, Doc to his friends, did not consider himself to be a hero. When he'd joined the Navy five years ago, he'd been a simple, relaxed, laid-back kid from Tennessee, best described by the kids in his boot company as "Old Mellow." He'd volunteered for BUD/S because Joe Saraglio, a good friend at his first duty station, had done so. It had sounded like a lark, learning to scuba dive and to blow things up. Certainly it would be more fun than bedpan duty and morning reports on a naval hospital ward.

One of the first things he'd learned at Coronado was that laid back and relaxed simply didn't cut it. A dozen times during Hell Week he'd come *that* close to quitting . . . and rejoining the sane world of showers and clean uniforms and six or eight hours of blissful, uninterrupted sleep.

Why hadn't he quit? Even now, two years later, he wasn't sure. Part of it, at least at first, had been the knowledge that he'd already signed for an extension to his original four-year hitch so that he could take SEAL training. If he left, he was still obligated, and he would be facing ten years of bedpan duty instead of four.

But gradually, he'd realized that there was more to it than that. He loved the Teams, loved the feeling of belonging. Loved the people most, he guessed, though some of them were thoroughgoing bastards. He'd toughed it out because he'd wanted to belong, and because BUD/S had already taught him that he could do things that he'd never thought himself capable of doing before.

He couldn't think of any other reason to carry on, especially after Joe had managed to get himself killed in a training accident, the silly bastard. *That* episode had nearly killed Ellsworth, left him feeling like he was caught between two worlds, the SEALs and the rest of the Navy. He couldn't go back . . . so all that was left was to go ahead.

He'd changed a lot in the years since. Laid-back and relaxed cut it no better as an active-duty SEAL than it had at Coronado. He had a wild rep now, one that he worked hard to live up to. The guys in his platoon joked that Doc's idea of the SEAL acronym wasn't even Sleep, EAt, and Live it up, but that he'd improved on that by changing to SEx and ALcohol.

Okay, so some small, tucked-away part of himself kept telling him that he was trying to die. Like Joe. But Doc's reason for living was the Team, the other guys in the Team, and he wasn't going to let them down. He might get there late, but by hell he would get there!

With the CAW as a crutch, he began hobbling painfully along the hillside, making for the castle lights.

0128 hours
Below Gorazamak
Lake Ohrid, Macedonia
"Okay, Red," Murdock said softly, punching the man's shoulder. "You're on."

The SEAL Teams tended to assemble odd accumulations of talent. Both Murdock and Jaybird had experience sailing, for instance, and Kosciuszko had a pilot's license and flew his own Beachcraft. Red Nicholson's means of unwinding before he'd joined the Navy had been mountain climbing, both free climbing and with all the trimmings. He stood at the bottom of the crevice now, a light nylon line snapped to his belt and trailing out behind. He removed his gloves, stooped to tighten the laces of his boots, then pulled his gloves back on and cinched them snug.

"Heads up," he said. "Climbing."

Murdock and MacKenzie watched as Nicholson ascended the cliff, one arm up, then one foot . . . then the other arm . . . the other foot. From there at the bottom, the cliff looked unscalable, at least without pitons and climbing gear, but they were too close to the sentries on those castle ramparts to risk striking steel to rock. At this point, the ravine was perhaps thirty meters deep, a little taller than two telephone poles stacked atop one another.

Nicholson vanished into shadow almost at once. Even in the soft green glow of NVD goggles, it was almost impossible to separate his form from that of the cliff, though Murdock's electronic optics picked up enough IR to pick him out from the cold, black rock.

Leaving Mac to pay out the line as Nicholson climbed, Murdock picked his way back down the steeply slanted floor of the ravine, to where the remaining members of Blue Squad were waiting. Roselli, Magic Brown, Professor Higgins. Nick the Greek Papagos. So few, with both Garcia and Doc missing. Damn! What had happened to Doc? Jaybird Sterling, along with Nicholson because of his climbing skills, had been shifted over to Blue Squad to fill out the numbers. DeWitt and the other five had already left to carry out their part of the mission approach.

From here, if you craned your head all the way back, you could just see the edge of the castle wall rising from the top of the cliff. The sky was lighter now with moonrise, and the overcast had given way to the scud of broken, patchwork clouds, now revealing, now concealing the stars.

"All I vant is your blood," Magic Brown intoned in low and sepulchral tones, looking up at the castle silhouetted against the ominous sky.

"Wrong country," Papagos said quietly, and a little nervously. "You want Romania." He pointed north. "That way."

"Yeah, I always knew you were a blood-sucker, Magic," Sterling said.

"No, man," Higgins said. "That's Doc. Where the hell is our platoon vampire anyway?"

"If I know Doc," Roselli said, "he's making it right now with some Albanian shepherdess."

"Yeah," Magic added. "Or her sheep."

Their voices were barely audible, their humor tight and hard beneath pre-combat nerves. Murdock considered ordering them to be quiet—they were breaking mission routine—but decided to let it go. They couldn't possibly be heard more than a few feet away.

And it sounded like they needed to talk about Doc.

Damn. It might have been easier if they knew what had happened to him. In over thirty years of operations, SEALs had never left a man behind, and no SEAL had ever been taken prisoner. Not knowing whether he'd died somewhere in Albania or made it as far as Lake Ohrid but come down in the wrong place made it worse. If he was still out there somewhere, alive but wounded, with his radio out . . .

"Papagos," he whispered sharply. "Roselli. Go do it. And keep it quiet. The rest of you, with me. We've got some climbing to do."

"Yes, sir."

"Aye, aye, Skipper."

He watched as they slipped into darkness.

"Sst. L-T."

Murdock looked back over his shoulder. Mac was signaling. Red had reached the top of the cliff and secured his end of the line. It was time to go.

"Let's move out," he told the others.

He'd already decided that he would be the first up the cliff after Nicholson.

0156 hours
Outer courtyard
Gorazamak

Sergeant Jankovic stepped out of the castle's main building, paused for a moment on the stone steps outside, then started walking across the outer courtyard toward the long, low buildings inside the west wall that served the garrison as barracks. He would start his night rounds there.

Jankovic had arrived at Gorazamak only that afternoon and been dismayed to find out that he'd been assigned the two-to-six watch that very night. He well understood the need for nighttime sentry-go—any hypothetical enemy was not going to be so considerate as to delay his attack until dawn—but he could have wished for a little time to get acclimated to the new place. This Ottoman monstrosity filled him with a deep foreboding—what he'd heard Americans liked to call "giving someone the creeps." The Ottoman Turks had had so much blood on their hands. It was easy to imagine these rough, brown stones crying out for more.

He was still recovering from that night of blood and terror on the beach near Dubrovnik. His personal report to Mihajlovic had been concise and factual. He was pretty sure that that was why the general had asked if he would like temporary assignment to this operation.

At least, that was part of the reason. Some part of Jankovic thought that the larger reason was that he'd encountered what were probably American commandos at Dubrovnik, and Mihajlovic seemed obsessed with the idea that those same commandos might attempt an assault here. Of course, they shouldn't know yet that their politician was being held here. Still, Jankovic was not at all convinced that the Americans hadn't somehow found out that this was where they were keeping her. Their spy satellites . . .

Jankovic glanced up, uncomfortable, and stared for a moment at low-drifting clouds and brilliant stars. He'd heard that the American satellites could see in the dark, could read a newspaper over a man's shoulder, could eavesdrop even on a whispered conversation. . . . Such powers were awesome, and terrifying.

He looked down at the initials tattooed into the back of his hand. *Only Solidarity Can Save the Serbs.*

Jankovic had seen and done terrible things in the past few years, things he was not proud of. At first he'd taken part because he believed in the holy war for homeland and for brother Serbs. Then he'd taken part because not doing so would have marked him.

But God in heaven, how could he continue? Stories kept circulating about Muslim or Croat atrocities against Serbs . . . but he'd learned to distrust camp talk and official propaganda both. He had *seen* the concentration camps at Manjaca and Kereterm, however, and had a good idea of what went on there, even if the details were never openly discussed. He'd heard screams, seen the bodies stacked in heaps behind a tool shed. And he'd heard of indescribable obscenities . . . made all the worse because the people he'd heard them from were boasting at the time. Maybe that was camp talk too, but he doubted it.

He'd seen the look in the boaster's eyes, and there were some stories too horrible to be fiction.

Would solidarity save the Serbs from the Americans, when they came?

They would come, Jankovic had no doubt about that. Mihajlovic was holding their people in that stone tower somewhere and Jankovic had no doubt at all that the Americans would find them with their magical technology . . . and come.

The only question was when.

The Americans could be out there right this moment, watching him through a sniper's nightscope. The thought made his skin crawl, and he hurried his steps across the compound.

0204 hours
Access road to Gorazamak
Lake Ohrid, Macedonia

Roselli adjusted the gain on his NVDs. The guards had started a small fire, and the glare tended to wash out the image in his night goggles when he looked toward it. It was the same four men, all sitting together now, backs to the night, hands to the fire, and paying no attention at all to their surroundings. Sloppy, sloppy . . .

He was just glancing at his watch when he heard a click in his Motorola's earpiece, followed by Murdock's voice. "Alex Three, this is One. In position. Over."

That meant that the SEALs in the L-T's group had made it up the cliff and were waiting outside the castle's walls.

He was so close to the four guards that he didn't dare speak in reply. Instead he reached up and pressed the squelch button three times, then twice: *Alex Three, okay.*

"Three, One. Alex Two in position," the voice said. "Your show, Three. Over."

Again, he pressed the squelch button three times, then twice: *Alex Three, okay.*

There was no use waiting any longer. Roselli disliked firing on men from ambush, especially these men who obviously didn't have the faintest idea about what they were doing. One of those people down there, he remembered, was little more than a kid.

A kid who was on the wrong side in a shitty war . . . and he should have known the risks when he first picked up an AK to play soldier with his big brothers. That was part of the trouble with the world today, Roselli thought. Too many child-soldiers all over the fucking planet. He pulled a flashbang from his thigh pouch, pulled the pin, let fly, ducking as he did so behind the shelter of the boulder. . . .

19

0205 hours
Access road to Gorazamak
Lake Ohrid, Macedonia

Flashbangs had originally been developed by the German GSG-9, a weapon in their war against international terrorism. The SEALs, Delta, the SAS, and a few other special-operations units had picked them up since. A cardboard tube filled with five separate charges timed to burst in rapid succession, the flashbang did exactly that—detonate with a chain of flashes that were momentarily blinding, and with a savage concussion that could leave the target helplessly stunned.

The grenade landed just short of the fire. Roselli heard someone shout . . . and then the night was filled with crackling thunder and shrill screams. As the echo of the final blast was still ringing in the air, Roselli and Sterling rose together atop the boulder. The four Serb soldiers sprawled in a circle about the fire, two lying flat, two on hands and knees. Roselli saw the black trickle of blood from the ear of one, from the nose of another.

One shouted something and groped for his AK assault rifle. Roselli squeezed the trigger on his H&K, a feather-light caress, and the man pitched up and backward onto the fire. Roselli tensed, waiting for ammo the man might be

243

carrying to cook off . . . but evidently any spare mags he had were in one of the rucksacks nearby. He fired again, knocking down a second, just as Sterling nailed numbers three and four.

Four up, four down. "Alex One, this is Three. Clear."

"We heard you, Three," came the reply. "The party's just beginning!"

0205 hours
West wall
Gorazamak

"What the shit was that?"

Jankovic ran to the stone parapet, along with the sentry he'd just been inspecting. Those flashes, those explosions, they'd been from the northwest, about where the castle access road came down to join the highway. What had it been . . . gunfire? Grenades? It was silent enough now. . . .

He reached into his back pocket and extracted a radio. "Command Center, this is Sergeant Jankovic, west wall. Something is happening at Post One."

"We heard, Sergeant," Captain Cherny's voice snapped back. "We are investigating."

Yes, investigating, Jankovic thought savagely. *With your head tucked up your ass . . .*

Jankovic's immediate thought was to lead a party of men down to Sentry Post One to find out what had happened. It could have been an accident . . . a grenade or some ammo dropped in a fire.

But Jankovic didn't believe that for a moment, not when the night still held the memory of Dubrovnik, and every shadow held the threat of nightmare. If this was an assault of some kind, why would they attack a sentry post outside the walls so noisily? . . .

. . . unless they wanted a diversion. Where did they, whoever "they" were, *not* want the garrison to look?

Jankovic turned, sweeping the compound, searching for anything out of the ordinary. Damn Mihajlovic. It was so brightly lit inside the place that it was hard to see much of anything outside. It would have been better to light the outside and keep the inside dark.

The courtyard below was occupied by a number of confused-looking troops. Four guards stood inside the front gate, and two more in the gate tower above. The east wall was manned by half-a-dozen sentries, including one with a bulky Mitrajez M80 machine gun. An officer stumbled out of the main building, still buckling his trousers as he shouted orders. He was gathering a squad to go down the hill. Someone started up one of the jeeps, backing it out into the courtyard.

Something caught Jankovic's attention, some movement near the gate. He looked back and saw nothing. Three guards . . .

No, there'd been four. Where was the fourth? As he watched, horrified, part of the shadow behind one of the sentries by the gate seemed to solidify, flowing about the man's neck from behind, dragging him back.

He lifted the radio to his mouth again. "Commander! This is Jankovic! They're inside the castle. Repeat, they're *inside the castle, front gate!*"

There was a heavy thump from somewhere outside, and the lights went out.

0205 hours
Outer courtyard
Gorazamak

Murdock dropped from the top of the wall and landed in the courtyard, letting his momentum carry him into a low crouch. To his right, the Professor lowered a dead Serb to the flagstone pavement. Another guard stepped out of a low doorway on the west side of the gate tower, and Murdock stopped him with a single three-round burst that punched him back into the room he'd been leaving. Nicholson followed up, tossing a concussion grenade through the stone opening.

"Grenade!" Nicholson yelled, and Murdock flattened

himself against his side of the gate tower. The blast, a heavy thump that struck him through the soles of his boots, blew out the twentieth-century glass windows that had been installed in sixteenth-century window slits.

Across the courtyard, four more Serbian soldiers appeared bursting out of the barracks door. Murdock dropped two with quick, three-round bursts, tapping the trigger twice and sending both men tumbling across the ground. The other two ran another couple of steps, and then the thunder of Mac's Maremont opened up from the parapet wall above and behind Murdock's position, the muzzle flash stabbing and stuttering against the night. Both Serbs collapsed as though their legs had been yanked out from under them. "This is Alex One-Two" sounded in Murdock's earphone, Mac's call sign. "I'm moving."

The SEALs possessed a considerable advantage in the M-60E3s they were humping, two weapons that could provide them with tremendous portable firepower. The disadvantage was that the gunner had to move each time he gave away his position with the gun's muzzle flash.

For this op, however, that was not a serious problem, since the SEALs were going to be moving constantly anyway. If they stopped in one position for more than a few seconds, the enemy would move in troops enough to pin them down like butterflies on a board. If they kept moving, the Serb defenders of Gorazamak would never be able to organize an effective defense, would never even be able to guess how many invaders they were fighting or where they were coming from.

Kick ass and take initials, the SEAL saying went, *'cause we're gonna be moving too fast to take names!*

When Mac had cut the main outside power lines leading to the castle, the defenders had been left in blind confusion, but the SEALs couldn't expect that to last for long. They had to take advantage of the darkness—and their high-tech night-vision gear—before the Serbs found their generator.

"Alex One!" Murdock called to his men over the tactical channel. "One-One! Move!"

0205 hours
Officers' quarters, main building
Gorazamak

Mihajlovic had just fallen asleep; it felt as though he'd only just closed his eyes. The crump of a grenade blast, followed by the rattle of a machine gun, instantly brought him wide awake. An attack! Rolling over in bed, he fumbled for his bedside lamp, then cursed when he turned the switch and the light didn't come on. He rose, fumbling about in the dark. Someone pounded on the door to his room.

"Enter, damn it!"

The door opened, and a soldier entered, an assault rifle in one hand, a heavy-duty flashlight in the other. The movements of the light sent fantastic shadows dancing around the room. "My General!"

"What is it?"

"An attack, my General!"

"Yes, yes, I can hear that, damn you!" More explosions, and the crackle of automatic weapons, were sounding outside. "Who? Where?"

"Sir!" The man snapped to attention and tried to deliver an official report. "Sir, unknown forces of unknown strength and composition have entered the compound at the gate tower! Sir!" Another rumbling boom echoed through the stone walls of the tower.

Mihajlovic was already pulling his uniform trousers up over his pajama bottoms. "Has Communications reported the attack?"

"Sir . . . I . . . I'm not sure—"

"Go to Communications. Have the duty officer flash a Priority One message to Ohrid Command Center, my authorization. Tell them we're under attack and require immediate assistance. Understood?"

"Yes, my General!"

"Next. Go down to the basement. To the generator room. If you don't know how to start the generator, find someone who can. Get us some power, damn it!"

"Yes, sir!"

"Go! Do it!"

"Sir!"

Mihajlovic found his way to a dresser drawer, opened it, and fumbled inside. His hand closed on the small, cold, stamped-metal shape of an M61(j), the Yugoslav version of the Czech-made vz.61 machine pistol. By touch, he checked that the twenty-round magazine was in place, then snicked back the charging knob, chambering a round.

Continuing to rummage in the drawer, at last he found the other necessity . . . a flashlight. Flicking it on, he hurried to the door of his room and stepped out into the corridor.

Whoever was attacking Gorazamak would be professional, well-trained, and moving hellishly fast. He had to get to the prisoners before they did.

0205 hours
Gate tower, northwest wall
Gorazamak

Magic Brown hunched a little lower, his right eye pressed against the rubber-rimmed eyepiece of his low-light sniperscope. From this vantage point thirty feet above the bailey courtyard, he had a clear view of nearly the entire inside of the castle's ward. To his right, along the base of the east wall, was a long, low building that satellite photos had identified as a barracks. To the left was a smaller building that had once been a stable and was now a motor pool. A dozen cars, small trucks, and military vehicles were parked outside. Directly opposite was the castle keep, a five-story tower with an irregular circumference, topped by a spiky array of communications antennae.

Nicholson and Papagos had gone right, moving along the front of the barracks, stopping at each doorway to toss in a grenade. Murdock had gone left, sweeping through the motor pool, while Mac, with his 60-gun, had paced Murdock on the stable roof.

The courtyard had been transformed into a bloody slaughter pen, swept by fire from three directions now, and with a dozen bodies sprawled on the flagstone pavement already. The detonations of hand grenades from left and right followed one after another with metronomic precision. The thump and roar of 40mm grenades fired from M203s added to both the confusion and the slaughter.

Defenders continued to show themselves, despite the casualties they'd suffered already.

"Target," Higgins said at his right side. "Right of the tower, on the parapet walk." The Professor was pulling double duty, as communications center for the platoon and as Magic's spotter.

Magic eased the muzzle of his Remington to the right, and the crosshairs centered on the magnified image of a Serb militiaman standing in a half crouch, holding a general-purpose machine gun.

"Got him."

Part of Magic's pre-mission studies had involved going over dozens of satellite photos with calipers and a scale, measuring out ranges. This target was close, as sniping went—about eighty meters. Magic drew down slightly, since his rifle was sighted in at the lowest possible adjustment of 150 meters.

Aim . . . hold . . . squeeze . . .

The Remington's report was lost in the general cacophony of battle. The target staggered and went down like a sack of meal.

"Hit," Higgins said. "Clean kill."

"Damn straight."

"Target. Top of the tower, left side."

Nothing visible there but a shape filling an opening against the sky . . . someone peeking through one of the rampart openings, looking for a clear shot. Another sniper. Magic wondered if the target was engaged in a counter-sniper role right now, searching for Magic at the same moment Magic was lining up on him. . . .

"Hit," Higgins reported. "He's down. Can't tell if he's out."

"He's out," Magic said. "Saw his brains splatter."

"Nice. Target . . ."

The slaughter continued.

0206 hours
Main tower, east wall
Gorazamak

"Okay!" DeWitt called. "Alex Two, we're climbing!"

DeWitt and Gold Squad—minus Nicholson and Sterling—
had worked their way around to the southeastern side of the
castle. Built partly into the side of the mountain, the outer wall
was only fifteen feet high here, as opposed to the thirty feet of
the west wall, and it was an easy climb. The rocks set into the
outer wall, roughly cut and crudely mortared, protruded
enough that a good climber could have made it without the
rope. The trouble, of course, was that there were more sentries
back here, precisely because the enemy knew that the physical
layout of Gorazamak was vulnerable at this point.

The moment the grenade and machine-gun bursts went
off, however, most of the soldiers atop those walls would be
turning their backs on the mountain, staring across the
courtyard to see what was going on at the main gate. They
were human, after all . . . and not particularly well trained
or disciplined.'

Holt and Kosciuszko tossed the grapnels, using easy,
overhand tosses that cleanly paid out the trailing lines. The
three-pronged hooks snagged across the top of the battlements; Holt and Kos gave the lines experimental tugs, then
pulled them taut. DeWitt and Stepano started climbing,
swarming up the line in a rapid hand-over-hand ascent, their
feet only occasionally using projecting stones for leverage
up. At the top, they clung to their lines with their left hands,
keeping their suppressed H&Ks at the ready in their right.
DeWitt edged his NVD-encased head above the opening of
one of the parapet firing slots and caught sight of the back
of a soldier vanishing into the main tower. He paused,
looked both ways, then hauled himself through the opening
and onto the parapet walk. Some thirty feet below the walk
on the other side, gunfire blazed across the bailey, and an

explosion shattered one of the doors leading to the barracks. He glimpsed running men, saw them jerk and twist and fall.

He nearly stepped on a body lying sprawled across the parapet walk, a Serb soldier with a neat, round hole just below his right eye and the back of his head missing. DeWitt heard scuffing sounds—boots on stone steps—and looked up; another trooper was just reaching the parapet walk from a stairway coming up the inside of the wall from the bailey. Before DeWitt could trigger his H&K, however, the soldier gave an odd, forced sigh, then toppled sideways off the stairs. DeWitt turned his electronic gaze to the northwest, across the courtyard to the gate tower.

He couldn't see anyone there, but he knew that Magic Brown was behind one of those windows above the main gate, and that he'd just silently marked down these two guards at least. DeWitt gave a jaunty salute in the direction of the gate, knowing that Magic would be watching him through his scope, then turned and headed for the back of the main tower.

The main tower—the castle keep—was directly adjacent to the east wall, with only the width of the parapet walk separating it from the ramparts. A single door in the keep's eastern wall gave access from the walk directly to the tower's third floor. Overhead, the keep rose for another forty feet to the very top of the tower.

"Alex One, Alex Two!" he called over his Motorola. "We're on the parapet okay. Moving."

"Two, One, roger" was the reply. AK fire rattled nearby, echoing off stone. "Good hunting!"

Tactically, Gold Squad had a tough choice to make. Since they had no idea where the hostages were being held, they would have to search the entire structure, clearing it as they went. The enemy could be counted on to be keeping the prisoners someplace inconvenient for any invading HRU, someplace easily sealed off and easily defended. Given the architecture of the castle, that meant either all the way down in the basement—possibly even in the old dungeons that had been Gorazamak's principal tourist attraction—or at the

very top, in one or several of the rooms that had been
remodeled as hotel suites for visitors. The question was
whether to take the castle tower from the bottom up or the
top down. A wrong decision could cost the hostages their
lives.

The preferred means of clearing any building was to go in
on the roof, since it was far harder to fight your way up a
staircase than down. That wouldn't work here, though,
because the enemy had almost certainly posted people on
the tower's roof. The gun battle had probably pulled them
around to the side facing the bailey, and Magic would be
picking them off right now with his usual murderous
accuracy . . . but Magic's vantage point in the gate tower
was still well below the top of the keep. He couldn't see
inside the ramparts up there, so it was all too possible that
someone would still be up there, waiting when Gold Squad
fired their climbing lines over the top of the keep.

If they'd been able to carry out a heloborne assault, or if
they'd had time to place a sniper on the mountain above
the level of the keep and with a clear field of fire onto the
roof enclosure, Murdock would almost certainly have decided to have Gold take the roof first and work down. As it
was, however, there was a convenient compromise available. Murdock's squad, after knocking loudly at the front
gate, would force the front door to the keep and get two men
into the basement to check out the rooms down there. The
six men of Gold Squad, meanwhile, would take the tower
from the middle, going in by way of that wooden door set
into the east side of the keep.

All of Gold Squad was on the parapet walk now, Kos and
Stepano breaking left and right to cover the flanks, Holt and
Frazier aiming their weapons almost straight up, ready to
target any curious head that showed itself from the roof.
Rattler Fernandez had his CAW unlimbered. As the other
members of the squad took up positions against the stonework to the left and right of the door, Fernandez leveled the
assault shotgun at the door and opened fire.

There was no way to silence a shotgun. On full auto, the

big weapon bellowed a deep-throated *slam-slam-slam* that
echoed back from the cliffs behind them. Rattler had loaded
his first mag with slugs rather than shot. The door, an
inch-thick, solid wood instead of hollow-core, bucked and
cratered under the impacts of the first three one-ounce slugs,
then cracked open in a whirlwind of lead and flying
splinters. Fernandez shifted his aim and sent two more
rounds, a light tap on the trigger for each, slamming into
the door's hinges. The ruined door crashed back into the
corridor beyond, as Fernandez went full auto, emptying the
last of his magazine in a sweep designed to take down any
unwanted ambushers guarding the door from the inside.

"Avon calling!" Kos yelled, and he tossed in a concussion
grenade as the SEALs pressed back against the wall; the
blast rang through the tower like the tolling of a huge bell.
Frazier hurled a flashbang, and as the last detonation died,
Holt went through the door, his big M-60 leveled from his
hip.

"Passageway clear!" Holt shouted. The other SEALs
rushed in, leapfrogging down a darkened corridor that
was littered with wood splinters and blast-loosened stones
and—yes—two shredded bodies.

"Alex One, Alex Two! We're in! Two tangos down!"

"Copy, Two. We're at the front door!"

Holt's machine gun thundered in the passageway ahead,
an ear-splitting blast of hellfury announcing quite definitely
that the SEALs had just come calling.

0207 hours
Main tower, main entrance
Gorazamak

"One, this is Three!" Roselli's voice said in Murdock's ear.
"We're coming in the front gate!"

"That's right," Sterling's voice added. "None of this
'friendly fire' shit."

"Come on through," Murdock replied. "Rally at the
tower's front door!"

Murdock, crouched next to the main door in the tower,

turned to face the front gate. A moment later, Roselli and
Sterling trotted through the arch, emerging from the battle
fog that wreathed the baileylike specters, their gear-heavy
vests and the NVDs worn beneath their helmets transforming them into nightmare apparitions.

"Set at the road entrance?" Murdock asked.

"Claymores are out, Skipper," Sterling told him. "Anybody comes up that way, we'll hear it."

"Okay. Let's get inside. Positions!"

Roselli, Sterling, and Papagos took their places to either
side of the front door, weapons ready. Murdock and
Nicholson tossed a pair of flashbangs through the door
together, averting their electronic gaze as the first floor of
the castle keep lit up in a stuttering chain of light bursts and
sense-numbing blasts. They charged through the opening as
plaster continued to rain from the ceiling, both as a fine
cloud of dust and as chunks the size of dinner plates. A
guard staggered erect behind a counter to the left and
Murdock shot him down. Another man lay on the stone
floor across the room, fumbling with the receiver on his AK
until Nicholson put a burst into his head and back.

Left, beyond the counters, an unsteady light spilled
through a partly open door. The door opened and an officer
emerged, backlit by an emergency battle lantern.

"I'm on him," Murdock said, thumbing his H&K to full
auto and spraying a burst across the officer at the level of his
chest. The man shrieked and went facedown. Sterling pulled
the pin on a fragmentation grenade, let it cook off for two
seconds, then yelled "Grenade" and hurled it through the
open door. There was a tinkling of smashed glass, then a
shattering blast that blew out the door. Roselli ducked in,
then came back out. "Clear! Three tangos down inside!
Looks like the commo shack!"

"One-One," Murdock called into his lip mike. "We're in
the front door."

"You're clear outside," Higgins said. "And Two-Eyes is
on the third floor."

"Roger that. Keep an eye out for unfriendly neighbors. The commo shack was occupied in here."

"Ay-firmative."

The soft stutter of suppressed fire clattered at Murdock's back. Turning, he saw Nicholson and Sterling in the middle of the rotunda, firing full auto at a trio of half-glimpsed shapes moving on the second-floor balcony at the top of the stairs. One shape slumped over the banister, then dropped to the stone floor below; another spilled onto the stairs, thumping loudly as it rolled halfway down. The third slipped through a door to the left, vanishing.

The lights came on.

"Hello," Jaybird said, reaching up to adjust his night goggles. "Somebody's home!"

"Jaybird! Red!" Murdock snapped. "You've got the basement! Nick, you're with me."

"Right, Skipper."

Together, Murdock and Papagos stormed up the stairs.

0208 hours
Main tower, fifth floor
Gorazamak

"What's *happening*? What's *happening*?"

"Easy, Celia," Kingston said quietly. "Worst thing we can do now is panic."

"That's right, Celie," Bunny added. "The Marines have landed and the situation is well in hand."

Another explosion sounded, much closer this time, and Kingston was certain she could hear someone screaming in pain. She wondered if the lights would stay on this time.

The women were all in the same room, lying flat on the floor behind the bed with their arms over one another, listening to the approaching thunder. Never in her life had Ellen Kingston felt so utterly and completely helpless. There were six of them, Kingston, the four of her staffers who were women, and one female sergeant who was on Colonel Winters's staff. So far they'd held up remarkably well, Kingston thought, all except Celia, who'd been on the verge of hysterics the whole time and who was certain that they were all going to be raped.

Celia, unfortunately, was the Army sergeant. In Congress, Kingston had delivered speeches several times in favor of bills that would allow women to serve in combat. After observing Celia these past few days, she was beginning to question her stand.

So far, and despite Celia's shrill fears, none of them had been mistreated in any way . . . none of the women, anyway. She'd not seen any of the male hostages since they'd arrived here—wherever "here" was—and she didn't know where they'd been taken. The soldiers watching them had been stiffly formal and correct, even courteous with an Old World formality; the women had been fed, and several times a day a uniformed woman had escorted them one at a time to the toilet.

But no one had so much as questioned the women or come to tell them why they were being held or what demands were being made for their release. Hour after hour was an agony of not knowing, of wondering what each new sounding of footsteps in the corridor heralded.

Footsteps sounded outside the door, and the rattle of the lock as someone turned the knob. Kingston, braced for the worst, prayed that it would be Americans who opened it. . . .

Celia began to scream.

20

The door banged open, and Kingston's prayers dissolved in sick horror. The man was in uniform, but not of any U.S. military service. There was a lot of gold braid on the unbuttoned jacket, and he held a vicious-looking little pistol with a curved magazine in front of the trigger. Two more soldiers crowded in behind him, brandishing assault weapons.

"Up ladies," the man said, his accent thick and Slavic-sounding. "Everybody up!"

"What do you want with us?" Beth Leary cried from behind the bed.

"He's going to rape us!" Celia screamed.

"I will kill you if you don't do precisely what I tell you!" the man snapped. He added something in a rasping, Slavic tongue, and the two men with him came in and shut the door, taking up positions on either side of it.

The officer shoved his way through the women until he was face to face with Kingston. "You," he said, "will come with me." Moving around behind her, he reached around her with his left arm, not circling her throat as she'd thought he was going to do, but slipping it under her left arm and across

257

her breasts. She caught the sharp tang of his cologne
mingled with his sweat. He jerked back suddenly, lifting her
off her feet, swinging her about to hold her between his
body and the door, backing farther away from the door until
his back was up against the wall. Bunny screamed.

"Shut up!" the officer shouted. Still holding Kingston
inches above the floor with one arm, he reached out with
the deadly-looking little gun, until the muzzle was only a
couple of inches from Bunny's right eye. "Shut up, bitch, or
you die this instant!"

The woman fell quiet. "That is better," the man said, but
he did not relax at all. "Now, we wait."

0208 hours
Main tower, stairs
Gorazamak

Stepano had point going up the stairs; Kosciuszko was at his
back, moving up the steps backward with his M-16 trained
up the stairwell, insurance against someone pulling a
hop-and-pop surprise from further up the steps. Frazier
followed, then Holt, packing his big M-60 like a child's toy.
DeWitt and Fernandez brought up the rear.

"Looks clear," Stepano was saying as he went, a kind of
mantra, a chant. "Looks clear . . . looks clear . . ."

It was one of those tightly wound spiral stairs, all of
stone, winding up the middle of the castle keep. If there was
a good place for an ambush . . .

Movement . . . a face, a weapon at the landing just
above. Stepano fired instinctively, the silenced weapon
thuttering briefly as he sent a burst snapping into the target.
Stepano took the next few steps three at a time, bounding
onto the landing, stepping across the body. The man was
still alive, his eyes starting from his head, his hands
scrabbling weakly at his chest and shoulder, which were
already slick with blood.

He was wearing an officer's uniform . . . a captain in
the JNA.

Stepano grabbed the man's collar beneath his chin. *"Kade*

e Gospogya Kingston?" he demanded. "Where is Ms. Kingston?" Then he repeated it in Serbian, the words almost identical. *"Gde ye Gospogya Kingston?"*

"Top floor," the wounded man answered, speaking Serbian. He seemed anxious to talk, and Stepano wondered whether that was because he thought he was dying, or because he was terrified of the black-clad apparition looming over him. "Room twelve."

"Are the hostages all together? Or did you spread them out?"

"Women . . . in room twelve. Men are . . . are room three. Please. I didn't—" And then he was dead.

"Room twelve and three," Stepano told DeWitt.

"Room twelve and room three, people," DeWitt echoed. "Let's go!"

"You wanna split up and take 'em down together?" Holt asked.

"Sounds good," DeWitt said. "Three and three. Kos, you take Bearcat and Scotty. Steponit and Rattler, you two with me. Watch out for a trap."

Stepano didn't think the dying man had lied, but it was certainly a possibility. At the top of the stairs the SEAL squad turned right and pounded down a corridor. Room eight . . . room ten . . . there! Room twelve.

Silently, DeWitt deployed his men, Stepano to the left of the door, himself to the right, both crouched below the level of the doorknob in case the opposition tried firing through the door. Rattler took up a crouched position slightly on the right of the door, his shotgun switched to single-shot.

DeWitt held up three fingers . . . two . . . one . . .

0208 hours
Main tower, fifth floor
Gorazamak

Blam! Blam! And the door splintered inward, flying off shattered hinges. Kingston screamed; she couldn't help herself . . . and then her ears rang with a deafening

quickfire chain of explosions and a blinding light like a
news reporter's camera strobe set off inches from her face.

She squeezed her eyes tightly shut, seeing that blinding
light even through her closed eyelids, feeling something like
a hot blast of air slap her face and clothing and set her skin
tingling. When she opened her tear-streaming eyes again,
she had a glimpse—just a glimpse—of monsters crashing
through the shattered door. They were dressed head to foot
in black, with vests heavily laden with arcane and technical-
looking gadgets, with visored helmets and with the visible
parts of their faces thickly smeared with green and black
paint. Their weapons were submachine guns of some kind,
but with muzzles as long and as thick as her forearm.

The first man through rolled to the right, so low he might
have been sitting down, his weapon held high and stiff-
armed; he nearly collided with the soldier crouched in the
corner, who had fallen to the floor and had his hand over his
eyes. The submachine gun spoke—a fluttering whisper—
and the stunned soldier's face came apart.

A second black-clad figure had rolled through the door to
the left close behind the first. The other Serb soldier had had
his head turned away from that dazzling light and was still
on his feet. As the black apparitions burst into the room, he
tried to raise his assault rifle, but before he could fire he was
slammed back against the wall by the attacker's shot and the
gun went clattering into the floor.

"Stop!" the officer holding Kingston screamed, his mouth
an inch from her right ear, the muzzle of his machine pistol
pressed against her head. She knew he was shouting, could
feel his chest moving and feel the breath on her face, but her
ears were still ringing from the explosions and his voice
seemed very far away. "Stop now or I kill them!"

"American Special Forces," one of the men shouted back.
"Hurt her and you're dead, y'hear me? You can't get out of
here. Best thing for you to do is drop your gun and give it
up!"

Everything seemed suspended in time and space. Both
invaders had their weapons turned now, aimed—she was

certain—directly at her, and there was a third invader still in the hallway, covering them all with something that didn't even look wholly like a gun. Kingston found herself looking straight down the black openings at the fronts of those heavy barrels. The women were flat on their faces or on their hands and knees, knocked down by the explosions; only Ellen Kingston was still upright, and that was only because her captor was still holding her up off the floor. She swung her legs, kicking at him, but he only tightened his grip painfully across her chest.

"No! You will drop weapons!" her captor shouted. "Now! Then back out of the way!"

It happened so fast she could scarcely tell what had happened. The black figure on the right took two steps further to the right, the muzzle of his gun still aiming at a point directly behind Kingston's head. He said something . . . and it wasn't English. What was he saying? The words were liquid and Slavic-sounding, spilling out so quickly she felt completely bewildered. She'd assumed her rescuers would be Americans, not . . . God, was that *Russian* he was speaking?

Her captor stiffened; the muzzle of his gun left her head, sweeping across an arc to aim at the Russian-sounding man. Her captor screamed something. . . .

The other invader's strange weapon spoke twice, a sound like the double slam of a door. At almost the same instant, her captor's gun fired, and the rattling crack it made was far louder in that narrow hotel room than the gunfire from the other weapon.

And the Russian-sounding man was already lunging toward her; she saw the bullets striking his vest, opening holes in the nylon fabric, and the little gun was still firing, the muzzle flash dragging up across the black-clad body. . . .

And then she was on the ground, and her captor was limp beneath her and her deliverer was a dead weight lying on top of her and Celia was screaming and screaming and Ellen thought if this went on much longer she would surely shoot Celia herself.

The weight was lifted off her and she sat up, gasping for breath. Bunny knelt beside her, holding her upright, helping her over to the bed.

"It's okay!" the man was saying, shouting to be heard above Celia. "Everybody stay down! I'm Lieutenant j.g. DeWitt, and we're here to get you out. Stay calm, stay quiet, and stay on the floor. Okay?"

"You're . . . American?" Monica Patterson asked.

"They're American!" Celia cried.

. . . and then the women were leaping to their feet, screaming now for sheer, adrenaline-shaking joy.

"Stay down!" DeWitt bellowed, and the screaming stopped as though cut short by the throwing of a switch. As the women parted before him, he moved across the room to kneel above the body of the man who'd somehow called her captor's shots to himself. The man in the hallway with the strange gun came in and checked each of the uniformed soldiers briefly, then knelt beside the other two. The women watched quietly, sensing the life-and-death drama, afraid to speak, afraid almost to breathe.

"This one's still alive," the man with the strange gun told DeWitt.

"I don't give a fuck about him. Tie him and then mount guard at the door."

"Aye, aye, sir."

DeWitt kept working with the wounded man, pulling a first-aid kit from one of his pouches, opening the man's vest. There was a lot of blood. "Aw, shit, Steponit! Shit! Talk to me! *Shit!*"

"He gonna make it, sir?"

"Watch that door!"

"Yessir."

"Shit, Steponit. What the fuck did you tell the bastard to piss him off so bad?"

"Told him . . . he was coward," the wounded man said. God, he was smiling. "Called him . . . filthy coward, hide behind women, small . . . small penis. Called him . . . everything I could think of. Then . . . said his wife was probably making it with his neighbor while he terrorized innocent women . . ."

"Shit, Steponit. Didn't anybody ever tell you it isn't a good idea to piss off a guy who had a gun?"

"Can . . . can we help get him on the bed?" Kingston asked, sitting up. Her hearing was fully recovered now, though there was still a faint ringing in her ears. She tasted salt on her lips, and she realized her nose was bleeding.

"Thanks, ma'am, but we'd better leave him where he is for now."

"What about this one?" Unsteadily, she moved over to the body of the man who'd been holding her. The braid on his uniform suggested that he was of very high rank. A general? She thought so. He was lying on his stomach, his wrists strapped behind his back with a length of white plastic. Gently, she rolled him onto his side. For a moment, his eyes locked with hers, and she thought she saw recognition there.

"Katrina," he said.

And then the eyes were no longer focused. He was dead.

"Shit! *No!*" DeWitt shouted. "No, Goddamn it!"

"He's gone, XO."

Kingston moved over to DeWitt's side. "He . . . he saved my life, Lieutenant. He may have saved all of us."

"Yeah." DeWitt looked up at her as though seeing her for the first time. "Yeah, but that's why we're here, isn't it? You're Congresswoman Kingston?"

"That's me."

"Okay." He drew himself up straighter. "I want you to be in charge of your people here. Is anybody missing from your party now? Anybody taken someplace else? To the bathroom? Whatever?"

"The women are all here, Lieutenant," she said. "I don't know about the men."

"Some of our boys are taking care of the men right now," DeWitt told her. "Is anyone in here hurt? Does anyone need medical attention?"

"We're all fine, Lieutenant," Kingston told him.

"You've got some blood on your face."

"From that, that explosion."

"Flashbang. Got your attention, didn't it?"

"I'm okay." She smeared at the blood on her lip and decided that she didn't want to see what she looked like right now. Gunfire crackled in the distance. "Is . . . I mean, are you still fighting?"

The lieutenant's mouth, almost invisible under layers of black and green paint, quirked upward. "Yes, ma'am. But it'll be okay. You ladies just do what you're told and everything'll work out fine." He turned away then and crouched inside the shattered door.

With a jolt of insight, she realized that these young men had fought their way to her, one had died for her, and now the others had placed themselves between her and her former captors. From the look of those two, she wouldn't care to be in the army boots of anyone trying to recapture the hostages.

As she lowered herself to the floor, however, she caught sight of one of the soldiers lying in the corner, the first one to be shot when the Americans had burst in. His head was turned to face her; the lower jaw was missing, and one of the eyes had popped out of its socket. There was blood everywhere, all over the shattered face, draining down the front of his tunic, pooling on the floor, splattered across the wall behind him.

Grimly, Kingston turned her eyes away and told herself that she would *not* be sick.

For a moment, she'd been caught up with the traditional, romantic image of heroes to the rescue. That body, in a way words never could, snapped her back to reality. There was *nothing* romantic about war. . . .

Sitting on the House Military Affairs Committee, Kingston knew a fair amount about things military. DeWitt had said he was Special Forces when he came through the door . . . but he'd given his rank as lieutenant j.g. There were no junior-grade lieutenants in the Army. That was a Navy rank, equivalent to an Army first lieutenant. If he was Navy, he had to be a SEAL.

An elite murder squad she'd once called the SEALs. *Shit!* Ellen Kingston lay on the floor and thought about her distinguished colleague from Virginia, the one that had a son who was a Navy SEAL.

God help me, she thought. *The next time I see Charles Fitzhugh Murdock, I'm going to grab the guy, kiss him on the mouth, and swear never, never, never to vote against Navy Special Warfare appropriations again!*

"One-One, this is Two-One." DeWitt was speaking so quietly Kingston almost couldn't catch the words. He seemed to be talking into a pencil mike extending from his helmet around to just in front of his paint-smeared lips. "I have six women, fifth floor back. All safe, no injuries." He took a breath. "Three tangos down. One of ours down."

She couldn't hear the reply.

"Steponit, L-T. He's dead." Another long pause. "Roger that," he said after a moment. And then: "I copy."

He turned slightly, facing the women. "Okay, ladies," he said. "We're gonna have a short wait. The other guys outside have pretty much mopped up on the tangos—the terrorists, I mean. The other hostages, the men, are all safe. Twelve men, including the five guys on your staff, ma'am. They were being held in another room on the other side of the building."

"Thank God," she said. "What about the airplane's crew?"

"I don't know about them, ma'am. They may still be with the plane, and someone else'll be taking care of them. Now, we have helos inbound for you. What we're gonna do is wait until the helos are here. Then we're gonna walk down the stairs, go out into the courtyard, and climb aboard. Ms. Kingston, I want you to be in charge of the people in this room, okay? You feel up to that?"

"Yes, Lieutenant."

"I want you to make sure everyone's with us when we start to move and to make sure everyone stays together. Hold hands, so no one gets lost. If anyone wanders off, we won't be able to come back for them, understand?"

"Perfectly, Lieutenant."

"Okay. Just sit tight for now. You'll be on that chopper and on your way home before you know it."

The women started cheering again, a sound that seemed incongruous with so much death and sadness in that room . . . and yet Kingston felt the overwhelming sense of relief as well. They were going . . . *home!* Bunny leaned over and tried to kiss DeWitt and got black grease-paint smeared on her cheek.

"Settle down, all of you," DeWitt said, easing Bunny aside with one hand. "I'm afraid we're not out of this yet."

The women withdrew to the back of the room and at DeWitt's orders got back down on the floor, but they continued to talk among themselves in excited whispers. Kingston wanted to cry. Home! Thanks to . . . what was his name? Steponit, DeWitt had called him. Thanks to Steponit, they were going home.

She wondered, though, as they crouched on that blood-smeared floor.

Who was the "Katrina" that her captor had confused her with?

0211 hours
Gate tower
Gorazamak

"Olympus, Olympus, this is Phalanx." Higgins crouched on the stone floor of the gate tower, speaking into the mike of his sat comm. "Olympus, come in."

"Phalanx, this is Olympus," a voice said in his headset. "Go ahead."

"Olympus, Nike. I say again, Nike."

With scrambled encryption on both ends, there was no real need for special code phrases, and communications protocol even suggested using clear language on an encrypted channel for clarity's sake. With the Greek theme of this mission, however—Alexander, Olympus, and Phalanx—the name of the Greek goddess of victory had been too perfect not to incorporate as well. The word *Nike* meant "Mission successful, all hostages safe." Had he instead said *Samothrace*, the reference would have been to the Nike of Samothrace, the famous statue of victory lacking arms and a head.

It would have been the grim announcement that the mission had been successful, but that some of the hostages had been wounded or killed.

Medusa was the code word that had been chosen to announce disaster.

"Well done, Phalanx," the voice in the headset said. "Well done!" There was a burst of static, and Higgins thought he heard a babble of voices in the background. No . . . that was cheering.

Damn it, he thought. *Don't start celebrating yet! How about getting us out of here first?*

"Okay, Phalanx," the voice of Olympus said after a moment. "Here's the word! Chariot and Achilles left San Vito twelve minutes ago. They're on the way and should be over your position in . . . make it thirty-nine minutes. That's three-niner minutes. Think you boys can hold out that long?"

"Copy that as three-niner minutes, roger. We'll manage till then."

A dull thump sounded from outside the castle walls, toward the northwest. Higgins looked up, meeting Magic's eyes.

"Phalanx out," he added.

"Thirty-nine minutes, huh?" Magic said. Another thump echoed from the woods outside. "From the sound of things, someone just stumbled across ol' Razor's and Jaybird's handiwork down there. Thirty-nine minutes just might be too long."

0215 hours
Main tower
Gorazamak

"Spit it out, Mac."

Murdock was standing in the rotunda just inside the entrance to the keep. The sounds of battle had died out minutes ago, and the SEALs had been systematically moving through the building. Mac, his M-60 balanced over his shoulder, his helmet off and his NVDs pushed back up on his forehead, looked haggard. The actual firefight had lasted less than five minutes, but combat could drain a man in seconds. Especially *this* kind of combat, driving, close-quarters, unrelenting, and unimaginably vicious.

"The XO and Rattler are with the women," MacKenzie said. "Bearcat and Scotty are with the men. The compound is secure, but don't take that as gospel, 'cause there are a hell of a lot of places to hide in this rat's nest. We've counted twenty-nine dead-uns so far, but the estimate was anywhere up to fifty bad guys inside the walls. Some may have jumped the walls and run. Some may still be hiding."

"Everybody okay so far?"

"Everybody except Steponit."

"Yeah." From what DeWitt had told him over the radio, Steponit had drawn the enemy commander's attention enough for DeWitt to shoot the bastard. Unfortunately, the bastard had killed Stepano before he'd died.

Damn! First Doc, now this.

"Now, the kicker," Mac was saying. "Magic and the Prof report activity on the access road. At least two claymores that Razor and Jaybird set up down there were triggered about five minutes ago. No other contact, no sign of the enemy. We have to assume that they're out there watching us, probably trying to figure how to get at us."

"It would be nice to know what we're facing out there," Murdock said, considering the tactical aspects of the situation.

"You thinking of a sneak-and-peek, L-T?"

Murdock sighed. "Negative. We don't have the manpower, and I don't want anyone left behind when the helos show. Ammo?"

"Not a problem. Most of the boys are down to a couple of clips or so on their original loadouts, but Jaybird and Red just secured the basement to the tower. They've found a couple of rooms down there full of toys."

"Ah."

"Mostly Automat M64s and M70s—the old Yugoslav versions of AKs and AKMs. Plenty of seven-six-two by thirty-nine to go with 'em. No five-five-six or seven-six-two NATO. No nine-mils."

Which meant that when the ammo for the SEALs' M-16s and H&Ks was exhausted, they could use Yugoslav AKs, but they couldn't resupply their own weapons from the Yugoslav stores. The ammo didn't match.

"There's a bonus, Skipper."

"Yeah?"

"Two RPGs."

"Like you said," Murdock told him. "Toys. With a little luck, we won't get to play with 'em. I expect our friends in the trees are going to be kind of cautious for a bit. They might even decide to wait until sunup, by which time we'll be gone with the wind."

"Yes, sir."

"But we can't take chances. I want everyone not doing anything else on the walls. How's the front gate?"

Mac frowned. "Wrought-iron bars, and I'm not even sure the thing works. It's probably for show."

"That's what I thought. We need a barricade up. Maybe one of those army trucks?"

"I'll get on it, Skipper."

"And have Scotty rig something down there to make some noise after we leave. Something in memory of Doc and Steponit."

"Yes, *sir!*" And he was gone.

0221 hours
Access road to Gorazamak
Lake Ohrid

"Halt! Halt or we fire!"

Sergeant Jankovic staggered to a halt, then sank to his knees. His heart was pounding, his breathing coming in ragged, painful gasps. His face and hands were bleeding; he'd slipped on the rocks below the castle and slid perhaps twenty meters to the main road, clawing desperately at the wet rock face all the way down.

He'd thought he was going to have to stagger all the way to Ohrid, but he'd encountered the head of the relief column on the main road, stopped at the point where the castle access road wound down off the hill. The main road was crowded with vehicles of all types, and the soldiers stood about in small groups, nervously fingering their weapons and staring up the hill into the forest.

Four JNA privates advanced, keeping their assault rifles on him. A major walked with them, a TT33 Tokarev pistol in his hand, a furious expression on his face.

"Who the hell are you?" the major demanded. His voice was shaking.

"Sergeant Jankovic, Major, Yugoslav National Army."

"You're from Gorazamak?"

Jakovic nodded. *God,* he was tired. . . .

"What the hell is going on up there? What's Mihajlovic playing at? Look what happened to my lead element!"

Jankovic looked past the major. At first, the scene scarcely registered on his fire-numbed brain. Only gradually did it dawn on him that those red objects bathed in the headlights of a truck were *men* . . . or had been. A jeep sat crossways on the road, its motor still running. Its side had been scoured as though by a titanic shotgun blast; what was left of three or four passengers—it was impossible to tell how many—had literally been blown out of their seats.

"Some kind of booby trap," the major was saying. "If this is Mihajlovic's idea of a training exercise—"

"It is real, Major," Jankovic said as two of the soldiers helped him to his feet. "Gorazamak has been . . . has been taken by commandos."

"Commandos! Those fantasies again!"

"Not fantasies, Major. I was there, up north, four days ago. Now they're here."

"What commandos? Whose?"

"I don't know, sir. American, I think. Probably parachutists. They hold the castle now."

"And the general?"

"I don't know, sir. I was on one of the walls when they attacked. I . . . I saw it was hopeless and climbed down the outside of the wall."

"Deserting your post."

Anger flared in Jankovic . . . but quickly faded. It was the truth, after all. "Sir, the enemy was slaughtering the garrison. *Slaughtering* them, sir. I . . . felt it would be best if I could get help."

"You're under arrest."

"Yes, sir."

The officer was staring up the hill, into the forest in the direction of the castle.

"You will ride with me. As guide. Acquit yourself well, and the arrest will be rescinded."

Jankovic sagged, almost falling again. He wanted to tell the major to go to hell, to throw him in prison and be done with it. He didn't want to face these nightmares that appeared out of the night to kill, and kill again. He'd faced them at the monastery, and again on the beach. Now they were here, and Jankovic was beginning to think these night terrors had singled him out personally.

But discipline and training reasserted themselves. "Yes, sir. Thank you, sir."

"Commandos, eh?" the major said. "We'll see how they stand up to the 434 Motorized."

Only then did Jankovic notice the line of flat, ugly vehicles squatting on their tracks astride the main road, their engines thuttering noisily at idle.

The major grinned at Jankovic's expression. "Parachutists don't stand a chance against armored fighting vehicles, eh?"

21

They could all hear it now, the metallic clattering of an armored vehicle's tracks. "What the hell?" Magic said. "They sending tanks after us?"

"Not quite," Murdock said, leaning against the parapet and holding a Varo AN/PVS-4 nightscope to his eye. "Looks to me like a couple of bumps."

Bumps—BMP-1s, to be precise—were tracked infantry combat vehicles, a primitive version of the modern M2 Bradley AFV in the U.S. Army's inventory. Originally introduced by the Soviets in the early 1960s, the BMP-1 was the first AFV ever employed by any army, a low, boxy vehicle running on tank tracks, carrying a crew of three and up to eight troops. The top was completely flat except for a small, squat turret mounting a 73mm gun; a launch rail mounted just above the gun carried an AT-3 Sagger antitank missile. A single coaxial machine gun completed its weapons inventory, though the troops also had firing ports along the side of the low-slung, armored hull.

Through the nightscope, Murdock could see the two vehicles just coming around the curve in the access road on the far side of the stone bridge, grinding their way toward the castle's gate, one following the other in stately line-ahead.

"Higgins!" Murdock snapped. "Get on the horn and tell 'em we got company, at least two BMP-1s. If they don't get our air support here stat, those things are going to be all over us."

"Yes, sir!"

He opened his tactical channel. "Mac!"

"Yeah, Boss!"

"We've got bumps knocking at the front gate. Where's that truck?"

"Roselli's got it started. He's on the way!"

But it might already be too late.

"Get those RPGs up here, gate tower, on the double."

"Yes, sir!"

Murdock heard the truck's engine behind him, just audible over the ragged purr of the BMPs. The Yugoslav vehicles had slewed to a stop a few meters beyond the bridge and appeared to be waiting there. Murdock shifted his nightscope, checking the woods to either side. Yes . . . there was some movement. Troops were moving among the trees. There was also some movement at the bridge abutments on the far side of the ravine . . . men checking for mines or booby traps, he thought.

Blowing that bridge would have been a nice idea, Murdock thought, but the team had been so heavily loaded for Alexander already that they'd brought a minimum of explosives with them. Frazier had a kilo or so of plastic explosives and the usual assembly of detonators and prima-cord, but that bridge was solid built, all steel and concrete. A good twenty kilos or more would have been necessary, and it had been assumed that the stuff wouldn't be needed for a quick in-and-out like this one.

"I think we'd better get clear of this tower," Murdock told the other men with him. "These walls aren't going to stand up to a seventy-three."

"My antenna's on the roof," Higgins said.

"Bring it. We can realign—"

The coaxial gun of the lead BMP opened fire, the
stuttering yellow muzzle flash stabbing out of the night.
Bullets whined and shrieked off stone or thudded heavily
into the barricade at the gate. Murdock turned to look out of
the tower's southeast window; Roselli was backing a
two-and-a-half-ton truck into position, blocking the open
gateway.

"Out!" Murdock yelled. "Everybody out! Roselli! Get the
hell out of there!"

The BMP's 73mm gun spoke, the shot a hollow boom
that echoed off the mountain above. The round slammed
squarely into the truck and detonated, the concussion jolting
Murdock in the gate tower directly above the blast. The
SEALs scrambled out through the narrow doorway leading
to the parapet walk northeast of the gate tower.

"Razor! You okay?"

"I'm clear, Boss," Roselli's voice replied. "A little singed."

From his new position on the ramparts, and using his
nightscope, Murdock could see small details of the vehicle
now, including the semicircle of small ports around the
driver's hatch and on the commander's hatch just behind.
Firing at those slits with small arms, though, would be
futile . . . and a great way of drawing fire. Automatic
weapons were flashing and stuttering from the forest.
Bullets sang off the castle walls or sighed overhead. The
lead BMP was moving again, starting toward the bridge.

"Holt," he called over the radio. "Where are you?"

"West wall, L-T. Just got here."

"Anyone with you?"

"Nick the Greek," another voice said. "I'm up here with
Bearcat."

"Okay. I want you two guys on top of the keep. Holt, use
your sixty to sweep bad guys off the walls. Papagos, you
spot. Watch out for our people."

"You got it, L-T. Let's move it, Bearcat."

Another explosion boomed from beneath the archway of
the main gate. For a moment, Murdock thought the BMP
had fired again, but it was the gasoline tank in the

truck-barricade cooking off. Orange flame spilled skyward, licking at ancient stone, and Murdock was very glad that they'd cleared the gate tower. Assault rifles chattered wildly from across the ravine.

"Magic!" he called. "Professor! I want you two up on the tower as well."

"I need my sat antenna, L-T," Higgins said.

"Forget it." The roof of the gate tower would be well covered by fire from below. "Achilles will be in line-of-sight soon enough. Now haul ass!"

"Here we go, Boss," Mac said. Murdock turned. Behind him, Mac was cradling an RPG-7 under one arm and holding a case of four rocket grenades in the other.

"Great! What kind of rounds we got? Any AP?"

"'Fraid not, Boss. Couldn't find anything down there but HE."

"Never mind. At least we'll shake the bastards up. Gimme a hand here."

Together, they prepared the first grenade, screwing a cylinder containing the rocket propellant into the warhead section, then snapping the complete round into the launch unit's muzzle. Mac snapped off the warhead's nose cap and pulled the safety pin. Murdock hefted the weapon to his shoulder.

"You ever fire one of these things, L-T?"

"In training, sure. Exotic Weapons 101. Anyway, if a terrorist can learn how to use the thing, how tough can it be?"

"Remember your back-blast." Mac slapped Murdock on top of his helmet. "You're go!"

The lead BMP was almost all the way across the bridge now, less than thirty yards away and grinding slowly toward the front gate. If they could kill it while it was still on the bridge, the enemy assault would be stopped cold . . . at least for as long as it would take Chariot and Achilles to reach the castle.

Murdock squeezed the trigger. A jolt flung the grenade clear of the muzzle, and then the igniter caught and the rocket-propelled round swooped toward the target with a hiss, but lower than Murdock had expected. It struck the stonework of the bridge with a flash and a bark of thunder. Rock and shattered concrete cascaded into the ravine, but the BMP kept coming, untouched, clearing the near side of the bridge.

"Shit!" Murdock said.

"Back to summer school for you, L-T. Duck and move!" Together, they scurried on hands and knees further to the right, keeping below the line of parapet openings. An explosion ripped through the ancient stonework, throwing both SEALs flat. Looking back over his shoulder, Murdock saw that the BMP's 73mm round had slammed into the parapet just below where he and Mac had been hiding.

The BMP slewed off the road and kept coming. The gun barked again, striking just below the last impact. Rocks showered into the bailey. Clearly, the latest in sixteenth-century fortifications weren't going to last long against an AFV.

"Shit!" Murdock said. "They're gonna come straight through the wall!" He opened the mike to his Motorola. "Okay, all Alexanders, all Alexanders, off the walls. Fall back to the tower, everyone! We'll make our stand there! Move it!"

"Can we manage another shot?" Mac wanted to know.

"I think so. He's close, but I think so."

"Okay," Mac said, screwing the propellant onto a second grenade. "Let's try that again, shall we? Allow for the rocket's dip this time."

"Yes, teacher." RPG rounds had a curious dip to their trajectory, the result of being kicked clear of the muzzle before the rocket ignited, and at close range it could result in the projectile striking considerably lower than the aim point. Murdock hefted the weapon to his shoulder once more, peering through a parapet firing slot. The BMP was so close to the wall now that he couldn't get a clear shot and still stay under cover.

"I'll have to hop, pop, and drop, Mac."

"Shit, L-T. They'll nail you."

"Where's your hog?"

"Left it at the tower. I couldn't carry all this shit and a sixty-gun too."

"I'll just have to do it fast, then."

"Let me."

"Negative. Here goes."

In one smooth motion, Murdock rose, aimed, and fired. This time the round swooped down from the battlements, leveling off just before it struck the ground and slamming into the BMP's left side, below and a little in front of the turret. The fireball enveloped the front half of the vehicle; the blast jolted it to the right.

Gunfire from the woods exploded around him. Chips flew from the top of the parapet, and something stung his cheek. He dropped behind the safety of the ramparts as the second BMP's coaxial gun opened up, sending a line of dazzling green tracers searing overhead with a curious snapping sound. Another machine gun joined in. A third BMP had just joined the fight, and the topmost stones on the rampart shattered and sprayed beneath that hosing of 7.62mm rounds.

"Move!" They scrambled clear as another 73mm round slammed into the wall, searching for the troublesome snipers.

"A for the day," Mac cried as they dropped flat once again, further down the parapet walk. "You dropped that one right in the commander's seat!"

"We're not going to get another shot from up here," Murdock said. "Let's pull back to the tower."

"Roger that. You okay? Your face is bleeding."

"Just a sting. Piece of stone, I think."

"We got two more rounds here."

"We'll save 'em for when they come through the wall. Come on."

"You know, Skipper, that we're in a world of shit. The

choppers won't be able to come in with an army camped right outside our front door."

"Yeah. It's gonna be up to the flyboys now."

0229 hours
AC-130 gunship
Over Lake Ohrid

Major Peter K. Selby keyed his microphone. "Alexander, Alexander, this is Night Rider. Do you copy? Over."

The AC-130 gunship had flown across Albania at treetop level. Now it was above Lake Ohrid at ten thousand feet, banking into its left-hand turn to bring the weaponry packed into its port side to bear.

"Alexander, this is Night Rider. Do you copy? Over."

"Night Rider, Alexander!" a voice called back. "Seems like you're always riding to our rescue! Over!"

"Shoot, is that Nomad?"

"Affirmative, Night Rider. Different call sign, same problem. We're inside the fort on the hill. We got some bad guy Injuns coming at us from the northwest. Think you can do something about that?"

Selby was studying the infrared sensor screens. The landscape below was ablaze with heat; the main gate of the castle was burning, the fireball lighting up the surrounding walls. A tracked AFV was burning just outside the wall, and he could see the engine heat from several more vehicles along the road leading to the castle.

The main road, however, was packed with military vehicles, trucks and jeeps mostly, loaded with troops, but there were some more tracked vehicles as well.

"Alexander, this is Night Rider. Confirm your ID with a flash, over."

"Roger, Night Rider."

An IR beacon strobed from the castle tower.

"Okay, Alexander, we have you. Confirm your position inside the castle walls."

"Roger, Night Rider. That is affirmative."

"Alexander, it looks like we have a number of vehicles on

the main road by the lake, approximately regimental strength. You want 'em boxed, or you want 'em on the run?"

There was a moment's delay. When Alexander came back on the air, it was a different voice. "Night Rider, this is Alexander, Charlie Oscar. The faster those people run, the better. Our real problem is going to be the head of the snake."

"We copy that, Alexander. Stand by."

Standard procedure for taking down a column confined to a road like the one below was to disable vehicles at both the front and the rear of the column, trapping those in between for a leisurely and thorough kill later. Alexander's CO—that's what the "Charlie Oscar" meant—was telling him to leave an escape route. Hit the head of the column hard enough, and maybe most of the hostiles would turn around and head back to Ohrid.

"Sergeant Zanowski, we'll be taking the targets from south to north. Not too close. We don't want to bounce any inside the compound."

"Yes, sir."

Selby reached for an intercom switch. "Colonel Carlotti," he said. "We have Alexander on-line, positive identification."

"Very well. Permission to fire."

"Gunners, this is Selby. Stand by. We have firing command. Set, Sergeant?"

"Locked in, sir." The sensor operator said, reaching for the armament safeties.

"Punch it!"

0229 hours
Main tower
Gorazamak

Night turned to day as fire rained from the sky, a lightning bolt, save that this bolt was ruler-drawn straight, and where it touched the earth beyond the castle walls, it erupted in blazing fire. Trees whipped back and forth beneath the touch of that hot breath, then cracked and fell, trunks splintered by lethal hail.

A meteor streaked down the shaft of fire. An explosion detonated down the hill among the trees. A second meteor followed, almost too quick to see . . . and a third . . . and a fourth.

A skilled Specter gun crew could work the aircraft's 105mm howitzer so quickly that they were firing the gun while one round was still in the air between the aircraft and the ground, and a third round was just slamming into the target. Murdock wasn't sure what they were hitting out there, but it was something big. The roar of rapid-fire explosions was deafening, drowning out the eerie, low-pitched, moaning shriek of incoming Gatling rounds. The northwest wall was backlit by fire.

Murdock peered down from the battlements of the castle keep, watching the incoming hellfire. Through his night-scope, he could see a line of Serb soldiers, dozens of them, running out of the trees beyond the ravine.

Then the pencil of fire drifted across them, caressing them, lifting them, tearing them apart as a sleet of lead slashed through them like a whirlwind, leaving bodies and body parts and a thin, bloody spray in its wake. The circle of destruction widened, as a two-and-a-half-ton truck exploded in flame, as a jeep overturned, shattered, as a BMP exploded violently in orange flame and hurtling bits of armor, as soldiers crumpled and twisted and died, and that moaning howl went on and on like the grating shriek of a banshee.

The flame moved on, reaching lower down the slope, but an explosion against the castle wall to the right of the gate tower grabbed Murdock's attention. He swung the night-scope onto this new threat, caught the spilling of rocks and broken mortar into the courtyard.

A stray round? He thought so at first but quickly changed his mind. The AC-130 was having to be conservative for fear of striking inside Gorazamak's walls; ricochets bounding around inside the walls could be deadly, and there was a hell of a lot of gasoline—and maybe ammo as well—inside the vehicles parked by the stables. Probably the Specter was restricting its fire to the far side of the ravine . . . but something was on this side of the ravine and it was coming in through the wall.

The second BMP was coming through the breach in the wall now, its coaxial gun chattering as it blindly swept the courtyard. No one was left in the bailey, though. All the SEALs had pulled back to the keep and were either up here on the roof, in the back of the tower with the hostages, or on the lower floor, bracing for the assault. Murdock had ordered the male hostages moved from their room near the front of the tower to the room where the women had been held. The problem was deciding where, inside the keep, was the safest place.

Probably there was no such thing as a safest place, not if the Serbs started shelling the keep. He was counting now on air support to stop the enemy assault.

But leakers were coming through, despite the deadly, controlled lightning from above. The BMP ground over the spill of stone and rubble. Its main gun fired, and the castle keep shuddered as the round exploded at the front door.

"Damned pesky salesman," Papagos said.

"Maybe we can discourage him," Murdock said. Rising, he shouldered the RPG again, aimed, squeezed on the trigger. . . .

The round arrowed down from the tower top, striking the BMP squarely on its glacis. The explosion was shattering, halting the vehicle's advance . . . but as the smoke cleared it was obvious that the high-explosive round hadn't pierced the armor. Its main gun fired again, and Murdock felt the tower shudder.

This close, the BMP probably couldn't elevate its main gun high enough to reach the SEALs on the tower roof. On the other hand, all it had to do was keep slamming rounds in through the front door. Sooner or later, this old tower was going to come down, taking a lot of people with it.

The fire from the sky had ceased.

"Prof! Lemme have the horn."

"Here you go, L-T."

"Night Rider, Night Rider," Murdock called. "Alexander. Do you copy? Over."

"Alexander, Night Rider copies."

"That was right on the money. Can you hit a bit closer? We're all inside the big tower. You can come right down inside the compound if you can."

"Ah, that's a negative, Alexander. We're moving into the north leg of our orbit. The mountain's in our way."

Specter gunships, with all of their armament on the port side, had to engage the enemy in a constant left-hand bank. The Specter had been circling counterclockwise in from the lake, passing south of the castle while continuing to smash at targets to the north. Now, however, it was passing to the east, and the mountains and the trees were blocking its view not only of the road, but of the castle itself.

"Copy that, Rider. See you on the other side." *I hope.*

"Watch it!" Mac shouted. "Here comes the grunts!"

Soldiers were following the BMP through on foot, and more were piling out of the AFV's rear, scattering across the courtyard. Murdock thought they must be charging at least in part because moving forward against a fortified position was preferable to staying on that road long enough for the Specter to get another crack at them.

Mac's M-60 opened up, a sustained, crashing volley that cut down running men one after another. Holt, sent up to the rooftop with his M-60, opened up as well, and was quickly joined by Papagos with his H&K, and by Magic Brown, who was calmly and steadily dropping enemy soldiers one at a time with his Remington.

Murdock raised himself above the parapet, his last RPG round loaded and ready to fire. "Watch my back-blast!" he yelled, and he sent the last HE round streaking toward the BMP.

The charge struck the turret with a crash; the Sagger exploded an instant later, adding to the destruction. The turret, its gun barrel twisted, hung over the side of the AFV, as smoke boiled from the interior.

But the eight troops inside were already out and clear, sheltering behind the dead BMP and the vehicles by the motor pool. Gunfire barked and crackled from the courtyard below. Sooner or later, they would try a rush. Kos and four SEALs were on the ground floor waiting for them, but if they went in using a lot of grenades, the way the SEALs had done on their entry, the affair could have only one ending.

Part of the trouble was that SEALs, probably the best-trained fighters in the world, were at their best with offensive combat, not with holding a fixed position.

The gunfire from the tower sputtered out. With the JNA under cover, they were no targets . . . and ammo for the M-60s was running low now . . . about two hundred rounds left apiece.

"Alex Two, this is One! Do you read me?"

"Loud and clear, Skipper," Kosciuszko replied.

"You guys hanging on down there?"

"So far."

"The bump's dead, but we've got bad guys getting ready for a rush, looks like. We'll hold them from up here as long as we can, but they're probably working up close to the walls by now, down where we can't see 'em. Watch out for grenades."

"We're ready. L-T. Rattler and Jaybird moved some of these counters around to make a barricade, and we're up on the balcony now with a good field of fire."

"Okay. Just hang on. When Night Rider makes another pass, I'm going to have him dump a load inside the perimeter."

There was a long pause. "Copy that."

It was a desperate measure, but Murdock had just run out of options. The helos wouldn't be here for another fifteen minutes or a bit more. He could try to take the hostages out the tower back door and into the woods, but those woods were probably crawling with JNA troops by now. Besides, getting untrained civilians to rappel down a wall at night would be inviting disaster.

Fifteen more minutes!

"Here they come!"

Gunfire volleyed from the courtyard, shrieking off the ramparts at the top of the tower. A fresh wave of JNA soldiers were coming through the breach in the wall, firing wildly. Murdock dropped the RPG and unslung his H&K. Leaning over the parapet, he took aim. . . .

"What the *fuck*?" Holt said.

The Serb soldiers charging through the gap in the wall were being hit, and hit hard. No one in the tower had started firing yet, but the enemy troops were going down in twos and threes and fours, and the rest were scattering. Mac's 60-gun began hammering away in short, sharp bursts, but the enemy's charge had already broken.

A lone figure was crouched in the breach in the wall, firing into the JNA troops from behind, his weapon scything down men with a deadly *thud-thud-thud* of full-auto shot-gun fire.

"Doc!" Roselli's voice yelled over the tactical channel. "Jesus Christ, hold your fire upstairs, it's Doc!"

The Yugoslav soldiers still on their feet in the courtyard were surrendering now, throwing down their AK-copies and raising their hands. Doc's shotgun fell silent.

"Kos!" Murdock snapped. "Doc's at the wall, the bad guys are surrendering. Get your people out there and round 'em up!"

"Already on it, L-T." SEALs were spilling out into the courtyard, rounding up soldiers who'd suddenly been trans-formed from desperate, charging fanaticism to a kind of dazed and accepting docility.

Thunder pealed across the sky. Murdock looked up, half expecting to see Night Rider on his way in for another pass . . . but what he saw instead was the glow of after-burners, the too-quick-to-follow shadows of low-flying jets.

"Skipper!" Higgins called. "Night Rider's on the line. He says the Javelins are here."

"Javelin?" The code names were running together. He didn't remember that one. Was his mind starting to play tricks on him? *God*, he was tired. . . .

"That's VFA-161, L-T. A Hornet squadron off the *Jefferson*."

Hornets! That's why he hadn't remembered the code name; "Javelins" was the unit name for a squadron of F/A-18s, deadly, carrier-borne aircraft with dual roles, both air-to-air and air-to-ground. The U.S. Marines swore by them for close ground support. Two of the aircraft were streaking in low above the lake, moving south to north. By the firelight, Murdock thought he could see the elongated shapes of bombs tumbling off the aircraft's wing racks, and a moment later, he heard the popcorn stuttering of cluster-bomb bomblets detonating along the main highway. With a roar of exploding gasoline, fresh fires lit the night beyond the trees to the northwest.

"Skipper?" Higgins called. "I've got Chariot on the horn. Chariot and Achilles are inbound, ETA eight minutes."

Explosions roared from the direction of the road. More Hornets circled out of the night, their thunder pealing across the lake and echoing off the mountainside.

"I think," Murdock said slowly, "that we can hold out that long. No problem."

He wondered if anyone else could see that his hands were shaking.

22

"Here they come, Boss."

Murdock looked up. A shadow moved in from the lake, slowing as it neared the castle, drifting above the courtyard, as black as death, the wind from its rotor wash blasting across the bailey like a hurricane. Orange flame spat from the Gatling in its starboard side, the cyclic so high that the gun didn't chatter, it moaned, a low-pitched groan that set Murdock's teeth on edge as it fired at some unseen target in the forest beyond the wall.

"Pave Low," MacKenzie said, almost reverently. "Come to Poppa, baby!"

The MH-53J—socially the Pave Low III—was a direct descendant of the Super Jolly Green Giants of Vietnam, a Sikorsky CH-53 updated for the '90s and extensively re-engineered. Equipped with infrared sensors and FLIR, inertial navigation, multi-mode radar, and a 7.62mm Gatling gun protruding from the starboard side behind the pilot's seat, the Pave Low could streak across the landscape at two hundred miles per hour in pitch blackness at an altitude of one hundred feet or less, navigating anywhere in the world through a GPS link. Its range was limited only by pilot fatigue, for the massive boom protruding forward from the starboard side of its nose could be used for in-flight refueling. A device called a hover coupler allowed the Pave Low III to perform that almost miraculous maneuver for a helicopter—a stable hover—even in darkness or in bad weather. By processing signals from five gyroscopes, an inertial guidance system, and a radar altimeter, the hover coupler literally took over the fine adjustments of pitch for both main and tail rotors, allowing the Pave Low to correct instantly for pitch, roll, yaw, and the effects of unexpected updrafts, downdrafts, crosswinds, and even the jolting change in weight as troops exited the aircraft.

One Pave Low III could carry thirty men. Four had been dispatched for the Alexander extraction, two under the code name Achilles, two under the name Chariot. There would be no aborted rescue mission this time, as there had been in the 1980 Iran hostage rescue, with the mission called off because too many of the helicopters developed mechanical difficulties on the way in.

The first Achilles Pave Low moved slowly across the sky until it was hovering forty feet above the castle keep, where Frazier and Papagos had only recently taken down the antenna array mounted there. The rear hatch was down— Murdock could see the green gleam of the go-light winking at him from inside the troop bay. Suddenly, a line spilled from the rear of the Pave Low, uncoiling to the tower roof, and then heavily armed men in black were fast-roping their way down, each hitting the tower, then moving aside as the next man in line dropped after him. Murdock had once participated in an exercise where thirty men had exited from a Pave Low in five seconds flat.

The first Pave Low hovered a moment longer, then moved off toward the south. A second Achilles chopper moved in, hovering above the bailey. A rope uncoiled, and men began spilling out, dropping rapidly and silently into the courtyard and spreading out with practiced efficiency, taking up positions around the castle perimeter. Seconds later, a SEAL in black combat gear and helmet, his face almost invisible beneath his camouflage paint, trotted up to Murdock. "Well, Blake," the figure said. "Been keeping yourself busy?"

Murdock didn't salute. SEALs don't in the field, not when an enemy sniper might be watching. "Busy enough, Captain Coburn," he said. Then he blurted it out. "One of my men is dead."

"I heard the report on the way in. The Slavic kid, Stepano."

"Yes, sir."

"Sorry to hear that."

"Yeah." SEALs expect to take losses in the field. People die in combat, and in a close-knit band of brothers like the Teams, those people were going to be guys you cared about.

Stepano hadn't been with Third Platoon long, but he was still one of them.

"You also saved the lives of one of our congressmen and her staff," Coburn said. "That was a damned fine piece of work. What's your situation here now?"

"No enemy contact since the Hornets arrived, sir. I've been in radio contact with Night Rider, and he's been keeping us posted on their movements. Looks like they're heading north just as fast as they can manage, with the Hornets snapping at their heels."

The second Achilles helicopter had moved off, joining the first in a slow, round-and-round circuit of Gorazamak, half a mile out.

Chariot came in next, another Pave Low III identical to the others, black and menacing. This time the helicopter moved in lower, barely skimming the castle's ramparts, turning slightly, then lowering itself toward the pavement.

It was a tight fit. Standard procedure for preparing a chopper landing zone called for clearing an area fifty meters across, with a further twenty meters beyond that cleared to within three feet of the ground. To do that, though, they'd have had to level the castle walls; the bailey was well over one hundred meters long but only about forty wide. The Pave Low III's fuselage was thirty meters long, and the rotors, when turning, reached twenty-four meters across. That left very little room at all for error.

The Air Force special-ops squadron pilots who flew the Pave Lows, however, were used to making the impossible routine. Besides, it was widely acknowledged that *nothing* could excite a helicopter pilot. Chariot One hovered briefly, aligned north and south to give it some takeoff room, while a SEAL with a pair of Chemlites gave instructions from the ground. Then gently . . . gently . . . the big machine settled onto the flagstone pavement, the rear ramp already coming down.

"Let's get the hostages out of there," Coburn said.

Murdock was already pumping his arm up and down, signaling to DeWitt. "Go!" Murdock shouted above the whopping sound of the Pave Low's rotor. "Move! Move! Move!"

The line of former hostages darted out from the main building, doubled over low as they passed beneath the shining arc of the helicopter rotors, the line kept straight by SEAL flankers, who stood to either side with weapons pointed at the sky, waving them along. Escorted by a determined-looking young SEAL, Congresswoman Kingston was first up the Pave Low's ramp. Her chief aide was next, then Colonel Winters, his head wrapped in white gauze. He looked tired and haggard, but when he glanced up and saw Murdock and Coburn watching him, he grinned and gave them a jaunty thumbs-up.

"Thought you might like to know," Coburn said as the rest of the hostages began filing past. "A Delta detachment hit Skopje Airport two hours ago. They took down five tangos and secured the Olympic aircraft, just like clockwork. The flight crew was still being held on board. They're all safe. The Yugoslav Macedonian government forces are in charge now. I imagine the headlines tomorrow will explain how Macedonian troops successfully stormed the aircraft. Our State Department will want to use the incident to strengthen Macedonia's hand in this region."

"So everyone's accounted for then?"

"Everyone."

"Hey, L-T!" DeWitt trotted toward them from the keep. He was holding a sheaf of manila file folders and what looked like a couple of videotapes. "Oh, excuse me, Captain."

"No problem, Lieutenant," Coburn said.

"Whatcha got, Two-Eyes?"

"Scotty blew that safe we found in one of the rooms. Thought you might like a look."

The videotapes were unmarked, but Murdock imagined that they would be important, if for no other reason than that they'd been found in a safe. He accepted the folders from DeWitt and began leafing through them. Most of the papers they contained looked like records, pay vouchers, muster logs, the usual paraphernalia of any military unit, though the entries were made in the Cyrillic alphabet, and the language, Murdock thought, was probably Serbo-Croatian.

One manila envelope tied shut with string, however, contained a stack of 8x10 black-and-white photographs. Murdock shuffled through several of them, then handed the stack to Coburn. "I don't recognize any of these people, sir. Do you?"

"Can't say that I do. I imagine there are some folks back at Langley who could identify them, though." He tapped one of the photographs. "Especially this guy."

All of the photographs featured one particular man, white-haired, in his fifties, perhaps. He might have looked distinguished had he been wearing clothes; as it was, he looked ridiculous, and a bit sad. The photos showed him in a variety of positions with a number of other people, male and female. Whips, leather, and chains were in evidence as well.

"Blackmail, L-T?" DeWitt asked.

"These were in a safe?"

"Yup. In Mihajlovic's office."

"Blackmail, then. Or insurance." Murdock slipped the photos back into the envelope. He felt dirty, having handled them. "In any case, these will tell us who Mihajlovic's man in the Greek government is. He had to have someone there to arrange for the DEA to be infiltrated the way it was. You know, at one point I thought Mihajlovic hijacked that plane in response to our op at the monastery. But he's had this under way for a long time."

Coburn accepted the files from Murdock. "It was probably coincidence that Mihajlovic showed up at the monastery. But I gather the intel boys have quite a bit of material on him. He was ambitious, probably had his eye on a seat in the Yugoslav parliament. Maybe he was aiming higher than that."

"Was he going to use the hostages to bargain with us?" Murdock asked. "Or was he going to stage a faked rescue, be a hero?"

"Maybe these papers will tell us. It's not really our business, though, is it? Our people were being held against their will, maybe being used as a part of Mihajlovic's power games. They could have been killed . . . and if things had gone bad, we could have ended up with World War III right here. Your people did an excellent job, Lieutenant. *You* did an excellent job."

"Thank you, sir."

The last of the hostages had vanished up the Pave Low's ramp, which slowly closed after them. The aircraft paused there a moment, rotors spinning faster, and then the SEAL with the light sticks signaled and the machine raised itself, very slowly, off the ground. Moving up and a little forward, it cleared the castle's north wall with fifteen feet to spare, then banked sharply away toward the lake.

The second Chariot came in hard on the heels of the first, settling to the pavement. Almost the moment its ramp touched the pavement, four SEALs holding a stokes stretcher hurried across from the castle tower.

"Excuse me, sir," Murdock said.

He trotted over to the medical team. Doc was lying in the stretcher, looking haggard, his face almost unrecognizable beneath the smeared greasepaint.

"Damn it, Doc," Murdock said. "You're not supposed to be a patient."

"Hey," Doc replied grinning. "If God had meant us to jump out of perfectly good airplanes, he'd have seen to it that the damned things never got off the ground."

Murdock didn't want to hold up the line. "See you on board, buddy."

"Sure thing, L-T."

Four more SEALs were carrying another Stokes out of the tower now, the motionless form inside wrapped head to toe in a dark blue blanket. SEALs never leave their own behind. Never.

"The boys're ready to mount up," Mac said, materializing at Murdock's side.

"Let's get the hell out of Dodge, Mac."

Minutes later, Murdock was aboard the Pave Low as the special-ops helo lifted up out of the courtyard, banked over the northwest wall, and set a course west for Albania and, beyond that, the waters of the Adriatic.

Doc's Stokes had been slung in a rack designed to carry medevac stretchers. Murdock leaned over the injured SEAL.

"You going to be okay?"

"Ah, sure, Skipper. Just a sprain. You don't think a little thing like that'd keep me away from a party, do ya?"

"Not you, Doc. But you had us worried. I thought you'd gone AWOL. We were taking bets on whether you'd shacked up with some local girl or with a sheep."

"Shit, L-T. Don't lay money on the sheep. You know I never do sheep unless they're really good-looking."

"Good-bye, Macedonia," Roselli said. He was standing nearby, leaning against the Pave Low's fuselage and staring out through one of the few side windows. "Shit, L-T, look at 'em burn!"

Murdock joined Roselli, peering aft. The Pave Low was now well out over the lake, and he could see the eastern shore all the way from the castle to the city of Ohrid, in the north. A good third of that line was dotted with orange points of light, the funeral pyres of burning vehicles.

He couldn't see the attack aircraft that had wreaked that destruction, of course, any more than he could see the Navy Tomcats that would be flying a protective umbrella over the Pave Lows all the way back to San Vito. The scene looked deceptively peaceful from here.

He couldn't see the castle either, or the two Achilles Pave Lows. The SEALs of First and Second Platoon would hold the perimeter until both Chariots were well clear, and then they would board the last two choppers and extract as well. They would leave the fortress of Gorazamak behind them untouched, the explosives Scotty had rigged in the ammo storage area disconnected; over forty JNA prisoners were locked up inside the keep, and indiscriminate slaughter was not part of the SEAL repertoire.

Murdock managed a smile at the thought. SEALs specialized in only the most highly discriminating slaughter. . . .

0315 hours
Access road to Gorazamak
Southwestern Macedonia

Narednik Andonov Jankovic looked up from the snowbank in which he'd been lying. When the major's command car had been pitched over onto its side, he'd been hurled here to the side of the access road, less than ten meters from the ravine bridge and perhaps another twenty or thirty meters from the castle's main gate. The walls loomed high against the forest and the night, illuminated by the ruddy sky-glow.

Burning vehicles. Half of the motorized regiment must be in flames by now, stretched along the road from here halfway back to Ohrid. The air stank of burning rubber and diesel fumes and other, less pleasant smells.

The last of the American helicopters rose steadily above the walls, a huge, ominous black insect silhouetted against the glowing sky. It hovered there a moment as though sniffing the air, searching for any last, lingering survivors like Jankovic. Then it nodded, as though convinced the job was done, swung to the right, and with a droning flutter of its rotors, headed off toward the east.

With the last helicopter gone, the sounds of the battlefield rose all around him—the crackle of fires, the shouts of men calling to one another in the woods, and most horribly, the piercing shrieks of men in agony, the cries for *voda*—water—the moanings and pleadings of the dying.

Some minutes ago, Jankovic had been astonished to find that he was unhurt. He'd continued to lie there in the snow, however, unmoving, convinced that the Americans would see him if he so much as twitched. Now that they were gone, he slowly stood up.

The major who'd put him under arrest lay nearby. Jankovic recognized him by the uniform; his head was missing.

Jankovic staggered back down the access road, coming at last to the intersection with the coast road along the lake. North, burning vehicles littered the highway. He could see other soldiers, other survivors, moving among the wrecks, helping the wounded or simply wandering about in a shell-shocked daze.

What now?

The accumulated horror hit him in that moment, and Jankovic was violently sick, vomiting into a ditch on the side of the road. When he pulled himself erect again, he felt a little better.

He also knew what he had to do.

Only Solidarity Can Save the Serbs. The hell with that. Andonov Jankovic had had enough of war. He was sick of a bullying and inefficient army, sick of power-hungry and manipulative politicians and officers, sick of rape squads and ethnic cleansing and concentration camps and a war that long ago had lost any point, any vestige of the holy righteousness he'd once thought it possessed.

He'd had enough.

North on the coast road was Ohrid. The survivors of the JNA units at Gorazamak would be rallying there.

South, the coast road wound along the lake to the border with Albania. A side road split off to the left, wound up over the mountains, and eventually rejoined M26, the main road between Ohrid and the southern city of Bitola. From Bitola, it was a short twelve-kilometer walk to the Greek border.

The jeep he'd seen earlier, the one scoured by a booby-trap blast, was still sitting nearby, its engine still idling. It would let him stay ahead of the military police at least as far as the main road. After that, he could find some civilian clothes, maybe find a farmer who'd be willing to smuggle him across the border. Anyway, things were going to be hellishly confused in this corner of Macedonia, while the Serb military tried to figure out just what had hit them.

Yes, he would go to Greece. And after that?

Jankovic bore the Americans no ill will. Mihajlovic had provoked them by holding their people hostage; the Americans had struck back with overwhelming and devastating might. He was sure now the commandos had been Americans. No other nation on Earth had such magical technology.

Or such warriors.

That was it. Once he'd reached Greece, Andonov Jankovic would look for an American consulate. There would be one at Salonika.

He wondered if they allowed Serbians to become citizens of the United States of America. . . .